Praise

THE
WALK-ON

"An interesting read where star linebacker Mike Stalowski confronts the inevitable challenges every NFL player faces as they transition to their post-football life. His experiences may seem exaggerated, but they are still very real."

Gary Fencik, Chicago Bears, Super Bowl XX Champion

"I am not a football fan. I've never lived the fast life in the big city. So I approached Richard Podkowski's new book, *The Walk-On,* with some trepidation, fearing it might simply be about the selfish glitz and grift of professional football and its hangers-on, both male and female. Imagine my joy when I discovered that there was another major character in this book, one personally dear to me: the city of Chicago itself, with all its rawness, rich ethnicity and beating heart. This book was written by a person who knows the city and its neighborhoods, its restaurants and bars, its patchwork of streets and human networks. And then, once you are hooked by these stories, you'll find yourself increasingly drawn to its two lead characters—the football player known as the Steelman, and the young woman whose caring soul counterbalances her flashy lifestyle. Don't be surprised when faith and its formation make an appearance; that's part of the real Chicago, too. Just like in football, there's some great game day action in the book, even for a football amateur. You'll be glad you picked this one up."

**Barbara Dembski, Retired Milwaukee
newspaper journalist and Chicago native**

"*The Walk-On* is a fascinating story of self-sabotage and redemption. A page-turner!!!!"

Mary Pat Kelly, Bestselling author of
Galway Bay, Of Irish Blood, **and** *Irish Above All*

"Just like the protagonist's very fast sports car, *The Walk-On* will leave you, from the very first paragraph, just a little breathless as you navigate all the sharp turns that come fast and furious at the reader. Yet, at the end of day, Richard Podkowski's story of a fading football hero from Chicago's Southeast Side will mostly—and unexpectedly—touch your heart."

Jean Becker, Author of *The New York Times* **bestseller,**
The Man I Knew: The Amazing Story of George H. W. Bush's Post-Presidency

"As a former college football player, I was cheering for Stalowski. As a police chaplain for over a decade who has been called to numerous fatal accidents and delivered too many death notifications, I wanted Stalowski to be severely punished. As a Catholic Deacon for the past twelve years, I have preached forgiveness and redemption from the pulpit. Podkowski does an excellent job writing about the complexity of emotions and consequences of actions. I, along with many, love a great comeback story. *The Walk-On* is one you will love."

Deacon Greg Gitschier, Former police officer, retired Secret Service agent,
current police chaplain, and author of the award-winning book,
Sneakin' Deacon: From Secret Service to Sacred Service

"Sometimes a story is told that reaches us all on some level. *The Walk-On* is just that story. Mike "the Steelman" Stalowski is a man who has achieved legendary status in his NFL professional life while at the same time his personal life is in a steady downward spiral, gaining momentum almost daily. At the NFC Championship game, the two collide.

"As Podkowski tells his story, we follow the Steelman's struggle to the top—his fame on the field—but as for a hero in a Greek play, the tragedy awaits. All comes in turn; all leads to the fall. But with failure there can be triumph. By losing everything, one can acquire insight and focus. With insight and focus, a path can be found for redemption and *this* is what *The Walk-On* is really about. *The Walk-On* is a story of love as much as it is about football. The superb telling of the story takes you from the Steelman's first real emotional breakthrough with a woman to the Sunday gladiator events that earned him his name. I was hooked on this novel from the first to the last page. It's an excellent story that will touch us all."

William L. Albracht, Author of the award-winning memoir, *Abandoned in Hell: The Fight For Vietnam's Firebase Kate*

"From the first to last page, I was immersed in Mike "the Steelman" Stalowski's story, alternating between loving and hating Mike depending on the scene. Despite his NFL fame and bad-boy attitude and antics, I empathized with the humble guy from a blue-collar background fighting painful emotional and physical demons. Podkowski clearly knows and loves the city of Chicago: the ethnic neighborhoods, the grit, the glitz, the lakefront, the diverse people who make it truly unique. Ultimately, *The Walk-On* is an incredible story of love and loss, with faith and mentorship fostering hope for the future."

Bill Rancic, Entrepreneur, Chicago native, and Author of *The New York Times* bestseller, *You're Hired*

THE
WALK-ON

A NOVEL

RICHARD
PODKOWSKI

FROM THE TINY ACORN . . .
GROWS THE MIGHTY OAK

www.AcornPublishingLLC.com

For information, address:
Acorn Publishing, LLC
3943 Irvine Blvd. Ste. 218
Irvine, CA 92602

The Walk-On

Edited by Molly Lewis
Cover design by Damonza.com
Interior design and formatting by Debra Cranfield Kennedy

Printed in the United States of America

ISBN-13: 979-8-88528-034-1 (hardcover)
ISBN-13: 979-8-88528-033-4 (paperback)

This story is dedicated

to those of us

who took a wrong turn

on life's highway.

St. Michael the Archangel,

Defend us in the day of battle,

Be our safeguard against the wickedness

and snares of the Devil . . .

Table of Contents

Troubled Times—Fall 2006–Winter 2007

Road to Redemption—Spring (2007) Forward

ORIGINAL SIN

January 2007

Eve of Destruction—Part One
The First Domino Falls

THE NFC CHAMPIONSHIP HYPE WAS GETTING ON MIKE'S NERVES. WHILE leaving Storm headquarters after the final team meeting, Mike answered a call from his attorney, Steve Kendall. "Why the fuck are you callin' me the day before the championship? Need a couple of tickets? Cash?"

"Mike, it's business. I wanted to tell you because I think the media knows."

"Tell me what?" barked Mike.

"You just got served. Lisa finally filed for divorce. The process server knew he'd never get near you today, so I got the papers. The timing gets her media attention with everyone looking for a story on you this close to the Super Bowl. Allegedly, she already told some Hollywood tabloid she wants out because of your crazy behavior. I think she's out to ruin you, Mike. I don't get it. McClellon assured me we were going to work it out quietly."

Motherfucker! Mike knew the marriage was beyond repair, but he didn't expect Lisa to make the first move by dishing hot lava to the media. By his calculations, a divorce would lower her standard of living to reality, especially if his contract wasn't renewed.

"The complaint makes serious allegations: mental cruelty, irreconcilable differences, binge drinking and narcotic use, extramarital affairs, assault with a deadly weapon. We have to meet as soon as possible. I know it's bad timing, but we can't wait past next week."

"NASTY bitch! She's probably screwing some asshole right now, and she's on top. Fuck her and her papers and her fucking interview!" bellowed Mike. "I've got nothing to hide. She can kiss my ass. I'll see her in court. No fuckin' way she's gonna bleed me dry. I fuckin' made that leech and this is my payback?"

1

Steve let him vent. Nearby players and coaches stopped talking and stared.

"Let HER knock heads on a fucking football field instead of sitting in the stands wearing tight-assed $500 jeans and push-up bras holding her big tits. Fuck her and her fucking Dago disposition. Bring it on man . . ."

Finally, Steve interrupted. "Mike, calm down. We'll deal with it after the game. Don't worry about Lisa, just bring the Steelman's game! Call me Monday after the win."

Mike jammed the phone into his hoodie pocket.

"Hey, Mike, you okay?" asked Castro.

Mike sneered and continued walking down the hall. Don Castro did not like to be ignored.

He yelled through cupped hands. "Stalowski! Is your fuckin' mute button on? What am I? A fuckin' clown in your circus or your Head Coach? I asked *is everything all right*?"

"Yeah, I'm good, Coach," Mike grumbled. "I'm good! Don't worry. See you tomorrow by five o'clock."

"Everybody else is 5:00. You make it 3:30! And read your goddamn game plan tonight!"

Numerous staff members in the Storm front office believed Stalowski wasn't the player he had been, even two years ago. Although he wouldn't agree in meetings, Castro felt Mike's chronic neck pain did sometimes hamper his level of play. But tomorrow the championship was at stake and Castro needed the Steelman to show up to play. He silently hoped Mike Stalowski would remain angry.

Mike's mood suddenly changed when he got to the parking lot. Although cold, the snow had held off that week. No worries about street salt eating his "bitchin" Chevelle Super Sport's freshly painted metal.

When he had picked it up, the Chevy looked like it had just rolled off the 1970 GM production floor. Completely dismantled and rebuilt part-by-part to original specs, the muscle car was meticulously finished with midnight blue paint and white racing stripes. The Steelman went wild when he saw it. As he imagined his father and Uncle Mike would have.

The Speed Shoppe's owner explained the $57,000 process in excruciating detail before handing over the keys. Mike mostly tuned him out, picturing his Uncle Mike behind the wheel, his dad in the front seat, and him as a little kid in the back, holding on for dear life while they cruised Hegewisch.

"One last thing, Mike. Seat belts are backordered. You're screwed if you get pulled over."

"Only if they catch me," laughed Mike.

Forgetting his troubles with Lisa, he unlocked the door. The Chevelle SS turned heads and begged to be pushed to its limits. Mike was happy to oblige. The dual Flo Master exhaust pipes responded with a deep, throaty rumble. He revved the engine in neutral and then shifted into first. The rear tires smoked and the beast fishtailed. He abruptly hit the brakes and stopped with a screech.

Castro and some assistants, who were still walking to their cars, watched in disbelief as Mike power shifted through the gears, hitting the I-355 on-ramp at 80 mph. He unleashed a pavement-scorching demon from its thirty-seven-year sleep.

"When the fuck is he gonna grow up?" asked Castro.

Beaming, Mike listened to the engine whine as the cowl induction flap on the hood sucked air into the quadra-jet carburetor.

Traffic was unusually light for Friday night. Reaching into the back seat, he pulled a beer out of a cooler and popped the cap with his teeth. Downtown lights beckoned. The SS would hasten his arrival. Thank God there weren't any state troopers to slow him down. Passing County Line Road, he flipped off an imaginary Lisa and hoisted the beer. *See ya in court, baby!*

Mike desperately wanted to see Kim, but he knew the Sunset Grill would be packed. With his luck, full of Seattle fans. Mike called her cell. No answer. He tried two more times.

Fuck it! I'm going anyway.

Mike glanced at the speedometer. Almost 90 mph. The engine whined and the SS jerked when he downshifted to take the North I-94 exit. Mike knew people were staring at the classic car. He even got a few beeps and thumbs up. Probably after they deciphered the *Storm 52* tag.

At the Sunset, Mike waved the valet over. "Park this thing somewhere safe. I don't want it within twenty feet of another car, okay? You know how to shift gears, right Smitty?"

"Sure thing, Mr. Steelman!"

Mike peeled off a $20 and smacked it in his palm. "Be careful. I'll be back in about twenty minutes."

Smitty lurched the Chevelle out of first gear, chirping the back tires. The Steelman winced. "Hey, watch the fucking clutch!"

Mike rode the VIP elevator to the fortieth floor. He snuck into the kitchen through a back door and grabbed Mauricio, the head waiter.

"Hey, Mo, tell Kim to come to the kitchen."

"Sure, Mr. Mike. It's very, very busy behind the bar, but I'll let her know."

Mike was seated on two milk crates wolfing down a prime rib sandwich from Mauricio when Kim walked in. "Is eating all you ever do?"

"What's up?" In between bites he noticed her boobs stressing her shirt and vest. "You look pretty good . . . but beat. Tired, huh?"

"I am! God, I'm so ready to get off! I've been here since lunch and still have five hours to go." For weeks, Kim had been afraid to tell Mike why she was exhausted. "Good to see you, baby, but shouldn't you be locked in a hotel by now?"

"Tough practice so Castro threw us a bone. Pre-game hotel's not mandatory."

Kim planted a kiss on his forehead and fanned her face with both hands. A hot flash was coming.

"I stopped to say hello before I go home to study the game plan."

"You study? Seriously?"

Mauricio shot through the door. "Would you like dessert? I have good Key lime pie."

"Sure, I love Key lime pie. It's tart yet sweet." Mike surprised Kim by putting his arms around her. "Like you."

Kim rolled her eyes and groaned at Mike's lame humor. "Oh my God! Please stop." She took Mike's unexpected PDA as a sign to tell him tonight and whispered sexily in his ear. "I've got a surprise for you later, baby."

Mauricio reappeared with a huge section of pie.

"Thanks man, you're the best. Hey, you wanna go to the game tomorrow?"

"No thank you, Mr. Mike. I don't know your game very well. In my country, the football is round. But thanks."

After gobbling the pie, Mike turned to Kim. "Listen baby, I've had a tough day at the office. I'm sore as hell. Tomorrow night a million people expect me to tear the quarterback's head off or snap a ball carrier in two. And to be honest, I don't even feel like playing." He paused. "Oh yeah, I was served with divorce papers today."

Kim was speechless.

"Pretty soon I'm out from underneath her thumb. Then things will be good, Kim. I'll be at the condo when you get off." Mike kissed her cheek and hugged her tightly. "Hey, remember to reserve the room overlooking Mag Mile for the defense victory party. Once the media bullshit is over, we're coming for some R & R."

Kim nodded as Mike stood up to leave.

"See you later," he said and headed for the door.

For the first time in his career, Mike was "this close" to the Super Bowl. Deep down, he knew it was probably his last shot at a ring, but he didn't want Kim at the game where she might be singled out on camera, or worse yet, cornered for an interview. Mike wanted to shield her from the madness . . .

North Lake Shore Drive— Where Beat 645 Meets #52

January 21, 2007, 3:00 a.m.

OFFICER GEORGE GIBSON SAT IN HIS SQUAD CAR. ASSIGNED TO THE TRAFFIC detail, he was parked conspicuously in a northbound curb-cut lane on Lake Shore Drive near the La Salle Drive exit. Gibson lit another Marlboro, hoping his midnight shift would end without incident. He hated early morning car stops even more than floater retrievals.

Unfortunately, he knew tonight might prove to be busy. A few hours ago, the Storm, Chicago's beloved football team, lost the heartbreakingly close NFC championship. Fans drowned their sorrows after Super Bowl dreams were dashed. Following "last call" they drove home.

Gibson's eyelids were heavy when he caught the glare of headlights in his rearview mirror. They were getting bigger—faster. Two vehicles roared past, almost side by side. Pursuit in these icy conditions would be suicide for one, both, or all three vehicles. He let them go and then, did in fact nod off.

"Unit 6-4-5," called the 911 dispatcher. "CFD notified a pin-in involving possible vehicle rollover... northbound LSD at Belmont exit... nothing further... ALS 42 and 11 responding... what is your status?"

George shook his head and saw it was 3:12 a.m. *Oh fuck! Here we go.*

"Squad, 10-4 Squad... en route... 2-minute ETA."

"6-4-5."

"Go ahead, Squad."

"Truck 3 and Squad 1 en route."

Not surprised, might be a fatality. Gibson raced up the Drive as fast as slick streets allowed. Near Belmont Avenue, George saw headlights beaming east, toward the black abyss of Lake Michigan. Something wasn't right. No road was there.

Approaching the off-ramp, he observed skid marks that jumped the curb and disappeared down the embankment. Through the sleet, he saw the silhouette of a vehicle a few hundred feet away, against a tall thick tree. Gibson pulled over without seeing anyone. No witnesses.

He fumbled for his radio. "Squad . . . 645. Confirmed vehicular rollover at Belmont Avenue exit, Lake Shore Drive. Send CFD stat, copy . . . stat."

"645, copy. CFD en route."

He ran toward the vehicle, an older coupe with big tires and mag wheels. A wet blanket appeared to be wrapped around the base of a nearby tree trunk.

Pointing his LED flashlight in that direction, George discovered a young woman with a gaping laceration above her left eye. Her head and neck were snapped back like a broken Pez candy dispenser. Glass shards were sprinkled over her bloody face. Her eyes were fixed and vacant. A shredded sweater exposed her torso and a wingless angel tattoo above her left hip. Gibson checked for a pulse—her slender wrist was limp and lifeless.

Gibson noted the *STORM 52* vanity plate, assuming it was a football fan's show of affection. The driver, a tall stocky white male wearing sweats and a hoodie, was alive. His forehead oozed blood. The front seat passenger, a smaller black male, also had a bad head wound. Both were unconscious. Neither wore a seatbelt.

Their legs appeared to be trapped under the twisted remains of the mangled dashboard. The car's front end had collapsed into the engine compartment. *Probably lost control and rolled it.*

Gibson took another look inside the wreck, stunned by his sudden recognition of the driver's long, blue-streaked blond hair, wet and matted with blood. He quickly called for license plate verification. After what seemed an eternity, his radio crackled.

"Unit 645, Illinois plate STORM 5-2 comes back on a passenger car. A 1970 Chevrolet coupe registered to Steel Trap, Inc., 2020 North Lincoln Park West, Chicago." The dispatcher hesitated. "Registered owner is Michael J. Stalowski." An eerie pause. "Copy?" Gibson shivered and recalled two vehicles blow past him minutes before he was dispatched to the scene.

It wasn't long before the fire department rolled in with a show of force, working quickly and methodically with the Jaws of Life to peel back the classic Chevy's roof like a tuna can lid. Both male victims' legs were trapped. Every precious second mattered in the race to extricate them. Within minutes, their stretchers were loaded into waiting ambulances.

The paramedics' preliminary assessment of Mike Stalowski's injuries indicated a broken right tibia and severely lacerated right wrist and forearm, gouged by flying glass. The passenger's right foot was almost severed at the ankle by shards of jagged steel. The paramedics, fearful the skin and muscle connecting his shattered ankle bones were in danger of tearing off, hoped they could get him in the hands of surgeons before he bled out.

The lifeless female was carefully loaded onto a backboard. A neck collar was secured and an oxygen unit began to pump into her lungs. Paramedics worked feverishly to establish vital signs. Defibrillator paddles failed to jolt her heart. Despite the monitor's stubborn flat line, they continued their valiant efforts all the way to the Northeast Metro ER. The wails of the three sirens overlapped in the stillness of the early morning hour.

By the time the ambulance trio arrived at Northeast Metro, a Channel 5 news minicam van was already positioned at the ER ramp, after picking up emergency responder radio transmissions about a vehicle crash possibly involving two Storm players. Gibson and three CPD escort squads set up a security perimeter to keep the ambulance entrance ramp free and clear. Quickly challenged by the arrival of additional media jockeying for position and curious early-rising pedestrians, the perimeter was expanded, sending the cameras and reporters down the block.

Despite their efforts, by dawn the hospital was swarming with local and national media. Head Coach Don Castro and Mike Stalowski's agent, Shel Harris, rushed to the hospital. No one could fathom the catastrophic tragedy unfolding on the heels of last night's devastating loss.

Reporters and camera crews engulfed Shel Harris as he approached the emergency entrance. Local Channel 7 sports reporter Ryan Donegan stuck his microphone in Shel's face. "Mr. Harris, what can you tell us about the accident that put the Steelman and Christian Blackwell in the hospital?"

Shel glared at Donegan and emphatically pushed the mike away. "Storm management will issue a statement when information is available. NO further comment." He forced his way past the cameras, into the ER.

For months, Shel and the Steelman had not seen eye to eye on contract negotiations. Primarily because, despite Mike's denials, Shel believed he played hurt most of the time. Additionally, Shel's advice to straighten out his personal life had fallen on deaf ears.

Mike Stalowski—a.k.a. the Steelman—was a runaway train that had officially derailed.

Post Mortem

ALS UNIT 11 KNEW THE FEMALE WAS DEAD ON ARRIVAL. KIM RICHARDSON was officially pronounced at 4:42 a.m. by Dr. Valdez, the attending ER physician. The trauma team's final attempt to revive her, shooting adrenalin directly into her flatlined heart, failed. Her face was peaceful when her battered body was covered with a clean white sheet.

It was almost 11:00 a.m. by the time Hillsboro Beach Police located Kim's parents at their club. The Richardsons were in shock. Minutes later, they received a call from Dr. Philip Scanlon, Northeast Metro Chief Pathologist, requesting consent to conduct Kim's post mortem. The Cook County Medical Examiner required a forensic autopsy to determine cause of death in an accident. Kate was too distraught, so Bryce Richardson reluctantly authorized it.

Shortly before noon, Dr. Benjamin Wilson, Chief Hospital Administrator, was at his desk drinking his eighth cup of coffee and preparing for the unavoidable press circus. By 12:05 p.m., two pathologists were scrubbed.

Dr. Scanlon pulled the sheet off Kim's head, temporarily startled by her lacerated but stunning face. He read the ER report, then turned to the attending pathologist who was securing the body diagram to a clipboard so they could note their observations.

"How long have you been here now, Jake? I'm curious how Chicago winter looks to a bona fide West Coast surfer. Can't surf on Lake Michigan in the winter."

"Or any other time! All I know, dude, is when I got done for the day at UCLA Medical Center, I put the top down and headed west on the 10 to clear my nostrils and ride my board at the beach. In the '60s, my old man hung out with the Beach Boys, so I guess it's in my genes. California's bitchin'—Chicago is a bitch!" He took up his position across Kim's body.

His emphatic Southern California surfer inflections got a chuckle from

Scanlon. A little levity was always good during a forensic post mortem that was absolutely serious, potentially making or breaking a case.

"I remember on my one trip to Los Angeles the traffic was horrible, but the smog was even worse."

"Well, I lived in La Cañada, in the foothills above LA. On a clear day, you could see the Pacific. Can't say the same here any day."

They both focused intently on their observation of Kim's upper body trauma.

"You ever cut on any Hollywood stars who met an untimely death?"

"None you would consider famous. I did a lot of drug overdoses and suicides out of Beverly Hills and the Sunset Strip clubs. The cops were in and out of our ER all the time. There were always wannabe stars coming in from a Hollywood Hills party gone wild. I do remember being fresh out of residency when the whole O.J. thing happened. I wasn't there when they brought the bodies in, but I've seen *ALL* the LAPD crime scene photos. It's frightening what a little rage will do to a body."

"So why did you move to Chicago?"

"Back in residency, I'm on a ski trip in Lake Tahoe, and I meet this Chicago girl. We hit it off and lived together near Manhattan Beach. I followed her when she got homesick. Two kids later, I'm in the suburbs and shoveling snow. It's a wonderful life!"

Despite his surfer-boy appearance, complete with ponytail and dolphin tattoo on his left wrist, Jake Davis was known for being one of the hospital's most detail-oriented pathologists. His laid-back attitude complemented his quiet and methodical approach. Dr. Scanlon called on him when he needed solid conclusions with legal and criminal implications. If there were any problems with this one, Scanlon would be called on the carpet.

Davis moved alongside the table, ready to begin examining her torso.

Dr. Valdez walked in. "Hey, guys, just finished talking to the cops. Things are not looking good for our hometown hero."

"This little lady's name is probably all over the news," said Davis. "I'm not surprised he had a girl like this on his arm. What a waste! I'm not a big football fan, but I recognize his name. I know he's pretty popular, especially here, but I understand he's a real asshole."

"Yeah," Scanlon admitted. "I follow the Storm so I can converse intelligently on the golf course. He's still a hell of a football player, but I think he's developed some big problems. He's been jammed up with the cops and in the news a lot. Seems like the media hounds him, but he never says much. Personally, I think knocking heads caught up with him. Keep it quiet, but I know a surgeon who sees him."

While noting the location and description of Kim's tattoo, Dr. Scanlon asked, "What do you make of this?"

Dr. Davis leaned over and peered closely. "I see an angel with no wings."

"Agree."

"Face kind of looks like the Precious Moments figurines my mother used to have."

"Ouch! We still have some around the house."

After Kim's external examination was completed, she lay naked and exposed. Shards of windshield glass had been removed from her face and shoulders. Dried and congealed blood stains had been cleaned, but several gaping lacerations still oozed red against her graying skin. Her golden hair remained matted with blood, brushed off to the sides of her face.

Dr. Scanlon performed the Y-incision which would allow access to Kim's major organs. Jake Davis began to record signs of obvious internal trauma.

"Hey, Jake, if you move the block up a little more, we can start to look at her vertebrae. So far, no real trauma to the pelvic region I can see. No broken ribs. Her pericardial sac looks pretty normal for a twenty-three-year-old."

"Here you go, Dr. Scanlon. Hot off the presses." A pathology lab technician placed a report on the desk and turned to leave.

"Thanks, Vincent." Dr. Scanlon resumed navigating his way through Kim's large intestine and noted aloud that her uterus looked slightly puffy.

"I guess the accident happened a few hours after the game. I watched the second half with my little guy. Our hero, Mike the Steelman, lost the championship for the Storm with about a minute left. According to sportscasters, he blew the last play himself. The Storm should have won and gone to the Super Bowl. Now he's in the ER, and she's on the slab." Jake Davis shook his head. "Did you see the scowling picture of him this morning? He's walking off the field and ripping off his armband with the plays. He looked plenty pissed at that point."

After dictating notes into his voice recorder, Dr. Scanlon took a scalpel to some flesh attached to Kim's liver, which he was balancing in his left hand, just above her stomach. Jake Davis was focused on something in the abdominal cavity. His eyes scanned the lab results, stopping at her hCG level.

Vincent burst in the lab again, coming right up to the table where Kim was being dissected. "Dr. Scanlon, I'm sorry! Dr. Wilson called the lab and told me the newspapers and TV stations are bombarding Media Affairs. He insisted I interrupt the post right now to find out when you'll be done."

Phil Scanlon was usually reserved, but he didn't care for Ben Wilson's hospital impression of Al "I'm in charge here" Haig. "Why don't you tell him to get off his ass and come here himself? I know it's been a while since he smelled an autopsy, but he's a big boy. Look Vincent, you tell our illustrious leader that if he wants this thing done right, he better let those important people know it's at least another ninety minutes. I know he has a press conference to prepare for, but it's MY signature on the autopsy report."

Vincent was a little taken aback. "Got it, Dr. Scanlon, I'll do my best to stall him. FYI, ER labs confirmed Stalowski's alcohol blood level was off the chart. The players are still in intensive but going to make it. Blackwell lost his right foot above the ankle." He looked down at Kim. "I guess everyone is anxious to learn about her."

In the conference room, a swarm of print and live media jockeyed for position while sharing whispered rumors and opinions about the accident. Tom Trahey, the long-time Chicago Storm GM, huddled near the front, alongside coaches Don Castro and Ernie Wallace. They were engaged with Stalowski's agent, who simultaneously conducted a phone conversation.

Janice Miller, Superintendent of the Chicago Police Department, and her Chief of Detectives conferred with Kenneth Hairston, the Cook County First Assistant State's Attorney. The Chicago Fire Department spokesperson was present too.

Dr. Wilson strode purposefully to the podium. "Good afternoon. At this time, I can only confirm the crash victim was a female. There will be no further information for at least two hours, pending completion of her post mortem." He nearly sprinted to the door to escape the inevitable barrage of questions. He thought about stopping by the pathology lab but decided not to.

"Phil, I just read the labs." Jake Davis put the lab report down. "Man, this girl's hCG level is way up! You were right. Look at her uterus. I think it's a first trimester baby bump. I'm guessing somewhere between nine to eleven weeks pregnant. No alcohol or drugs at all in her system. She probably knew she was pregnant. What do you think? This doesn't look good for the steel guy."

Dr. Scanlon stripped off his gloves. He wiped his hands and read the report. There was nothing abnormal about Kim's lab analysis except for the elevated hCG reading. He knew the only way to make sure was to cut into Kim's uterus.

"Shit, Jake! This is probably not one but two fatalities! You know we'll be subpoenaed when this goes to court. Everything has to be documented on the up and up. We'll need forensic proof of the fetus, including gender."

A very unpleasant task faced the two veteran pathologists: identification of a fetus likely less than two inches in length. Slowly and methodically, they revealed and removed the tiny form from Kim's uterus. They worked in silence, except for anecdotal recordings. The fetus measured 1.78 inches, consistent with a pregnancy well into the first trimester. They noted development was consistent with an eight-to-ten-week period of gestation. Though some gender differentiation was taking place, both pathologists agreed that for the official report, gender could not be positively determined. Once the fetus was returned to its mother's womb, Jake Davis quietly remarked he thought he observed male development.

Kim's post mortem concluded at precisely 2:45 p.m. Official cause of death was "a severing of the spine between the C3 and C4 vertebrae from trauma likely received upon ejection through the front windshield of a vehicle involved in a rollover accident." The broken bones, massive hemorrhaging, and numerous lacerations were collateral damage.

Scanlon shook his head as he visualized Kim launching through the windshield and hitting the tree. "It's better this way. She'd be a quadriplegic if she somehow survived, not to mention brain damage. Let's close up and get out of here. Ben will want a play-by-play before his press conference."

"I'll let him know we're done."

Vincent returned as Kim was being rolled back into the cooler. "Dr. Scanlon, the girl's parents evidently want her cremated. A livery service is scheduled to pick her up tomorrow morning."

"Understood, Vincent. I'll tell Dr. Wilson. It's on him to deal with potential legal issues."

Twenty minutes later, they were ushered into Ben Wilson's sixteenth floor office. Phil Scanlon looked out at the green-gray waves crashing against the Lake Shore Drive breakwater. The sleet had stopped, but the horizon was typical for January, bleak and foreboding.

"Ben, I'm still jealous of your tremendous view. Sure hope that telescope isn't trained on Oak Street Beach during the summer. It must be loaded with sunbathers getting a head start on skin damage. Come June, I'll trade you for my office in the Path Lab."

"No thanks."

Jake Davis began to read the autopsy results to Dr. Wilson, who only half-listened. Midsentence, Janice Miller, Kenneth Hairston, and Calvin Pletcher (the Cook County Medical Examiner's Chief Investigator) barged into the office. Pletcher, a political hack in a ceremonial position, stood back silently.

"Excuse the interruption, Dr. Davis." Ben Wilson directed his stern gaze to the officials. "I understand you are anxious for an update, which I planned to provide after I was finished with this meeting. Since you are here, I will share that the charge nurse recently informed me that Michael Stalowski and Christian Blackwell are critical but stable. Stalowski's blood alcohol was .30—more than three times the legal limit. Blood and urine labs revealed drugs in his system. Blackwell's blood alcohol level wasn't as high, but he too was far beyond .08. They remain under police guard. Stalowski is drifting in and out of consciousness. Blackwell is under heavy sedation. We have to agree what will be shared with the media. But first, I need to finish my briefing on the Richardson autopsy."

A short time later, Dr. Wilson began the press conference.

"Ladies and gentlemen, I have information regarding three accident victims transported to the ER early this morning. Both males have multiple injuries and are being monitored in critical but stable condition. They were identified as Michael Stalowski and Christian Blackwell. The female, whose identity is being withheld pending verification by next of kin, was pronounced dead upon arrival from the accident scene. I will not take questions."

Dr. Wilson concluded without taking a breath. He knew they really wanted to hear from the first responders. Those details made for better headlines, providing solemn newscasters enticing *Breaking News* tidbits.

Janice Miller approached the podium, and she wasn't happy about it. As superintendent, it shouldn't be her job to brief the press on DUI accidents and fatalities.

"At this time, the Chicago Police Department is conducting an ongoing investigation. We are working with the Chicago Fire Department to complete a thorough accident reconstruction. I have no further comments." The media was frustrated with the prolonged wait and lack of salacious details.

During Monday's law enforcement press briefing, Kim Richardson was identified to the public. Storm faithful digested horrendous news about the Steelman and Blackwell. Mike was regaining consciousness, coming out of one nightmare only to enter another.

The Steelman's right leg was in a full cast, elevated in a sling. His broken tibia was laid open in surgery and screwed together in three places. God only knew what the long-term impact would be. He had multiple contusions and cuts to his head, arms, and torso. The more serious lacerations to his right wrist and forearm, requiring over fifty stitches, barely missed major arteries. The deep gash in his forehead from the unpadded 1970 steering wheel needed thirty stitches. Mike Stalowski was battered and bruised, unlike any punishment the Steelman had ever doled out or received on the football field.

Blackwell remained under heavy sedation after the amputation of his right foot, just above his ankle. His multiple contusions and lacerations were the least of his worries. The promising career of the talented rookie had been ended by Mike Stalowski and the raging horsepower of his out-of-control muscle car.

Wednesday, the news of Kim's death was broken to Mike by his distraught mother and her husband. Although the former emergency room nurse and her husband, a homicide police commander, knew all too well how to break bad news to victims' loved ones, this was personal.

Late Thursday morning, Mike's doctors determined he was well enough to understand the charges leveled against him. A uniformed Chicago police officer stood watch outside the Steelman's hospital room. Michael J. Stalowski was placed under arrest for the aggravated reckless vehicular homicide of Kimberly Richardson and her unborn child.

Mike stared vacantly with swollen and blackened eyes. He slowly nodded yes when asked if he understood the nature of the charges against him. A reluctant CPD detective read his Miranda Rights in the presence of Kenneth Hairston. The Steelman did in fact remain silent and was then handcuffed to the bed railing.

Mike lay back on his pillow, staring at the bright ceiling lights. The narcotic painkillers may have played tricks on him because he thought he saw Kim's face in a radiant light, looking down at him, expressionless except for her soulful hazel eyes.

Tom knew Janet would not be able to bear seeing her son shackled to the bed, so he entered Mike's room alone.

The Steelman opened his eyes but couldn't seem to focus.

"Mike, this is Tom Dennison, your mother's husband." He reached out his hand.

Though groggy, Mike grabbed it. "Where is she?"

"In the hall. I told her I'd come in first to see how you're doing."

The Steelman slowly nodded. In a raspy whisper, before drifting off again, he commanded, "Don't bring her . . . don't want to see . . . me . . . like this."

AT THE BEGINNING

Summer 2006

The Bikini Bust Out

Kim Richardson was fresh out of college and ready to pursue her dreams in the Windy City. She wanted to be an actress. And that wasn't about to happen below the Mason-Dixon line.

"Why Chicago?" her mother asked. "It's sooo... blue-collar. And you'll freeze."

Katrina (Kate) Mayfield-Richardson expected Kim to marry a rich southern boy with a comparable trust fund. Mickey Mouse had made the Mayfields very wealthy. After plans for Walt Disney World were made public, her father made a killing selling ten thousand acres he owned outside Orlando.

"Momma, for what I want to do, Chicago is the place to be now. I heard living downtown in the Loop is the ultimate, and I'm going."

"I don't know who's filling your head with such nonsense. You know, your father thinks with your looks and charm, you could be a corporate Vice President in five years. Or at least married to one."

Kim stood her ground. "I'm not cut out to be a business executive. Acting is what I want to do. New York and Los Angeles are better known, but I think the opportunity is in Chicago. They always had a lot going on with theater, but movie and TV filming is really taking off there too. They just finished *Batman Begins*."

"We can't forbid you, Kimberly, but we aren't funding your frivolity indefinitely, so you need to hand over your credit cards." She pulled out her checkbook and furiously scribbled. "This will get you started. Make it last until you come to your senses."

"I didn't ask for money, but thank you, Momma." Kim tucked the check in her pocket. "Remember when I got my tattoo and you laughed? Said no one ever heard of a wingless angel except George Bailey? I told you then she'd get her wings when I spread mine. Well, it's time... and I'm following my heart. Something good is waiting for me in Chicago. You'll see!"

21

After leasing a tiny studio outside the Loop, Kim got hired at the exclusive Sunset Grill. In between working long shifts, she took acting classes, attended open auditions and tried to get an agent to represent her.

One day, while hustling as a bartender, she was distracted by the expansive Chicago lakefront and skyline views. *Definitely something to this Third Coast thing. I almost feel like I'm on . . ."*

"Hey, baby!" She was jolted back to the bar by Kevin Corbin, a loathsome attorney.

"Yes, Mr. Corbin?"

"A client took me to the Crunch Bar. You could make serious cash at their bikini contests." Kim had long, sandy colored hair with blonde highlights. Her big hazel eyes were soft yet piercing. Five feet, eight inches of slender beauty, she was tan, poised, and elegant, exuding confidence. "Or I could pay all your bills."

Keep dreaming! "No thanks! I take care of myself."

"The prize money's good and I don't see anybody coming close with your package." He dropped a $20 bill. "My number's on it. Call me for dinner."

Kim wanted to throw it at him, but she really needed the money. Between her security deposit, some secondhand furniture and professional headshots, the $5,000 from her parents was almost gone. Determined to succeed on her own, she had no intention of asking for more, even though she knew they would give her whatever she needed.

A few weeks later, short on August rent, Kim found herself in the Crunch Bar "Bikini Bust Out" final curtain call. Being ogled by a bunch of drunks was the last thing she wanted, but the $2,500 prize would cover two months' rent. Griffin Burke, the owner, welcomed the six contestants onto the stage. He sported a graying '80s mullet and loose Hawaiian shirts to hide his protruding gut. "Girls, SHAKE your moneymaker!"

Griff was a retired All-Pro defensive tackle released from Houston in 1987 after twelve years. Near the end of the regular season, the Storm's starting defensive tackle got hurt, so they bought cheap services from Griff, hoping he had a little more left to give. They never figured he'd help them win a ring, let alone post three sacks and recover a fumble in the 1988 Super Bowl.

A good ol' boy from Texas, he earned the nickname "Crunch" after knocking several quarterbacks out of key games. Too many times, he led with his helmet, which may have contributed to his often appearing a bit punch drunk. Realistically, he probably was a little drunk a lot of the time. Instantly accepted by rabid Chicago fans, Griff was inspired to play two more seasons. The Crunch Bar, where he liked to hang out with fans he thought still cared about the Super Bowl victory, became home after he retired.

The Steelman knew him from sports engagements around town. Mike felt sorry for Griff, who often stayed at his bar after hours, retelling his favorite football stories, known to be exaggerations, half-truths, and false memories. Some people thought he was loud and obnoxious. But Mike liked him. He saw Griff as a football legend, a throwback who played with his heart and led with his head, much like the Steelman.

Knowing he would be a lucrative attraction, Griff had asked the Steelman to be a Bikini Bust Out celebrity judge before leaving for training camp. Mike liked being at Marian College in central Wisconsin because the lake on campus was filled with smallmouth bass and crappie. After dinner when most players socialized or pretended to read the play book, he could fish, often accompanied by Cecil "the Diesel" Cummings, a veteran running back. Mike never joined the end zone prayer circles led by Cecil, but they found common ground watching their lines and bobbers dance in the lake.

The other judges were TV sports personalities Mike didn't care for and definitely did not want questioning him about the upcoming season. Plus, the loudmouth yuppies at Crunch Bar were prone to making stupid remarks. For Griff, though, he would put on his game face and agreed to round out the panel.

Kim's Chicago stage debut, parading around a sweaty sports bar wearing a yellow bikini, wowed the Bust Out crowd. The vote was unanimous.

Mike wanted to escape before his fellow judges asked for off-camera interviews to use on the 10:00 news. He stood up, intending to skip out the kitchen door, but was blocked by Griff who led Kim by the elbow. Now dressed in a black mini-skirt, white tank top with spaghetti straps, and black pumps which showed off she worked out, Mike thought she looked like an NFL cheerleader fresh out of college. He was half right.

"Steelman, meet the winner . . . the lovely Miss . . . What was your name again, honey?"

Kim assumed Mike was lecherous like most of the audience and held out her hand reluctantly. "Hi, I'm Kim," she shouted over the din.

"Mike, Kim's from Florida. I thought she might like to meet a nice hometown boy." Griff smiled like the Cheshire cat. "This is a tough city. People need friends."

"Kim, Mike Stalowski is a football star like me . . . but still plays for the Storm. You've probably seen the Steelman on billboards."

Mike blurted out, "Hey, welcome to Crunch Bar."

Even in heels, Kim was nowhere near eye to eye with him, so she tipped her head back. Mike was an imposing figure. She wasn't up on NFL players but knew from the Grill he was popular.

"Nice to meet you." Mike felt her eyes bore right through him. Trying not to look her up and down, he nervously crossed his arms which made his massive biceps appear bigger.

Close up, Kim was a bit taken aback by the infamous steel trap tattoos. *Guy's over the top.* She stood silently, staring at his long blond locks, streaked Storm blue. *That's one heck of a cut and color! But he's actually kinda cute . . . beautiful blue eyes. Although I don't know what on earth we'd talk about.*

The Steelman felt compelled to break the silence. "You got a hell of a tan for Chicago."

"Well, I've only been here a few weeks. Moved from Florida."

"Oh, right." At a loss for words, Mike stared at the floor. "Hey, how about I buy you a victory drink?"

He seemed like a dumb jock. She wasn't impressed by the bad-boy reputation she'd heard about.

"Ummm," Kim hesitated, "I usually don't mingle with NFL linebackers moonlighting as judges, but I'll make an exception. Just one."

"How do you know what position I play?"

"I read the papers and watch TV sometimes." She continued, "This place does some business. I should bartend here instead of the Sunset Grill."

"You're a bartender? I thought you were like a bikini model or something."

"I'm a better bartender. I feel a little shy walking around in bikinis."

"You didn't look too shy on stage."

"It's an act. I need the money. Anyway, I'm bartending to pay the bills. One of the regulars said I should enter this contest. I REALLY want to be an actress. That's why I moved here. There's a lot going on with theatre and filming more TV and movies. I'm taking on-camera classes and trying to get a talent agent."

Jesus, another starving actress wannabe.

"That's great, Kim. I know people in the business. I've done some endorsements and stuff." Mike hoped she didn't know about his music video fiasco.

"What about you? I saw the Harley bandana in your pocket. Do you ride or do you just want people to think you do?"

He half-smiled, figuring she was busting his balls. "I've had a few bikes. Do you?" He took a swig of beer. "Or did you wear yellow bikinis and drive your red convertible with BEACHBABE vanity plates? Maybe you shoot whiskey and play pool? Or does a girl like you dress up like you wanna ride, but won't get on?" *That might'a crossed the line!* But Kim played along.

"What do you mean," she coyly inquired in her soft sexy southern drawl, "a girl like me?" Laughing, "Okay, okay, I dated this guy who owned a Harley. He was a real estate salesman who thought he was a Hell's Angel. You know, a weekend warrior? He thought I looked good on the back of his bike." She kidded Mike. "I dated him until he traded me in for a Hooter's girl. That was it for motorcycles and me." Kim pouted and flashed her heavily made-up eyes.

Mike took another gulp of beer. *She definitely has my attention.*

When patrons asked, Mike quickly scribbled his autograph and then threw himself back into conversation with Kim. Despite the public spectacle of her victory, she seemed out of place in Crunch Bar. He pictured Kim on his boat— soaking up the sun in her yellow bikini or cruising the lakefront at night—before quickly remembering where that got him with Barbi doll.

Mike took the plunge. "Hey, my bike's out back. How about me and you take a ride? I'll show you parts of Chicago nobody else will."

"Oh, I see," She stared Mike down. "Me and you on the back of your Harley, huh? I don't think it's very ladylike to ride in a miniskirt. Plus, I don't know you that well and you've had a few beers." Sensing he was different than his reputation, she added, "I had a really long day and I'm meeting a friend for breakfast. Maybe a rain check."

Mike took another swig of beer and looked her straight in the eye. "All right then," he matter-of-factly announced. "I'll pick you up tomorrow at 2:00."

"Let me think about it. I'll call you after breakfast."

Hegewisch

TRUE TO HIS WORD, MIKE ARRIVED AT 2:00 SHARP. HE SMILED WHEN KIM walked out. She would be noticed at red lights and roaring past other drivers. Her hair was swept up. She sported large silver hoop earrings and Ray-Ban aviators. She wore tight faded jeans, short black boots, and an aqua blue T-shirt, which would stand out against Mike's black and gold-trimmed Harley.

"Michael, nice to see you're punctual."

"Heck, yeah. Climb on!"

They headed westbound on the Eisenhower expressway, the Steelman's blue-blond hair blowing in the wind. About an hour later, in west suburban Lisle, Mike stopped on Connie Everett Way and turned the engine off.

Kim asked, "Where are we?"

"Where I work. Wanna see my office and cubicle?"

Kim shrugged. "Sure."

Mike fished out his access card and opened the glass door etched with the Chicago Storm logo. He saluted the lobby security guard. Harry McCabe, a retired Illinois State Trooper, was constantly asked to help players get out of speeding tickets.

"Mr. Stalowski, what are you doing here? Forget something?"

"Nope. I just brought this poor stranded motorist to use the bathroom. Her car broke down on 355."

Harry grinned. "You know, sir, some guys have ALL the luck."

"He's lying. I'm his fiancée." Kim elbowed the Steelman. "Come on, baby boy. Let's go." She tucked her arm under his and got close.

Speechless, the Steelman smiled big-time. *Shit, she's feisty too.*

"I thought you played football. This place looks like an insurance sales office."

Kim stopped dead in her tracks when she saw the 3D Chicago Storm logo, a lightning bolt and fierce storm cloud, spanning an entire wall. Then she looked over the action photos encircling the atrium, including a few of #52, sans steel trap tattoos and sporting short blond hair.

"Oh my God, is that you?" she gasped. "You look like you're in high school."

"I get better looking with age," he replied nonchalantly.

Mike led her past the front office to the locker room. Just inside was the trainer's area, where bruised and battered bodies were fixed, like at an auto body shop.

"I'm surprised girls are allowed in here."

"They're not!"

Kim looked around and pointed to a huge stainless-steel tub. "What is that thing?"

"The ice tub. I feel like a beer on ice when I'm in it."

"Really? No way you'd get me in that frigid thing!"

"Ha!" Mike played along. "Maybe I will."

"You're not going to take advantage of a poor helpless motorist are you, Mr. Steelman?"

"Why do you think I brought you here? To work out?"

Mike led her to the locker stall labeled STALOWSKI #52. It was loaded with athletic cleats, gym shoes, practice jerseys, pads, and his helmet. Framed pictures of two boats and his Harley were prominently displayed.

"Nice, huh?" he asked like a proud parent. "Boats and bikes run hard and don't talk back. So this is all my stuff for work. How do you like my office?"

"It's pretty compact. Where's your desk?" Glancing over his gridiron body armor, she noticed the dings, scuffs, and deep scratches on his helmet. Its condition indicated one thing: the Steelman loved to hit hard. "You could use a new helmet, Michael."

He shrugged. "That's an old one. The new ones are a little more durable."

Kim saw more pictures in the corner of the locker. She stood on tiptoes and squinted to see a boy with a flat-top haircut standing on big rocks, holding a fish on his hook. A good-looking man holding a fishing pole was next to him.

"Who's that?"

"Me and my dad."

"Doesn't look like you. That little guy is really cute."

"I was five or six years old I think, maybe seven." Mike hesitated. "Almost every day in early and late summer we went perch fishing after work."

She pointed to a stick-figure crayon drawing of a blond-haired boy and a man fishing on a wooden dock. *Gone fishin' with my dad* was scrawled in crooked green letters. "Why don't you get a buzzcut like that now? You might get a few more endorsement deals." She poked his arm. "Kidding! Are you still close with your dad? I'll bet you are."

"Nope. He died a couple of years after a bad stroke. I was in eighth grade." Mike's eyes dropped to the floor.

"Oh, I'm sorry!" Kim tried shifting the solemn gears. "Hey, that's a big boat. You know, I went swordfishing with my dad when I was little. Southern girls aren't afraid of live bait. Where is it? In Lake Michigan or the ocean?"

"Lake Michigan is my ocean. It's in the harbor near my condo. If you want, I'll take you out."

"Only if you're Coast Guard certified. I bet you have your own crew."

"I do, and they're all hot, including the first mate."

"Yeah, figures."

Mike felt compelled to know her better. She was kind of a sweet smart-ass.

Kim pointed to the last photo. "He looks like your dad, so who's the other guy?"

"His brother, my Uncle Mike. I was named after him. They loved old muscle cars. Supposedly they built that red '62 Chevy 409 and street-raced for money. My mom actually just gave me my uncle's 1970 Chevelle SS. I'm having it restored even though it was barely driven. Just sat under a tarp for years."

"I knew guys in high school who were into old muscle cars and custom pick-up trucks. Thought it was a Florida thing. My mother warned me to stay away because they'd only get me in trouble."

"When my car's done, we should go cruisin' on a Friday night."

"Yeah, maybe." She was definitely interested but didn't want to seem too eager.

"Tell you what. Let's head back to my old South Side neighborhood." He held open the locker room door for her. "I'll show you some of my old haunts and introduce you to real Chicago food. Thin crust pizza at Mancuso's. The food's great! I only take my agent or special dates there." Mike hadn't strung that many sentences together in months.

Mentioning Mancuso's brought back memories of his first date with Lisa. He pictured her with big '80s dark hair, wearing his St. Michael's practice jersey and playing their song, "Living in Sin," by Bon Jovi, over and over on the juke box. *No way she woulda spent the day riding with me—only sat on my bike long enough for the damn newsies to get photos.*

As they approached the lobby, Harry stood up. "Good night, Mr. Stalowski. Congratulations on the engagement!" They all shared a laugh before Mike and Kim left.

"Know what? I like him! Jury's still out on you. First you ride me all over the place on your big Harley and impress me with your NFL stuff. Then you'll butter me up with food and wine. Next, you'll take advantage of me, a poor defenseless girl from Florida trying to make it in the city of big shoulders."

"What? You write fiction?" Mike poked her arm much harder than he should have.

"Hey! That wasn't nice #53! I was just kidding."

"Uh, it's #52."

Kim was surprised he wanted to show her his old neighborhood. Kate had made sure to tell her about the crime-ridden South Side of Chicago, but Hegewisch was an old working-class and tightly-knit neighborhood, culturally stuck in time when the steel mills operated at full force and neighbors looked out for one another.

Kim climbed back on his Harley. "C'mon, let's go! I thought you're buying me dinner at some expensive Italian restaurant."

They rode toward the city, Sears Tower and other skyscrapers looming in the distance. Past McCormick Place, an ever-expanding lakefront convention center, they turned southbound onto picturesque Lake Shore Drive. Gentle blue waves were rolling on Lake Michigan, and the sailboats took advantage of a southerly breeze. Bike riders and joggers filled the lakefront path.

The scene changed a few miles later where Lake Shore Drive merged with South Shore Drive and the lake was no longer visible. Mike navigated through an area mired in poverty. Part of the complex quilt of Chicago neighborhoods, urban decay stood in stark contrast to the stately homes a few blocks east.

Kim saw the Skyway bridge arching high over a neighborhood of row houses and two-flats, where steel mills and the immigrants who toiled in them had prospered until the industry dried up. Most storefront businesses were vacant and shuttered.

"Hey, you're not taking me over that thing, are you?"

"Why? Scared of heights? Don't worry. We're staying on the ground. But we can head back to the Loop that way."

"I am! And no thanks!"

Impulsively, Kim wrapped her arms around his waist. Mike looked down and saw her tanned, toned arms and slender fingers locked around his abs. *Good to have someone besides an offensive lineman cling to me.* His heart raced.

At 95th Street, Mike turned into Calumet Park, which curved along Lake Michigan's shoreline toward the Indiana border a few miles away. For over a hundred years, it had been a green oasis within the industrial landscape. Its popular sand beach provided respite from blue-collar grit for residents of the Southeast Side. Mike parked by the boat launch ramps surrounded by a breakwall, constructed of large, stacked boulders. Extending a couple of hundred yards into the lake, they created an inlet for boats seeking calmer waters. It was also where die-hard fishermen hung out. Mike sat down on a boulder and motioned Kim to join him.

"Remember that picture in my locker? This is the spot. I used to fish for perch here with my dad. Then I met my friend Ric here. And see over there . . . the Indiana border is right past that old power plant with the big black smokestacks. That's all closed now."

"Does your mom still live here?"

"Yeah, but not for long. She's getting married soon and moving to Arizona with her husband. I'm happy for her. She had it tough as an ER nurse in a shitty neighborhood. She worked a lot of overtime to feed me and my sister. And I ate a lot.

"So I used to have to come straight home after school and take care of my dad and Anna until my mom got home from work." Mike avoided eye contact, whispering, "He was in the wheelchair all the time and couldn't talk. He was paralyzed really bad on one side of his body. I had to do everything for him and he never answered because he couldn't. He just drooled a lot and grunted every now and then, but I guess we kind of had our own way of communicating."

"I'm so sorry. That must have been really hard. Where's your sister?"

Mike chuckled. "Anna's a free spirit. She wanted to be a babysitter in France, then a travel writer, then a theatre actress, then a rock guitarist." He shook his head. "It was good to see her on a trip to LA recently. She's chasing the Hollywood dream. Anna's three years younger than me and we don't have much in common, but she's a good kid. Maybe you'd hit it off."

Kim took that as a compliment. "Maybe I'll get a chance to meet her. Free spirit, huh? Runs in the family, I guess. This looks like a place where you could sit in a convertible, listening to tunes and watching the moon and stars at night. In Hillsboro, I'd hang out at the beach with my friends until the cops kicked us out after curfew. A lot of times I'd just go there by myself. I love being by the beach when the sun goes down. It's peaceful and not crowded.

"When I was little, my Momma would take me there to play with my friend Maddie, and we'd run around digging in the sand. You should see the lighthouse at Hillsboro Beach. It stands out like a beacon. I dreamed it was my house and the ocean was my backyard. In high school, I'd go to clear my head. Lay in the sun or look at the stars. It still makes me happy when I think about being there." She looked out over the lake, then turned back to Mike. "So, did you come here often with your special dates, like after pizza?"

"Yeah, sometimes I brought my date here, but only to point out the constellations. Maybe we'll come back later and I'll show you."

Laughing, Kim exclaimed, "I'm sure you will! Mr. Steelman, how do you spell constellation?"

"S-T-A-R-S or B-I-G-D-I-P-P-E-R."

"Very impressive, Michael!"

Only his mother called him that. Mike felt light-headed and not from a concussion for once. He liked the soft, slow, and sexy way Kim said Michael.

Kim slipped her hands in the front pockets of her jeans, wistfully scanning the horizon.

"What are you thinking about?" he asked.

"Nothing in particular. Just comparing the lake to the Atlantic. Looking out over the water kinda reminded me of Hillsboro Beach."

He sensed she was homesick. "So you saw, I got this big boat. We'll go out on it sometime and I'll show you the skyline from the lake. It's way cool, especially at night!"

Kim winked. "Sure, why not. If we have another date!"

They continued to Hegewisch. Kim checked out the neat brick bungalows, two-flats, and old frame houses, all in a row. Mike slowed down to a roll.

Like a schoolboy during show and tell, he proclaimed, "That's my old house— 13011 South Carondelet Street, Chicago, Illinois 60633. The one with the For Sale sign. I grew up there. I hung out across the street in Patriot's Park and played baseball and pick-up football. I also might have snuck a few beers with my buddies when I was fourteen or fifteen."

"Did you ever kiss a girl behind that big old tree?"

Mike immediately thought about kissing Kim there.

"Every chance I got. I had a crush on Brenda Collins, the neighborhood hottie who developed Playboy bunny boobs in sixth grade. She was a year older than me and lived on the next block. Speaking of bunnies, my mom said my Uncle Mike dated a girl from around here who actually became a Playboy bunny and moved to LA."

Kim wiped her brow with the back of her hand. "I guess it comes from drinking the lake water!" Mike looked puzzled until he realized she was busting his balls.

She noticed a sweet-looking old man, sitting on the porch of his brick bungalow, wearing a worn USS Indiana cap, undershirt and faded jeans held up with big black suspenders. He waved the cane resting between his legs when he saw Mike, who flashed a thumbs-up. At the corner, Mike pulled over to the curb and rummaged around in the saddle bag for his phone, which he then put in his back pocket.

"Michael, do you know that old guy we just passed?"

"Very well! That's Chester Janowik. He's a World War II vet—a battleship gunner in the Pacific. They got the shit bombed out of them by the Japs. Almost lost both his legs from shrapnel. Got sent home with one leg and a Purple Heart. His wife died pretty young and they never had kids. Chester sits on that porch most of the time and keeps an eye on the neighborhood.

"When I was a kid, he owned a bait shop near the lake. That's where we got our worms and minnows. He used to tell me and Ric corny jokes and war stories, then plied us with free cans of soda and chips. Sometimes he'd slip me a five and say, 'Go get a hot dog, Mike.' He'd yell at us, too, when he thought we were smartasses, which was most of the time. For as long as I remember, he's worn that old Navy hat. Might be glued to his head! He's probably like ninety and still going strong.

"When I'm in the 'hood I enjoy a few beers with the old guys at Old Tyme Tap, but I like to get them out. I hook him up with tickets for the warmer home games. Chester and some of his VFW buddies get picked up in a van, fed in the

Stormcloud Club skybox, and brought back. They're pretty good guys. Best part, none of them hit me up for autographs."

"That's really sweet, Michael! They must love that."

"After my dad died, Chester kept me in line. He's the only guy I listened to."

While Mike stepped back to make a phone call, Kim tried to sort through the past few hours. The Steelman seemed to be an innocent kid, stuck in an oversized body, who looked like he rode with the Hell's Angels. The sensitive guy she suspected was beneath the wild and crazy exterior definitely piqued her interest.

There must be more to him than all that news nonsense.

They drove past a crowd out front and parked around the corner from Mancuso's. Like the neighborhood, it was stuck in time, starting with the vintage red neon sign in the front window. Everyone loved Mancuso's—cops, firefighters, teachers, and streets and sanitation workers who had to live in the city—lawyers, doctors and professionals no longer bound by residency requirements but who returned in droves on weekends. A recent "neighborhood best restaurant" news segment caused a surge of far-flung city and suburban diners to downtown Hegewisch. They weren't necessarily welcomed by the locals.

Mike hit a speed dial number on his cell. Seconds later, the side door opened. A guy with salt and pepper hair, wearing a white apron, waved them in. Mike fist-bumped Rosario, the head pizza maker and unofficial manager. Like many artifacts inside, Rosy, a cousin from Italy, was a Mancuso's fixture for years.

"Thanks, Rosy! Good to see you, man. Got a quiet booth?"

"Always for you, Mike. Follow me. Very busy today!"

They were led to a booth in an intimate room, off the main restaurant. Rosy took their drink order and rushed off. Kim was surprised by the coin-operated jukebox mounted above the table. The lighting was dim and the song list dingy, but she made out Dean Martin, Frank Sinatra, and the Four Seasons. Also old rock and Motown songs. The early '90s was as contemporary as it got.

"What the heck is this contraption? Something from the Happy Days set? Songs are kind of dated."

"Be careful! I grew up on some of those."

"Real golden oldies, don't you think?"

"They're never old around here. Got any quarters?"

Kim reached into her right front pocket and came up empty. "Sorry, baby!"

Mike's heart skipped a beat. "Hey, Kim . . ."

"Michael," bellowed the one and only Gina Mancuso, in a purple dress and white apron, "my Michael . . . how are you Mikey?" She grabbed Mike's neck in a bear-hug and scowled at Kim. He winced in pain.

Gina's father Antonino used his family recipes from Sicily to satisfy WWII veterans' cravings for the food they had loved while fighting overseas. Sixty years later, Mike made the drive whenever his Mancuso pizza cravings were insatiable. And every time, Gina treated him like a neighborhood kid, despite his football fame and fortune. The portly 5' 2" Italian matron, with a no-nonsense disposition, was larger than life. Her husband had died young, leaving her with four kids to raise. None of them joined the family business. Now in her eighties, Gina still spent time with her customers and spoke her mind.

She gave him another hug and kiss on the cheek. "Mikey, it's good to see you." Gina pulled at his ponytail and shook her meaty finger when she noticed the blue highlights. "You need a new barber. I think the one you got is color-blind." Gina laughed heartily. "Come back to the neighborhood and get a real haircut, eh? You look like some crazy rock star." Mike bit his lip thinking about his recent LA performance fiasco.

"Okay, Gina, you win. Just for you, I'll get a buzz before the season starts."

While a waiter set their drinks on the table, Gina turned her full attention to Kim, giving her the head to toe once over. Gina loved Lisa and her extended family who were good friends and customers. Ever since Mike and Lisa were in high school, she thought they made a cute couple. Her instincts told her this blonde chick, who looked much younger than her dear Mike, was definitely not from anywhere near Hegewisch.

She crossed her chunky arms next to Kim's shoulder. "Hello, honey." Politely she asked, "Are you a relative or friend of Mike's?"

"Yes, I am." She extended her hand. "My name is Kim."

"Uh, which is it honey? You Mike's friend or cousin?"

"Kim and I are friends from promotional stuff downtown. We were out on my motorcycle. She's from Florida so I wanted to show her where to get the best pizza in Chicago." Mike stepped in quickly, expecting Gina to ask a lot of questions Kim definitely did not know how to answer.

"Oh, I see . . ." said Gina, nodding her head slowly. "You know, Kim, people from the South don't know good pizza. Tastes like cardboard with ketchup and Velveeta cheese there. You know like those chains on TV. I guess southerners don't know good food unless it's greasy and fried." Gina let out a loud belly laugh and poked Kim's shoulder.

"Thanks, I'll remember that." Kim forced a curt smile and took a long sip of her house red wine.

"Mike, when you going to play football? Everybody in the neighborhood comes when you play."

"Camp begins Monday for me, Gina. After I see my doctor. The season starts in September. If we go to the Super Bowl, we'll bring the team for dinner and make a commercial. You'll be famous."

Kim sat quietly, pondering his doctor remark.

Gina put her arm around Mike's shoulder and tussled his hair. "I'm famous already, Mikey! Whatta you talkin' about, huh?" She pinched Mike's cheek and kissed the spot. "Mikey, you guys have fun. Say hello to your mother and Tom. They make a great couple. God bless them. You don't get hurt, eh? Nice to meet you, Linda." Gina smiled and made the sign of the cross before moving on to the next table.

"I don't think she liked me too much. Sure loves you, though! And why do you have to see a doctor before camp?"

Mike sidestepped her last question. "No, that's just Gina. I started working here when I was thirteen. Rosy taught me how to wash dishes and bus tables. She still thinks I'm sixteen, hangin' around with my teammates." He knew Kim would eventually learn about Lisa, the missing puzzle piece to Gina's cool reception.

The rest of dinner went well. Kim had two small pieces of thin crust pie and another glass of red wine. The Steelman ate the rest, plus a huge antipasto appetizer, but no beer. He remembered what Kim said about mixing bikes and beer. Never one to open up, especially about his family or football, he was surprised to feel comfortable around Kim. He didn't even mind the first date small talk.

She told him about growing up in south Florida and hanging out at the Panhandle beaches near Florida State University. Clearly, she loved being near the ocean. Mike shared his love of boating on Lake Michigan's open water.

Eventually, Kim talked about her parents' dreams for her future. "My dad owns BRDI, Bryce Richardson Distribution Incorporated, a big string of consumer goods warehouses in Florida, Alabama, and Georgia. He's filthy rich. I grew up on Millionaire Mile in an oceanfront mansion. He's also President of the Hillsboro Beach Chamber of Commerce, a scratch golfer, and a big fundraiser for the Florida Republican Party. Since I'm an only child, he wanted me to join the family business and get involved in politics. He said I had a lot going for me and I should develop my talents. He never bought into my acting dreams. Claims theatre is a waste of time.

"Never spoke to him much after his *second* affair." She continued matter-of-factly. "My mother is a kept woman. She spends most of her time on her cell phone or playing tennis before lunch with the girls at the Hillsboro Club. When I was little, she'd dump me at the kids' activity center for most of the day and pick me up after mimosas or martinis."

Mike couldn't believe she was so candid. He was enthralled, listening to her soft southern drawl and rapid fire delivery, while looking into her mesmerizing eyes.

"Kate Richardson loves her lifestyle even though my dad is a jerk to her." Kim shrugged. "Although she tells me not to put up with a cheating husband." Kim smiled as she twirled her glass. "She wasn't too supportive of my move to Chicago either. Guess I showed them, right?"

"Sounds like you got quite a family thing going on. No wonder you left."

"I'm in no hurry to go back and visit. Let them come up and see me." Kim brushed her hair back with her fingers and looked straight into Mike's blue eyes. "That's me," she smiled, "a Southern girl in the Windy City, trying to make her way."

Unsure how to respond, he changed the topic.

"You know when I worked here as a busboy, Gina always let me eat at the end of my shift. My family came here since I was a little kid. I grew up on this stuff and still think it's good. How about you? Like it?"

"I really like this pizza. So I cheated today. I eat well most of the time and I like to work out. I had a cruiser bike down in Hillsboro I loved to ride up and down the beach. Believe it or not, I also took kickboxing and ran a marathon."

"I run like I'm dragging a piano," Mike laughed.

By the time they left Mancuso's, stars shone brightly over the lake. Mike made a quick right turn at 95th Street, into Cal Park. They sat on the beach, looking out over the water. The moon rose higher, casting its glow on the gentle tide.

"I like being out on my boat at night. It's quiet, and the city is all lit up. You have a standing offer to join me sometime. You'll be glad you did."

"That sure sounds like a come-on, Michael! I won't have anywhere to escape—and neither will you," she winked.

She unpinned her hair and Mike watched it gently blowing in the wind. Their eyes met and they drew closer. Their first kiss began tenderly—but after a long time—ended voraciously.

After cruising around downtown, he finally pulled up to Kim's West Loop condo about 1:00 a.m. Mike felt himself turning down a road he hadn't traveled in a long time: real interest in a woman.

"Kim, what are you doing tomorrow morning? I've got some time before I have to get ready for training camp and was wondering if we could get breakfast? The Palace Grill is only a few blocks from here."

"Michael, I can't. I have to work Sunday brunch until 3:00, although maybe you could call me later." Kim paused. "But I have to get home early because I have an 8:00 a.m. appointment at Elite Modeling Agency."

"How about I pick you up at 6:00? We'll go to Taylor Street for Italian ice. It's close."

Kim was definitely interested but decided to drive a hard bargain. He broke the mold of the guys she dated before—college preps and privileged southern boys who drove souped-up Jeeps on the beach and expensive convertibles at night.

"Maybe. Call me around 4:00. I'll let you know."

"Okay, I'll see you at 6:00." Mike smiled to himself and started the bike, letting it idle at a low rumble while she walked inside the glass-skinned condo tower. She stepped in the elevator and turned around. As the doors were closing, she blew him a kiss and mouthed, "Thank you." He flashed a thumbs-up.

Not wanting the night to end, he thought about following Kim upstairs. He hadn't felt a rush of emotion like this in years. The separation from Lisa seemed to have destroyed his ability to be happy with anyone, let alone a recent college coed. Post-Lisa, he'd been "sworn to fun and loyal to none." Who would expect Kim Richardson of Hillsboro Beach to have such an impact on his life—and he on hers.

Wrigleyville

Mike pulled up in his newly washed Chevy pick-up truck at exactly 6:00, and they headed to Martino's. For over fifty years, the hole-in-the-wall Taylor Street landmark served the best Italian ice in Chicago. Kim looked great again, in a T-shirt and shorts, with her hair pulled back. Mike wore his standard disguise: ponytail with a backwards Old Style beer baseball cap, wraparound shades, jeans and a long sleeve T-shirt covering his steel traps. Blending a 6' 5", 255-pound NFL middle linebacker into a crowd was not easy, but it was particularly important he kept a low profile here. People in Little Italy had long memories and his last visit had ended with his arrest.

As soon as they finished their signature watermelon Italian ice, Mike drove north on Halsted Street and surprisingly found a parking spot on Waveland. He figured Kim might like the North Side better because it was more like her roots.

He was a lifelong South Side White Sox baseball fan, but Mike happily walked near Wrigley Field where the Cubs reigned. Waiting to cross the busy intersection of Clark and Addison, he spontaneously grabbed her hand and intertwined their fingers. Kim didn't pull back. O'Rourke's Irish bar, underneath the Red Line "L" tracks, wasn't too crowded so they went in.

After grabbing drinks at the bar, they settled in at a booth. Kim shared exciting news.

"I have an audition for *A Christmas Carol* in two weeks. It's for young Scrooge's girlfriend Belle. Before he became an old money-grubbing tyrant. Never did a British accent, but I'm working on it."

"Oh, yeah! I know about that one. Scrooge and the ghosts. Last year a few guys from the team were in it for charity. They did background stuff like singing. Those big top hats are the best. Maybe I'll do it this year if you make the cut."

"Oh, I can see it! You'd look cute, Michael, with that blue and blond ponytail sticking out of your hat." Kim laughed and took a sip of wine. "Scowling like Scrooge himself!"

After a few beers, Mike's concentration waned. Kim was beautiful and idealistic, full of life and dreams, and all he could think about was the total mess his life had become. A divorce showdown with Lisa seemed inevitable. Connie Everett, the Storm team owner, was pissed about sensationalized media reports concerning his social life and missteps with the law. Not helpful for upcoming contract negotiations. And his physical aches and pains were a constant reminder his playing days had a timestamp.

"Are you looking forward to the season? I'll bet you get excited this time of year. How do you live with all your fans wanting you to be the Steelman or Steeltrap or whatever steel thing they call you?"

"Sometimes it's tough. I try not to believe that b.s. too much. I just like playing football. It's what I know."

Kim suspected Mike was uneasy in the public circus of his life.

He thought about asking her over to his place but didn't, figuring she would decline the invitation. They headed back much earlier than he wanted. Outside her building, Mike wished with all his might Kim would make the first move and invite him upstairs. She leaned over the center console and looked directly at the Steelman. Her hazel eyes drew him in.

"Michael, I don't know why we met the way we did. I don't usually open up easy about personal stuff. This is all fast and crazy! It feels like two months have passed in just two days. But here's what I *do* know—you're a famous football player and kinda intimidating, but I think you're sweet." Kim paused and almost whispered, "I want to be careful about this, but I do want to see you again soon. How about you?"

Mike couldn't believe it. Fumbling for words, he answered awkwardly. "Yeah! I mean yes. You're nice too. And you smell pretty good."

Kim giggled. "Gee, thanks! I can't wait until you say something really flattering. Well, I hope you think of me at camp. You've made me feel like I belong in Chicago. However, Mr. Steelman, I don't want you to think I'm a pushover."

After a short but tender kiss on the cheek, she exited. Mike watched her walking away. This good-bye was turning into something he never expected. He had to say something before she got inside. Mike dropped the window. "Hey, Kimberly, can I call you from camp? No phones during the day, but I can call at night."

She turned around and nodded approval. Kim closed her eyes, kissed two fingers and blew a hurricane of emotion toward the Steelman.

———————•———————

Brandon Stokes, Mike's roommate this year, was a nine-year veteran outside linebacker traded to the Storm in the off-season. Stokes played the strong side with almost as much fury as Mike in the middle.

Stokes had four stair-step boys, aged 2–7, and a needy wife. Clarice left him messages all day long about the trouble the kids got into and how much she needed him at home. After his evening check-in, he turned his ringer off. He was a great father, but dog-tired.

After several days of toiling side by side on the field, Stokes was comfortable enough to needle his roommate. "Steelman, if you want to talk to your girlfriend, how 'bout you do it in the lounge down the hall. I'm tired man! Need some peace and quiet to watch CSI."

"I got me a woman, brother. I'm in . . . don't cramp my style!" Mike laid his head on the pillow, arms crossed behind his neck, staring dreamily at the ceiling.

"You're in what, brother? Love?" Brandon laughed.

"None of your business, bro! Just read the playbook."

After two weeks in camp and a preseason away game in Minneapolis, Mike couldn't wait to see Kim. Despite chronic neck pain, he looked like he'd regained some of his old Pro Bowl form and the intensity he lacked last season. The coaches wondered what put the fire back into him. If they had listened in on his nightly conversations in the student lounge, they would realize he found someone to believe in again.

———————•———————

Finally wheels down at O'Hare the week before Labor Day. The last preseason game would be Thursday night at Veterans Stadium. Mike couldn't wait to see Kim and called to make dinner plans. Fishbone, near the Oprah Winfrey Studios and just a few blocks from Kim's studio, was one of Mike's favorites.

Kim primped a long time, finally deciding on a yellow sundress with white polka dots and black stiletto heels she knew he'd notice. Especially since she tuned up her Florida tan studying lines on the sundeck. Eager to see Mike, she would have jogged all five blocks if not for the damn heels.

Kim made it there in time for one last look in the bathroom mirror. *Nearly perfect.* She wet her lips with gloss and went to wait at the bar. Someone tapped her shoulder. She knew guys were staring at her and turned around to shut them down. Her heart beat faster. It was Mike.

The spark from a few weeks ago was now blazing. They embraced and she momentarily brushed her lips against his.

Kim pulled back, gave him her biggest puppy dog eyes and grabbed both of his hands. "Hi, baby! I've got a million things to tell you. Remember I was really super bummed I didn't get that part in *A Christmas Carol*. Well, guess what I found out today? *GREASE*—yes, *GREASE, the Musical*, is holding November auditions! It's one of my all-time favorites. We have to watch the movie together soon."

"Sure! God, you look good! Nice heels by the way."

Kim playfully threw her hair back across her shoulders. "I bought them for you."

"Really? Well, that's great, but how about let's eat. I'm hungry as hell and ready to stick a fork in your leather purse if we don't order soon."

After dinner, Mike didn't have to work too hard to get Kim back to his condo so they could talk uninterrupted. Not that they talked much anyway. When he opened his eyes the next morning, Kim was asleep. A newly minted college graduate—much different from Lisa—had caught him hook, line, and sinker.

For the last preseason game, Kim sat in the Storm's Family and Friends section. Assuming she was a temporary trophy girlfriend, most of the wives gave Kim the cold shoulder when she politely announced she was a friend of #52. Clarice Stokes was one of the few to engage her in conversation. She was from Jacksonville, Florida which at least gave them something to talk about.

On the final Tampa Bay drive, even though he was double-teamed, Mike sacked the quarterback. The crowd went wild. Diesel Cummings scored on the next play for a Storm win. Many Storm faithful had visions of Super Bowl rings in their heads.

Mike instinctively tugged his faceguard when he saw Kim. She didn't notice the gesture and wouldn't have understood the significance anyway. In recent years, Lisa no longer noticed because she was too busy making sure she was front and center for the cameras.

After the game, Mike and Kim retired to his condo. She came out of the bathroom with #52 written in sparkly pink lip gloss on her cheek. Mike smiled and shook his head. For a fleeting moment, he thought of Lisa and high school football games, but easily shrugged it off. Soon the Steelman sacked another Florida native. This time—HE scored on the next play.

BEFORE
THE FALL

St. Michael the Archangel High School

Chicago, Illinois; October 22, 1993

As a freshman, Mike Stalowski first inhaled the pungent smell of St. Michael's chapel, a distinct mixture of incense and floor wax. He had brought up the rear on his initial holy trek from the locker room. Now a senior, he led the charge of cleats clattering down the gleaming tiled corridor. Dressed in silver and blue battle gear, the team prayed in unison near a life-size portrait of St. Michael the Archangel, whose huge, muscled arms wielded a mighty sword to vanquish the devil.

"St. Michael the Archangel, defend us in the day of battle. Be our safeguard against the wickedness and snares of the Devil. May God rebuke him, we humbly pray, . . ."

The Crusaders fervently prayed to vanquish the Resurrection Ramblers, their North Side rivals. The Chicago Catholic League Gold Division championship title and a shot at the state playoffs were at stake. During his twenty-two-year head-coaching tenure, Coach Grogan had won the state championship twelve times, most recently in 1990, the year Mike Stalowski began his football career as an average defensive back.

He had grown quickly, both as a teenager and a player, currently 6′ 2″ and 220 pounds of ripped muscle. With each passing game, the starting middle linebacker's sacks and tackles increased in number and ferocity. Mike developed quite a reputation in the almighty Chicago Catholic League. The mere mention of his name caused opposing running backs and receivers to cringe. College scouts took notice.

Along with fervent pregame prayer, discipline was instilled in every facet of the program, on and off the field. Each player was drilled endlessly in St. Michael's football fundamentals: ferocious tackling, blocking, and ass-kicking. Discipline and ass-kicking were the job of the assistant coaches, including Father John L. MacKenzie.

45

Still sporting the same flat-top haircut—now sparse and white—MacKenzie had been a fixture at St. Michael's since 1963.

Father Mac, as he preferred to be called, was also the St. Michael's Dean of Discipline. An imposing figure with a blue-eyed steel gaze like John Wayne, his stare made students tremble. His instructions were loud; his punishment was corporal, usually consisting of a solid whack to the back of the perpetrator's head. For emphasis, Father Mac would turn his Notre Dame class ring around so the stone made first contact with the student's skull. But that was tame compared to what he was capable of when he was pissed.

He grew up in Canaryville, next to the city's stockyards, in a tough, shanty Irish neighborhood not known for turning out Catholic priests. There was a tavern on every corner where patrons settled their differences with fists. As a boy, he used his to resist joining a gang. Named after John L. Sullivan, the Irish boxing legend, Father Mac must have picked up some of his prowess, winning the coveted Chicago Golden Gloves boxing title as a teen.

He took up football in high school when his raw talent was noticed by an assistant coach during a lunchtime pick-up game. He became a standout defensive tackle at Notre Dame and likely would have gone on to the NFL, if not for divine intervention in the form of a career-ending knee injury. Working toward a teaching degree, Father Mac heard the calling and followed it to St. Mary's Seminary, north of Chicago. After two years as a parish priest, he was assigned to St. Michael the Archangel High School, where he was feared but fair.

The Dean of Discipline was quick to pass out jugs for the usual high school infractions and to players who were late to practice or forgot plays. It's an urban myth in Catholic high schools that jug, otherwise known as after school detention, means "justice under God." It's derived from Latin *sub jugum* or "under the burden." Mike Stalowski was religiously under the burden of Father Mac.

No one intentionally crossed Father Mac. He sometimes gave rule breakers the choice to attend jug or go five rounds in the ring with him. Ninety-nine percent chose jug. The other one percent wished they had. Father Mac rarely showed it, but under his gruff exterior, he had a soft side for kids he thought needed extra help to "find their way."

Long before Father Mac's arrival, St. Michael's had a rich history of academic and athletic success, based on a solid foundation of discipline and mentoring. Built in 1910, the Gothic-looking campus, at 71st Street and South Cottage Grove Avenue, near the lakefront on the Southeast Side of Chicago, was clean and in good repair due to strong alumni support. The Jesuits taught, mentored, and disciplined the sons of European ethnic enclaves, mostly city workers, tradesmen, and steel workers who toiled in the nearby smoke-belching mills. In the mid-'70s, the school enrolled the growing influx of black and Hispanic students. Despite "white flight" from the city, suburban boys continued to attend based on the school's academic reputation and perennially successful football program. A lengthy commute to St. Michael's did not concern recruited football players or those who thought they had a chance to walk-on the storied team.

"*. . . and do Thou, O prince of the Heavenly Host, by the power of God, cast into hell, Satan and all the other evil spirits, who prowl through the world, seeking the ruin of souls. Amen.*"

After the traditional prayer, Mike didn't engage in the usual banter. He was pissed off when Ricky Bell, who was getting looked at by Ohio State and Michigan scouts, slapped him on the shoulder.

"Hey! STEEL . . . LAKOWSKI—Stall . . . LOVESKI—Steel . . . LOWSKI. Brother, your name is too fuckin' weird! You and that fuckin' defense better be on your game, man. Everybody's lookin' at us. Right STEEL-MAN?"

Dan Boskovich, the quarterback, and tight-end Brendan O'Connor also slapped Mike on his shoulder pads. O'Connor added, "Yeah, Steelman, we better win this fuckin' game. I ain't losing to these assholes, especially White. The offense will take care of the score. You and the defense take care of the milk and cookies!"

Mike flipped them off. He wasn't fond of the nickname.

In Polish, "stal" meant steel, and Stalowski sounded out as Stah-lov-ski. Most people mangled the pronunciation. His teammates shortened it to Stal-man which morphed into Steelman. The quiet but intense kid, from the hardscrabble Southeast Side in the shadows of the steel mills, was destined to carry his high school nickname his entire life.

The team boarded the school bus for the short ride to Pullman Stadium, their inner-city home turf shared by nearby public and Catholic schools. Landlocked by poverty and crime, it was in dire need of a facelift, especially the circa 1975 Astroturf. The stadium was more worn green-carpet-covered concrete than it was a field. Despite conditions that caused more injuries than the violent game of football itself, Pullman Stadium was a field of dreams for young football players looking for their ticket to a Division I school—and, for a select few, the NFL.

The windows were a bit fogged up. Playing in the cold never bothered Mike. He imagined players would look like charging bulls, heads lowered and snorting visible breaths across from each other at the line of scrimmage. Mike often sat alone to deal with his pregame anxiety. Tonight, he pondered his future. It was senior year. All he knew was he wanted to play football. He didn't care where. Mike and academics were often at odds. Luckily, his girlfriend Lisa Morello, who attended McKinley High, was a whiz at math and English. She helped him with assignments, keeping him on track to graduate. He expected they would probably go to different colleges.

Mike wiped part of the window clear and gazed at the boarded-up and graffiti-filled storefronts on South Cottage Grove Avenue. A well-known sign caught his attention. Sullivan's Drive-In was THE neighborhood hangout for years. The dust-covered neon sign outlining a huge Chicago-style hot dog (mustard, no ketchup) was once a beacon of light for hungry teenagers and Gresham neighborhood families looking for soft serve ice cream cones on hot summer nights.

Mike loved hearing Father Mac's stories about Sullivan's during religion class. A friend of Patrick and Maura Sullivan, Father Mac had been a frequent patron himself since he began coaching in the '60s, often treating players after football practice. After school, St. Michael's boys had gone there to meet girls from nearby Mother Seton High School. After dances in the '50s and '60s, it would be packed. Mother Seton "mixers" had been the basis for many a lecture on how young men and women should behave. The students were also frequently warned not to pick fights with the "publics" from nearby McKinley High School. Many high school crushes had begun at Sullivan's. Some relationships had endured, providing the next generation of student-patrons. Not surprisingly, there had been a few fistfights over girls or neighborhood turf. Father Mac's stories always concluded with the social and moral lessons a young man should learn from hanging out at Sullivan's.

After Maura succumbed to cancer in 1972, "Sully" decided it was time to move on. The city's demographics were radically changing. Sparked by the assassination of Martin Luther King, the 1968 race riots accelerated "block-busting" real estate practices. To maintain segregation, families and businesses fled farther south and west in the city or settled in new suburban subdivisions carved from farms. Twenty years later, Sullivan's remained vacant and lifeless. Vandalized repeatedly, it was a dangerous eyesore, almost begging for a wrecking ball to turn the memories to dust. In contrast, just a few miles south where Mike lived, the residents of Hegewisch stood firm and refused to move.

The bus bounced through a rough patch of potholes, jolting Mike. Time to focus on stopping Lorenzo White from gaining yardage and moving the sideline chains closer to a touchdown. White, the son of a prominent Black attorney, was the Catholic League's premier running back, playing for a team that was big, fast and well-coached. His politically connected father was one of the first to move his family from the South Side to Edgebrook, at the northwestern corner of the city, where mostly white, well-to-do parents sent their indulged kids to play sports at privileged schools. Lorenzo was a bright, articulate student-athlete on the fast track to a Division I football scholarship, with most of the Big Ten schools and beyond trying to recruit him.

But Mike knew White as a cocky running back and receiver, very capable of running around or over defenders. Lorenzo was well-aware of the ferocious hits Stalowski delivered. Mike feared White would run hard, trying to bust big runs through the secondary, to impress college scouts in the stands. Lorenzo wouldn't want Mike making him look bad.

All year, coaches told Mike if he wanted to get noticed by Division I scouts, he needed a break-out game to complement his likely All-Conference and All-State season. Only seventeen, he looked twenty-one. His style of play mirrored several NFL defensive legends known for their intensity and ability to instill fear in opponents—Nitschke, Butkus, and Lambert—all rolled into one. Mike wasn't worried about impressing college scouts; he simply wanted to stop the Ramblers offense, specifically White.

Yesterday, Coach Grogan had looked intently at each and every defensive player. "Guys, show your opponents with the first hit that you came to play. When you get the chance—knock someone on their ass. You're either gonna be the hammer or the nail. Make your choice." Tonight, the choice was evident.

The Crusaders scored quickly on Boskovich's pass to the tight end. They held the Ramblers to a single field goal during a defensive battle throughout the first half. Mike was at the bottom of gang piles and completed bruising mid-air solo tackles—most often leading with his helmet.

Late in the fourth quarter, the score was St. Michael's 14, Resurrection 9. The Crusaders' defense held the Ramblers to three field goals. Suddenly, left defensive end Max Calavano missed a tackle, allowing Lorenzo White to turn the edge and break a 45-yard sideline run to the Crusaders 11-yard line. On a last-chance drive to the end zone, less than a minute to go, Lorenzo was relentlessly clawing for yardage, determined to score the winning touchdown himself, earning a trip downstate and a Division I scholarship. After two broken pass plays, including a near fumble, it was 4th and 11, with 27 seconds left. The final chance to score—and win—came down to Lorenzo White's powerful legs.

Both sides of the stadium were rocking, drowning out the quarterback's cadence. Stalowski, gasping for air, knew his defense was tired. He was sure White would try an end run or bull his way up the middle. He looked to the sideline. Father Mac signaled "Blue 47," an all-out safety blitz. Remembering *hammer or nail*, Mike understood it was on him to stop White.

The ball was snapped. A straight-ahead run by White, through daylight in the B-gap, challenged the front four of the Crusaders' defensive line. He saw the blitz coming and knew if he could get past the linebackers, he could outrun the secondary—untouched into the end zone. Double-teamed, White blew past the nose guard and tackle.

Stalowski saw him on the periphery and instinctively cut left in midstep to square off. Mike put his shoulder down and led with his helmet, planting it between the numbers on Lorenzo's chest, almost causing a fumble.

He followed the obvious spear hit with his entire center of mass, standing White straight up—separating the soles of his cleats from the turf by a good six inches. Not only did he stop Lorenzo dead in his tracks at the 5-yard line, avoiding an end zone romp, he drove White back, planting him face first on the turf. White stayed down. No one noticed "Holy shit!" emanating from Father Mac's pursed lips.

After what seemed an eternity, White got up slowly, humiliated, and was helped off the field. The St. Michael's fans nearly imploded Pullman Stadium. The Crusader quarterback took a knee to let the play clock expire. Prayers answered. Victorious in battle. The scoreboard blazed 14-9.

"STEELMAN ... STEELMAN!" The crowd stomped on the metal bleachers and roared. Mike bent over on the goal line. His ears were ringing. His eyes were sensitive to the blazing Friday night lights. He refused to be carried by his teammates. Battle-weary, he just wanted to get to the locker room. His head ached. His neck was stinging like he'd been hit with a baseball bat. He thought he saw Lisa in the midst of cheering fans. Her cheek painted with #52. She held up her hand and blew him a kiss. Normally, he'd tug on his face guard—his "I Love You" signal—but Mike pulled off his helmet and stumbled to the locker room. Collapsing on the bench, he buried his head in his hands. The team rallied around him, whooping and hollering. The Steelman slowly raised his head and acknowledged his teammates with a half-smile. Eyes glazed—ears ringing—head aching—neck stinging—he pounded on a locker with both fists and shouted, "YES... YES... YES... We fucking did it!"

Two weeks later, Mike Stalowski racked up five more devastating solo tackles, a sack, and a fumble recovery for positive yardage. The Crusaders won their thirteenth IHSA Class 8-A Championship, beating downstate powerhouse Taylorville Central, 31-3. He accepted a full scholarship to play Division I football at the University of Illinois, following in the footsteps of Dick Butkus, a former NFL linebacker also from the South Side of Chicago. Shortly before graduation, in the spring of 1998, Mike Stalowski was drafted by the Chicago Storm in the seventh round. Surprised scouts said he'd never make it in the NFL—not too smart and not too fast. Ecstatic Chicago football fans looked forward to the storm Mike would bring to the field, but there was no predicting the serious storm coming for this hometown kid who played with a chip on his shoulder and hit with the intensity and power of a wrecking ball.

Affairs to Remember

Joe "Stacks" Stachowiak was the first guy to befriend Frank Stalowski, Mike's dad, when he and his family immigrated to Chicago from Poland in seventh grade. The rumor was Joe's nickname came from his proficiency winning and stacking poker chips. Or maybe—like Steelman—it was an abbreviated version of his surname.

Frank only knew a few English phrases, and Joe only knew a few Polish words, but they quickly became close friends, playing sports and hanging out in Patriot's Park. Unlike Frank, Joe was outgoing and did well in school.

A gifted athlete, he played football at Dominican Catholic which churned out Catholic League All-Stars like Ford turned out Galaxies at the Torrence Avenue plant. Sophomore year at Notre Dame, he tore ligaments in his right knee recovering a fumble. He transferred to Loyola in Chicago to finish his degree and began his ascent to social and career heights not normally available to kids who hung out in Patriot's Park.

The Stalowski brothers were fortunate too. Just two years apart, they were close. Frank relied on his older brother when he got in a jam or other kids made fun of his accent. Mike was always there for him.

They followed their father to U.S. Steel South Works, working side by side in one of the last operating steel mills on the southern shore of Lake Michigan. At one time, native Poles comprised forty percent of the workforce. Frank's old world work ethic quickly got him promoted to the blast furnace; while Mike eventually left the mills and became a car mechanic. In 1971, shortly after Mike died, Frank was promoted to heavy crane operator, earning another raise and working more overtime.

He went to work, came home, and played softball four nights a week with the "Men of Steel," a local park district team. Frank learned "16 inch" in Patriot's Park pick-up games. He loved Chicago-style softball; it was his only interest outside work. Although Joe Stacks didn't work at the mill, he was allowed to join Frank when the team needed a ringer with a heavy bat.

Four hundred family members and friends, primarily the bride's, attended Joe Stacks' June 1972 wedding at the exclusive Beverly Ridge Country Club. The Irish bride from affluent Beverly and the Polish groom from the Southeast Side met at Loyola University. Colleen never really intended to pursue a career; she went to college to find a worthy husband. After law school graduation, Joe was fortunate to be "recruited" by the Cook County State's Attorney's Office. Colleen's dad, the Chief Cook County Circuit Court Judge, just happened to know of an opening.

"Frankie, have I got a girl for you!" exclaimed Joe. "Wait until you see her!" Joe steered the reluctant Frank toward Colleen who was chatting with a guest.

Janet Krolik had become friends with Colleen freshman year at Longwood Academy for girls. They stayed in touch when Colleen headed downtown for her "Mrs. degree." Janet attended nursing school while working as a nurse's aide at Little Company of Mary Hospital. She lived nearby in Mount Greenwood. At the southwestern corner of the city, the neighborhood was popular with City of Chicago employees who had a residency requirement, mostly firefighters and police officers.

Joe Stacks started the silly skit he and Colleen outlined. "Hey, Coll, who is the vision of loveliness next to you?"

"Oh, you mean Janet, my competition for the last ten years? Who's the handsome guy with you? You know, you're lucky I saw you first."

"Hey! Watch it, honey! The ink isn't dry on our marriage certificate. Me and Frank left a trail of broken hearts in Hegewisch. Besides, baby, you and me, we're a match made in heaven!"

Joe dipped Colleen for a big, long kiss. Janet, who had just gotten out a bad relationship, clutched her purse and smiled. Frank's hands were awkwardly stuffed in his tux pants pockets and he shuffled his feet nervously.

After coming up for air, Colleen Stachowiak directed, "Janet, meet Frank. Frank, meet Janet. You guys should get to know one another." Joe grabbed Colleen's hand and scurried her away.

"Hi. Nice to meet you, Frank." Janet politely extended her hand.

"Yes, me too," Frank mumbled. He looked down at his uncomfortable shiny black patent leather shoes.

Somehow he mustered the courage to ask if Janet wanted a drink. It took two beers for Frank to relax enough to look at the petite blonde with big blue eyes when speaking. Finally, he asked her to dance to the love ballad, "The First Time Ever I Saw Your Face." Frank's heart raced. He felt light-headed with one arm barely around her waist and her hand clasped in his. By the end of the song, their fingers were intertwined.

Janet was instantly attracted to Frank's blond hair and blue eyes, which were honest and sincere. He was rock-solid from working at U.S. Steel. Frank swayed to the music, barely able to breathe. Usually uncomfortable around girls, his mind was racing with crazy thoughts by their third dance, like how Janet would look in his passenger seat heading to Warren Dunes.

The band played "Beer Barrel Polka" next, prompting Frank to ask, "You have a Polish name. Do you speak any?"

"Not much. When I was little my grandma and grandpa always said *Daj mi buzi* and *dobranoc* at bedtime. I think that means give me a kiss and good night."

Frank beamed. "It does—and that's all you need to know."

Later that evening, on her way to the ladies room, Janet was stunned to see her ex-boyfriend waiting for her.

"What are you doing here?"

"I saw you talking to that asshole in the tux, Jan. What's up with that?"

"None of your business, Mario! Can't you get it through your head we're done? Please, leave me alone."

"Shut the fuck up! As far as I'm concerned, we're still together." Mario grabbed her arm. "Come on, we're leaving."

Back on the dance floor, Frank paced and wondered if she was coming back. Unable to contain himself, he headed toward the lobby and turned the corner just in time to see Mario yank Janet's arm. Instinctively, Frank grabbed him from behind and spun him around. Mario went down, out cold from Frank's single punch.

Joe ran over. "Shit, Frank, you almost killed the guy!" Several bystanders picked Mario up off the floor to wait for the police. Frank and Janet were inseparable the rest of the night.

For the next five months, they dated steadily. Movies, Janet cheering at his "16 inch" games, Phil Schmidt's frog leg dinners in nearby Hammond, Rainbow Cone ice cream, 95th Street Beach picnics in Calumet Park, and Sunday Mass at St. Florian's or Queen of Martyrs in Mount Greenwood. Frank popped the question at Thanksgiving. Janet thought she should finish nursing school first, but followed her heart and completed her studies as a young bride. Everyone agreed Janet and Frank Stalowski looked like Barbie and Ken come to life when they walked out of Queen of Martyrs as husband and wife on July 28, 1973.

Shortly after, U.S. Steel began to scale back for an eventual shutdown. After his father's death, Frank supported his mother until she died. The same year, 1976, "Little Mike" was born with his parents' baby blues and curly blond hair on a stormy April 27.

As the steel trade died, Frank couldn't sustain the family with his mill pay. He rented out the flat where his parents had lived. His father was a bricklayer and taught the boys the basics. Frank was pleased to discover brickwork was always available and started a construction business with several skilled Polish craftsmen.

To Little Mike, their hands were the size of shovels. They worked hard from dawn until dusk, laboring for the almighty American dollar they heard so much about in Communist Poland. Sometimes, Mike went along and picked up the scrap pieces of brick strewn about in exchange for a dollar and a cold Pepsi. When Mike was in high school, Stash, the new boss, let him work during summer. Good money for Mike and the old crew loved having him around. He pushed the wheelbarrow of wet cement around like it was a baby buggy.

Mike looked forward to the Patriot's Park Fourth of July picnic. He was only ten, but it was the first time Mike could remember Frank inviting people over to celebrate. The last big neighborhood patriotic celebration was the 1976 Bicentennial picnic when Jimmy Carter had made a campaign stop in Patriot's Park looking for votes from the steel mill and city workers.

Frank asked Mike to help him carry a folding table out of the garage. It was leaning against a dusty tarp laden with boxes of holiday decorations and miscellaneous odds and ends.

"When are you gonna tell me about that car, Daddy?"

"That's your Uncle Mike's car under there." Frank fought back tears and swallowed hard before his face took on a faraway look. "He was so happy to be coming home from war in Vietnam for good and drive that car. I remember we went to the bank so he could take $3,750 out from savings. 'You'll pick it up for me, Frank, and hold on to it,' he told me. 'We're gonna have us some fun when I get back.' But he never got the chance.

"Sixteen long years, Mikey." Saying his son's name brought Frank back to the present. He looked sorrowfully at Mike. "I coulda never bring myself to drive it after your Uncle Mike died—but you gonna get this car when you grow up and learn how to drive. I saved it for you."

"Can I learn to drive tomorrow?"

"No, not yet." Frank grinned. "You drive it when you can pay the gas and insurance."

The temperature climbed to the upper 90s. It was partly sunny and very muggy. By late afternoon, the picnic was well under way and the tangy aroma of barbecued meat wafted through the thick air.

About five o'clock Alderman Santiago got up on the small stage, flanked by his wife, daughters and the American and Chicago flags. "Please stand and join me and my family in singing the Star Spangled Banner."

Most everybody sang loudly and waved small American flags. Mike noticed his father remained seated with his back to the stage. Mike didn't understand that every time Frank saw an American flag, it was draped on his brother's casket.

Dark and ominous clouds rolled east. At the first flash of lightning, everyone rushed to gather their belongings for a quick exit. Mike helped pack up and saw his father fall to the ground. There were shouts and screams as a crowd of people encircled his father.

Mike couldn't get close enough to see him, but found Anna. Within a few minutes, an ambulance pulled up. Paramedics rushed to Frank and loaded him onto the gurney. He was secured in the ambulance and Janet jumped in, then a moment later, emerged with her hand over her mouth, wide eyes seeming to search for Anna and Mike. He knew from the look on her face that their father was seriously ill or worse. A neighbor put an arm around Mike and Anna, pulling them in close. She motioned for their mother to get back in the ambulance.

THE WALK-ON

Mike watched the Chicago Fire Department ambulance, lights flashing and sirens blaring—marked with a big red "52" on its side—speed away.

The Odd Couple and the Special Grand Jury

MIKE'S RELATIONSHIP WITH HIS FATHER CHANGED AFTER FRANK'S MASSIVE stroke. No fishing off the 95th Street breakwater. No scoldings for picking on Anna. No playing catch or hide-and-seek in the park. Instead, Mike helped his father in and out of his wheelchair and bed. After two years of rehab and therapy, Frank took a turn for the worse, needing 'round-the-clock care due to total paralysis of his right side. He spent his days in a wheelchair or hospital bed, looking out the living room window. A far cry from scorching the Torrence Avenue pavement in his '62 Chevy 409 or working at the mill.

His care drained the family's meager resources. Janet worked as an ER nurse. Fortunately, Father Stanek kept the St. Florian's tuition to a minimum. Mike got a job at Mancuso's hauling bus trays of heavy dishes. He also had plenty of responsibility at home. Mike's loathing of changing bedpans and spoon-feeding his formerly robust father often overwhelmed his love for Frank, usually followed by intense guilt.

Mike grew from a ten-year-old boy who idolized his dad to a brooding teenager who resented the shell of the person his father had become. His feelings didn't change much the September day Frank's day nurse found his vacant eyes staring out the front window. Frank was finally at peace.

Shortly after Frank's death, Mike begged Janet to let him go fishing at 95th Street Beach. She didn't want him to go alone, but he hadn't really hung out with any friends since Frank's stroke. Too much responsibility at home. Finally, Janet relented, knowing the nearby bait shop owner was an old friend of Frank's. Since the 1950s, Chester had sold bait, told tall tales, and looked after the neighborhood kids hanging around Cal Park beach. If anyone would keep an eye on Mike, he would.

Mike and Ric Flores met at the breakwater one Saturday morning. They became fast friends with two common interests: food and fishing. Ricardo Flores was a short, heavy-set boy who lived in the growing Hispanic section of Hegewisch, bordering Cal Park. The deteriorating bungalows and two-flats were turning over to the next generation of immigrant families seeking the American dream. After enjoying the delicious homemade tamales and tacos at the Flores stand near the Indiana/Illinois border, Mike could see why they caught on with the traditional hot dog eating crowd in Hegewisch.

An unlikely pair, the quiet loner Mike Stalowski and Ric Flores, a street-wise hustler and entrepreneur of sorts, remained *mijos*. In high school, Ric had a reputation for getting things done, like securing beer kegs for unchaperoned parties or procuring desirable merchandise including illegal fireworks, high-end gym shoes, and gold chains. Mike called him "Slide" because he was always "slidin' in and out of shit."

After graduating, Ric turned the family taco recipes into Rico's Tacos, a string of popular Mexican eateries in the city's gentrifying neighborhoods. In 2004, Ric looked to expand his empire by opening an upscale dance club downtown. When he needed help, Mike became a silent investor in Bluewater. Unfortunately, Ric was silent too. He didn't tell Mike he was afraid to tell the notorious Spanish Counts street gang "no" when they "offered" to invest drug money cash in return for "investor dividends." Flores knew all too well from years of paying taco stand "protection" money that the Counts ran their financial operations like the Mafia, protecting, laundering and diversifying their illicit profits at all costs.

"Mr. O'Connor, December 12 presents a conflict for our client due to the previously scheduled Monday Night Football game in New York. His absence will no doubt have an effect on the team and their ability to win the Division title. My colleagues and I respectfully request a continuance to appear before the Special Grand Jury after February 10, 2006. Can we approach the bench in agreement?"

Assistant U.S. Attorney Neal O'Connor's Irish temper usually caused his neck to turn beet red when he thought he was being taken advantage of in the courtroom, especially by private practice attorneys who looked down on government prosecutors. He kept his cool, however.

"Look guys, you know your client has an obligation to this process regardless of what he does to earn a paycheck. This is the second time you've asked for an extension. We could have done this right the first time—three months ago, by deposition in your spacious and well-furnished conference room. My inclination is to ask Judge Scalise to compel his appearance."

———————●———————

Earlier that year, in February 2005, Ric Flores was desperate. Bluewater was $1.5 million over budget. The $2.5 million construction line of credit was maxed out and subcontractors were screaming for payment. Ric needed a fast cash infusion. He called Mike Stalowski, his boyhood fishing buddy, with a business proposal.

"*Mijo!* I need help, man, big time! I'm outta dough and the bank won't plus up the loan unless I secure more investors. I need a mil' from you right now, brother. You get 20% of the place and your money back in two years—guaranteed. Mike, this place is gonna be big: stars, top shelf babes, sports guys, politicians. We'll be rich and even more famous than you are now. You gotta come through, *mijo*. It's the chance of a lifetime. We open New York and LA next!"

The Steelman agreed to meet that evening. Ric suggested Agave, a trendy tequila bar on Randolph Street in the West Loop. He was involved with one of the bartenders. For a short, stocky guy sporting twin diamond pinky rings, Ric did okay with the ladies, especially blonde *gringas*.

After several shots each of Cuervo Gold and a big plate of stuffed nachos, the Steelman pointed a finger at Ric. "Okay, man, we're on. But Lisa never knows, right? Things are bad and I don't need her asking questions, got it?"

Ric nodded his head, glancing at his gold Rolex and then the bar.

Mike glared at Ric like he was across the line of scrimmage and tossed back a cold beer in two gulps. "Hey, man! Focus! I can front you five hundred grand now, but no one ever knows I'm in, right? The team doesn't want us to fuck around investing in gambling joints, upscale bars attracting rich assholes, or gentlemen's clubs. It'll send the old man up the wall and get me traded to St. Louis. Plus, my accountant will have my ass if he doesn't know about it first. Lisa did a pretty good job of blowing enough of my dough already."

Ric was distracted by his bartender *chica* who was flirting with two guys in suits. But he knew he had to get back to the business at hand. Ric looked Mike directly in the eye and slowly and deliberately stated, "No one—will ever fucking know—that Mike Stalowski—is a silent partner in the Bluewater venture—period. I swear on my grandmother."

"Right, no one knows. Just me and you. No paperwork. I'll get you the money. You'll get a check from my foundation. I can always say it was for some kids' charity your restaurant sponsors or some other bullshit."

Ric nodded his head in agreement. It was done. The Steelman's word was lock tight. Ric reached up and put his arm around Mike's massive neck. "Steelman, you're the best, *mijo*. I love you, man. You bailed me out. We're gonna be famous from this, you'll see."

———————•———————

Neal O'Connor was a twenty-year veteran of the Chicago Organized Crime Strike Force. For many years, the Strike Force focused on criminal activity masterminded by a largely select group of Italian mobsters known as the "Outfit." It was common knowledge the roots of the Outfit began during Prohibition, beginning with Al Capone's vast and lucrative empire funded by Chicago's thirst for alcohol and vice. The business was supported by crooked politicians and police officers, along with a never-ending line of patrons.

Over the years, Chicago's organized crime changed along with demographics. No longer just Italian wise guys, the gangs that controlled street corners, businesses, and even entire neighborhoods involved various nationalities. They reaped illicit profits from drug and gun trades, extortion, and vice, sucking the lifeblood of hope out of infested communities through intimidation, violence, and death.

A routine Chicago Police Narcotics Unit investigation had grown into a joint federal, state, and local task force that eventually revealed the inner-workings of a sophisticated and structured money-laundering machine. Unfortunately, the problems with Bluewater made Ric the perfect partner in crime for the Spanish Counts. By laundering gang profits through his legitimate business, he became a target of the Strike Force.

The Counts prospered selling fake IDs or *micas*. For a few hundred dollars, a fake Social Security card, driver's license, and birth certificate created an identity for scores of illegal immigrants needing them to work. Many a suburban teenager looking to buy alcohol made the trek to 26th Street in Little Village. Additionally, the Counts extorted a street tax known as "protection," from businessmen who paid or were "counseled" to comply.

The current U.S. Attorney, Carmen Pullido, son of Mexican immigrants, often visited the bustling Little Village neighborhood filled with busy restaurants, clothing stores, and Mexican *carnicerias*, most run by decent and honest immigrants. His mother had helped pay his law school tuition with earnings from a nearby sweatshop. He took it personally when the Spanish Counts utilized *beso de la muerte*, or the kiss of death, to enforce compliance.

Shortly after Mike bailed Ric out with the loan, Miguel "Loco Mickey" Castaneda paid a visit to Flores. Loco Mickey had heard Bluewater was in financial trouble and decided to help. The feared and revered *veterano* was well into his fifties, having survived his early and violent gang-banging years, and considered himself a businessman. He was the last person Ric Flores wanted to see, particularly regarding business.

"The deal is simple. We will give you $100,000 as a goodwill loan for now. Then every month after you open, you will take more cash from me and report it as sales. A percentage of monthly profits comes back to us as 'payment with interest for services rendered.' *Comprende?*" Castaneda patted Ric on the shoulder before straightening his two-carat diamond pinky ring. The point was made.

"Mr. Castaneda, I have other investors. How do I deal with them?"

"That's your problem now, isn't it?"

Ric knew he was dancing with the devil but felt he had no choice. *Beso de la muerte*. He couldn't share the Counts' interest in Bluewater with Mike. And he certainly had no idea his conversations with Miguel Castaneda were intercepted and would lead the Strike Force to discover the loan from Mike.

Several months later, the U.S. Attorney's Office for the Northern District of Illinois presented him two options: testify before the Special Grand Jury about his business dealings with the Spanish Counts or Chicago's most famous NFL football player would face a grand jury appearance and possible indictment as a money laundering co-conspirator. Either way meant trouble. Ric chose to remain silent about the Counts and face the legal consequences. His life expectancy would not be cut short. Mike would understand and forgive him.

———————●———————

Judge Scalise, a former prosecutor who had previously served on the Strike Force compelling the Steelman's grand jury testimony, was a diehard Storm fan, season ticket holder, and long-time friend of Connie Everett. Nevertheless, Judge Scalise ordered Mike Stalowski not to leave Chicago on December 12. Mike's personal obligations were superseded by his judicial responsibility—as Judge Scalise's personal affinity for the Storm was superseded by his judicial responsibility.

The Special Grand Jury rendered a "true bill" indicting the Spanish Counts gang and Ric Flores in a highly publicized money laundering case. In a 24/7 news cycle, bad news always sells, especially if it concerns pro athletes or celebrities. Mike Stalowski was in the middle of another controversy.

The government stipulated to his grand jury testimony, sparing Mike the trial circus. Prosecutors determined Mike's testimony wouldn't help the government's case. It would only reveal Mike's innocent desire to help a friend.

Ric Flores honestly thought if he did what Castaneda "asked" everything would be fine. He had almost five years of his seven-year sentence, which began shortly after Mike met Kim, to contemplate his actions. While in federal prison, Ric watched the news and read papers, so he saw his *mijo's* nightmare unfold. He knew Cook County Jail was a hellhole: a place for stone badasses, gangbangers, and fuck-ups. Mike Stalowski could hold his own, but Ric didn't think he deserved to be in County—even on reckless manslaughter charges for killing his girlfriend.

Billy Reardon

ON A BEAUTIFUL SPRING AFTERNOON, ANNA TOOK HER RABBIT TO THE PARK across the street. Measles, named for the red spots on its face, had received lots of extra hugs and cuddles since Frank died. The park was empty except for Billy Reardon, an acne-infested, lanky ne'er-do-well who ruled Patriot's Park. He sauntered over to confront Anna.

"Your rabbit's a freak," taunted Billy. He grabbed a stick and poked Measles, who ran away.

Anna screamed at the top of her lungs—loud enough for Mike to hear in his room, over the heavy metal music he was blaring. She tried hitting Billy, who grabbed her little fist in midair and knocked it away. "Jerk!" she shrieked. Both fists clenched, she lashed out again, landing one solidly on his pimpled nose and drawing blood.

By this time, Mike had bolted out of the house and across the street. He slammed into Reardon, blindsiding him in an aerial assault. He hit Billy so hard with his left shoulder that he flew back ten feet before slamming his head against the sidewalk. Mike Stalowski stood over the neighborhood bully. For a brief moment, he wanted to pick him up and slam him down again. Mike's blood boiled and his fists remained clenched at his sides.

Mrs. Fabian saw the commotion from her front porch and ran over. Billy lay limp and still. Mrs. Fabian knew Billy was a troublemaker—and the son of a politically heavy Democratic precinct captain. It broke her heart that Janet would have another problem to deal with.

"Michael, take your sister and get out of here."

By the time they were inside, Mrs. Fabian had called 911. Billy was attempting to sit up, and blood ran down the back of his neck.

Later that evening, Janet was surprised by two plainclothes detectives investigating an assault on Billy Reardon. "He was diagnosed with a severe concussion and sprained neck," explained Detective Carmody. "Needed sixteen stitches in his head."

"I was at work today until 7:00 p.m. and have no idea what you're talking about."

"His father wants charges pressed against your son for assault and battery. Billy stated he was in the park and wanted to pet a rabbit. Next thing he knows, your son knocked him out. His head was bleeding when he came to."

"What happened, Michael?" asked Janet.

Mike hung his head. Quickly, Anna chimed in, explaining what Billy did. The detectives knew Billy had numerous police encounters for vandalism, bullying, and petty thefts. They also knew nothing ever stuck. His father, the precinct captain, made sure of that.

Looking Detective Gorrence in the eye, Mike said, "He's an asshole and deserved it."

Secretly, Janet was proud Mike came to his sister's defense, but she was fearful that he could not control his emotions or brute force. In a twist of fate, Mike's aggression against Billy Reardon—which brought detectives to her door—was encouraged, cheered for, and handsomely rewarded on the gridiron.

Uncle Case

AFTER THE BILLY REARDON ALTERCATION, JANET'S COUSIN CASEY KROLIK officially introduced Mike to the game of football. He had no children of his own and was a frequent visitor after Frank took ill, helping with house repairs and trying to look out for the family.

At 6′ 3″, Uncle Case was built like an all-pro defensive tackle. He walked with a slight limp, due to perennial knee abuse from sports and commercial construction. Casey had a perpetually unlit cigar as a chew-toy. His stomach bulge revealed a love of Old Style beer. He often patted his girth and joked, "Hey, don't give me no hard time—it's bought and paid for!" Casey played high school and college football and currently volunteered as an assistant varsity coach for suburban Marquette Catholic High School. They churned out the most Division I college athletes in the metro area after St. Michael's.

On Saturdays, Casey often tossed the football with Mike in Patriot's Park. Mike liked Uncle Case's construction site humor and was happy to put down his Nintendo Game Boy. Plus afterwards, Casey took him to Uncle Eddie's, the popular fast food joint, for his usual hero sub and two chili tamales.

Case recognized Mike's natural athleticism. He was strong, fluid and agile. He might even make a good running back or tight end. However, Case sensed the killer instinct in Mike, which likely pointed to the defensive side.

Walking across the park, Casey asked, "Mike, do you think you'd like playing offense or defense?"

"Defense," Mike replied without hesitation. "I like to hit. Like a wrecking ball."

"Is that so?" Case figured the kid wasn't serious. "Well, let's see. Maybe the best position for you is linebacker, in the middle. Linebackers can do all that and more. You're quick. If you have a nose for where the ball is going, you'll have an opportunity to do some damage." He brought out a blocking pad and held it up.

"Okay, let's go Mike! I'm the ball carrier. Give me all you got!"

Case braced himself against the back of the handheld pad. Mike came at him, legs churning and eyes focused. Lowering his head and left shoulder for the hit, he knocked Case down.

Monday morning, Casey called Tim Grogan, an old friend and varsity football coach at St. Michael the Archangel High School. St. Michael's remained a popular all-boys parochial school, despite its location in an increasingly crime-ridden neighborhood. He knew he could never get Mike out to a suburban school, so this was the next best thing.

"Tim, I think I've got a freshman prospect for you. He's my cousin's son, but I'm calling because you rarely see a kid like this. He's big for his age, about 5′ 10″, and he moves like a cat. He's quick *and* strong. He hasn't played grammar school ball, but he's got raw instincts. I can see it. I mess around with him in the park. His dad died last fall, and he's a little introverted. With the right coaches, he'll make a hell of a linebacker or tight end. Thing is Tim, he'll need financial assistance. Another problem will be convincing his mother."

Grogan respected Casey's opinion and scouting ability. If he didn't give him a look, another Catholic League coach would. "All right, Case, can you set up a meeting Saturday at his house? The mother should be there too. I'll talk to the AD and see where we stand with tuition 'leadership' awards."

Janet was not interested in Mike playing a sport where he could get hurt, or worse, with his temper, hurt someone else. Casey spoke of St. Michael's heritage and solid academics. He reminded Janet this was an opportunity for Mike to have male interaction and oversight. She reluctantly agreed to listen to the coach's pitch.

Saturday afternoon, Coach Grogan showed up in a St. Michaels's football jacket and gave Mike a Crusaders T-shirt. He always talked to prospective recruits about the school first.

"Mike, what do you think about playing football at St. Michael's?"

Mike shrugged and looked at his mother who smiled nervously. "Sir, I think I would like to come to your school and play sports, football for sure. I know a few guys who go there."

Grogan never dreamt the polite introverted kid would turn into a blue-chip high school and Division I athlete—then come home to play in the NFL. When he looked Mike in the eye, he wanted to see fire and bravado, but he saw a shy kid with a protective mother. Nevertheless, he trusted Casey's word enough to tell Janet straight-up he might be able to get financial assistance.

"Thank you, Mr. Grogan. I'll talk it over with Mike and get back to you. I don't know much about football, except we get an awful lot of injuries in the ER." Janet continued nervously, "I'm a trauma nurse."

A scholarship to a revered school would be a godsend. But she feared a growing boy with a temper could be a recipe for disaster in a school with lots of rules and discipline. Janet called Casey for advice.

Casey reminded her it was a great school with a rich scholastic and athletic legacy. Although it was located in a tough neighborhood, Mike would get a good education, a religious foundation, and male support during his formative years.

Janet was grateful for $6,000 annual tuition assistance and relieved that a charter bus would pick Mike up. "But I see all those injuries in the ER. Broken bones, stitches . . ."

Casey interrupted, "Jan, football's less dangerous than having a teenage kid with a few beers behind the wheel."

Lisa & Mike

"For Better, For Worse"

THE FORMER LISA MORELLO MET MIKE AT A FRIDAY NIGHT PEP RALLY. THEY were popular with Hegewisch High School girls or "publics" looking to meet the highly desired Crusader football players.

Although getting a lot of female attention on and off the field, Mike was not very confident around girls. He couldn't help but stare at Lisa. She was standing in a group of girls wearing tight sweaters, jumping around his fellow defensemen to garner attention. Lisa looked directly at him with a big smile and tossed her mane of long auburn hair. The connection was instant. Lisa finagled an introduction in typical high school fashion. One of her friends, who was a cheerleader, told one of Mike's teammates that Lisa wanted to meet him.

Their conversation fumbled through football, hair metal bands, and mutual hangouts on the Southeast Side. He couldn't believe his good fortune when Lisa said they should get together sometime and go to Mancuso's. Saturday night, Mike borrowed $40 and his mother's Chevy Impala. Fifteen minutes into the date, Lisa decided she was in love with Mike and his football popularity—not necessarily in that order. She determined she would have him for herself. Starting tonight.

"C'mon, Mike, it's nice outside tonight. Let's go hang out at Cal Park."

"Sure! I go there a lot."

"Really?"

"My favorite place to fish."

Lisa had other plans. "I got IDs . . ."

Mike looked blankly at her.

"We can get a few beers from AJ's and watch the waves."

"Okay. Yeah, I guess."

They picked up the beer and drove to Cal Park.

"It's cool watching the waves from the breakwall," said Mike as they turned into the parking lot.

"I'm not looking to get wet. Let's just kick back in the car."

Lisa popped the cap off an Old Style and passed it to him. She inched closer as Mike nursed his beer. The alcohol kicked in by the time Lisa leaned her head on his shoulder and rested her hand on his leg.

Nature was too much to handle. Mike Stalowski was not well-versed in these matters. Lisa Morello evidently was and told Mike she was "safe." He didn't know what that meant, but learned rather quickly. Luckily, no cops knocked on the fogged windows while the radio blared "Living in Sin."

They became inseparable. She was half-Italian and half-Czech, with deep roots in Hegewisch. The Morellos worked long hours during the week but spent time together on the weekends. Her father ran the family asphalt paving business, employing many relatives. Mike especially loved the huge Sunday dinners where they embraced Mike as one of their own.

Lisa was the first in the family to express an interest in college and followed Mike to the University of Illinois. Lisa pretty much told him what to do and when, freeing him to focus on playing football. Junior year, Mike pledged his love to the girl who helped him keep up with his academics and manage the social demands of being a Big Ten football standout.

Lisa and Mike's wedding, a lavish affair held between graduation and his rookie season training camp, seemed like a fantasy to most people in Hegewisch. Lisa officially charted their course from that day forward, quickly adapting to the spoils of the NFL.

The Stalowski newlyweds left their blue-collar backgrounds behind with $7.5 million from Mike's three-year NFL contract and signing bonus. Lisa got the Burr Ridge McMansion with a pool, tennis court, and full-time maid. She had luxury vehicles, custom jewelry, and no real limits on her spending. Her clothing budget exploded, with nothing less than exclusively branded merchandise in her overstuffed closets. Mike spent his money on cars, motorcycles, boats, and exotic fishing trips.

Possessions and schedules diverted their attention from each other.

Unlike Mike, Lisa relished the social aspect of his career. She never missed a social event, game, or interview and became President of the Chicago Storm Wives'

Club. Lisa headed up the annual fashion show, as well as "Snow Ball," a black-tie gala benefiting Children's Hospital.

Mike hated the day-to-day chore of managing finances. A year or so after they were married, Mike turned everything over to Lisa. He was too busy and didn't care. Until early in 2005.

On Valentine's Day, no love was lost during a lunch meeting with his agent Shel Harris, who'd represented Mike since he was drafted. Like Lisa, Shel loved the finer things in life and being seen in public with his clients. Mike wanted to cut to the chase of contract negotiations without distractions at Shel's office, but grudgingly agreed to meet him at Hugo's Frog Bar on Rush Street. It gave him an excuse to stop by Diversey Harbor and see if he was moving up the waitlist for a more private boat slip. They got down to business while waiting for their entrées.

"I've reviewed their offer, Mike, and I'm advising you take the money and run. Let's get it done." He passed a one-page summary to Mike for his review.

"What d'ya mean I better take this first offer?" Mike's voice got louder with each word. "A one-year contract with a right of rescission if I don't pass a team physical?"

"Most guys your age are thinking about retirement because they can't play at the level they're used to. Plus, there's two guys behind you at half the money."

"What kind of bullshit is that for a guy making them all kinds of dough?"

Hesitantly, the waiter approached with their food. He scurried away after making sure they didn't need anything else.

"Mike, you're in the league seven years. You're almost thirty and you've had both knees 'scoped what, two-three times each?"

"My knees are fine!"

"What about your neck, man? That's Trahey's real concern. What are you hiding?"

"Fuck it, Shel. If old man Everett wants to release me, I'll take free agency. I can go another five. This meeting's over!"

Mike stormed out without touching his food and headed to Griff's to console himself with a liquid lunch of Jack Black shots and beer. The Steelman knew he still had gas in the tank. He didn't want to hear about some body dents and rust.

When he got home, Lisa's black Maserati with *STORMED* vanity plates was gone. *Probably still at the club, gossiping over a glass of wine.* He dropped his keys on the foyer table. Looking for any distraction from his lunch meeting, he picked up the heavy pile of envelopes and catalogs from today's mail. *How many fucking catalogs does she get?* After opening the first envelope, he shook his head, trying to clear the alcohol-induced haze. Lisa's car payment was three months in arrears. Mike ripped open another envelope to find their $7,000 mortgage hadn't been paid in six months.

Lisa sashayed through the door in a designer tennis outfit, carrying her carbon fiber racket and flashing a $20,000 tennis bracelet from Asher and Klein. She tried to look past the fact Mike had clearly been drinking heavily.

"Happy fucking Valentine's Day to me." He waved some of the mail in her face. "I'm looking at all these fucking bills and credit card statements. What's up with the fucking finances? Are you out of cash? Why the fuck aren't the bills being paid?"

She dropped her racket and broke down in tears. "Mike, I got sucked into a deal that was supposed to make us a fortune. Karen Rodgers from Hinsdale told me about a big real estate partnership her husband was heading up. We bought into the group putting up multi-million-dollar houses on the last open land around Hinsdale and a big downtown condo building on the Chicago River. But her husband took the investor money and pissed it away in Vegas. Now he's bankrupt."

"I always hated that little asshole husband of hers. Drivin' around in that red fucking Bentley ragtop, smokin' his big cigar, telling me we should win a Super Bowl. I should tape him to the fucking goal posts, not the rookies. So how much did you give him?"

"T . . . Ten . . . million."

"Are you fucking crazy? You gave away that kind of cash without telling me! Are you fucking crazy?" he repeated.

"I'm sorry. I was gonna tell you when the profits rolled in. Then the whole fucking thing blew up! I didn't know what to do. And we barely talk since . . ." She looked at the floor and sobbed.

Living in a fishbowl—which only Lisa enjoyed—and having different interests had caused the Stalowskis to slowly grow apart over the years. The tragic stillbirth of their son last fall was an accelerant to the smoldering fire. Since Lisa and Mike dealt with their pain and grief individually, not as a couple, the loss drove them even further apart.

Increasingly angry about their financial situation in the months that followed,

Mike started keeping late nights in downtown bars, not caring one bit who saw him drunk or who he was with. Based on gossip columns and news reports, Lisa accused him of having one-night-stands. Mike's counteraccusation was Lisa was having an affair with Larry Rodgers and funneling him money through Rodgers real estate partnership.

In April, the police responded to the Stalowski house in suburban Burr Ridge for domestic disturbances—twice in two weeks. The first time, Mike came home drunk and late for the Burr Ridge Youth Football awards dinner. He was in no shape to say a few words. Lisa was pissed she couldn't hobnob with the Burr Ridge elite. Mike didn't give a shit.

The second incident began after the Steelman was stopped for speeding and weaving on I-55, near his home. The young State Police trooper, a Storm fan, tried not to agitate him.

"Mr. Stalowski, it's your choice to decline the Breathalyzer. You have another choice. I either call my supervisor to join us while we sort this out or I follow you to your residence." Mike chose the latter. Once safe in his driveway, the trooper sternly instructed him not to get behind the wheel for the rest of the night.

The arguing began the moment he walked in. Lisa was fed up with Mike's drinking. Mike was tired of Lisa directing his every move off the football field. Two hours later, Lisa Stalowski frantically called 911.

"My husband is going crazy! He just threw a football trophy through the wall. Pulled it off a shelf and launched it at me." Panicked and gasping for air, she continued. "Probably only missed because he's drunk and out of control. I'm locked in a bedroom now, but I'm terrified he'll break down the damn door. Please hurry! Hurry!"

"Stay away from him," the dispatcher instructed. "Officers are on the way. I'll remain on the line with you."

Three police squads and a shift supervisor quickly responded, startling Mike in the driveway. He'd stepped outside to get a breath of fresh air and away from Lisa. The arguing was exhausting. Tomorrow, he'd have to patch a hole in the drywall. She kept following him around the house and wouldn't stop screaming. He wasn't proud of it, but launching a trophy at a picture of them with their wedding cake did finally shut her up.

One officer approached with his Taser out. The other two had batons extended and pepper spray. Lisa ran outside. Even though he was still inebriated, the Steelman realized he was in really deep shit. He threw up both of his huge, tattooed arms as if surrendering.

"Look man, she's driving me fucking nuts! But I'll leave now. I promise. No bullshit. I like you guys," he slurred.

Lisa's Italian temper surfaced. "I'm tired of this shit. He tried to fucking kill me. Arrest him!"

"Mr. Stalowski, your wife told the dispatcher you threw a trophy at her head. That's assault with a deadly weapon, sir."

"No! No! I didn't. Not true!"

"Are you kidding me? Officer, just look at the damn wall!"

"Yeah, I guess I threw it, but not at her. I'm sorry man! I didn't mean it, Lisa." He turned to the officers. "I was aiming for the wedding picture . . . guess that's why I'm not a quarterback."

The ranking sergeant was also a huge Storm fan. "Look folks, I think it's best if Mr. Stalowski leaves and doesn't come back tonight. We'll follow you to I-55. You are not to come back tonight. Am I clear, Mr. Stalowski?" Mike nodded, doing his best to appear remorseful. "And I suggest you two get some outside support."

"Outside support? How about you idiots take him to sober up in a cell! He can't drive! He's drunk!" Lisa's dark eyes flashed angrily. "I'm calling the Chief. Let's see what he thinks about turning a blind eye to drunk drivers. Even if he's the infamous fucking Steelman."

"That won't be necessary. We're escorting him off the property."

"Don't worry, Lisa. I'm not coming back." Despite the earlier explicit directions from the state trooper, Mike got in his truck and drove slowly to the I-55 ramp under police escort; an hour later, he was in the Lincoln Park condo.

The next day, Lisa filed for an order of protection against her troubled husband in DuPage County Court. The line in the sand was drawn.

Mike was allowed to return to get what he needed: clothes, a few personal items and some football gear. He left everything else, including his precious modes of transportation. He had no regrets about leaving their wedding album, a picture of the football-shaped wedding cake on the cover. *Lisa and Mike—A Port in the Storm Together—52 to go!*

To Mike, it seemed a lifetime since the Italian sweet table had been loaded with football brownies and miniature pastries shaped like football helmets. Lisa didn't miss a trick to remind everyone she was "gonna be an NFL bride." Mike just wanted to get through the ceremony and reception—and survive his rookie year.

A few weeks after moving out, Steve Kendall called to review the proposed separation documents. "Mike, we gotta talk. She wants sole occupancy of the house, with you paying the mortgage, utilities and all maintenance, plus an additional $40,000 per month for living expenses."

Lisa may have helped him with math homework in high school and college, but Mike quickly recognized that was an outrageous allowance.

"She's out of her fucking mind! No way! Ten grand a week for what? She can kiss my ass! Steve, you draw up a fucking counteroffer telling her she can live in the fucking garage and collect fucking welfare!" bellowed Mike.

After a lengthy—and expensive—negotiation process, Mike and Lisa agreed to the financial terms of their separation. Lisa got the house and related expenses, plus $15,000 monthly for living expenses.

———————————— • ————————————

The first few years in the NFL Mike Stalowski had been low-key and quiet. He shunned the media spotlight and most post-game parties. "Self-expression" was becoming fashionable for players—dreadlocks, beaded hair extensions, and multiple tattoos were only the tip of the iceberg.

The Steelman's metamorphosis began imperceptibly. His growing legion of fans admired his ferocious and relentless style of play. Profitable endorsement opportunities increased exponentially. The media fed the frenzy by endlessly replaying game highlights of his brutal hits and providing constant color commentary about his life on and off the field—not all true. Fueled by alcohol consumption, intended to suppress his demons, the Steelman became bigger, badder, and more outrageous with each passing season.

By 2003, he was part outlaw biker, part superhero, and most importantly, the anchor of the "Steel Trap" defense. When #52 called their number across the line of scrimmage, most NFL opponents were uneasy. And then, almost as imperceptibly as the adoration began, some of the media turned on him. They blasted him as aloof and a bad image for pro football. Antics and attitudes, previously promoted, were now disparaged.

The Storm finished 2005 near the bottom of the Central Division. The media delighted in perpetuating rumors that Mike Stalowski, "leader of the Storm's vaunted Steel Trap defense," was affected by alleged drinking problems and run-ins with the police. They also rumbled about the Steelman's declining level of play. He seemed to have limited range of motion, often struggling to roam the secondary from sideline to sideline and fulfill his role as a headhunter. The speculation concerned Connie Everett and the Storm's front office.

The Steelman purposely continued to keep his neck stiffness secret. The pain, often accompanied by the sound of crunching glass from worn ligaments moving, had steadily increased for the last two seasons. Sooner than later, the degenerative bulging disc in his neck would need surgery. Years of football hits, often leading with his helmet, took their toll.

Only Head Trainer Tommy Johnston, who slipped Mike painkillers to get him through games, knew the intense recurrent pain he suffered. Mike unsuccessfully pleaded with Tommy to inject him with NFL-banned corticosteroids. Gambling with a black mark on his career, Mike relied on self-medication.

Mike grew increasingly withdrawn. He didn't want to admit it, but he was damaged goods at the age of thirty. Football had brought Lisa and Mike together, and it appeared to be tearing them apart.

Barbi Doll

Longtime 10th Ward Alderman Jose Santiago, who had his eye on city hall, was blessed with good looks, a silver tongue, a beautiful wife, and two high-maintenance daughters, Barbara and Nicole. Their mother Elena, who claimed Castilian blue-blood heritage, trained her daughters to be elegant, poised, and well-groomed. They always wore the latest chic fashions purchased on the Magnificent Mile. Even upscale boutiques in south suburban malls did not measure up.

Per city ordinance, Santiago had to reside in his ward. To satisfy his family's expectations of privilege, he purchased several adjacent properties on a secluded block in Hegewisch then razed the houses to build an enormous suburban-style home. Its high privacy fence surrounded a lavish yard with an in-ground pool and tennis court. Prominent Chicago politicians and businessmen jockeyed for invitations to his renowned summer barbecues. They wanted to be where decisions were made and deals were cut—long before votes were cast at City Hall. When she was young, Barbi Santiago would never have run into Mike Stalowski unless it was at a red light.

At Notre Dame, Barbi enjoyed her sideline privileges covering football games for the school newspaper. Being attractive with a killer figure didn't hurt her chances of hanging out with the players. Freshman year she became intimate friends with Lorenzo White, who faced Mike Stalowski in the 1993 Catholic League playoff game.

Lunching with her father at Riva's on Navy Pier shortly after graduation, Barbi got right to the point and asked who he could call because she wanted to work as a Channel 7 news reporter. "They have the best-looking correspondents, Daddy." Santiago, not thrilled with the idea of her wasting her Notre Dame education as a "bimbo with a microphone," offered to get her a spot in the Mayor's office. A toddler-like tantrum ensued. As usual, Jose acquiesced to her demands.

Following a call to the President of the Chicago ABC affiliate, Barbi was hired as a field correspondent for the 5:00 p.m. news. She covered everything from brutal murders to Cook County Board budget hearings, surprisingly managing to appear interested.

Truthfully, she was more concerned about how she looked on TV. Barbi pushed the envelope for attention. For many viewers, there were too many open buttons on Barbi's blouse. Wrapped around the microphone, her long, blood-red fingernails screamed *Look At Me*. But between her heritage and good looks, she survived in Chicago's competitive news market.

The alderman encouraged ABC to assign her to sporting events in August 2005. Management recognized an opportunity to showcase Barbi at Veterans Stadium. She loved being in the crowds. And she loved to confront players, resulting in great quotes and video footage.

Barbi thoroughly enjoyed being recognized around town and would do anything to stay in the limelight. Three years younger than the Steelman, she followed his career closely, as she did anyone in Chicago with fame or notoriety.

Although most Hegewisch people were beneath her, Mike Stalowski was now different. The Steelman was the ultimate rebel, playing his game the way she liked it, fast and furious. In late October, Barbi decided she would interview the elusive Mike Stalowski, rumored to be separated from his wife.

At Veterans Stadium, the minicam truck was positioned at the top of Ramp 41. Players would have to pass her to enter their garage. Barbi usually flirted to get players on camera. During the recent World Series playoffs, Barbi was repeatedly seen with one of the White Sox players. While there might be a date with a World Series ring in her future, football players were her favorite boy toys.

Quarterback Mark Meade drove up first. Meade loved the media and did interviews and color commentary whenever he could. He was a better TV announcer than a quarterback.

Meade slowed his Porsche Cayenne and dropped his window in response to Barbi's animated window crank gesture. Grinning widely, with flirtatious body language overkill, she asked softball questions about his game and how the Storm would do. Meade welcomed the opportunity to plant the seed for a date with Barbi. He offered to score a touchdown in exchange for her coverage of his foundation's charity event the next weekend. With no intention of showing up, Barbi said,

"Game on." Meade waved to the camera and descended to the garage thinking about how hot Barbi looked in her Storm colors and high heels. He chuckled to himself and envisioned throwing the touchdown in her honor. Instead, he would be sacked four times.

The *STLTRP* vanity plate on Mike's approaching pick-up was unmistakable. Barbi Santiago nearly stepped in front of the truck. Mike hit the brakes and scowled. *This chick has balls.* Although he had never met her, he had seen her on TV and had heard plenty from other guys.

Barbi tapped on his window. Grudgingly he lowered the glass. She bent over and put her microphone in his face, knowing full well he was fighting not to look at her ample cleavage while the camera rolled.

"Good morning, Number 52! Are you ready for some action? Word has it our defense has several points to prove against Minnesota today."

Mike hated talking to the media on a good day, even if the reporter was a popular and hot female. He especially hated it today, before an important Division game with his neck bothering him all week—exacerbated by taking painkillers for his back and passing out on the floor last night.

Mike avoided the camera lens and muttered, "Uh, yeah, we're playin' Green Bay. Don't really like those guys, never did." He inched his truck forward. The left rear tire almost ran over Barbi's foot in a 4″ stiletto heel.

"Oh, you're right," she said, embarrassed by her mistake. "I must have looked at the wrong game," she smiled to the camera.

Looking backward out of his window, the Steelman glared at Barbi. "When I get the chance, I'm going to show them how much."

He continued to inch forward.

She backed up, plunging her heel deep into soggy grass. She almost fell over with the camera still rolling. Barbi was not happy. Mike barely concealed his amusement when he stopped to offer assistance.

Barbi quickly turned the tables. In a very concerned tone she inquired, "Mike, how is your neck? Are you able to play today?"

"Everything's good. You'll see how good after kick-off."

She motioned for the camera to stop rolling. With wide eyes and bared cleavage, she asked, "Mike, could a former Hegewisch girl like me get a one-on-one interview with Chicago's biggest football star? Please? I planned a piece this week on the daily life of a Storm player and YOU'RE the one I WANT."

Mike's eyes darted side to side, then he looked at her from the ground up and back down again. "What's in it for me?"

Coyly, she replied, "You get to know me better."

Against his better judgment, figuring he would simply answer a couple of questions over the phone, the Steelman provided his cell number. "Call me."

But Barbi wanted to cause a "little stir" in the city.

The Midnight Hour

ALMOST SIX MONTHS INTO HIS SINGLE LIFESTYLE, MIKE ENJOYED HAVING AS many beers as he wanted and coming home to his conflict-free condo. After shopping or lunch, Lisa used to bring her girlfriends there to show off the expansive Lake Michigan and skyline views, well worth the condo's million plus price tag. Mike could park his Silverado and motorcycle, but he really missed the Burr Ridge six-car garage for his toys. He loved opening the overhead doors and seeing his full-dress Harley, '63 Corvette Stingray, and completely accessorized 25' glitter-finished 400 hp fishing boat.

Two days after the Storm's big loss to Green Bay (34-3) Mike was watching ESPN highlights. He was full after his fourth beer and wolfing down a signature "El Gigante" foot-long burrito from one of Ric Flores' popular Rico's Tacos. It satisfied even the Steelman's appetite. When his cell phone rang, he ignored it.

The game put the Storm 3-5 at midseason and planted seeds of doubt for the playoffs. ESPN announcer Rick Hanhardt focused on the 4-3 defensive scheme not working. He claimed the Storm defense looked "asleep at the wheel" and allowed a mediocre Green Bay running game to gain over 300 yards. Stalowski was singled out.

Mike flipped off the screen. "Fuck you, dipshit!" he yelled. "The only football you played was with a joystick."

Mike's cell phone rang again. He didn't recognize the number with a desirable 312 area code. Gruffly he answered. "Yeah?"

"Hello, is this number 52?" inquired a soft and sultry voice.

"Who's asking?" He heard a sexy deep-throated giggle.

"I'm your biggest fan, Steelman."

"I've got lots of fans. Which one are you?" he asked sternly.

"Why don't you come out and meet me tonight? We can talk and get to know one another."

Mike shook his head. *Of course she'd have a 312.* "Hey, Barbi, is this you?"

"All right, all right, Mike, you win," she confessed. "It's me, Barbi Santiago, ABC news correspondent, reporting from Lincoln Park," she said in her most professional voice.

"What's up?"

"Can we meet for about thirty minutes? You promised me some time for my story."

"Nothing like some notice, huh?" Mike felt kind of mellow. It was almost 10:00 p.m. He paused for effect. "Okay, you got me. But only for a little while. I've got to get some sleep."

"Great! I'll meet you at the Midnight Hour. I'm wearing jeans and a purple top."

I'll bet your sweater's two sizes too tight. "Yeah, that's good. I'm not far away. I've got on camo cargo shorts and a gray T-shirt. My hair is blond and blue."

"I know what you look like," she laughed. "You probably scare people no matter what you wear. I can't wait."

Mike hung up and looked at himself in the mirror. His eyes settled on his latest tattoo, courtesy of "Inked" in Wrigleyville. Two separate silver "jaws" dripping blood and hinged at his elbow adorned his left forearm and lower bicep. As the Storm's vaunted Steel Trap grim reaper, they symbolized his death grip on opponents, closing into a "steel trap" when he flexed his arm. Lisa, who hated tattoos, would be out of her mind when she saw it on TV. His first tattoo, a brooding St. Michael holding his mighty sword and shield, seemed less colorful.

Me? Scary? You're fuckin' A right I'm scary. Alcohol seemed to have the same effect on the Steelman as whatever Kool-Aid the media and fans drank.

Mike took a cab. His Harley's tank sported newly painted purple ghost flames, and he didn't want some gawker touching it. A careless valet almost hit it last week near Bluewater, flirting with premature death.

The Midnight Hour was more crowded than expected for Tuesday night. Mike instinctively pulled the crushed ballcap out of his pocket, placing it backwards over the distinct blond and blue ponytail. He sat at a two-seat high-boy near the bar and ordered a beer.

Meanwhile Barbi parked her white BMW 330ci convertible with *BDOLL* vanity plates in a tow zone. She tossed her police-issued ABC-TV News placard on the dashboard.

Her cell phone rang. "Yes, yes, I'm meeting with him right now. Get a good picture, hear me?"

Barbi's CFM heels tapped cadence on the concrete floor. Her mere presence demanded and received attention. Brushing past patrons, some thinking she looked familiar, she searched for the largest person she could find. Barbi jiggled right up to Mike, held out her perfectly manicured right hand and smiled demurely. "Hi, Mr. Stalowski. I'm so happy to see you."

"Hello to you, Miss Newsie." Mike tried like hell not to stare her up and down. "What d'ya want to drink?"

"Oh, a glass of red wine is fine. Merlot or something. Thank you." Barbi smiled as innocently as possible. "Miss Newsie, huh? I'm getting the feeling you don't like media folks."

"Not really. Have you fallen down lately?"

"Funny! I just wanted to capture your smiling face and comments about the game."

"Okay, so what's up now at 10:15 on Tuesday night?"

"I always wanted to do a one-on-one interview with an interesting Storm player, a little bit of a character," explained Barbi.

"So, I'm a character? Don't think so. I'm just a regular guy from the Southeast Side of Chicago—like you."

"Right, except I can't bench press small cars."

The Steelman ordered two shots of expensive tequila. Barbi politely refused, so Mike downed both. He sucked on a lime wedge and stared at her. A little uneasy, Barbi flashed her big pearly whites. Mike noticed a couple taking pictures of them.

"Hey, I'm gonna go tell them to put that damn camera away."

Barbi shrugged it off. "Happens a lot lately. Fans I guess. Let them alone, Michael. I'm sure they mean no harm."

"I don't like pictures, especially in public. Let's get out of here."

"Relax, Michael. They'll get their little Nikon shots and brag about running into someone famous."

He didn't like her calling him Michael. "Okay, on with it then. What d'ya want to know?"

"I want to know what this guy called *the Steelman* is all about. We come from the same neighborhood, but I never had the pleasure of meeting you before."

Mike almost laughed out loud. "You know, we didn't run in the same social circles. Your dad's a big shot politician and you lived on the better side of Hegewisch. Besides, I hear you're a Notre Dame fan." Mike lowered his forehead and looked straight at Barbi with his steel-eyed glare. "I'm not. I look for ND guys in the league and let 'em know who hit 'em! Write that down!"

Barbi imagined that's what the opposing offense saw on the field. It was unnerving.

"Well, Mike, what I want to know is how a regular guy from the Southeast Side became the Chicago Storm Steelman. The way you play is legendary. I want to know about the guy nobody sees."

"Not much to say. Since I was a kid, I play to win. Some say being a linebacker makes me a headhunter. I try to play it clean. But sometimes I get really pissed during a game, and that's when I put the hurt on somebody. As for my personal life, that's *personal*."

She leaned in close, with a coy smile. "Come on, Steelman. We both know I need more than that," she implored.

Mike was cautious. "Okay . . . I do like fast cars, motorcycles, my boats and fishing. I listen to hair-metal bands when I work out and '60s Motown music when I fish. I like to listen to old guys who know a little about everything. It's something I guess I missed out on when my old man died young. My favorite food is all food. My favorite pizza is Mancuso's back on the Southeast Side. That's me, my life, Miss Newsie. Now how about some more wine?"

"Sure, one more." She didn't like the way Mike was treating her or the interview. "I remember Mancuso's . . . the small dumpy place. But tell me more about your boat? Do you keep it on the lakefront?"

"Mancuso's isn't dumpy!" Mike was irked. "And my boat's about five minutes from here in Diversey Harbor. I'm getting ready to put it up for the season."

"I love boats. Can I see it sometime?"

Normally, Mike would not even entertain the idea of bringing a newsie aboard his boat, but he was feeling no pain and not blind to the assets Barbi constantly promoted. He pictured her in a hot pink bikini, her blood red nails wrapped around a margarita glass.

"C'mon! It's a nice night. Let's take a quick cruise along the lakeshore to Navy Pier and back."

Barbi voraciously fed off the free press she got being seen around town with celebrities. She knew this would make a great picture for her confidante Brooke Benett, author of the Tribune gossip column. She excused herself and made a beeline to the ladies' room to text the photo crew.

> Going to his boat in Diversey Harbor. Now!

Barbi and Mike made their way to her car. She put the top down to enjoy the warm night.

"Hey, how do you move this freakin' seat back?" asked Mike, his sore knees now close to his chin.

"Hold on, Steelman. We'll be there quick." Barbi did a U-turn on Clark Street. In her rearview mirror she saw Joe, one of the best stealth photographers, driving an unmarked white van.

The skyline twinkled as they walked along the wooden dock to Mike's slip. He pointed toward Navy Pier's lights. "That's where we're heading, the playpen. Ever been aboard a boat on Lake Michigan? It's supposed to stay calm tonight, but this thing can kick up some waves of its own."

"In high school, I dated a guy whose family had a place in New Buffalo. We used to sneak beer and make out on his dad's speedboat. He was a little crazy and scared me when he drove it too fast."

Barbi failed to mention she was currently involved with Bobby Nolitano, a hotshot commodities trader and rich asshole from Little Italy, who had a huge yacht in Burnham Harbor. After several months, Barbi was tiring of his possessiveness.

The gentle southwestern breeze felt good against her skin. Barbi saw *Wage Burner* splashed across the back of the transom in Storm silver and blue letters. They climbed aboard and Mike uncovered the cockpit of the 42' Sea Ray.

"Nice name for your little boat, Michael," Barbi teased.

"You wouldn't want to feed this thing gas and keep up the maintenance," Mike replied. "It'll remind me when I negotiate my next contract."

He fired up the engines and they were underway. Mike switched on the sound system, looking for the softer rock he played when guests were onboard.

Barbi was a bit apprehensive because of the shots and beer, but Mike was definitely in command of the cockpit, initiating and reviewing all the controls, focusing on the task at hand. She sat on the double lounge seat across from him while he cruised by Oak Street Beach. The Steelman was intense, yet serene, behind the wheel. With his blond mane blowing in the breeze, he looked like a pirate ship deckhand.

Mike broke the silence. "You know if we head south about nine miles as the crow flies, we'll hit our old neighborhood. I'll bet 95th Street Beach is empty now."

"I guess we can head that way, but I kind of like looking at the skyline from this end."

"Yeah, it's weird how different our lives are now from where we grew up," mused an unusually pensive Mike. "When I was a kid, I was happy sitting by the beach, not knowing how big the lake really was. I didn't even go downtown until high school. Sometimes I don't know if I belong on this end of the city. Maybe it was better on the poor side of town."

Unsure how to respond, Barbi chose tongue-in-cheek and flirtatious. "Steelman, you're the hottest thing to come out of Hegewisch since molten steel." Mike immediately realized sharing his innermost thoughts with a superficial chick was a mistake.

Barbi's crew would never be able to get photos on the water. She texted to call them off and was pleased with the reply.

> Mission accomplished. Some good harbor shots.

Mike cruised inside the breakwater near the Chicago Water Filtration Plant to the "playpen," a popular boating haunt to anchor, tie up together and party, above and below deck.

"How about another glass of wine?"

"Okay, one more."

"So what else do you want to know, Miss Newscaster? You want to know my fishing secrets or how many cars I own? Or, do you want to know about my hairdresser?" Mike laughed and dramatically ran his fingers through his hair.

"Michael, tell me about your personal life. I must be honest with you. The media hasn't been kind to you in that department." She hesitated, then boldly continued. "I know you and your wife had some problems along the way." Barbi fully expected that would either open the door or unleash Hell's fury.

Once again, Mike's eyes hardened into the Steelman glare. *Is Barbi Santiago looking for a story or to hook up with an NFL player?* "That's got nothing to do with this interview."

"I'm sorry. That must be difficult. Let's rewind the tape."

Slowing the engines, he admitted, "I'm on my own. Yeah, we're split up right now. That's all you need to know."

Mike was surprising himself by admitting snippets of his personal life to a "newsie." They sat quietly looking at the city lights. He fired up the boat's engines when they drifted close to the breakwater. He pulled out a bottle of vintage California red wine, one of Lisa's favorites. He thought about tossing it overboard, but not at fifty bucks a bottle. Mike filled a large foam cup halfway. He handed it to Barbi, killed the engine and sat back in his captain's chair.

Barbi saw a man who thoroughly enjoyed his present surroundings. Mike looked calm and peaceful—the polar opposite of the Steelman on the field. She raised her hand to his shoulder. "I didn't mean to dig too deep. It's really no one's business how you live your life, although a lot of people would love to know." Barbi leaned seductively against the side of the boat. "Tell me about your favorite rock song instead."

"'Paradise City'—Guns N' Roses."

Mike reached in the cooler for a beer. He took a long swig, almost emptying it. The music had stopped so the only sound was waves lapping against the boat. "You're actually all right, Ms. Newscaster. I guess you're just looking for your story, your angle. I know how you guys work. No harm no foul. Just no more questions, deal?"

"It's a deal, Steelman." Barbi extended her right hand as a conciliatory gesture. When they shook on it, Mike felt her long blood red nails dig into the palm of his hand. He figured they would do the trick for a backrub.

He saw goosebumps on her bare arms and offered his sweatshirt. Underneath he wore a Storm jersey with cut-off sleeves. Barbi couldn't help but stare at his arms and the steel trap tattoo. Genuinely grateful for his chivalry, she spontaneously kissed him on the cheek. Mike pulled her into his lap and kissed her. He hit the windlass' down button. The sound of the chain and anchor hitting the water broke the silence. *Wage Burner* was the only boat anchored in the playpen overnight.

Sunlight streamed through the bedroom portholes.

Mike threw off the sheet at 6:05 a.m. He rubbed his eyes and realized he was not at home. Mike tried but could not remember much of what happened last night, thanks to another blackout from alcohol and painkillers.

Barbi was pulling on her jeans. "Get me out of here, Steelman. I've got to be at the station. Now!"

He did remember team meetings started at 8:00 a.m. sharp. "Holy shit, we are out of here!" Mike fought with his crumpled shorts and tee shirt. Fifteen minutes later, without a word spoken, they pulled into his slip at Diversey Harbor.

"I think I cabbed it to the bar last night. Can you drop me at my condo? I gotta get on the road quick or I'll be in deep shit."

"Sure, Michael, get in. After all, it's my fault. I'm the one who asked you for a boat ride." In daylight, downtown looked impersonal and business-like, not seductive like the night before. Not much else was said.

They pulled up to Mike's building and he turned to face her. "Did we mess around last night, and if we did, did we take precautions?"

Pissed, she glared at him. "Don't worry, Michael! I'm a big girl who doesn't take chances. You're protected," she sneered. Then Barbi blew him a kiss. "Bye-bye, Steelman." She sped away from the curb.

Mike realized his boat keys were in her console. *Shit! Now I have to fucking call her.*

Two days later, on his way home from practice, Shel Harris called.

"Mike, did you read today's paper yet?"

"Shel, I don't read the paper. The stories are all bullshit except for the fishing report in the Sports section. What's up?"

"Well, you'll find *The Steelman and His Barbi Doll* in the Tribune's *About Last Night* column. There's a grainy night shot of you with that Mexican babe from Channel 7 on the back of your boat. Kind of like one of those grocery store rags. You're holding a beer bottle, and it looks like you two are real close. Christ, Mike! You're still on fuckin' probation from your last fuck-up. According to the story, you two are an item since splitting with Lisa. You're legally separated, right?"

"Yeah, it looks that way," Mike quietly acknowledged, understanding he would pay a steep price for his first one-night stand. To make matters worse, after April's bad press, the front office made it clear they did not want to see Mike's name in the news unless it was regarding football.

"All the more reason to make it a story," Shel pointed out. "Old man Everett doesn't need to see this shit in the paper while I'm trying to portray you as a solid citizen and role model. You know he's as straight as they come. Goes to church every day. He's old school Irish Catholic, Mike. A big family guy. Always telling me about his seventeen grandkids. He wants you guys to play it straight. We're in the middle of contract negotiations. And let's face it, this hasn't been a Pro-Bowl season for you,

Mike. This shit is definitely another distraction. What's with that broad anyway? Are you bangin' that?"

Mike stopped for a paper. There on page ten was the column, and sure as shit, a grainy picture of him and Barbi on the back of his boat captioned *Sports news reporter Barbi Santiago gets late-night interview with the Steelman.*

It started sinking in that the alderman's spoiled little brat set him up. She knew a fling with the Steelman would put her in the spotlight.

Mike knew Lisa read garbage like this religiously because she liked to see her name in the paper. *What a fuckin' idiot I am! Trust a fuckin' broad and this is your payback.* Mike was sure Lisa immediately called her asshole lawyer.

The Steelman decided to confront Barbi. He got her voicemail and left a message that he wanted to see her right away. She called back.

Mike played dumb. "Who is this?"

Tersely, Barbi replied, "You know who this is. What can I do for you, Steelman? I'm kind of busy having dinner with a friend at the Rose." Barbi caught herself letting the angry Steelman know where she was.

Friend, my ass! Probably fucking some other guy over.

"I really don't have time to talk now."

"You have my boat keys in your car. Oh yeah, I read today's Trib. I didn't know we were posing on my boat for guys with long lenses. What kind of bullshit did you feed me to get that picture taken? There's no fucking news article about me. You're a fucking liar, a bitch, and a leech! Hooking up with anyone who gets you fifteen minutes of fucking fame! We can talk about this in person because I'm coming now to get my fucking boat keys. Got it, Barbi—*Doll*?"

"I have nothing to say to you. I'll mail your damn keys to the Storm office. Leave me alone. If you call again, I'll tell the police you're stalking me and making threats!"

Mike heard the click. *I don't fucking believe this.*

Barbi's panties were in a knot. She was afraid of what the Steelman might do. To make matters worse, she was with Bobby Nolitano, at his unofficial office, Divina Rosa Café on Taylor Street in Little Italy. He had hit it big trading at the Merc in the mid-'90s and never looked back at his blue-collar roots. She met him while reporting at a political fundraiser. Enamored with the flirty Barbi who looked good on his arm and was recognized in public, Bobby wanted her to be one of his many possessions.

Bobby regularly held court at the restaurant with his posse, gangster wannabes who thought they were real wise guys. Their primary purpose was to stoke Bobby's short-man's ego. Bobby's coveted brass plaque on the wall of fame identified him as someone special. The valet always parked his black Mercedes right near the door in the No Parking zone. No one ever messed with it, not even the CPD beat cops or parking enforcement drones who plastered cars with tickets. Outsiders weren't welcome at the Rose. She'd never explain this away if Mike showed up.

Totally unaware of what was in the Tribune, Bobby was enjoying dinner with Barbi, who almost choked on her whole wheat pasta marinara when she saw a black Chevy pick-up at the valet stand. There was no mistaking the blond-and-blue-haired Steelman, his silhouette filling the entire front door. She slunk down in her seat, hoping he wouldn't notice her. Mike walked right up to her table, startling Bobby and everyone nearby.

"Hey, Barbi!"

"Who the fuck are you and what do you think you're doing here? Don't you know where the fuck you are?" Bobby threw his cloth napkin on the floor and stood up to face Mike. He was almost a foot shorter. Scowling, he backed up. "Who is this guy, Barbi?" Clearly he was not a football fan.

"A friend, Bobby. Calm down. Mike, what are you doing here? I told you we would talk later."

"What the hell are you going to say? We looked cute in the picture? You set me up! You used me to plant a bullshit story to get you attention. You think I'm an idiot?"

"What the fuck are you two talking about, and who the fuck is this clown?" Bobby yelled.

"I play football asshole, and if I were you, I'd stay out of this. Who the fuck are you, anyway?"

Bobby waved over two of his goons.

"Mike, you should leave," warned Barbi. "Don't do anything stupid. I'm not going to take this shit. I'm telling you one last time. Leave me alone!"

Bobby was emboldened by his posse and her warning. "Look motherfucker, I don't care who you are and what the fuck you do. You don't want me to make your bad day worse. So listen to the lady, and get the fuck out of here before I call the cops."

Mike grabbed a big handful of Bobby's jacket and shoulder and sat him down in his chair. Hovering close to his face, he snarled, "I'll talk to you outside if you want, *little man*, and explain what the fuck I'm here for. Only you're not going through the door." He paused, "See that window?"

Bobby fumed. All his life he hated being reminded he was short. "Call the cops, Dom. This asshole's threatening me and my date."

Mike knew he didn't stand a chance. Everyone was staring and half the patrons recognized him. But he would have the last word. "Hey, Barbi *Doll*, we'll pick this up another time when your *little* friend isn't around."

Mike got in his truck and started to pull away but was boxed in by two police squads. After bracing him on the hood of his truck, four of Chicago's finest cuffed him and took him into custody.

The next 24-hour news cycle starred Mike Stalowski. The Steelman bonded out the next afternoon. Don Castro and Carl LeFevour were waiting for him in the lobby of the 11th District police station. Nobody was happy.

Carl had been around pro football as an attorney-consultant almost forty years. He saw the generational changes of players, from flat-topped jocks to reality-show stars prospering from their notoriety. Now, instead of toiling on the gridiron for low salaries and no benefits, they wanted to be superstars with multimillion-dollar contracts and big endorsements. Increasingly flagrant bad behavior garnered 24/7 media attention.

"Don, I thought Mike would be the last guy to get jammed up when he was drafted. A local kid with a good upbringing gets his big chance to be the hometown hero. What the hell has happened to him the last few years?"

"I wish I had the answers, Carl. Mike's basically a good guy. He trains and plays hard. He's still got heart, even after years in the league."

"Looks like he's really starting to believe all that *Steelman* bullshit!"

"I think getting kicked out by his wife messed him up bad. More than we first thought. I don't think he's focused. But that doesn't make it right."

"For Chrissake, Don, his freakin' hair is blue! And the steel trap tattoo! Connie's getting pissed with his antics. I don't get it. Guys messed around before but never caused this much trouble. He needs to man up and cut this shit out!"

"I know the old man isn't happy with all the negative media exposure Mike's getting himself and the organization. I also know I can't cover for him if this continues."

Mike was escorted from the holding cell and brought to the lobby. LeFevour and Castro saw he was fuming.

"Get me the fuck out of here. The lock-up guy wants my picture with him."

"Mike, news crews are outside. Don't say anything."

"Fuck them! Where's my pick-up?"

"Carl and I will drive you home. Your truck's impounded."

"My fuckin' house keys are in the console. How am I supposed to get in my condo?" He began walking, shoving away microphones stuck in his face.

Luckily, the doorman had an extra key. Otherwise, Mike probably would have broken the door down.

Over the next few days, Mike's trials and tribulations kept him and Barbi Santiago in the public eye. In one of her numerous interviews, she explained, "It was all a big mistake. Just the result of someone's publicity stunt, using me and Mike Stalowski to cause a stir." She never speculated on who "someone" might be.

Midnight Blue and
Scorched Pavement

JULY 2006 STARTED OUT HOT AND MUGGY, SO LAKE MICHIGAN PERCH schooled out in deeper, cooler water. Nevertheless, Mike and Ric decided to take the Steelman's glittering fishing boat, *Grim Reaper #52,* out for a quick spin. Mike loved the look of the creepy lime green letters scrawled across the black hull.

"This thing will tear up some water when I open it up. Let's hope the fuck it doesn't flip over."

"Are you fucking crazy?" Ric clutched his seat with both hands and screamed. "Slow the fuck down, bro! Did you learn how to drive this thing on a video game?" His right hand let go momentarily to make the sign of the cross. "I got reasons to live, *mijo*. There are women who will cry if I die!"

Mike laughed as the speedometer reached 50 mph. Too damn fast for a flat-bottomed fishing boat. Nearing the breakwater, he abruptly slowed the boat. Backwash surged over the transom and doused the two fishermen.

"Hey, Steelman! Can't you buy a goddamned fishing boat with a 20-horse motor like everyone else?"

Mike floated the boat into a small cove. "Give me a beer and let's nail 'em. Gotta get in and out, man. I got things to do."

An hour later, after a 12-pack between them, the friends were feeling good, despite no action on their rods. They reminisced about the "good old days" when neither of them had any money, cares, or problems.

"Brother," Ric wistfully proclaimed, "I would trade it all. No headaches back when we hung around here. Old Chester kept us in line, *mijo*!"

Mike felt the first tug of the day on his bait. Maybe the perch were finally biting. If not, it was still worth it, being out on the lake, off the breakwater they had navigated together since they were boys. Mike's phone vibrated in his shorts pocket. He tried setting the hook while checking his caller ID. The rod went straight. "Shit." The fish took his bait, so he answered the call.

"Hi, Mom. What's up?"

"I hope I'm not disturbing you, Michael. I planned to leave a message because I thought you'd be in a meeting."

"I had neck therapy and snuck out afterwards to fish."

"How *is* your neck? Still taking muscle relaxers?"

"Yeah, and they make me dopey. More than I already am. Don't worry, team trainers are on it," he lied.

"Just be careful you don't wind up on opiates like Oxycontin, God forbid. Anyway, I have something to tell you. Can you come over after 6:00 p.m.?"

"Sure, Mom, when we're done." He was scheduled for a private appearance at a Sox game but could stop in briefly. It seemed important to her.

When he arrived at his boyhood home, Janet was waiting on the porch. She hugged him and tussled his blue hair tips. "Michael, aren't you over this yet?"

"For my public. Kinda matches the team colors."

Janet shook her head. He seemed to enjoy the notoriety now. Sometimes she wondered if it was still an act, or if he had truly become the outrageous and brazen Steelman? What she did know was that right now she intended to enjoy a rare solo visit with her son.

"How was fishing? And Ric? I read in the Trib his club is all the rage. Are you hanging out there now that you and Lisa aren't together?"

"Sometimes." No need to add that when he wasn't in a bar, he still had plenty of alcohol on hand to dull his pain.

"Michael, isn't there anything you two can do to save your marriage? How about counseling? You've known each other since high school. The fact you can't have kids shouldn't drive you apart. Lisa told me she brought up adoption but you wouldn't talk about it. What happened . . . carrying a baby to term . . . only to have him stillborn . . . it's devastating for a woman, especially after the miscarriages."

No response.

"It's not just Lisa's loss, Michael. You share that grief."

No response.

"What's going on? Another woman?"

Still no response.

"Seriously, do you really have to be the team bad-boy? I didn't raise you to act this way. And neither did your father!"

A wave of bitterness overcame Mike when Frank got dragged into the lecture. "What do you have to tell me, Mom? I'm not talking about Lisa. I've heard enough about her shit and my fucked-up marriage from everyone. Leaving home last year was the best fucking thing I did in a long time."

"Watch your language!" Janet reprimanded. "And as your mother, I have a right to ask questions about your life."

The Steelman hung his head. "I'm sorry, Mom."

Janet thought how ridiculous this must look, all 5′ 5″ of her, yelling at her 6′ 5″, 255-pound son. She remembered when he was little and she towered over him like it was yesterday. She'd catch him with his hand in the cookie jar and shake her head, asking "Mikey, what did you do?"

She looked closely at Mike under the glare of the kitchen light. He was big and imposing with earrings, tattoos, and his long, blond hair tipped blue. But when Janet peered into his bright blue eyes, she saw a young boy, trying to impress his sister with never-ending superhero imitations. Her eyes suddenly welled up, recalling Mike sitting in the same chair shortly after Frank was buried. He'd told her, "Mom, don't worry. I'll take care of you and Anna."

Looking around the tiny kitchen, Mike reminisced aloud. "Remember when Grandma cooked all that Polish food, especially at Easter and Christmas? That was some good stuff."

His comment brought Janet and her spot-on maternal instinct back to the present. "Mike, why are you wearing a long sleeve T-shirt in this sweltering heat and humidity? Hiding something? Show me your arms!"

The Steelman hesitated, but slowly pulled back his right sleeve, above his elbow. Janet's eyes opened wide when she saw another steel trap hinged at the elbow. Now he had a matched set to catch defenseless prey.

"Don't you have enough ridiculous body art for your fans? When you're eighty, your skin will look like a faded comic book."

"Look Mom, I'm the captain of the *steel trap defense*. It's my job to trap some poor running back and make him pay for coming on our side of the ball. My fans expect me to look fierce. It's part of the costume."

"Can't you play without looking like you belong in a circus sideshow? You make more money per game than this whole block makes annually. You don't need to look like a Hell's Angels biker to impress anyone. And players wear uniforms—not costumes!"

"Well, that's what the fans want. It's not really me, Mom. Well, maybe. Besides, Lisa hated them. She'll really be happy when she sees it on TV," he added sarcastically. "You know the blade on my right forearm covers her name I put on in college."

"Great way to salvage your marriage!"

"I'm not here to discuss that. Thought you had something to tell me."

Janet blurted out her news. "Tom and I are getting married soon and moving to Phoenix. You're the first person I've told. You need to know I've had no interest in any other relationship since your father died. But my friendship with Tom has grown and we believe we have a future together. He's a good and decent man, and he treats me like a queen."

Mike played with the placemat. Being back here triggered long forgotten memories. Good and bad. When he finally spoke, it wasn't anything she expected.

"Tom was in Vietnam like Uncle Mike, right?"

"Yes, Tom was wounded bad. But he made it back. He hardly talks about it."

"Hey, you don't have any beer in the fridge, do you?"

"No, how about some iced tea?"

"No thanks." Mike was pensive again.

Janet wondered if he was lost in memories or at a loss for conversation. "What's going through your head? Did you hear anything I said about me and Tom?"

"I'm thinking . . . good for you and Tom. He seems like an okay guy from the couple of times I saw him. Arizona is a good place for you to be. Although I could buy you a condo there myself and you wouldn't have to get married." Mike laughed. "Just kidding, Mom! Maybe you guys'll have more marriage luck than I did with that lousy bitch!"

Janet frowned. "Michael, watch your language! I don't care how big you are or what costume you're wearing! And you should be glad she stuck by you as long as she did with all of your nonsense."

"Stuck by me?" He laughed. "She's still trying to take me to the cleaners."

"Don't you have a hand in this, too?"

No response.

"It looks to me like you're trying to self-destruct. You've been blessed but chose to turn your career and private life into a public soap opera."

Mike glossed over Janet's comments. "You know I'll miss you, Mom. And you never know, I might get traded to the Arizona Rattlers." He glanced over at the wall clock. "I really need to get going."

"One minute, please, Mike. I have something for you." Janet dangled a ring with two odd-looking keys. "Remember the car that sat in the garage? With all the junk piled on it? You probably haven't even noticed it since searching for your high school football spikes. Anyway, Tom and I were looking at everything that needs to go. He said it's a classic 1970 Chevy muscle car and could potentially be worth a lot of money.

"I know your father intended to give it to you eventually. So here you go, Mike. Take it, fix it up—restore it—whatever. It's your link to your father's and uncle's past. They loved fast cars and raced all around here, mostly illegally." Janet smiled. "Just promise me you'll be careful. Nothing foolish for your fans!"

"Hell, yes, I'd love to take it! I know a little about muscle cars. You won't recognize it after I get through with it."

His enthusiasm made Janet happy.

"The guys on the team will be jealous. Lots of them are into exotic and expensive rides. Who knows. I might even have another garage to keep it in by that time." Grinning, he grabbed the keys from his mother. "Thanks!"

Mike stood up, bumping his head on the old overhead kitchen light, and prepared to leave Janet and his boyhood home. "When's the wedding? In case Shel has to rearrange some big endorsements coming up." Without giving her a chance to answer, he continued. "Hey, guess what? I'm gonna be in a music video! Can you believe it?" Mike laughed. "I've got a cameo in a remake of a '90s rock video. The lyrics are a little raunchier than the original, but I guess my fans will think it's way cool."

"That's great, Mike. Anyway, we don't know the date for sure, but probably right after your season starts. Don't worry, we'll give plenty of notice. It'll be simple. Maybe just an afternoon service at St. Florian's for family and a few friends. No big honeymoon either. We'll probably take a weekend trip to the Grand Hotel on

Mackinac Island. No cars, only horses and bikes on the island. And lots of fudge! It also depends on when Anna can come home."

"How is she? I haven't heard from her in a while. I think the last time I saw her was like a year ago."

"She's fine. And you should pick up the phone to call her occasionally."

"I know, I know. Promise I'll look her up next week in LA. Maybe I can get her in the video or something. I'll see, but gotta go. Promo gig at Sox Park in an hour."

He turned to leave, but Janet tugged on his shirt sleeve.

"Wait! I have an important question for you."

A bit puzzled, he turned back to face her. She clasped his hands in hers, looking up in his anxious eyes. "Will you walk me down the aisle?"

"Sure, Mom! I may even shave and put on a nice shirt and tie—or not!"

Mike's smile reassured Janet about Tom, but she noticed he'd had a hard time turning his neck. "Mike, what's really wrong with your neck?"

"I'm good. Guess sixteen years of football is starting to wear out the warranty. Just a little stiff. I'm fine, Mom. Really."

He looked over her to a tabletop photo display in the adjacent living room. His eyes were immediately drawn to one. It was from the annual Chicago Park District 95th Street Beach Father and Son Fishing Tournament many years ago. He walked over, picked it up and saw himself sporting a wide grin and crew cut. He had a tiny perch dangling from his rod. Frank was beaming, his arm around Mike.

"Can I have this?"

Janet nodded.

"Hey, how come he didn't take us to Disneyland or on summer vacations like other families? I remember Stevie, from down the block, bragging every time they were going somewhere. I was jealous because we never went anywhere, except 95th Street Beach on Sundays. Always wanted to go to Disneyland. When we win the damn Superbowl, I'm doing the 'I'm going to Disneyland' line . . ."

Stunned, Janet interrupted him. "I knew concussions would take their toll! After he lost his job at the mill, we struggled to make ends meet. Don't you remember having to help on the bricklaying job sites?"

Mike nodded and looked intently at the photo again.

"Today me and Ric were right on the spot where I used to go with him. I remember we'd stop at Chester's Bait Shop on 94th and Commercial. Dad would bullshit with him in broken Polish, I think."

"Your father was a good guy who left us too soon." Janet looked away as her eyes filled with tears. Good and bad memories for both of them today.

"Yeah, I know. It's been a long time since I went to the cemetery. Honestly, I haven't been back since they buried the baby. I can't handle it."

"I'm sorry. I know you and Lisa had a tough time. As for your father, before I move, I'm going to go through those old pictures and movies from when you and Anna were little and make some keepsakes for both of you."

He kissed her on the cheek. "Thanks!" Then he bounded out the door, into the evening shadows. Just like hot summer nights many years ago when he raced outside to meet his buddies in Patriot's Park.

The Rock Star

At the baggage carousel, Mike looked around for his driver and felt a tug on his back pocket. He spun around, ready to vaporize whoever was going for his wallet.

"Welcome to the land of the golden sun!"

He broke into a huge smile and pulled out his earbuds. "Well, well, if it isn't my long lost littlest sister!"

Mike bent down to all 5′ 3″ of Anna Marie Stalowski and engulfed her with his arms.

His baseball cap tumbled off, revealing his signature hairdo. "How are you, kid? You look great but must be blind! What sun?" Mike had heard of LA June Gloom, but it was almost August and there was no sun in sight. Just a gray haze.

"Very funny, biggest brother! I'm good. Jeez, Mike, it's great to see you! I thought you'd be getting ready for summer camp, not out here for more fame and fortune. You know you could answer my texts once in a while. And what's with this hair? It's at least eight or nine inches longer than mine!" Anna still talked a mile a minute.

"My thumbs are too big so my replies read like a two-year-old texted."

"The phone actually makes calls too!"

"And my hair's ready for the shoot."

"Your hair is VERY Venice Beach. You'd fit right in with the rollerblading, chain-saw jugglers wearing Jesus tunics."

"Yeah, now you're talking."

The siblings laughed.

"Come on, I got all my stuff. We can talk in the car."

Mike warily eyed Anna's faded red convertible VW Beetle-bug with a butterfly antenna topper. "Relax, it's old, but a great ride." She gave him a once-over. "I hope you fit."

Crawling down the ramp to wedge onto the always busy 405 freeway, Mike's stomach rumbled. "Can we stop to eat somewhere that doesn't sell tofu and bean sprouts? I need real food."

Only a few miles, but forty-five minutes later, they parked near Westwood Village, full of trendy eateries close to UCLA. Despite his desire for "real" food, Anna talked Mike into Tiger Sushi. They ate outdoors so Mike could enjoy the sights of LA.

"So where are you living? Hollywood?"

"Burbank. Not too far from here. It's kinda near Disney offices and NBC Studios where they film *The Tonight Show*. Remember how much Mom loved watching Johnny Carson! Anyway, I rent a studio from a really sweet lady who was a '50s B-movie actress. Mrs. Conway's late husband was in *I Was A Teenage Frankenstein*. You know, the one with the pizza face and dangling eyeball."

"Wow, very cool. I bet she could tell some stories. Hey, if we have time, can we go to Disneyland? Just me and you. We never went as kids."

"We never went a lot of places as kids, Michael. But here we are together in Los Angeles, and you have an acting gig! Who would have guessed?"

"I don't really act."

"Have you ever done a music video?"

"No, but I watch them. I've done beer advertising stuff and Chevy commercials. There's one where I'm in my uniform, having a tug of war with a Silverado truck going in reverse. It was a bitch, but I won. So for this gig, we're filming a pool scene where I've got two bunnies in a headlock. Then there's a football cut where I'm walking off the field after a game, into a stretch limo with cheerleaders following me. Pretty wild, huh?"

"How on earth did you get picked?"

"Because I'm THE STEELMAN! And I play for the Chicago Storm, that's why. Don't you read Sports Illustrated or watch ESPN?"

"No, not really. I love you, but I can't see why you get paid millions of dollars to play a game that's really just barbaric staged violence. Basically, a step up from being a Roman gladiator."

"Well, they want sports guys, TV celebrities, and rock singers doing cameos. But you know Anna, I think they really picked me because of these . . ." Mike slowly rolled up his sleeves, expecting to shock her. "Everyone in football knows me as the leader of the Steel Trap defense, get it?"

Anna didn't even blink. "Yep, I can see you and the cheerleader bunnies, bro. You know, I still like your St. Michael tattoo. He's hot."

"If you say so. Well, thank God I'm just supposed to mouth the words while they're captive. You remember how I sing, right?"

"Oh-h YES!" Anna stuck her forefingers in her ears and laughed. "Lalalalalala, can't hear you!"

She dropped Mike off at the Century Plaza Hotel near Beverly Hills, with plans to meet for breakfast at 7:00 a.m. Tired and jet lagged, Mike plopped on his bed to watch the KTLA breaking news—Malibu fires and Compton shootings.

Next morning at the MTV office, Mike presented Anna as his agent's assistant. The entourage departed for the stand-in Playboy mansion. Extras, posing as poolside bunnies in neon bikinis, were being prepped by the director Murray and his staff. Everyone noticed when the Steelman walked on set and removed his shirt, revealing his ripped physique.

Mike finally got it right after four screwed-up takes. The camera panned a pool party with lots of skin, beer, and the Steelman in the center of the action. A blonde and a redhead, their necks between each of his steel traps, smiled and flashed four barely covered boobs before they all fell backwards into the pool.

Walking into the Rose Bowl stadium for the second scene, Mike recalled how desperate he was to get to Pasadena senior year for the granddaddy of all college bowl games on New Year's Day. After the second cameo wrapped, Mike was more than ready to call it quits. The day had required more social interaction than he could tolerate for a week, let alone one day. He glanced around looking for Anna and saw her talking to Murray's assistant.

Murray asked the Steelman to autograph promo pictures. Mike reluctantly penned #52 with a big "S" and squiggly line. He figured it was part of earning his $500,000 fee. He even managed small talk. Then Murray asked him to pose for some stills with the cheerleaders. For the last shot, the photographer positioned him close to an auburn-haired goddess with big green eyes who winked at him.

Mike winked back and went to his trailer, eager to get the hell out of there. He was ready to step in the shower when he heard a knock on the door. "Hey, Anna is that you? I'll be out in a minute."

No response. Mike cracked the door and was stunned to see the auburn-haired goddess.

She pulled a business card out of her ample cleavage. Stepping closer, she pressed it into Mike's hand and whispered, "Call me later. It's worth it."

The card simply read *Emerald* and a phone number.

Anna took Mike to Divina Cucina in nearby Glendale where they enjoyed a quiet dinner. The unrecognized NFL star inhaled a huge plate of homemade pasta and two bread baskets, washing it down with four glasses of California Merlot to Anna's one. After dinner, Mike stuffed himself into Anna's VW bug and they cruised down the 2 freeway toward Los Angeles.

"What a day! Thanks for letting me tag along, Mike. I got quite a bump up the ladder of success! Murray asked for my number. Said he might use me on an upcoming video for a hot new female singer. Lady... something or other."

"That's great. Glad I could help. I'll see you soon at Mom's wedding, right?"

"Of course! I'm so happy for her. You know, it was only recently I realized she kept a lid on everything after Dad died. She worked, cooked, pulled the sled, made your games and my recitals and plays. Mom was two parents all of the time."

"Yeah, you're right. Don't hand me up, but I'm giving them a Hawaiian cruise for their honeymoon. On a "shore excursion" in Kauai, they'll get the keys to a condo I'm buying them."

"Hard to believe, but you do have a heart in there, Michael. Sometimes, I miss you lots."

"Yeah, Anna, me too. Come back and visit more. I'll even take you to some plays in the Theatre District. It's not far from the Lincoln Park condo."

"I'm sorry about you and Lisa."

"No worries, it's all good." Mike reached in his back pocket and handed her a crumpled envelope. "Open this tomorrow when I'm gone, okay?"

"Why tomorrow?"

"Because I said so!" He gave Anna his football glare, softened with brotherly love. Anna nodded and stuck it in her purse. Back at the Century Plaza, Mike unfolded himself from the little red Bug. He hugged Anna and watched her drive off.

————————•————————

Two days later, she would find the envelope while rummaging for her keys and discover a check for $250,000 along with a scribbled note.

You better cash this! Pay your rent, buy some groceries, new clothes, and a puppy. Name it something that reminds you of me. And put the change in the bank!

Anna's fingers would fly across her phone.

> Thank you . . . thank you . . . thank you! Still my
> guardian angel, Michael. The puppy will be a
> Chihuahua named Marshmallow. I luv you always!

———————————•———————————

Yawning and fumbling for his keycard in the lobby, Mike glanced at his phone and saw it was 10:45 p.m. Only a few hours before his flight. Out of the corner of his eye, he saw Emerald, the trailer-visiting cheerleader, sitting at the end of the bar, twirling a half-filled wineglass. *Holy shit! That's her, a body double, or too much merlot.*

She looked around as though waiting for someone. Her eyes widened when she noticed him staring at her. She waved him over. "Hello, Rock Star #52. It's about time you showed up. I've been waiting since 9:00 o'clock."

She looked elegant—older than the twenty-one or twenty-two he guessed her to be—dressed in a short, low-cut black sundress with spike heel sandals. Big hoop earrings shone brightly underneath her auburn mane. Her glossy lips were stained red from the wine. She took another sip.

"Aren't you the cheerleader from the Rose Bowl today?"

"Yes."

"What are you doing here?"

Matter-of-factly, Emerald replied, "I was hoping I would run into you. Figured you might want some company."

"Expected me to be alone, huh?"

Although very tired, he figured one more drink would let him spend a little time with the video extra before offering his autograph and going to his room—alone. Mike sat down next to her and waved over the well-coiffed bartender whose name tag said Lexx. Mike didn't like guys that looked like Lexx or had names like

Lexx. He pulled out a wad of cash and Emerald's card tumbled to the floor. She smiled knowingly. Mike retrieved it and threw a one-hundred-dollar bill on the bar.

"Hey, Lexx, let me have a draft." Mike winked at the bartender, half taunting and half pitying him.

Lexx smirked arrogantly. He hated when guys, who clearly weren't A-listers, tossed big bills around pretending they were.

Mike looked at Emerald. "How about you, mystery lady, do you want another glass of whatever you're about to finish?"

"Yes. Thank you."

Lexx put Mike's beer on a coaster and stared at him. "Here you go, sir. By the way, your hair is stunning!"

Mike couldn't decide if Lexx was coming on to him or messing with him. Mike downed half the beer in one gulp. "I'll have another. And so will she." He turned back to Emerald.

"I couldn't believe it when I got the casting call from my agent! I'm one of your biggest fans."

Shoulda known better! Damn Barbi Doll was one of my "biggest fans," too.

"So you decided to stalk me in a public place like a hotel bar. Where's the paparazzi or whatever you call the news slimeballs out here? And what do you mean, agent? Are you an actress?" Even though he was upset, he couldn't stop thinking that Emerald was put together like a California show car—bright headlights, nice clean lines, and glossy finish.

"Sorry, Mike Stalowski. I guess that didn't come out right. I do act and I do have an agent."

"Yeah, what have you acted in?"

"Some TV extra stuff, indie movies, lots of commercial auditions, stuff you probably haven't seen."

"What do you mean, indie?"

"You know, independent films. Kind of artsy."

Elbows on the bar rail, Emerald interlaced her fingers, with perfectly manicured dark red nails, and rested her chin on them. She looked deeply into Mike's fierce blue eyes and smiled coyly. He wondered how old she really was—and how much lower the sundress could be cut before her cleavage had a wardrobe malfunction.

"I'll bet you're really from Cleveland and your name is like Ginny O'Rourke. How old are you?"

"Close, Mike Stalowski. Actually, I'm from Cincinnati. I'm half-Irish and half-French. My real name is Michelle Redden, and I'm twenty-five. My family calls me Mickey, like Mouse. Next question."

"You can't be twenty-five. You look barely old enough to drink."

Two more beers for Mike and another glass of wine later, Mickey's speech was slurred. She decided to come clean.

"Okay, Steelman, you win. I'm really twenty and I quit Ohio State my sophomore year to be an actress. I was captain of the cheerleading squad."

"Nice! Real nice! I'm sitting here with Minnie Mouse who's not old enough to drink. You're gonna get me busted for sure. Holy shit, I've been buying wine for an underage wannabe actress. And I hate Ohio State! They beat us bad senior year when I was out with a concussion."

"It's Mickey, not Minnie, Steelman!" Emerald proudly pulled something out of her purse. "I have my SAG card."

"What the hell is that? A credit card?"

"No, silly! It means I can act. I started doing bit parts in adult films, like background stuff as an extra. So, I don't really *do* it. I just flash my boobs for the most part. They get a lot of attention, don't you think?" Emerald, quickly deteriorating into a drunken stupor, cupped her breasts in her hands.

Mike had a buzz on and was having a little fun. But he almost fell out of his seat when he realized what she just admitted.

"You mean indie films are porno movies and you're in them? Holy shit! Now I'm really gonna get busted!"

"Look, it was only to get started as an actress, and the money's pretty good. I don't socialize with those people."

This chick would probably say anything. Mickey Redden looked like she was going to slide off the barstool, so Mike grabbed her shoulder and propped her up. "Hey, are you gonna be all right? How did you get here anyway?"

Mickey tried to focus. "Um, I took a cab. I'm just gonna put my head down for a little bit."

Mike was pissed at himself for letting her drink that much and watching her slide into oblivion. He could call her a cab but was afraid she might not make it home.

"Hey, Mickey, I'm out of here real early to catch a 7:00 a.m. flight. I've got a big suite upstairs. You can crash. I'll stay in the other room. When you wake up, I'll be gone." Mike put his arm around her waist and lifted her off the barstool, supporting her while she limply shuffled her heels.

When they got to his floor, she barely opened her eyes. "Where's the bathroom, Steelman? I think I'm gonna be sick."

"Shit! Hold on, we're almost at my room. Don't puke!"

Mike inserted the key card and pushed the door open. He flipped on the light and quickly led Emerald to the bathroom.

"Listen, Mickey, you just kneel down and you'll feel better. I'm gonna call for some coffee. I'll be right back."

While dialing, he heard the wretched sound of her puking her guts out. *Better she gets it out in there instead of here.* Impatiently waiting for room service to answer, he heard a loud thud. *What the hell was that?* He rushed to the bathroom. Emerald was passed out next to the toilet. Blood flowed steadily from her forehead onto the marble floor.

He carefully positioned Mickey on her back, with a towel under her head. Thankfully her chest was rising up and down, so she was at least breathing. He bit his lip when he saw her left boob was almost exposed.

"Hey, Mickey, wake up! Are you okay?" She groaned a little. He tried to stop the bleeding with a washcloth but knew he had to call 911, so he left her on the floor.

"Hey, this is room 1422. My girlfriend is sick. I think she passed out in the bathroom and hit her head pretty hard. It's bleeding. You gotta call the paramedics."

"Mr. Stalowski, security will be up shortly. 911 was called. Paramedics are on their way."

And right between the eyes, with the force of a baseball bat, Mike was hit with the realization that he would be the KTLA 6:00 a.m. breaking news. *The Steelman, NFL Chicago Storm middle linebacker, sends porn starlet to the hospital.* The LAPD public information officer would release a statement and the voracious media would be relentless, trying to implicate him in some bullshit Hollywood scandal. And then, the NFL Commissioner would call Storm brass for an explanation of Mike Stalowski's latest escapade. Connie Everett would not be a happy man by the time Mike landed at O'Hare.

LAPD officers arrived right after paramedics put a groggy and sobbing Mickey on the stretcher. It was 1:00 a.m., only four hours before Mike needed to be at LAX. He spent those hours at the UCLA Medical Center ER, in the company of the LAPD officers and on the phone with his attorney. Sure enough, KTLA's minicam truck was first to arrive.

The sequence of events pretty much played out as Mike expected. Luckily—and contrary to the expectation of his attorney and popular opinion—Mike wasn't charged with assault and battery. Mickey Redden vouched for the Steelman's chivalry. He was only trying to help her. She came out on top for all of her troubles, including five stitches in her forehead. Her Emerald persona was no longer needed. Mickey Redden's newfound notoriety caught the eye of the entertainment industry. She was well on her way to fame with TV guest appearances, commercial offers and even a pitch for a reality TV show.

TROUBLED TIMES

Fall 2006-Winter 2007

Sunset and the Endless Summer

MIKE WAS EAGER TO ENJOY THE PERFECT INDIAN SUMMER DAY WITH A SCENIC motorcycle ride around the southern tip of the lake into Southwestern Michigan. He got an eyeful when he picked Kim up. On a scale of 1-10 for biker chicks, she was an 11.

Although he'd never admit it, Mike loved seeing the fall colors in Harbor Country. Quaint shops and restaurants beckoned travelers to stop and visit along Red Arrow Highway. After a late lunch and stroll through New Buffalo, they continued to Warren Dunes State Park, where tall sweeping sand dunes descended into the blue waters of Lake Michigan. He planned to watch the sun set over the lake. Walking down the wooded path from the parking lot, Mike realized he left his keys on the seat.

"How did you get to miss the meeting before this big Minnesota rivalry? Won't you be in trouble for playing hooky?" Kim looked over and realized she was talking to herself. "Hey, where the heck are you?" She kept walking toward the lake, half expecting him to do something stupid like jump out from behind a bush.

Up ahead, three young guys were sitting on rocks, drinking beer and throwing "F" bombs. Instinctively, she slowed down. There were at least a dozen bottles strewn about. Two wore beat up baseball hats and ragged sleeveless T-shirts. The third one was a skinny version of the Steelman, complete with long hair and heavily tattooed arms.

"Hey, baby . . . you lost? Join us for a beer. We'll show you a good time." Their disgusting howls turned Kim's stomach. She avoided eye contact.

"Maybe you didn't hear my partner. Get over here!" commanded the long-haired creep.

Kim heard wood chips crunching behind her. The Steelman, who instinctively sized-up and neutralized threats on the football field, heard a different kind of threat in their voices. This wasn't going to end well.

These rednecks were obviously not Storm fans. No one seemed to recognize him or his steel traps. Six inches taller and twice as wide across the chest, the Steelman grabbed the shoulders of the long-haired loudmouth who'd ordered Kim to join them.

"Aren't you assholes a little young to be drinking? How 'bout you shut the fuck up and pick up your shit? Apologize to my girlfriend and get the fuck out of here before I kick all three of your clown asses and lay you over these rocks to dry!"

"Hey, man, just because you think you look bad, don't mean you are. Why don't you and your little squeeze take a walk and maybe we won't kick YOUR ass!"

Mike tightened his grip and lifted him two feet off the ground. In an instant, there was an audible sickly thud after the Steelman threw him down on the rock. Then he leaned in, inches from the punk's face, and grabbed a handful of dirty T-shirt under his chin.

"Cletus," the Steelman barely whispered, "I would tear your fucking head off right now and shit in your lungs, but there's a lady present." Mike let him go and picked up the case of remaining beer. He slammed it over a nearby boulder sending beer and glass flying.

"Hey, man! We're not looking for trouble with you or your girl. Just partying. We good, man?" asked Cletus' friend.

Mike was in full combat mode. "No, we ain't good! Shut the fuck up and show some respect, asshole!"

Scared shitless, they helped their broken buddy up and guided him, wobbly at the knees, back to their truck. Kim was shocked by the spontaneous eruption of Mike's rage and grateful the cops or an ambulance weren't needed.

"Next time, don't flirt with a bunch of idiots." Mike grabbed her still trembling hand without looking at her and began walking.

Her eyes widened at the false accusation. Kim willed her legs to move. She smiled curtly. "Thanks for saving me, Sir Galahad."

"Sorry." He lightened up a little. "Guess I'm no day at the beach."

Emerging from the path, she gazed at the lakeshore stretching infinitely on either side of her. "Wow! Michael, it's beautiful here." The setting sun felt good on her face. Lake Michigan's rushing tide and rippling waves reminded her of her beloved Hillsboro Beach.

The tension of his grip almost imperceptibly loosened, and Mike's demeanor softened. The water and breeze transformed him. They stopped near some tall beach grass. Kim watched his eyes follow the shoreline west. She couldn't quite put her finger on it, but somewhere beneath 255 pounds of muscle and attitude she sensed a little boy searching for something. Then she remembered the photo in his locker.

"Hey, Kim, when I die, I want to be buried at sea like an old pirate. Just wrap me up and slide me off the back of my boat into Lake Michigan."

"Well, Captain Steelman, you kind of look like a pirate and you do have a big boat in Lake Michigan. So, I guess the rest is easy, right?"

"You catch on pretty quick for a blonde chick who grew up on a Florida beach."

"What the hell is that supposed to mean?" But she too became wistful. "When I die, I want my ashes spread by the ocean, carried by the wind across the waves, in front of a setting sun—kind of like now."

Kim pulled the clips out of her hair, letting it fall to her shoulder. She looked so vulnerable. Mike wanted to hold her, right there on the beach, and never let go. The sun continued moving lower in the sky, casting long shadows on the dunes behind them.

Mike gently nudged Kim toward the tall beach grass. He kissed her, gently first and then more passionately. Continuing down her neck, he tried to give her a hickey.

Kim shrieked and pushed him away. "Stop you knucklehead! What are you doing? I have a big audition next week . . ." Mike backed off, flashing a boyish grin. He whispered something in her ear. "Are you nuts? Besides, I'm not protected. Or do you want to have a baby?"

"Yeah, sometimes. Then I'll have a fishing partner. Unless it's a girl."

Mike led her by the hand into the grassy dunes. Later, they emerged in the dark, arms around each other, and headed back to his bike. The seemingly endless summer sun had given way to a soft ripple of moonlight reflecting over Lake Michigan. A momma duck led her brood of ducklings across their path.

"Look, Michael, aren't they just so awful cute?" Kim nestled into his chest. "Maybe it's an omen."

"You know, baby, that would be my luck. One of those little bastards swims his way up and hits the bullseye. Well, at least he'll have blond hair and blue eyes, like his dad!"

"Let's hope he doesn't eat and drink like you! But, what if SHE is just like her momma? Sweet and demure!"

Mike pulled Kim closer. "Demure? I'll give you sweet, but sassy! I don't think I can handle a mini-Kim just yet. You already take up enough of my time and resources."

When they reached the bike, she pulled out her phone and made him take a picture of themselves next to the Harley. Kim smiled widely. Even Mike half-grinned, instead of his usual scowl. Later, she made it his phone background.

Once seated, she wrapped her arms around the Steelman's waist and rested her head on his back. He looked down at her slender fingers and had a vision of a diamond ring. *What the fuck am I thinking? Not again, not yet with all the shit still going on with Lisa!*

The Harley roared down Red Arrow Highway, which became Route 12 in Indiana, paralleling the lake back to Hegewisch. Kim held on tightly, contemplating her involvement with this big, bad boyfriend who crunched quarterbacks for a living—sometimes fueled by uncontrollable rage. She wondered if she wanted to live with a guy whose persona was larger than life. But she believed the true Michael Stalowski was nothing like his fans expected—and she was falling in love with him. Recalling the locker photo of the happy little boy with a prize catch and his dad, Kim confirmed he found peace near open water—on the beach, a boat, or even on a breakwater rock—with a worm on his hook. At least they had that in common.

Kim smelled garlic the minute Mike opened Mancuso's door. This time Gina was a little warmer and even called Kim "honey" when seating them at the same booth. Now it was *their* booth. Kim dropped a coin into the mini jukebox and selected "Suspicious Minds" and "Living in Sin."

"I like some of the old stuff too, Steelman." Nervously, she asked, "Hey, Michael . . . what happened between you and your wife?"

Mike was mid-gulp and almost choked. The coincidence of his and Lisa's song beginning to play almost floored him. Blindsided, he decided to lay it all out.

"Look Kim, it's been a real roller-coaster ride for ten years. Love and girls scared the shit out of me in high school. We hooked up junior year. She was my first and only girlfriend. Honest!"

One girl? Really? But Kim listened intently, holding his hand across the table from time to time as he narrated the story of his marriage.

"Right out of college we got married. Things were good for a while but then went south, way south."

Based on his version, she felt Lisa screwed up the marriage; although interestingly, he didn't make Lisa out to be the witch he often described. Her heart broke for him—and Lisa—when she learned about their son. The uncertainty of their separation concerned Kim, but she wanted more than anything to believe his final words.

"Kim, it's over for me and Lisa. For sure. I'm done. It's up to the lawyers now."

She reached out to take his huge hand in hers. "Look Michael, *I love you, baby,*" she whispered. "I don't care about what you've been through with whoever—or who or what people think you are—I want to be with you for a long time."

They were one of the last two couples in the restaurant. Even Gina sensed something was serious and left them alone. Searching for something to say, he came up empty. He stood up.

"Come on, let's get out of here." Mike threw a hundred-dollar bill on the table and pulled her close. They donned leather jackets to block the wind blowing off the lake. Mike revved the engine and turned around to whisper in her ear. Kim grabbed his stubbled chin and gave him a voracious kiss.

Back at Mike's, they lay in bed, and he drifted off to sleep. Kim snuggled closer, looking at the star-filled sky and full moon through the floor to ceiling windows. She replayed everything he'd said at Mancuso's. Mike stirred and repositioned his St. Michael-tattooed arm, resting it across her soon-to-swell breasts. All was good that night.

Comfortably Numb

MIKE AND KIM LAY ACROSS *WAGE BURNER'S* BOW. HE MOSTLY THOUGHT about yesterday's game, but also how glad he was to have Kim in his life. *What a difference a year makes!* Last October, he'd anchored overnight in the "playpen" with the vixen who moonlighted as a newscaster. Today, he was with his sweet girlfriend on an unusually balmy Monday afternoon.

"Hey, Michael, you were right. It's nice looking backwards at the city. Sure as heck doesn't look like any of the beaches near Hillsboro." Kim wiggled her freshly polished red toes and adjusted her sunglasses. She tenderly intertwined her fingers with the Steelman's, being careful of his splinted right thumb, the casualty of a crushing hit to a fleeing running back.

"How much longer are we staying out here, baby?"

Mike looked at the lake, smooth as glass on the windless day. "Forever. Why? What's your hurry?"

"I have to be at the theatre at three o'clock."

"Well, I finally get a Monday off. The lake is calm and nobody else is out here. It's the only way to begin the week after an even greater weekend!"

"I have a life and career too!"

"Yeah, but I'm the Captain, so you do what I say." Grinning, Mike poked her top.

"No, I'm not taking it off."

Mike nodded yes. "You did last Saturday!"

"And you tried giving me a big ol' hickey like a damn vampire. I still have dunes sand in the crack of my butt! Okay, half an hour more, but you have to get your head off that damn ice bag and help me learn these lines!"

He leaned on his perpetually-scabbed right elbow. Mike usually discounted his weekly injuries as collateral damage. "You know I usually don't mind running your lines, but my fucking neck really hurts! My whole fucking body hurts after four solo tackles, three assists and a sack that caused a defensive fumble recovery. I was on fire, Kim! We kicked Miami's ass! You shoulda been there." He laid back down.

"I couldn't, remember? You only let me go to Veterans Stadium once. And then you banned me from Miami because it's too close to my hometown!"

He said nothing.

"Come on, you have to help me, Michael. Four commercial auditions this month and not even one callback. I'm not having much luck here and might try LA."

Only sound was the water lapping against the boat.

"I've got an incentive for you, baby. If I get this part, I can't go home for Christmas, so you won't have to meet my parents."

Surprised that didn't warrant a reaction, she nudged Mike. "If we do go to Florida, you've got to see my skating Santa Bear. When I was little, he'd roll up Christmas morning singing "Jingle Bells." I'll show you where he skated, right next to my bed. Sound good?"

Still nothing. Kim was getting pissed. "Did you hear a word I said?"

Mike just lifted his head off the ice bag and rubbed his neck.

"And what's that clicking sound?"

"My fucked-up neck. I didn't think you could hear it. Sometimes my left shoulder and knee kinda make noise too."

"Do you want me to massage it?"

"Only if you have a fucking death wish!"

Kim recognized he was serious. "Michael, baby! How much longer will you play this damn silly game?" she asked plaintively. "Look at you! You're like a big bear full of boo-boos. Boo-Boo Bear, that's what I'm gonna call you. Are you going to keep knocking heads until you can't move your neck at all? At this rate, will you even be able to walk or know your own name in fifteen years?"

Louder, she continued, "Aren't you tired of getting injured in the weekly wreck you call a game? *I love you baby*, but I don't understand why you beat yourself up every Sunday and take all week to recover—only to do it all over again. And it's not just you, *Steelman*. What about everyone else you batter, break and maim? Ever think about that?"

Kim removed her sunglasses and stared at Mike for the final jab. "Maybe you should just retire. I don't care how damn much money you make or whether your fans love you and your bullshit antics! I want YOU to be around and love ME!" She replaced her glasses and lay down.

Retire, huh? Mike heard her loud and clear. Just like he had heard what Dr. Mark Cowan, the team orthopedic surgeon and sideline physician, told him in July.

———————————•———————————

Mike had waited impatiently for the team doctor to review the preseason diagnostic tests with him. When Dr. Cowan entered with a serious look on his face, Mike knew it wasn't good news.

"I'll give it to you straight, Mike. In plain English your neck and spine are fucked up. In medical jargon, your degenerative disc disease has progressed. You have a herniated disc and I'm seeing the onset of osteoarthritis too."

"I feel fine."

"I don't know who you think you're fooling, but it's not me."

Mike sat stoically.

"Look, we've gone over this before, but it bears repeating. Think about a car accident where you hit your head on the windshield—repeatedly for fifteen years. The force on the neck is simply too much to absorb repetitive injury. What you've accumulated over years on the football field is the result."

Mike looked down at the floor.

"Your C-3 and C-4 vertebrae are bone on bone. They're grinding against each other with every tackle. Bottom line, there's no cushion left, Mike. What you've been doing to your body the last what? Fifteen . . . eighteen years has taken its toll. Quite frankly, I don't know how you've gone so long with the way you play—hit after hit, season after season. You know I thought you should have called it quits last season. You must have one hell of a threshold for pain!"

Mike shook his head repeatedly. "You know your business and I know mine."

Cowan looked Mike directly in the eyes. "I know the symptoms you aren't talking about. Your neck is less flexible and you probably have numbness, tingling, and weakness in your shoulders and arms at times."

Mike stared but nodded almost imperceptibly.

"Disc fusion surgery, rehab, and recovery to play again is a 50/50 shot. Honestly, more like 80-20 you can't play."

Mike began shaking his head. He stood up and paced in the exam room.

"We can try stretching your neck muscles to relieve some pain." He paused. "I know you. Just one more season and a Super Bowl ring, right? You're not going to quit until they carry you off the field. So here's what I'll do. I know guys at the Laser Spine Institute, near Phoenix, who are into stem cell research. They'll keep it quiet. You can also go to Europe for off-season experimental treatment. But you know damn well I'm going to have to say something eventually." Emphatically, he warned, "It's only going to get worse. You will eventually have to stop playing and get it fixed."

"Doc, you know I've been playing hurt for four seasons! Why the hell should I stop now?"

"Listen to me, Mike! Your playing days are numbered."

"I know I gotta face what's going on, but I need this season. Just one more," he pleaded.

"If you want to roll the dice on one more season, it's up to you. Professionally, I'm telling you to get help now for the long term."

"We're gonna win it this year. It's in the cards."

———————•———————

After replaying Cowan's prognosis, Mike adjusted the ice bag under his neck and lashed out at Kim. "Damn silly game, huh? Retire? I'm trying to get a new fucking contract and you think I'm done. Washed up? Bullshit! I'll quit when I get the ring. I need something to show for seventeen years of this," he bellowed, more to himself than Kim. *Besides, it's all I know.*

Kim rolled onto her left side but said nothing.

Mike propped himself up and grabbed a cold beer before pleading his case. "Who knows, baby. Only eight more games and the playoffs. We're going to the show—the first time for me. If the season keeps going this way, I'll have extra contract incentives and even more money."

Scornfully Kim retorted, "Not a big deal, Steelman! My daddy's a millionaire too—and I don't want YOUR money anymore than I wanted HIS." Kim fumbled to retrieve the folded script from her beach bag and began whispering lines to herself.

The Steelman put on his headphones and lay back down.

She couldn't concentrate. *How much longer can he give and take the punishment of NFL football?* She'd never been a fan. To her, the Super Bowl was funny TV commercials and greasy food. To the players who toiled in the trenches, it was the Holy Grail.

In just a few short months, weeks really, Kim had fallen for Michael Stalowski. He was really funny, sweet, and caring. But maybe their relationship had progressed too quickly.

She wasn't like Lisa, living the life of Riley financed by football, with no regard for the price Mike would ultimately pay for choosing to play through the pain. Though Mike's physique looked like it was chiseled in stone, Kim saw movements that were slow and deliberate. She wasn't the only one to notice. Customers talked at the Sunset Grill. Sportswriters and fans all buzzed with innuendo. Probably teammates and coaches, too.

She glanced sideways at Mike, a gallon-sized bag of ice cubes under his neck. He had drifted off with a slight smile. The Tylenol with codeine he secretly downed had finally kicked in. Kim tried to brush away her bleak thoughts. Although Mike was wearing headphones, Kim could hear "Comfortably Numb," Pink Floyd's dreamy hard rock ballad. Little did she know he often listened to it when he needed to escape his pain—and justify the painkillers.

She flipped through her script for a few minutes before putting it aside. She laid her head on the towel and closed her eyes. Wise beyond her years, she recognized Mike was in denial about his physical reality and he needed to make decisions about the next phase of his life, with or without her.

How the heck can I get him to let go of the Steelman and football? That is the question, and even more pressing than this damn audition.

Leader of the Pack

THE NOVEMBER SKY WAS PERPETUALLY GRAY. BETWEEN THE "HAWK" WIND and plummeting temperatures, Mike felt his football aches and pains more intensely.

"Hey, you gotta do this favor for Griff's 60th next week. He loves his frickin' karaoke night more than beer, blondes, and boobs altogether. He doesn't have anybody to do anything for him. Griff's a good guy. Just a little rough around the edges."

Kim muttered loud enough for Mike to hear, "Bring anyone else to mind?" She started the coffee and rubbed sleep out of her eyes. "No family? Like an ex-wife or illegitimate kids? And why are we talking about this at 6:00 Monday morning? I've got spin class to get to. Then a print job audition. Local clothing store I think. Maybe a bra ad you can ogle in the bathroom."

"He never talks about family. I want to do something nice. He introduced us, right? Come on, will you do it? You got almost a week to practice. Do it for me, please!"

"What's in it for me, baby?"

"Oh, you'll see!"

Mike guzzled his signature creatine-peanut butter-banana-protein smoothie straight out of the blender bowl. Some spilled onto his cherished Chicago Fire and Police Department charity football game T-shirt. He stayed in touch with some St. Michael's teammates who were firefighters.

Kim shook her head in amazement. "You're really somethin' to watch! What am I supposed to do? Jump out of a cake wearing a cheerleader outfit two sizes too small?" Kim put down her coffee to shake imaginary pom-poms over her head while bouncing up and down in her pink robe and slippers.

"You got talent, girl! Coulda been an NFL cheerleader instead of a struggling actress. This gives you a chance to play something different from all these little auditions."

"Screw you, Steelman! Little auditions!"

"It'll give you diversity and a chance to sing."

"Gee, Mike, for a second you almost sounded intelligent. Do you even know what diversity means?"

"Hell, yes! It means you and two singer friends are gonna be a '60s rock-and-roll girl group. Griff knows the Shangri-Las and Crystals better than guys he played with on the '85 Superbowl team. His mother was in one or knew someone who was. Anyway, I don't get his taste in music. Really, who's better than Guns N' Roses or Poison? But Griff'll get a big kick out of it. C'mon Kim, *you owe me*."

In her best Southern drawl, Kim retorted, "Owe you for what, big boy? You owe me for putting up with you!"

"I'm the best thing that's come along in Chicago," kidded the Steelman. "You know what else? You get to go home with me and . . ."

"Ooooh," she interrupted. "I get to go home with you. Lucky little me."

"And Griff's paying $1000 to the act with the loudest applause."

"You're the lucky one, Steelman! I'll do it because rent's due! But you also have to throw in a candlelight dinner after my *Grease* callback. I've got a good feeling about this one."

"Okay, kid, I'll come see you and take you someplace special."

Kim put her arms around Mike's chest and looked up playfully. "You know, I do kind of like you. Naw . . . I think I love you! Well, a little anyway."

Mike briefly thought about what it would be like to have her there *all* the time. They separated after some short kisses and Mike headed to the door.

"I like Griff. He's kind of crude, but he did hook us up. I don't really know any of those '60s songs, but I'll call my mom. She'll know. Or they're on YouTube."

"Perfect baby, that's great! Hey, what's you . . . tube?"

"Seriously?" She shook her head. "I'll reach out to a couple of girls I know who can sing back-up." Kim had something up her sleeve. "But I'll only do it if it's a surprise."

"Thanks, baby! I won't say anything. You know you can get all that song info off your computer. Just pick one or two. I know you'll sound good."

Kim poured more coffee and watched the sunrise over Lake Michigan. Shades of yellow, orange, and purple all competed to shatter the darkness. Things with Mike were moving quickly. When they were alone, his child-like innocence was almost impossible to resist. She was falling hard and normally would have shared that with her mom. But it was definitely not a topic for today's call.

"Hey, Momma, how's it going?"

Kate Richardson was ecstatic. "My stars, Kimberly! It's so good to hear from you!" It had been almost a month since Kim called. "How are you, baby girl, everything okay? You sound so far away. Is it snowing in that god-awful city?"

"Sorry I haven't called. I'm sooo bad! But I've been busy with auditions and taking classes. Don't worry. I'm doing fine."

"Well, you know Kimberly, they have this thing called texting!" Kate thought it best to let her keep in touch. She hoped if Kim got lonely, she'd come to her senses and return to Florida.

"Promise I'll be better about keeping in touch! Look, Momma, I'm kinda busy now, but I really need some help with this karaoke gig . . ."

"What kind of gig, honey? Are you joining a band? Oh my stars, you are into all sorts of things up there!"

"I need some 1960s rock-and-roll girl-group songs. Any ideas?"

"I thought you wanted to be a stage actress, not a nightclub singer! Should I be worried about the crowd you're with?"

If only she knew. Kim smiled. "Of course not! I'm just singing with my girlfriends for a good cause. Retired folk, honest!"

"Well, Kimberly, I was barely a teenager. I remember some songs, but the only girl group I remember was the Supremes. Just look on your computer. Everything's there these days."

"Okay, Momma, thanks. Everything okay with you guys?"

"We miss you terribly. Why don't you come home for the holidays?" Kate knew how to press Kim's buttons. "I didn't want to tell you I haven't been feeling well the last few weeks. Getting some tests done."

"Oh my God, why didn't you say something?"

"I'll be fine. Honey, listen, it would be great to have you down here for the holidays. Like being home from college. No curfew! I promise!" Kate laughed.

"I'll try, but I need to see if any auditions turn into gigs."

After practice the following Tuesday, Mike headed to Griff's on his Harley. Typical for Chicago, after last week's deep freeze today was sunny and 50-plus degrees.

"Steelman, what the hell are you doin' here, buddy?"

"Finally came to listen to Tuesday-night karaoke."

"C'mere son, let me buy you a beer. My birthday's tomorrow, but we're celebratin' big tonight. Figure I better celebrate early in case I don't make it to sixty!"

"What's tonight's theme, Griff? Country or country AND western?"

"You're gonna hear good '60s stuff! Mike, who you guys playin' this weekend?"

"You should know! Christ, it's your old team. Listen, I'm tired of talkin' about fucking football. Castro is driving me nuts with motivational speeches and threats." Mike took a long chug of beer. "We're hurtin' a little on defense. Stokes's hip is banged up with a pointer. Butler has a high ankle sprain, and Dino Rhoades is hopefully gonna be back from his concussion. Fucking Castro thinks I'm supposed to rally whoever the fuck is left against their fucking rookie running back who's averaging a hundred fucking yards a fucking game, plus their two Pro Bowl wide-outs. It's Houston, Griff!"

"I know their Head Coach. Was a cocky asshole back-up quarterback when I played against him. I blitzed his ass one time in a playoff game and he fuckin' taunted me to do it again."

"So what happened?"

"I blitzed his ass again on the next play and chased it backwards twenty yards. If I'da caught him, I'd a killed him. Steelman," glared Griff, "I'd blitz their asses every fucking chance I got!" Griff snorted and slapped the Steelman's back.

"I gotta eat, so let's talk about food. What's good tonight?"

"It's all good, son. Try some ribs! Tonight's special. They are so gooooood! But don't break 'em, Mike. Eat 'em! Get it?" Griff was annoying tonight, but in honor of his birthday Mike let it go. "Hey, Steelman, where's that cute little girl I introduced you to awhile back? The one I know you're taking advantage of these days." Griff winked. "If I was twenty years younger . . ." Mike was not amused.

Griff slapped him hard on the back again, surprising Mike with his strength. Watching him shuffle to another table, Mike figured it was likely twenty-five years since Griff touched a free weight. The rest of his body was but a shadow of his past thanks to pro football and osteoarthritis. As far as Mike knew, his only physical activity was getting in and out of his truck. Or if shoulder pain allowed, shooting pool in the bar. *Will that be me?*

Two beers and a slab and a half of ribs later, Mike wondered where Kim was.

He couldn't believe the characters filling Crunch Bar for karaoke. Approaching 7:30 and still no sign of her. *Typical chick—always fucking late.*

Breathless, Kim blew in the front door with two identically dressed ladies, looking like they'd stepped off a fifty-year-old album cover. Mike did a double-take when they strutted in, throwing their hips like runway models. Horizontal rows of tassels adorned their short, tight, strapless red dresses. The tassels shook when they sashayed in their white high heels. Hair was up high in bouffants. Heavy eye makeup, lipstick, and candy apple red fingernails completed their costume. Mike thought they looked trashy good. Kim led her entourage to his booth.

"Hey, baby, how are you? Practice okay?" Kim brushed back hair on the side of his face.

"No!" Mike took a swig of beer.

"You look a little windblown, baby. Like you rode your bike here, right? Maybe I'll let you ride me home later," teased Kim.

"In that dress? You'll get me arrested!"

"Hey, Syl and Clare, this is Mike. He plays football here and I hang around with him sometimes. Actually," Kim said coyly, "we're dating."

She turned to him. "Mike, meet Sylvia and Clarice. We're all in the same improv class at iO Theater. They agreed to help in exchange for game tickets and team-autographed Storm jerseys. We plan to steal the show. Just wait baby, this will be a big surprise—for you and Griff. Did you know girl-group music is making a comeback? Kinda grows on you. No wonder Griff likes it."

"Hey, ladies, thanks for lending your voices." Mike tried to be personable since it had been his idea. "Kim's voice isn't that good, so I'm glad you're here to drown her out."

"Hey, you big brute, that's not nice!"

"Mr. Steelman, I mean Mike. I am such a BIG fan of yours and the Storm and the rest of the defense." Clarice gushed. "You guys are like 9 and 2, right? I think you're gonna get to the Super Bowl this year."

Not knowing a thing about football, Sylvia smiled. "I hope you make it to the Super Bowl, too."

"They better," said Kim. "I want that Greek Islands cruise he promised me." Mike looked puzzled. Then inwardly he smiled, beginning to formulate a plan.

"Want a beer or glass of wine before the show? You know, to get your nerve up?"

"Michael, we're professionals. Don't need liquid courage. But, you can buy us a big bottle of champagne when we win!"

"Okay, you're on. What are you gonna sing?" Silence. "How about a clue?"

"Nope!" they replied unanimously.

They bolted to the ladies room. Griff was in for an eyeful, but not until showtime. As Kim hurried away, Mike watched her tassles shake. *Damn, she looks like a '60s singer. A smokin' hot one!*

Already buzzed, Griff was in rare form when he took to the stage wearing a Hawaiian shirt with green dollar signs and black music notes. Exactly what Griff believed karaoke was about. A few years ago, his favorite event was "Don't Wet the T-shirt." Female contestants tried to chug 32-ounce mugs of beer in twenty seconds, inevitably spilling all over their tight "Crunch Bar" T-shirts.

"Welcome, y'all Crunchlings and karaoke lovers to my little Tuesday night competition where it's fun and simple to win cold hard cash. Tonight's GRAND prize IS a cool GRAND! Simply sing like girls from the '60s—back when girls were girls and they sang about boys and broken hearts. Y'all know what I mean? HEY! WOW! TIME OUT, Y'ALL!"

Griff stopped speaking when the trio approached the stage stairs. Kim winked at him while her partners waved to the audience and blew kisses. "Well, HELLLOOO, ladies! Do my eyes deceive me? There's three angels walking up here and they sure as hell ain't Charlie's." Kim kissed him on the cheek and grabbed the mike. The Steelman was a little stunned at HIS girl, who quickly took command of the stage.

"Hi, everybody! I'm Kim. These two lovely ladies are Clarice and Syl, and we are NOT the Supremes! We planned to let other contestants do their thing first. But since it's Griff's birthday, we decided to get this party started singing "Happy Birthday" to the one and only Crunch. C'mon everyone, join in!"

Griff, too choked up to say anything, wiped what looked like a tear from his eyes. Everyone sang along. Even the Steelman mouthed the words!

"Great job! One more round of birthday applause for Crunch! Now on with the show. Fire up that VocoPro!"

As previously arranged, Tommy the Spin simultaneously tossed wireless mikes to Clarice and Syl who took up positions on either side of Kim. Griff's top quality sound system made singers sound really good or really bad. The VocoPro kicked on hard. Kim belted out lyrics, bringing rock legend Phil Spector's "wall of sound" to Crunch Bar.

One of The Crystals' biggest hits, "He's a Rebel," was about a girl who loved her guy, despite his bad-boy image. Coincidence? Kim worked the stage, gesturing and pointing, her smokey, hazel eyes full of emotion. Clarice and Syl were fabulous, but Kim stole the show. This was no drunken attempt to follow a bouncing ball. They took the audience by surprise and never let go. Kim's eyes scanned the crowd, stopping to look at Mike while pouring out her heart.

Mike's prediction was right on. Griff was immersed in the '60s flashback. Crunch Bar Karaoke would never be the same. They quickly segued into "Then He Kissed Me," another Crystals' hit.

Kim's lyric delivery hit Mike like a prizefighter's left hook. *That's our first date at 95th Street Beach . . . kissing under the stars.* He felt light-headed like never before—with or without painkillers and alcohol. Transfixed when Kim looked lovingly in his direction, Mike felt her songs were intended to send him a message. He fixated on the lyric about a bride. Watching her, Mike felt fate was putting them on the fast track to love and happiness.

"I hope y'all like our little performance so far." Kim addressed the clapping and cheering audience. "One last song!" The Shangri-Las were Jersey girls who sang about a rebel biker boyfriend who was "The Leader of the Pack."

Clarice and Syl began. *"Kim . . ."*

Kim smiled and looked at her empty finger as though her boyfriend's high school ring was there.

In a heartbeat, Mike envisioned Kim's reaction when he placed a sparkling ring on her finger.

The ballad ended with background sounds of screeching tires emanating from the karaoke machine while Kim cried out. In a few short months, everyone in Crunch's that night would recall the ominous lyrics that ended Kim's time on stage.

The Steelman stared into his crystal ball and saw visions of spending his life with Kim. That was it. His mind was made up. He wasn't sure how or when he would present a beautiful dazzling ring to Kim—maybe for Christmas—maybe in the early morning hours after winning the Super Bowl. But Mike definitely knew where to get the ball rolling.

Asher and Klein

THE STEELMAN RACED FROM PRACTICE TO A & K. THANKS TO LISA, MIKE WAS familiar with the one-block stretch of Oak Street off Mag Mile. Chicago's version of Rodeo Drive was lined with extravagantly priced boutiques and jewelry stores. Thanksgiving was a week away, so it was bustling with holiday shoppers. Parking was non-existent, but Mike squeezed his pick-up into a tow-zone at the end of the block.

After pulling his black hoodie over his blond and now-fading, blue-streaked mane, he resembled a street thug looking for a quick purse snatch. Or an undercover cop. Other neighborhoods had more crime, but it was politically and economically unacceptable in the Gold Coast.

Where the fuck is it? Lisa knew all of these fucking stores by name and address! He finally recognized the greystone storefront with curved display windows. The 12' glass entry door with metal grates didn't budge when he pulled it.

"We're closing."

It was all coming back, like a bad dream. Mike remembered two guys wearing bad suits, probably off-duty cops, guarded the store. Customers were usually scheduled, screened and buzzed in.

"Hey, man, can you please let Jerry know Mike is here? I'm a little late. Sorry, traffic was heavy."

That was enough to just get him through the front door of Asher and Klein Jewelers, an exclusive institution for over sixty years. Sales reps were busy securing the exorbitantly priced merchandise.

"Can I tell Mr. Klein who's calling?"

Old money shopped at Asher and Klein. He actually liked the owner Jerry Klein, who was in his early seventies but far from retired. Mike figured Jerry just humored him talking about exotic fishing excursions, but he played along to pass the time while Lisa tried on everything in the store. He appreciated that Jerry never hit him up for autographs or tickets.

"Mike from Burr Ridge. He's expecting me." Obviously no fans here.

Everyone at A&K knew Lisa. She enjoyed spending Mike's hard-earned NFL money, thriving on the attention Jerry and his staff lavished on her in a private viewing room. Right after they moved into the McMansion, Mike plunked down $80,000 so Lisa could "celebrate" with a limited-edition Swiss watch. A year later, they went back to get diamond earrings for a mere $37,000. Six months later, she dropped by to prepare for the upcoming summer social season by adding a $33,000 diamond tennis bracelet to her collection. At fundraisers, she loved to impress old money society mavens with her A&K relationship. The little blue-collar Italian girl from the Southeast Side had arrived!

Jerry emerged from the back office and Mike pushed Lisa out of his mind. He wasn't here to relive that holy mess, but to get something worthy of Kim.

"Michael, so good to see you. What a season you're having! Looks like a ring for you this year!" Jerry chuckled and led him to the back. "And how is Lisa? We haven't seen her in quite a while. Planning to surprise her?"

Mike couldn't help but smile. "Oh, Jerry, she is gonna be surprised *big time*! Listen man. I want your guy to make a special ring. Big, beautiful diamond to start. At least three carats! That's the only 'C' I know about!" he laughed. "Then circle it with smaller diamonds all around. And on the band, too. You know down the sides, maybe two rows each." The Steelman was emphatic. "Jerry, there's gotta be glittering diamonds everywhere!"

Mike had given this a lot of thought. The big center diamond symbolized Kim, and he wanted to surround her with his love. Show her that she was the center of his world and he would protect her. He knew it was kind of silly, but the rows of diamonds on the band reminded him of stage spotlights, where she wanted to make her dreams come true.

"So you want a halo setting, smaller stones encircling a large center stone. What cut were you thinking? Emerald, pear, round, oval, marquis, maybe a heart? Personally, I believe a round diamond is the most stunning and classic look."

A halo setting would be perfect for my little blonde angel. "Round, yeah that would be good, Jerry. But it has to be bright. Really sparkly. What do you call it?"

"You knew *carat* coming in and just selected the round *cut,* Mike. The other

C's that make a diamond sparkle are clarity and color. Of course, we only use the highest grade, flawless diamonds money can buy. But why another engagement-style ring? I'm sure Lisa would love a diamond encrusted anniversary band."

"Oh, I'm sure she would." Mike didn't give a rat's ass what Lisa wanted. It was time for him to make someone else as happy as she made him.

After working out the details, Mike dropped $36,000 for a flawless 3.2 carat diamond. For another $40,000, brilliant quarter-carat diamonds, set on a platinum band with three rows of pave diamonds, would surround it. It might weigh Kim's slender hand down at first, but there would be no mistaking his commitment to her.

"Jerry, I need this thing in two days. You gotta get it done for me. I'll pay you an extra ten grand, man."

"Absolutely, Michael! For you, Sergei will get this done. Lisa is one of our best customers, so just make it $5,000." He knew she would let all the wives know. "You and Lisa will not be disappointed."

One out of two isn't bad, Mike thought.

Two days later, Mike returned. He opened the black velvet box, embossed with a silver A&K. "Wow! Jerry, this is wild! It's unbelievable man. I owe you big time!"

"You made a great design, Michael. Lisa will be impressed."

"Jerry, *Lisa will be speechless!*" He knew it was the right ring for Kim. Just what he wanted—big, beautiful, and brilliant, casting light in every direction. The Steelman shook Jerry's hand a little too hard, making him wince. "Hey, Jerry, if this thing turns out like I want, you and nine of your best friends WILL be my guests at the Super Bowl. I promise." Turning to the guards, he added, "You guys are invited too."

Mike thought about when he should spring it on her. Maybe that very night. Kim's childhood skating Santa Bear popped into his head. It would have to be the best Christmas ever if he could get it to roll up, carrying the little black box. Only problem, he had to find one. He checked the time. *Shit! Gotta get going.*

The Cadillac Palace

It TOOK TWENTY MINUTES TO DRIVE A MERE 1.5 MILES TO THE HEART OF THE Theatre District. Leaving the garage, Mike saw Scrooge's crotchety face in *A Christmas Carol* plastered on the Goodman Theatre marquee. *They should have given her a fucking part.*

When he arrived at the Cadillac Palace Theater, Mike shook the locked glass door.

"Sorry, box office is closed." Suddenly, a security guard opened the door. "My God! #52! You're the Steelman, right?"

"Yeah. Hey, how about an autograph and you let me in for just a few minutes? There's someone I gotta see in that audition. We good, man?"

"Of course, Mr. Steelman. We ALL good! I'm Curtis, your biggest fan, brother. The Storm's going to The Show this year, right?"

"Yeah, we're tryin' Curtis." Mike sized him up about 6′ 2″ and 320 pounds. "Maybe I bring you along to play back-up defensive tackle. You could plug a hole, bro!" In gratitude, Mike's usual hastily scrawled MS #52 was actually legible and contained a few more letters. "Hey, man, just slip me in the back, okay?"

"Sure, follow me. You know, I did play some ball in high school," he chuckled. "Got some college looks. But grades man, they held me out. I'd take a run at it again, but I'm a little out of shape."

Mike nodded, estimating Curtis had a 60″ girth spilling over size 56″ pants. "Thanks, man!" He sat in the back row and caught the last minute or so of a group dance number.

"Great, everyone! Take five." Two bearded guys in flannel shirts, one with a bright purple scarf, huddled briefly.

Gut-wrenching anxiety was palpable all the way to the back row. Most actors paced onstage or made small talk. A few chose to tune out the world with earbuds.

Watching the mad scramble of actors when the cast list was posted, it was immediately clear who made the cut. It wasn't Kim. She stood dejectedly under the lights.

Shit! Mike felt the black velvet box between his fingers. *Poor kid's devastated again. Maybe I should propose tonight.*

Kim walked toward the wings. A handsome guy stopped her. They hugged for a few long seconds and held hands. Something about their embrace made Mike mad. *Let her go, asshole!*

The Steelman slipped out unnoticed and stopped by Griff's so Kim could get back to the condo first. Once home, he opened the door and overheard her making flight reservations to Miami.

Kim quickly finished the call, grabbed her acoustic guitar and quietly began singing her version of Jesse Colter's love ballad, "I'm Not Lisa."

Mike grabbed a beer and sat across from her. Kim looked up and forced a smile. He leaned forward to look at a glossy photograph on the coffee table. She looked like a vixen, dressed in a sleeveless black dress, with a thick band of glittery gold just above her chest. Blonde hair cascaded down the sides of her face—smoky and mysterious eyes—soft pink lips slightly parted. The "come take me now" vibe sent a chill down his spine.

"Hey, what's this?"

Avoiding eye contact, she muttered, "My new headshot proof."

"Very nice! Looks like you belong in a Victoria's Secret ad." He took a big gulp of beer. "I heard you on the phone when I walked in. Where you going? Leaving me?"

Kim strummed the guitar, looking a bit like the cat who swallowed a canary. Her eyes welled up with tears which rolled slowly down her face. He sat expressionless and still.

"I didn't get the damn *Grease* part!" She cried, "I'm not an actress. I'm a damn fucking failure! I can't even get a fucking ensemble part!" It was the first time Mike heard her utter f-bombs. "They made the final cuts tonight. Including me!" She was sobbing. "I worked really hard. This really fucking sucks!"

Kim took deep halting breaths. Suddenly she picked up the headshot and tore it in half. His heart was breaking for her, but he didn't know what to do or say. Unfortunately, the Steelman didn't realize that simply scooping her in his huge, tattooed arms and holding her tightly would help.

"Can you get some tissues, please?" Kim wiped her running mascara. "I'm going back to Florida for Thanksgiving. It's been over five months. I want to see my mother. I don't know . . . maybe I need a break to think about things." She sniffled and dabbed her nose. "Maybe I should stay through Christmas. I thought I'd have that commercial to film but didn't get that either. All these damn auditions and no parts or bookings really, really sucks."

This is it. Silently, the Steelman stared out at the city lights. *She's outta here. I fucked this one up, too.*

Mike went to get another beer. Kim quickly stood up, stopping him in his tracks, and whispered softly, "Michael, will you come with me?"

Mike breathed a big sigh of relief. His mind raced with thoughts about the engagement ring. *Maybe I can give it to her before Thanksgiving. No time to concoct a plan. Christmas is too far away.*

"I can't, Kim. We're playing fucking Dallas like we do every Thanksgiving. Plus, I don't know—me—your family—now? You wanna spring ME on them for Thanksgiving? Your old man probably remembers some of the shit that's been in the news about me."

"Sorry to burst your bubble, Michael. He's not a football fan. I don't know what's been in the news, but it wouldn't matter. My father doesn't care about pro football or pro anything. Just his damn money. And I don't care either. I have to go back, Michael. It's the right thing for me to do since I left the way I did. I want you to come too and meet them. I'll show you around. We can walk on Hillsboro Beach and hold hands . . . maybe more. I really don't care what they think or say." She stared at him with puppy eyes and whispered, "I love YOU."

Maybe I'll just show up at her house late Friday night in fuckin' Boca Raton or wherever they live and surprise the shit out of everybody. Give her the fucking ring right there. Or Saturday, on the damn beach. I'll put it in the sand or something. Float it to the beach in a bottle or have a plane fly by with a banner asking her to marry me. Then he decided. *Fuck! I'll just spring it on her before she goes home.*

"Look, I'm really sorry, but I can't do it, baby."

Kim watched as he pulled yet another beer from the fridge. Obviously disappointed, she stared out the window.

Mike fumbled for the box in his hoodie pocket. *I could just end all the drama tonight.*

Kim announced matter-of-factly, "Okay, Mike, then I'm going myself. Like I said, I have things to figure out."

What was I thinking, buying this damn ring?

"I'm leaving Wednesday morning, so I'll be back in time for Black Wednesday." Mike looked clueless. "You know about Black Wednesday, right? The night before Thanksgiving when college kids get together at home to party."

The thought of her partying with college kids didn't sit well with him. "Look, if you have to go—then go. Hey, who was that scrawny guy hugging you onstage tonight?"

Startled, Kim realized he was there when she got cut. Suddenly physically sick, she got up with her hand over her mouth and ran to the bathroom. Mike picked up the torn photograph and gently held both pieces together. He taped it and put it in his drawer with the ring.

They didn't communicate much for the rest of the night. They both had such high hopes for today—none of which materialized.

Holiday Lights

M IKE MERGED ONTO THE KENNEDY/I-94. HE APPEARED FOCUSED ON RUSH-hour traffic but was preoccupied with pain. Castro's upcoming Thanksgiving vendetta against Dallas required brutal reinforcement of blitzes, forced fumbles, and ball-strips.

Now on the Dan Ryan stretch of I-94, Mike reached into the left pocket of his hoodie to check for the little black velvet box. *Got it!* Near 31st Street, they passed a Chevy Silverado billboard with #52 flaunting his Steelman attitude.

"Look at you in all your scowling glory!"

No reply. Mike checked his pocket. *Maybe after dinner.*

"So listen, baby, there's these two training classes I just have to take." November auditions were 0 for 5, but Kim Richardson was determined to land her first acting job. "I signed up for them this afternoon. They start next week at this really good acting studio called, surprise, the Actors Studio! By the river somewhere. Sylvia, remember her? Well, she told me about it. I'm gonna take them on the same day, one after the other," she bubbled confidently.

He nodded. *She'll flip when she sees this thing.* Turning his head to change lanes, Mike felt the usual grinding. Kim was miffed about his brooding. He wasn't chatty by nature, but it was unusual for him not to say anything.

Mike punched the gas pedal to get around a slow-moving semi. "Move the fuck out of the way, asshole! Get in the right fucking lane," he barked. *What if she won't take it?*

"Wow, baby, you're friendly tonight!" She continued as though nothing was wrong. "I'll show these guys who can act! The classes are $300 each. One thing though, baby, I'm broke until I get paid. Can you help a struggling actor fund her continuing education? Promise I'll pay you back!" She leaned left and made big puppy eyes. The Steelman remained silent. Kim playfully stroked his right forearm. "Please, Michael?"

"Yeah, okay. Sure," he mumbled.

"Thank you! I really think it will help with auditions. Otherwise, I'm grabbing my headshots and moving back home."

Before dinner? Mike approached the apex of the Skyway bridge. Kim clutched her seat, but managed a peek at the vast glowing grid of streets and neighborhoods below.

"You're quiet tonight, Steelman. Bad practice or something else on your mind?" No reply. "Are you hurting inside or outside, baby? I'm leaving tomorrow and I need some answers."

Her serious tone finally got his attention. "Yeah, Kim, I'm hurting outside. Just a little."

"Well, I'm sorry, baby. I noticed you're more tired and beat up than usual gearing up for this big Thanksgiving game. But at least we're spending more time together. How long has it been now? Almost four months? Officially an item!"

If you only knew!

"Do you remember Clarice?" No answer. "Well, she landed an ensemble role in *A Christmas Carol*. Dancing and singing which she likes. I'm really happy for her. We're getting together one night after her show for coffee and girl talk. Next year she's going after a main role. I may too, unless I try Hollywood. Oh, you know what else? She told me about some holiday charity event for an orphanage that's supposedly a big deal. Lots of the city's Who's Who attend."

"I know the one you're talking about."

"They're always looking for Actors Guild volunteers to join the chorale and perform skits with the kids. I think I'm gonna do it. Sounds sweet and I like little kids. Especially ones that need lots of love like you!" Kim smiled and stroked Mike's stubbled cheek. "Why don't you come?"

"I got asked a couple of years ago but didn't go. Me and kids don't mix too well." Mike wasn't comfortable as an NFL role model. He quietly supported children's charities, avoiding public appearances, much to the chagrin of the Storm PR department. His annual $100,000 contribution to Toys for Tots was anonymous, although he did enjoy participating in their motorcycle ride.

"You could get holiday cheer and donate some cash. And you should shave, Michael." Kim began humming when "Neon Moon" by Brooks and Dunn came on the radio. "I love playing this on my guitar!"

Mike was impressed she could play without sheet music. Lately, he would catch Kim sitting on the couch, strumming country or old rock ballads while softly singing. Her gentleness was a welcome counterbalance to the controlled violence of his profession. Sometimes he almost fell asleep while Kim lovingly sang a "lullaby" to her big "baby."

He wanted to propose before she left for Florida and decided the perfect place was where he first shared his life story. Of course, she would ask about Lisa and he'd have to explain the separation hadn't progressed to divorce proceedings. Lisa would eventually come out on top, but at this point, he really didn't give a shit. Mike figured his contract extension would make up the financial loss from the inevitable settlement.

He parked around the block from Mancuso's. *This is it!* He clutched the velvet box. The Hawk's icy breath blew them toward the familiar corner.

"My God! I'm gonna die here this winter! That wind went right through me, even in this jacket! My nipples aren't hard; they're frozen! On top of being super sensitive today!"

Kim pulled her Moncler goose down jacket tightly around her. She looked like she stepped out of a fashion magazine, sporting a cashmere sweater and scarf, mink earmuffs and knee-high leather boots. Figuring she needed clothes to keep her warm, Mike had taken her shopping on Oak Street, kicking and screaming that she didn't shop where there were no price tags.

He put his arm around her shoulder and drew her near. Barely covered in his black hoodie, Mike laughed. "You're soft, Florida girl! Welcome to the Southeast Side. I'm taking you ice-fishing for perch when they start running. We'll catch a shit-load. Me and my dad used to go . . ."

"Can't wait," she rolled her eyes and interrupted. "Did the cold air finally wake you up? You've barely said a word."

Kim tucked her arm under Mike's and picked up her pace to get out of the wind. She was surprised they passed the side door. The *Use Front Door* sign did not apply to Mike. Kim stopped suddenly when they turned the corner.

"Oh my God! Holiday lights!"

Mike knew she would love the four-block stretch of "downtown" with the storefronts and streetlights all lit up. He hadn't parked closer because turning onto Baltimore Avenue provided the most awe-inspiring view of Hegewisch Christmas lights.

The lights reminded him of his youth; they were a welcome sight brightening the bleak winter. Going to Mancuso's to have pizza and see the Christmas lights had been a Stalowski tradition. Until Frank's stroke.

The despair of WWII, with so many neighborhood men fighting in faraway places, had taken its toll on most Hegewisch families. Some guys made it back okay. Some, like Chester, came back broken. Some never made it back. After the war, Nino Mancuso was one of the first local businessmen to decorate outside with brightly colored Italian Christmas lights. It was his way of providing light and hope. Several years ago, Alderman Santiago had old-fashioned lamp posts installed, making it even more charming.

"Here in Hegewisch, us Catholics call those *Christmas lights, not holiday lights.*"

"I'm not Catholic, but I am Christian, Steelman."

"They mean Santa Claus is coming to town."

"You know, Florida has Christmas, too!"

"I like them a hell of a lot more than the stupid Michigan Avenue Light Parade you dragged me to last Saturday. I still haven't recovered from wearing an elf suit and waving to everybody from a float a few years ago."

"Torture, huh? Tough being famous?"

Mike pulled her closer.

"Hey, Michael, can we walk around after dinner? It's so quaint and beautiful. We didn't have anything like this in Hillsboro. Just decorated palm trees. Look! Little snowflakes falling! My God, it's real snow." She stuck out her tongue to catch the flakes.

"Yep, it's real snow all right. Better get used to it! It looks like shit after it gets gray and slushy. Worse, the street salt they drop eats cars. Which reminds me I gotta eat! C'mon, let's head in."

"Hi, guys, can I help you?" An unfamiliar hostess, who looked about seventeen and didn't recognize Mike, greeted them.

"Can we get a booth in the back room?" he asked.

"Sorry, nothing open. A Christmas party." She led them to a table in plain view, in the middle of the restaurant.

"Any chance we can have one of those booths off to the side, please?" He wasn't expecting a Tuesday night crowd. "We'd like a little privacy."

"Uh, I guess." She seemed perturbed. "Follow me." It wasn't their booth, but it was better. Mike peeled off a $50. Without even a "thank you" she stuffed it in her pocket.

"I wonder where Gina found her," he muttered. "Must be a relative."

Before settling in, Mike waved the waiter over to order two beers and a glass of red wine. *I'll wait so we can have a toast.* He calculated the distance between the ring in his pocket and Kim's slender finger. He surreptitiously moved the black box onto his lap and gripped it tightly. When the drinks arrived, he ordered another beer and a shot of Jack Daniels.

"Jeez, Michael, take it easy. You don't need to drink the place dry. And I'm driving that truck back." Kim was concerned about his more frequent drinking and increasing quantities. "You know baby, at first, I didn't like this place much because of your history. But it's our spot now, right?" Kim's comment had the opposite effect she intended, putting Lisa's image in Mike's head at the worst possible time.

He stuck the black box back in his pocket. "I guess Gina's breaking in new help. I don't see Rosy either. Shit, maybe she sold the place."

"I doubt it. She would have told you. How come we came all the way here? I thought we were going to some Mexican place with big margaritas."

"El Jardin's on Clark Street. We'll check it out eventually. I craved a Mancuso's House Special pizza." Mike kept his hand on the box in his pocket, but the liquid courage wasn't enough. He decided to wait until after dinner before getting down to "getting engaged" business.

"What's on the House Special?"

"Like, everything in the kitchen."

Kim folded her fingers and rested her chin on them. "Sometimes you're *so quiet* Michael, it scares me. You never give me a clue about what you're thinking. What *are* you thinking now, baby?"

The Steelman threw back his second shot of Jack.

"I'm fucking sore right now, Kim. More than usual and all over." He slowly lowered his chin to stretch his neck and then twisted it from side to side as if to shake out the pain.

"It's your neck again isn't it, baby?" There was an edge in her voice. "I know you're hurt and figured that's why you're so damn silent. Either that or you're just being an ass ignoring me." Plaintively Kim continued. "I'm worried. You hurt most of the time. Is this really still worth it to you, Michael?"

Taken aback, he took a big swig of beer and let go of the velvet box before enlightening her. "Listen, Kim. I play in the fucking NFL which for some guys means "Not For Long." I been in this League goin' on a lot of years now. I see what happens. You make your reputation. Kick ass or get your ass kicked.

"Years go by and you realize now you're getting your ass kicked more and more. So you man up and play hurt or fold the tent and go home. During the season, I fuckin' hurt most days now. Whether I'm on or off the field. That's the truth. I can still dish it out when I have to—and it's *my choice* to take it."

Kim leaned back against the seat and crossed her arms.

"I know we're gonna win it this year. I know it! This year, Kim. Not next year! End of story."

She now understood there would be no reasoning with the Steelman about football. Not tonight. Not ever.

The food arrived. Kim, who opted for homemade pasta and chicken, barely touched hers. Mike grabbed a slice of the big pie. Two more slices quickly disappeared.

Stopping to take a breath, he asked, "When are you leaving tomorrow?"

"Why? Trying to get rid of me? Is this the big brush-off?"

"Nope, I thought maybe you need a ride to the airport, so I'd call for a car." The way the evening was progressing, Mike knew she'd be shocked when he pulled out the ring. He just needed the right moment.

"I'm not packed, and all my summer stuff is at my place. You know, more and more of my stuff migrates to your condo. Why's that?" She smiled and reached for a small corner of the pizza. "My flight is at 10:00 a.m. from that little airport. With holiday travel, what time should I get there?"

"You mean Midway. Okay, so I'll drop you at your place tonight and have the car pick you up at 7:30 a.m. It's not far."

"Thank God there's no 'Hawk' in Hillsboro Beach. As a matter of fact, weather's good this time of year so I'll take my yellow bikini. Why don't you come up while I pack? You never know what might happen . . ." she teased.

Mike knew what probably *wouldn't happen* if she accepted the ring. She probably wouldn't go home to Hillsboro Beach. Mike felt for the box again and pictured the ring's brilliance. Only a few tables were occupied. Realizing dinner was ending, he felt a sense of urgency, almost panic.

He had to make a move. The alcohol and pain meds finally alleviated his physical pain. He thought about popping a coin in the jukebox to set the mood, but couldn't think of the right song. *Ha! Wonder if "Comfortably Numb" is on the playlist.*

Kim had no idea the symbol of her future with Mike was so close, yet so far.

"Well, I guess you better get the check. It's getting late and I still have to pack."

It was time. "Hey, Kim, I gotta tell you something . . ."

Mancuso's door swung open and in walked the Steelman's worst royal pain in the ass. Jack Sawyer was the local Chicagoland Chevy Dealer who supplied his complimentary truck. He always hounded Mike for autographs and signed Storm memorabilia. Tonight of all nights, Mike was in no mood to sign autographs or pose for pictures with Jack, anyone in his family, or anyone else. Jack made a beeline for their booth.

"Oh, shit!" Mike muttered. To make matters worse, Sawyer was a good friend of Lisa's father.

"Mike Stalowski! Holy cripe, Steelman! Funny to see you here on a weeknight. Me and the family are just grabbing some pizza. Come on over. I want you to meet everybody." Jack realized he was not with Lisa.

"Hey, Jack, was just paying my bill. Tell you what, I'll stop by next week with tickets for the last home game. Great seats in the Cadillac Club." Mike threw two $100 bills on the table.

"No problem, Mike. Good luck with Dallas. You guys will need it!"

The Steelman almost knocked someone over while hustling Kim toward the door. Mike turned to apologize. "Hey, man, I'm sor . . ."

He was shocked to see Billy Reardon hadn't changed much since eighth grade. No longer a fool, when Billy realized who almost put him on his ass for the second time, he bolted for the bar.

"Hey! You didn't apologize to that poor guy!"

"Girl, you don't know the half of it. Come on, we're outta here!" Mike almost ran, with his arm around Kim, pulling her away from the holiday lights.

"Hey, what's up? SLOW down, Michael!" yelled Kim. "Can't we at least drive past the lights?"

He reached in his hoodie pocket to grab his keys and felt the box. Mike didn't say much on the ride to Kim's. He was pissed at himself for not having a back-up plan.

Kim was baffled by his behavior tonight. In front of her building, she leaned over and kissed Mike on the cheek. "I love you, Michael. I really do." She exited the truck without looking back.

The Surfside Shack

<hr>

"MOMMA, IT'S SOOO GOOD TO SEE YOU!" KIM AND KATE RICHARDSON exchanged an extra-long heartfelt hug.

"Honey, I'm ecstatic you're home!" They went into the family room overlooking their private ocean beach. "Of course, I wish you could stay longer. Your father is in New York with stuffy old bankers until tonight." Kate opened the patio door. "Drop your things and come sit outside. I want to hear all about your new life. I'll get us sweet iced tea, like old times."

A sudden wave of nausea washed over Kim, then subsided. "Sure, Momma. Let me freshen up a bit first. It was a long flight." She hadn't felt quite right for a week or so. But between last night's conversation with Mike and the Mancuso's entrée she was downright sick.

She grabbed her phone to check in as promised. It immediately went to voicemail. "Hey, Michael, I miss you already. Made it down okay. Remember, I'm probably going out tonight with high school girlfriends. Please call me later, Steelman. I love you."

Being in Hillsboro Beach felt a little strange. *This isn't home anymore. But where do I belong?* Kim had thought about Mike on the flight, reflecting on their relationship. She loved him. At first, she hadn't dwelled on his drinking. But lately it worried her that it was pretty much all the time. She wondered if it was to dull the pain from the never-ending collateral damage inflicted by the game or something else. Maybe a few days apart would do them both good.

"So Momma, I have this great apartment near downtown, and I'm an executive hostess at an exclusive restaurant called The Sunset Grill. It pays pretty well. And I've met important people, but that's not as important as you and your health. What's going on?"

"I thought you went there to be an actress."

"Of course! That's my night job. I've been super busy with acting classes and some really good auditions. Tell me more about the tests you mentioned recently."

"Turns out I didn't need any. Must have been a bug or something."

Of course she didn't. When will I learn?

"Classes and auditions won't pay your expenses, honey."

"I have a paying gig, too. I'm an understudy for a Broadway in Chicago show you might know. *Grease, the Musical.* My agency gets me out for tons of auditions. I can't believe how much money a national commercial pays."

"That's good to hear, but we worry about you being alone. Especially with the schedule you're describing."

"No worries, Momma! I've made new friends. And no, there is no love interest." She finished with the truth. "I have met a few interesting characters, though."

"Well, it sounds like things are going well." *If it's all true.* Kate substituted her favorite merlot for the iced tea. "I would think by now one of those wealthy Chicago boys would have noticed you. Preferably one with a trust fund. Hopefully you're not seeing someone beneath you."

No way Kim was springing the Steelman yet. "I'm going to see Bethany tonight."

"Okay, honey. Remember your father should be home by 8:30."

Oh, boy! Can't wait.

Hillsboro Beach didn't have casual nightspots. Kim and Bethany, high school and college BFFs, decided to meet in Deerfield Beach at Surfside Shack. Their old stomping grounds attracted locals and tourists with greasy bar food and scantily clad servers. Kim really needed to see her old wingman. She had to tell someone about the Steelman. Bethany would understand and could be trusted not to utter a word.

Kim put Kate's Mercedes top down and headed onto the familiar stretch of A1A. The Florida sun felt good. Especially compared to last night. It emphasized her life in Chicago was completely opposite of Hillsboro. She considered other paths she might have taken. She could be in Boca Raton working some corporate job her father set up or down in South Beach. She could have pursued her real dream in New York or LA. Any other way, there's no Steelman in her life.

"My God, girl, look at you all pasty white! Doesn't the sun shine up there?" Bethany laughed while looking her up and down.

Kim turned heads when she strutted in, wearing a black mini-skirt, heels and pink sleeveless blouse she filled out more than usual. She had smoky eyes and hoop earrings to complement her pinned-up hair. Bethany was a knock-out herself, with streaked auburn hair and big brown eyes.

Kim grabbed Bethany's hands and they sat down in the bar. "You look great! Sooo good to see you."

They laughed uproariously about their escapades for a while. Kim excused herself to go to the ladies room.

"Girl, have you eaten a lot of Chicago deep dish pizza? Your boobs look bigger and your hard belly seems to be softening up," teased Bethany. "You know, you always made me jealous with your ability to eat, drink and still look fabulous."

"You're nuts! But you think so, Beth?" Kim pushed her chest out and rubbed her abdomen. "I've been working out a lot more than I did here. Gotta be camera ready."

"By the way, that guy at the next table almost choked on his chicken wing when you walked by," she chuckled. The dynamic duo still left a trail of guys with their mouths hanging open. "Speaking of wings, let's eat something we'd never order before like loaded nachos and blazin' chicken wings."

"I don't know. I'm queasy today. Last night I went out with this guy I'm seeing and I think the chicken piccata was bad."

"Who might this lucky boy be?"

"You won't believe it! What the heck! Let's get the nachos, wings AND another round!"

Bethany took a swig of beer and cupped her ear. "Spill the beans!"

Excitedly, Kim recounted meeting Mike at the Bikini Bust Out and the last four whirlwind months. She barely had a bite of the appetizers.

"Oh my God, Kim!" Bethany almost choked when she put the puzzle pieces together. "I know who he is! They did an article about him last month when Chicago played Miami."

Kim clearly remembered being on his boat after that game. Mike was banged up and comfortably numb, snowed on painkillers and beer.

"You're dating an NFL bad boy, like a biker with an attitude and a football helmet. I saw his picture and have to say he is damn cute without the scowl!"

"Listen, Bethany, I'm in love with this guy." Kim took a big gulp of beer.

"Hey, girlfriend, look at you puttin' that beer down! Did he teach you that?"

"No, he didn't teach me to swig beers. He's not at all like what the media says. He's a big handsome, although sometimes scary-looking, teddy bear. Honestly! And I just may keep him!"

"Honey, wait until Bryce and Kate find out," Bethany giggled.

"Can you believe I was gonna bring him down? But he's got a damn game on Thanksgiving!"

"I promise, not a word until you tell them." They toasted with clinking bottles. "I can't wait to meet him!"

Kim threw her napkin on the table and made a beeline to the ladies room. She returned pale and glassy-eyed.

"Honey, you look like you threw up. I'm so sorry. We should have ordered fucking salads instead."

"No, I'm good. I think I just had too much stuff I don't normally eat. I'll be fine, but I do have to get going."

"So soon?"

"Time to face Bryce."

"Well, good luck with that. You've got to keep Friday open. I want you to meet my latest boy toy. Kyle's . . ."

"Bethany, I'm soooo sorry! I've just been going on and on about me. Bryce can wait a little more."

"No worries! He's an Ivy Leaguer and East Coast blue blood who moved down from Connecticut. The folks are happy even though he's a damn Yankee and talks funny! His daddy is a Boca high-rise developer who used to build hotels for that Celebrity Apprentice guy. He's really cute, but I'm just using him," she giggled.

Kim paid the bill with Kate's credit card while Bethany gave Kim the once over again. "Kimberly, honey, I hope you're not pregnant!"

"You're crazy, but I love you, baby girl! Talk Friday."

"The signs are all there." Bethany laughed, "I'll be an auntie!"

In the parking lot, Kim breathed in the salty air. She merged onto A1A and looked up at the star-filled sky. *Do you even know how to spell constellation?* She remembered their first kiss at 95th Street Beach and their ride to Warren Dunes. *He should be here right now, holding me on the beach.* Bethany's comments about her appearance popped in her head. *OMG! SHIT! Damn it! I didn't have birth control when we jumped each other's bones in that damn tall dune grass. Bethany girl, you better not be right!*

Back in Chicago Sunday night, the line on the test stick clearly confirmed Bethany's suspicions. Sobbing, Kim leaned on the doorframe and slid down to the floor, letting the tears flow. She didn't know who to tell—or how.

———————●———————

Bethany would stay true to her word—until they spread Kim's ashes near Lighthouse Point on Hillsboro Beach. Then she shared their conversation with Kate.

Eve of Destruction–Part Two
The Chain Reaction

January 19, 2007, 4:40 p.m.

... "OH, YEAH, I WAS SERVED WITH DIVORCE PAPERS TODAY."

Kim was speechless.

"Pretty soon I'm out from underneath her thumb. Then things will be good, Kim. I'll be at the condo when you get off." Mike kissed her cheek and hugged her tightly. "Hey, remember to reserve the room overlooking Mag Mile for the defense victory party. Once the media bullshit is over, we're coming for some R & R." He stood up to leave. . .

Waiting for the elevator, Mike could still hear the whooping and hollering of Storm fans inside Sunset Grill. And the game wasn't until tomorrow. *Still can't believe that Burr Ridge bitch picked today to stick it to me. Fuck her! Kim's the one I want anyway.* Back downstairs, he retrieved the 1970 Chevelle SS from the valet and headed home. *I gotta forget about these crazy chicks and focus on the freakin' championship.*

The Storm hadn't won the Super Bowl since Mike was in eighth grade. Now the Seattle Firehawks were the only thing standing in their way. Jamal Brookes, their brash rookie running back, was knocking on a 1,000-yard season and NFL Rookie of the Year.

Could the Steel Trap defense stop Brookes? Jeremy Butler could take on the double team and shed blocks to fracture an offensive line. The linebacker trio, Stokes, Stalowski and Rivers, jelled on the field. The secondary was fast and alert to the deep pass. Ten-year veteran and All-Pro free safety Dino Rhoades was questionable for the game with a high ankle sprain. His replacement, if necessary, was Christian Blackwell, the rookie first-round draft pick.

As defensive captain, Mike had been responsible for training camp rookie initiations. He'd told Blackwell to pick up the wet towels after the veterans showered. Blackwell had dashed to the dining hall instead.

"Welcome to the team, 'rook,'" Mike had laughed while he and Rhoades taped Blackwell to the goalpost. "We'll save you some scraps!"

Blackwell was the next breed of Storm player. Fast, strong, and smart. He had the tools to become a Pro-Bowler, but understood football was not his only ticket to success. An honors student, he planned to pursue a career in bio-engineering after his NFL stint.

The Storm, a wildcard seed, enjoyed an improved offense over the previous season. Quarterback Mark Meade retired, landing in the broadcast booth where he was more effective in a tailored suit and moussed hair than in his uniform and helmet. Third year back-up Aidan McNulty, a record-setter at Ohio State, replaced him. McNulty had a rocket arm and was mobile. He was becoming quite popular, especially with diehard Buckeye fans. His favorite target was receiver Trumaine Hastings who made tough catches on deep routes. Working the Chicago social scene into the wee hours was Hastings' second career, keeping some heat off the Steelman. Their bread-and-butter runner, Cecil Cummings, was built like a fireplug, low to the ground and wide at the shoulder. He was nicknamed "the Diesel" for running hard and steady, even after nine years in the league.

Finally done navigating the heavy Friday night traffic on Lake Shore Drive, Mike signaled his turn into the condo's garage. He never liked studying game plans but knew that's what he had to focus on. *We have to pull this off. Probably my last chance.*

After parking, Mike stretched the custom cover over the SS. He kissed his hand before patting the hood. "Good night. See you tomorrow. Don't leak any oil, okay?"

Around midnight, Mike was restlessly watching MTV. Tomorrow's game plan sat untouched on the coffee table. The lobby intercom buzzed.

"Who is it?" he cheerfully asked.

"It's me."

"Where's your key?"

"Open up, baby. I have a surprise for you."

Kim stood in the doorway, wearing her long, down-filled coat and black stiletto heels. In one hand, she held a large bottle of Mumm's champagne. A box with a giant slice of decadent chocolate cake from the Sunset was in the other. She closed the door and slowly opened her coat. The Steelman rubbed his eyes.

"Where the hell were you? Shopping at Victoria's Secret?"

"I thought you might want an early victory gift. Although the champagne is for us to enjoy tomorrow after the game." She hoped the sheer black teddy would put him in the right frame of mind for her announcement.

"How the heck am I supposed to concentrate on football when you're running around like that? You're really a Seattle spy sent to break me and learn the defense's game plan, right?"

"Yes, I am. So are you going to have dessert now or later?"

"Which one? You know hot blondes, football, and championship games don't mix well."

Kim dropped her coat and sashayed over like a high-class hooker. Despite her pregnancy, she still looked like a centerfold. If the shock didn't kill him after he digested her news, she expected Mike would fixate on the boob fairy visit. They were getting bigger and more sensitive, but the Steelman was evidently clueless.

"Castro told us to go to bed early and not fuck around tonight."

Against conventional wisdom, Castro didn't hole them up at their usual "pregame quarters." It was a mistake.

Mike had two shots of bourbon before consuming both of his desserts, right on the couch. They went to bed, unable to sleep. Together side-by-side, but lost in individual thought.

Mike was focused on the dresser drawer where the diamond ring, symbolizing his future with Kim, was in limbo. *Either way, when it's done, I'm finally giving Kim the ring. Maybe kidnap her and take her to a deserted beach. Away from all this bullshit. Just me and her. No fucking auditions or practices. No attorneys, games, or agents. Gotta get my Florida girl on the sand in the sun for some R & R. Poor thing, I think she needs it more than me. Awfully pale and tired these days.*

Still unable to muster the words to tell Mike she was pregnant, Kim felt truly alone.

The predawn minutes ticked away. Kendall's call weighed heavily on Mike. His personal thoughts co-mingled with professional anxiety. The Steelman knew he better get into the right frame of mind.

After a few fitful hours, Kim was finally out cold. Mike sat up in bed, feeling sharp pain and stiffness in his neck and hearing the crunching glass. *Damn it! Left my stash at the office.* Mike decided to let Kim sleep and head to Lisle.

The day dawned gray and ominous. He shuffled into the kitchen to make a pot of coffee and buried his face in his hands. Mike had no appetite. There was a huge knot in the pit of his stomach. He knew Storm fans expected him to be the field executioner. *I'd rather stay home!*

His personal life was crashing in. The divorce papers did exactly what Lisa intended: mess with his head when he needed to focus. Mike couldn't sort out his feelings. Since last night, he was consumed with venom for Lisa and now it was intruding on his feelings for Kim. *Everyone needs to just fucking leave me alone.*

After wallowing in self-pity, Mike decided his personal problems would not interfere with the game. Too many people depended on him to carry the Storm's defense to the Super Bowl. Mike pulled out his playbook and flipped through it, unable to focus on the formations.

Kim walked out of the bedroom, rubbing her eyes. He barely looked up. She hugged him around his neck and shoulders.

"Hey! Easy! My fucking neck hurts!"

"I'm sorry, baby!" Kim backed away. "Didn't mean to hurt you."

"Hey, man, I'm sorry Kim. I'm just getting myself torqued over this game and it's only six in the morning. Look, I'm gonna go to Lisle and sit in the whirlpool to loosen up and get my head straight with this fucking game plan. Then I'm gonna throw some weights around and go straight to the stadium."

"Can I come? I'll call in to work and go to the game." She needed to be near him. Since last night the atmosphere seemed charged with bad karma that she had to turn around.

"No, I don't want the bitch wives or fucking media making a spectacle of you. Lay low at the bar. I promise it'll be just us tonight after this shit winds down. I'll call when I'm on my way. It's still dry out, so I'm taking my SS." Mike never paid attention to weather forecasts unless he was out on the water. "It got lots of attention yesterday. Hey, we're all good keeping it small tonight, right? I don't want to see a bunch of idiots waiting to celebrate with us."

"Yes, sir!" She would keep her secret for one more day. "Mike, call me the minute you can after the game. I'll be waiting. One more thing, baby boy. Lisa's gone and I love you." *Am I reassuring him or me?* She desperately wanted to spill the baby secret but felt that after the game would be better.

Approaching County Line Road, Mike instinctively steered toward the exit. He wondered if Lisa was home and had company. Driving the loud and whining SS into the stately gated community would prompt a call to the Burr Ridge PD. He continued past the exit.

The parking lot was empty. He swiped his access card and walked, half-scowling, into the lobby.

"Good morning, Mr. Stalowski. I was told everyone was reporting directly to Veterans Stadium."

"Hey, Harry! I'm here to get some stuff and a quick workout in."

Mike hit the weight room. He wanted to loosen up a little on the bench press. Throwing up the straight bar with only one 45-pound plate on each side, he felt the same sharp pain as earlier.

He had no choice. He returned to his locker. Confident he was alone, he rifled through a gym bag for his last two 500 mg oxycodone pills. He popped half of one. Fighting off the possible side effects of dizziness, nausea, and anxiety before the game was not something he wanted to do. But he needed immediate pain relief to get through the morning and ideally most of the game. Hopefully, it wouldn't fuck up his head too much.

He fished out the bag stocked with substances he ingested almost daily to get through practices and games. The dangerous combinations of Celebrex, Vicodin, and Tylenol with Codeine clouded his judgment, exacerbated by his alcohol abuse. Mike had learned he could crush a Vicodin tablet and dissolve it in water. Then he could inject the fortified liquid directly into his most pained area for faster relief. He jammed the small needle into the base of his right trapezius and depressed the plunger. After zipping the spent syringe in his bag, he headed back to the weight room.

Within fifteen minutes he was back in the groove, pounding heavy metal, both on the weight bench and with the music reverberating in his earphones. Mike loaded the straight bar with three 45-pound plates on each side. He threw up the 315-pound bar ten times like it was stacked with puffy marshmallows.

He followed up with an ice water bath then a hot whirlpool. The Steelman was ready to face the grim reality of pro football. Almost pain-free. Mike sat down in the locker room to finally review the game plan. Unfortunately, between the drugs and a sleepless night, he couldn't keep his eyes open. Four hours later, Harry carefully nudged him.

"Sorry, Mr. Stalowski, but I figured I'd check on you."

"Holy shit! I'm okay. Just took a little nap. Thanks, man."

The Super Sport rumbled onto I-55 again, passing carloads of fans on their way to Veterans Stadium for tailgating. He chuckled because the show wouldn't start without him. Nearing Burr Ridge, he thought about Lisa who would normally be holding court with the wives.

Driving the old Chevy linked him to his past, flooding him with memories of his father and stories about his uncle. The Hawk was blowing off Lake Michigan. Light rain fell onto the windshield as the Steelman descended Ramp 41.

Shit! Fucking rain on my new paint job.

Mike felt a knot in his stomach. The season and his career were on the line. Winning the NFC championship would propel him to a possible Super Bowl ring. He remembered the ring he already had. For Kim, in the black velvet box from Lisa's favorite jeweler.

"1256 Tackles—186 Sacks—
432 Hurries—
29 Fumble Recoveries—
5 Pro Bowls"

MIKE PARKED DIAGONALLY ACROSS TWO SPACES TO PROTECT THE SS FROM door dings. He walked away while pressing his original leather Chevy fob. Silence. *No remotes in 1970. Ha! Gotta put the damn key in the door!* Mike turned back and admired the beautiful restoration. *Dad and Uncle Mike would have loved this!* He saw the splattered windshield. *Fuckin' rain! Maybe I shoulda driven the truck.*

The locker room was empty. Mike went about his pre-game ritual, taping his wrists and fingers. The Steelman refused to wear gloves. He relied on the traction and stability surgical tape provided, often masking wrist or finger injuries.

Thanks to Vicodin, his neck was under control for now. Unable to focus, he gulped an energy drink to combat the fog. His thoughts cycled erratically between two women; the rambling in his head drowning out the rock music blaring in his ears.

Don't wanna play this game. So fucking tired of this shit.

Lisa thinks she's so fuckin' smart screwing with me now. She better not show up in that suite expecting me to tug my helmet. I'll flip her off and I don't give a shit how many cameras see it!

Can't deal with these crazy broads anymore. Kim lost it over some stupid role. Running back to mommy at Thanksgiving and Christmas to think about shit.

Who the fuck thinks about me? Lisa fucks with me! Kim worries about me! She loves me.

What the hell am I waiting for? Gonna give Kim that ring tonight. No! After we win the Super Bowl.

Shit, I gotta play this goddamn game first . . .

"Hey, Steelman! What time you get here?" Mike didn't notice players filling the locker room with music, bravado, and jokes. Dino's locker was next to his. They both loved to hit and cause turnovers on the gridiron. However, their lifestyles, appearance, and reputations were polar opposite.

Rhoades was a great role model: good marriage, three kids, and a true leader of his foundation. The Rhoades' Scholars benefited the most challenged inner-city schools. The media loved that he always had something positive to say and never took issue with his play.

Before a game, Mike was usually coiled. If startled, he would strike. Dino knew it was risky tapping Mike's shoulder when he didn't answer.

"Dino, what's up man? It's you and me playing defense so far."

"Give it time, man. They get bonus checks if we win. They'll be here! Ready to go, Steelman? Only two games between us and a Super Bowl ring! What about this kid Jamal Brookes, man? He runs like he's possessed! Over a thousand yards and wants more!"

Dino donned his thermal skins. Temperatures hovered in the low 40s. Chicagoans know about the lake effect, warmer winter temperatures near the lake. But Storm players experienced the wind effect, feeling at least ten degrees colder on the field than the official wind chill. Mike played sleeveless.

Mike stopped taping his wrist to look squarely at Rhoades. "Dino, you're a fucking safety and the last fucking man to beat. If he gets that far, it's on you to stop his ass. Remember film? This guy runs sideways, backwards, and up and fucking down! Wherever the fuck he wants. If he sheds tackles, we're fucked on every third down. Can't let him get an edge. He can fucking catch, too, although his dread-locked head is a little too big for his rookie fucking helmet. I'm callin' blitzes all night long! Be ready, man. When he comes my way, I'm gonna clean his fucking clock. Every chance I get." Dino took a long look in the Steelman's vacant eyes and realized he was stone-cold, drop-dead serious.

"Hey, Steelman, do you EVER stop saying fuck? Don't always be picking on us small fast guys," chided Dino. "Get your damn outside linebackers to do something." Rhoades chuckled, trying to keep things lighthearted.

The Steelman took everything to heart on game day. Most players left him alone. He knew they needed a win but could not stop thinking about Kim and Lisa and divorce and rings. The clock was running out. This could be his last chance to go out on top.

At 5:30, the air was electrified in the locker room. Connie Everett addressed the team. "Gentlemen, when you walk on the field, honor those men and women who serve our country in distant lands and those who didn't make it home. A hero who earned a Purple Heart will sing the national anthem. He does not let physical limitations hold him down. Thank God for your talents and your families. Take the field with pride and determination. Play to win. I'm not Vince Lombardi, but I'm asking you to exceed expectations. Leave it all on the field. Walk off as NFC champions."

The Steelman silently looked straight ahead. Connie's words conjured the folded flag on the living room mantle, next to the Bronze Star, and a photo of the good-looking soldier who never got to drive his Chevy SS. It was left to him by his wheelchair-bound father, who died in the prime of his life and Mike's childhood.

Coach Castro spoke next. "You guys came this far. It's up to you individually and as a team to win. Bring it on! Take the next step toward becoming world champions."

Mike headed to the tunnel, helmet tucked under his left forearm. His mind still racing. *Wounded warriors—the flag—Uncle Mike—his father who wouldn't and then couldn't stand for the national anthem—Lisa—dark and despair—Kim—light and love—Kim and Lisa—ring and divorce—Super Bowl ring—the game—he had to focus on playing the game.*

No one paid much attention to the raindrops, forecast to become sleet, then snow. The remaining stadium lights powered on. Only a few minutes before the bloodthirsty masses descended. He loathed the fans who thought paying for a ticket gave them the right to be obnoxious. Mike especially hated when they screamed at players coming off the field. Often, he wanted to reach up and choke the idiots screaming obscenities, impressed by their own ability to spit out stats.

During warm-up drills, Mike was light-headed and weak. At first, he thought it was his "meds," but knew from experience that the energy drink should counter the side effects. Then it dawned on him that he hadn't eaten anything solid *all day*. Normally he consumed protein throughout the day.

Fuck me! With all the shit going on, I didn't even eat. No! Fuck Lisa! This is exactly what she wanted to do. Mess with me and this game I gotta play. I'll give Kim the ring and show that bitch! No more wives club and she's moving her ass out of Burr Ridge! Shit, I'm starving! I gotta play to win this fucking game!

Mike completed the drills without the intensity Wallace expected. Several times he looked bewildered. He was short of breath and out of sync.

Wallace caught up to him. "Mike, what the fuck is up with you? You're the leader and you're doggin' it. Step it up!" Mike didn't hear a word Wallace said. He was wondering how Kim was doing behind the Sunset's bar.

Thirty minutes to kickoff.

The Firehawks charged out of the locker room. Media technicians made last-minute equipment adjustments. The Storm Predictors, local AM 78.5 radio announcers Buzz Taylor, Octavius Bradley, and Tom O'Halleran, were up in a heated booth. Griffin Burke was a good friend and former teammate. Once a week, they held a lunchtime radio show from Crunch Bar. They added authentic color commentary based on their championship experience, even if it was over twenty-years old. They were cut-ups most of the time and spared no one.

"Hey, Taves," said Buzz. "I'm looking at Mike Stalowski going through the motions. He doesn't look fired up tonight. Normally this guy is pacing the sidelines."

"The Steelman will bring it when he has to. He knows what's at stake. These guys have come too far this year. Watch him in the second half. I predict some big stops by the defense."

Tom O'Halleran was less optimistic. "But you guys know as well as I do, everyone speculates Stalowski has been battling back and neck injuries for several seasons."

"This rookie running back Brookes will want to make some big plays," said Taves. "You know . . . ROLL TIDE! The Steelman knows that too! It's not the Steel Trap defense it was several years ago, but with the players we got, he could still lead it. Still bring it . . . in my opinion."

"We all agree he is one of the most feared tacklers in recent NFL history," concurred Tom. "But I think leading with his helmet since high school has taken its toll. Mike's a hell of a football player, but I wonder how much longer he can keep it up. He has to be hurting. Trust me! Been there, done that."

Taves paused to pick up his notes. "Remember brothers, this guy's stats to date are—1256 tackles—186 sacks—432 hurries—29 fumble recoveries—5 Pro Bowls! I know a lot of older guys in the league are still terrified of him. I AM!"

"Okay! Okay! The stats don't lie. I get it. No disputing he's a warrior. But I've watched his movements coming off the field this season. He's a wounded warrior. His body has given and taken a lot of punishment. Not counting the concussions he's had, known and unknown. Let's see what happens tonight."

At 7:10 p.m., the enormous gray storm cloud was inflated. Conrad Everett chose a decorated Illinois National Guard platoon leader to precede the charge out of the tunnel, carrying an American flag. The team followed, led by rookie safety Christian Blackwell. For the national anthem, the Stars and Stripes were planted next to a wheelchair-bound Iraq War vet, injured in the Second Battle of Fallujah. Troops held and undulated the playing-field-sized American flag. Connie Everett, a Korean War veteran and American patriot, thought it was the least his team could do.

The Steelman instinctively glanced up at the packed Family and Friends section. *Good thing Kim's not here.* He needed to worry about Jamal Brookes, not Kim sitting by herself in the skybox suite.

During the national anthem, cameras focused on the soldier's family: a boy with his right hand on the stump of his father's left thigh; a girl to the soldier's right, holding her mother's hand. Bits and pieces of Uncle Mike stories swirled through the Steelman's mind. *Loved street racing with your dad.* Air Force jets roared overhead. Suddenly, one rose vertically and departed, while the others flew together out of sight, completing the "Missing man" formation. *He was a hero . . . killed a few weeks before the end of his tour of duty.*

As the game got underway, rain fell and the temperature dropped. In short order, field conditions were less than ideal. Offensive game plans for both teams were altered accordingly. Play calling was conservative.

The Firehawks had little success moving the ball. Jamal Brookes was unable to run his usual end sweeps for big gains or tally positive yardage catching screen passes. JB and Stokes were tackling well on the strong side. The receivers tested the Storm secondary, without much success. Rhoades broke up two deep passes that seemed sure touchdowns and bobbled an interception that would have put the Storm in their red zone. Mike Stalowski didn't do much the 1st half. No usual solo tackles nor shoring up the gang tackles.

The Storm led 3-0 at the end of the 1st quarter, scoring on a 44-yard field goal. Aidan McNulty and Trumaine Hastings, his go-to receiver, only connected on one 3rd down conversion. McNulty, throwing the ball with bad footing on wet turf, narrowly avoided two interceptions. Diesel Cummings' straight-ahead runs were predictable. Productive yards were hard to get. The Storm's O-line wasn't sure-footed and would have to change their cleats at half-time. Both punters certainly earned their paychecks.

On the last drive of the 2nd quarter, with less than thirty-seconds on the clock and one time-out remaining, the Firehawks attempted to spring Brookes for a big gain by testing the middle of the line. At the very least, they could try to kick a tying field goal. On 3rd and 4 from the Storm 48, Brookes took a hand-off and charged the A-gap. The Steelman saw it coming. He got a step on Brookes and barked out an adjustment to stack the strong side. When Brookes blew past the front line, the Steelman instinctively buried his helmet in his numbers. Like a crack of thunder, the sound of #52's helmet colliding with Brookes' chest plate resonated throughout the stadium. Brookes' legs swung out forward when he hit the solid brick wall with two arms—steel jaws that wrapped around him like a vise.

Another Storm legend was born. The impact knocked Mike's dental bridge, for his four front teeth, out of his mouth and into the slush. The Steelman looked like an old prizefighter after one too many bloody fights. The vicious hit on Brookes was borderline illegal, but no flag was thrown. The Storm dodged a personal foul that could have kept the drive alive and put the 'Hawks in scoring range. The call, or lack of, ignited the Firehawks fans.

Brookes was stunned. "You better have more in the tank for the 2nd half, Steelman! You rustin' out, man. Like a broke-ass ride." Brookes moved closer to Mike. "I ain't slowin' down for your old ass next time. I'm gonna run right through it and carry you with me. We got thirty minutes of football left! Bring it on next quarter! Hey, where's your teeth? You need some dentures, old man!" he sneered. Brookes glanced over at Butler who was smiling at the rookie's tirade. "You too, brother. Time you step aside and go sell razor blades on TV."

Mike was oblivious. He would have pounced on him if he had heard the trash talk.

Veteran Firehawk offensive lineman Max Rivera pulled Brookes away, offering sage advice. "You better shut the fuck up! This guy will flip the switch and kill your young ass next play. He plays with rage. Don't fuckin' call it up. He's an animal and you're just a loudmouth rookie. Get it? Look at him without those fuckin' teeth! Looks like Dracula and he'll happily break your fuckin' neck to suck your blood. I been playin' against him for seven years. He's crazy! You understand? Stone... fucking...crazy! Be cool junior and play your game. Watch his eyes. They go blank like he's stoned...and that's when he'll crush your ass!"

Since high school, Mike Stalowski had made critical plays in critical games. But with every tackle, the Steelman's hourglass of cognitive health lost another grain of sand. The permanent damage in his neck amplified. With 00:24 on the play clock, some fans were shocked when McNulty took a knee to end the first half. Castro didn't want to risk a turnover with the rapidly deteriorating field conditions. Coming off the field, Mike realized he was seeing double.

Wounded Warrior

A STINGER WAS PART OF THE PRICE PAID FOR THE HIT ON BROOKES. PAIN radiated from the Steelman's left shoulder causing pins-and-needles in his fingers. The Vicodin wore off sooner than expected. Mike momentarily considered asking for Toradol, the popular NFL injectable, but shrugged it off. He'd swallow the pain and keep playing at a pain threshold most players couldn't bear.

Mike was pissed. He thought he'd suppressed the symptoms long enough to get through the game. Avoiding the trainer, he reached in his locker for icy hot analgesic cream and massaged his neck. *Son of a bitch! Eight minutes of half-time and two quarters to go. Fuck me!*

"What the fuck? You're dragging your ass!" Wallace was not happy. "You're the goddamn team captain and this is the damn conference championship. Play like the Pro Bowler people expect! Make some goddamn plays yourself! The other ten guys are playin' their asses off. Brookes can't run at either edge because they're doin' their jobs. He's pissed and it's gonna be on you! He's called your ass OUT! The offense ain't doin' shit. How the fuck are we gonna win without points? You need to score them on defense. Play like a unit! Get some damn takeaways! Go lead this fucking Steel Trap defense!"

Wallace stayed in his face. Mike hadn't expected a personal dress-down. The Steelman reared up.

"Calm the fuck down, Ernie! There's a second fucking half! What the fuck! They haven't scored one fucking touchdown yet!" The Steelman began pacing. The rage within boiled to the surface. He picked up a folding chair and threw it through the drywall. The rest of the defense braced themselves.

Joaquin Rivers boldly stepped in to pull Mike away. "C'mon Mike, cut the shit and let's go play. I wanna go to Disneyland, man! But first we gotta win this slippery-ass ice bowl."

Back on the field, the Steelman blocked out the crowd. Often, he incited near riots, waving his tattooed arms to energize the fans. Last year during warm-ups, fans tossed water balloons marked with the opposing running back's number. Occasionally he caught one, placed it between his "steel-trap" and slammed it shut, exploding the balloon. The fans went wild. The media raked him over the coals. Castro ended it.

Lisa was probably watching the game somewhere, pissed she wasn't mugging for cameras in the wives' box but satisfied yesterday's action affected him. Kim likely couldn't watch because the bar was busy. He reassured himself that keeping her away from the stadium was the right decision.

The Steelman refused an offered rain parka. His bare arms were unaffected by the deteriorating elements. He buried his head in his hands, lost in jumbled thoughts, most of which didn't involve X's and O's but his "ex" and Kim. The Storm received the kick to begin the 3rd quarter. Stokes sat down.

"These guys better move the fuckin' ball and put some fuckin' points up. You know well as I do Brookes is hungry to break one. Gotta keep his ass off the field."

Mike nodded, brushed back his dripping matted mane with his taped-up fingers, and looked straight ahead at the 50-yard line. The image of the disengaged Steelman provided superb sideline footage for anchors looking to stir up controversy.

Sleet continued to fall making field conditions sloppier. The kick-off return was almost fumbled at the 10-yard line. Kyle Branch was lucky to hold onto the slippery ball. Luckier to run it back to the Storm 30-yard line.

Straight ahead running for short yardage was the best strategy for field conditions. Cummings ground out difficult yards, his muscular legs churning like the pistons of a diesel engine. Only 5' 9" and 245 pounds, Diesel ran through or leaped over defenders.

McNulty took a surprise Shotgun snap and gave Diesel the ball on 2nd and 8 from the Storm 32. He dropped back 7 yards, catching the Firehawks defense off-guard, pump-faked to his right and handed off to Cummings. Diesel slipped and fumbled the ball. In a mad scramble, it was scooped up by the 'Hawks defensive tackle who rumbled ahead to the Storm 24, carrying a gang tackle of Storm players.

"Oh fuck! Diesel coughed it up!" Stokes threw his towel down in disgust. The defense had a potential Red Zone disaster to overcome. At the very least, the turnover would likely result in a field goal.

"Mother . . . fucker! Can't even get a god . . . damn 1st down!" Mike put on his helmet and walked to the 24-yard line. Not leading but bringing up the rear.

Off air, Tom O'Halleran did not mince words. "Fellas, the Steelman looks like he's really dragging ass and doesn't give a shit. They're gonna score on the first play. Something's up. That last play before the half must have really fucked him up."

On air, O'Halleran remarked, "The Storm defense has to shore up and stop the 'Hawks from gaining more momentum. Could be the game-changer. Watch the blitz."

The 'Hawks lined up three wide receivers. Wallace smelled a run by Brookes and was inclined to have Mike call a safety blitz. He thought better of it due to the short field. If someone missed an assignment, it was 6 points. It could also be a fake handoff to Brookes. The captain of the defense would make the call.

The Steelman surveyed the offensive line. They played many of their home games in the rain, which seemed to help their footing. He scanned the "hit list" on his wrist, stopping on "Sting-edge strong safety blitz." *That's it.* He pointed right and left, barking out, "23 Sting! Sting!"

Dino saw something developing behind the line of scrimmage. The veteran figured he and the corner would get tested, likely with a slant or deep end zone pass. He motioned emphatically and shouted, "Kill sting! Kill it, man!" To no avail.

For a split second, Dino glared at Mike and threw his arms in the air. "What the fuck?" He looked forward, just in time to see the ball snapped, and back-pedaled. Dino correctly anticipated the underneath pass on the slant route and did not blitz.

Two 'Hawks receivers took off, one on a slant, the other to the back of the end zone. The Steelman bit when Brookes took a faked handoff. Stokes slipped in the slush on a lateral cut and was leveled by the tight end. Slow to get up, he limped back to the huddle with an obvious ankle tweak.

6' 6" 'Hawks Pro Bowl receiver De'Shawn Jackson moved like a gazelle in full stride. Dino knew he could haul passes in from thin air, shedding defenders for positive yards, and was expecting a jump ball. He was right. Jackson caught the perfectly thrown spiral at the 7-yard line and crossed the goal line untouched as Dino writhed in pain on the wet turf.

The replay showed he'd twisted his knee. Reluctantly he rode a golf cart to the locker room. Dino waved his arm and gave a thumbs-up to the standing ovation while tears rolled down his cheeks. With a suspected ACL tear, it looked to be the end of an era for the Storm.

"I went up to bat it away," Dino told medical staff hustling him to the locker room, "and came within a fingertip of fuckin' doin' it. He beat me and hauled it in clean. I went up high and came down hard on my knee. My footing was bad, and I felt the rip then the sting, like an electric shock, man! My leg went out from underneath and bent like a fuckin' twig. I knew it was over." Dino shook his head, tears in his eyes. "It's the knee, man. Always this goddamn old knee." Against medical advice, he refused to go to the hospital.

The Steelman sustained a hefty gash on his left forearm from a cleat. He waved off the trainer's towel and assistance, wiping his bloody arm across his thigh. He'd gashed the same arm when he stood up Lorenzo White in the 14-9 win, propelling St. Michael's to the state championship. Tonight, the scoreboard read 7-3 Firehawks.

In slow motion, Mike had seen the play develop. He was manhandled by the Firehawks. He slipped and fell flat on his ass, looking almost helpless. Mike knew the touchdown was his critical mistake. He alone was responsible for the bad call and blown play that would be Dino's last.

The 3rd quarter remained a defensive battle. Neither team got into the red zone. Back and forth, they traded scoreless drives. Both defenses were weary. Mike was in most of the scrums but didn't produce any big plays or solo tackles. On the last drive of the 3rd quarter, the Storm offense finally moved the ball close to the 50-yard line, hoping to enter enemy territory.

Facing 3rd and 5 from their own 48, Aidan McNulty finally connected on a gun-slinging pass to Trumaine Hastings at the 'Hawks 25-yard line. Hastings reached back and grabbed the pass midstride, trying to gain control. Running for extra yardage, it was punched out from behind by the 'Hawks free safety—thankfully rolling out of bounds.

The Storm attempted two unsuccessful running plays. On 3rd down, the tight end dropped a screen pass. Struggling to stay ahead of sleet and snow, the groundskeepers kept the outline of the field and yard markers visible, but the field was covered with an inch of wet snow. On 4th down, Castro decided to attempt a field goal. The ball was kicked wide right.

Going into the 4th quarter, 7-3 looked like a baseball score. Not a championship football game with two potent offenses. The 'Hawks had first possession.

The Steelman looked up at the scoreboard and realized he had to make something happen.

He was tired of Jamal Brookes flapping his jaws throughout the 3rd quarter. Pain elevated his game anger. Cameras caught the visceral image of the combat-weary warrior: bloodstains on his uniform, no front teeth and fire in his eyes. Suddenly animated, the Steelman pointed his taped fingers and barked out orders. He grabbed his helmet and paced the sideline.

Of course, no one could see Mike's intermittent double vision from the hit on Brookes that closed the first half. Not that it mattered—neither the Steelman nor anyone else would want to address concussion symptoms in the 4th quarter of a championship game.

Still in uniform, Dino used crutches to stand on the sidelines. Back-up strong safety Donte Sutherland was shivering and vomiting.

Next man up was rookie safety Christian Blackwell. A first-round draft pick out of Tulane, he graduated magna cum laude as a pre-med major. He was quiet and cerebral, a quick study of the playbook. Blackwell knew Jamal's moves from four years in the SEC.

"Blackwell, get in there and play your ass off!"

A cold, wet, and tired Brandon Stokes looked the Steelman straight in the eye. "You finally gonna help us win this one? This kid Blackwell got some big shoes to fill with Dino out."

The Steelman nodded. "Let's go, brother!"

———————•———————

Corbin, who had urged Kim to enter the Bikini Bust Out, and his obnoxious asshole friends were holed up in a suite watching the game. "Hey, baby, can you hurry up? I need another round since it looks like our team will cost me a fortune. You know though, I'd love to have you as my consolation prize."

The thought made Kim even more nauseous.

The second suite was locked and empty, awaiting the victorious Storm defense. Hoping to spot Mike, Kim glanced up while delivering drinks and saw the 7-3 score. *Shit!*

Kim felt sick to her stomach. She made a beeline to the ladies room, dropping the tray and shattering glasses. Barely making it to the bathroom stall, Kim was simultaneously crying and retching.

Morning sickness at night? Screw it! I'm telling him tonight.

———————●———————

The Firehawks started at the 25-yard line with under thirteen minutes left. Coach Harrell chose the ground game to chew up precious time. Despite field conditions, Harrell initially thought about passing on 1st down, but he wanted vindication for the last play before halftime. The Steelman wanted to shut Jamal Brookes up once and for all.

Mike wanted a turnover to get the ball back to McNulty, or better yet, have the defense score. He audibled a safety blitz and had to checkdown Blackwell, who was 5 yards off his mark.

When the ball was snapped, the Steelman instinctively and purposely dropped back 10 yards in coverage. The rest of the defense converged at the line of scrimmage, waiting to blitz. A handoff to Jamal Brookes, who charged the A-gap. The tight end manhandled Blackwell. Stokes fought off a double-team and lunged at Brookes, who saw him coming and cut left, narrowly avoiding the tackle. Unfortunately, he did not see the Steelman. He lunged low, burying his helmet into Brookes for the second time that night.

Two hundred fifty-five pounds of Steelman muscle, delivered by a pissed off, rusty wrecking ball caused Brookes' left leg to buckle at a forty-five-degree angle. Completely tearing most knee ligaments and tendons in the process, his kneecap spun to the inside. His tibia snapped. His foot pointed outward at an unnerving angle.

The sickening image would be replayed endlessly. Many viewers no doubt turned away. Medical staff converged on the fallen player. The crowd was silent. After a pain-killer injection, Brookes was strapped onto a stretcher and loaded into an ambulance.

Players from both teams held hands while the ambulance pulled away. Coaches conferred with officials near the penalty marker, at the 35-yard line. The Steelman slowly got up and staggered away to the 50-yard line, as if to get ready for the next play. Down on one knee, his helmet was off. He appeared dazed. Only FOX Sports picked up on the Steelman's post-play whereabouts. The other networks were glued to Jamal Brookes. Stokes found the Steelman.

"You okay, man?" Mike didn't look up. Stokes knelt down and saw the thousand-mile stare. "Mike! You okay, man? Brookes is bad! You fucked him up real bad."

Mike saw two Brandons. He tried to stand up and fell to his knees. "Yeah man, I'm good. It's a fucking football game, isn't it?"

"Mike, stop! You ain't right. Stay the fuck there!" Stokes waved medical staff over.

Both head coaches were still in a heated discussion with the officials. The referee made sure his public address microphone was off. "Stalowski's getting a flagrant personal foul! One more play like that, he's out. Ejected! He was head-hunting, not tackling!"

"Listen! I don't teach my team to play that way. Everyone, including Brookes, knows this guy is a Pro Bowler who won't take any bullshit. Especially from a loudmouth rookie jawing on him the whole game!"

"Jesus Christ! This kid is done for the year and maybe next year," screamed Harrell. Two years of torturous physical rehab would not be enough to regain his athletic prowess. Jamal Brookes, a promising and attention-hungry rookie, was out of football.

Dr. Cowan hovered over Mike.

"What the fuck, Doc?"

"Don't talk to me like that! You know the rules."

"It's a fucking tackle football game with the fucking championship on the line."

"I'm required to examine you. And if you *don't* have a concussion, you're not human."

"Back off!"

Normally, Cowan pushed the envelope when players insisted on going back in. He marched over to Castro and Wallace. "Listen, he knew damn well he was going to take Brookes out using his head as a battering ram. He won't let me near him, but based on the two hits he pasted on Brookes, I know he's concussed. I say bench him!"

The officials positioned themselves to resume play. "Please reset the game clock to 12:48. After review of the last play, number 52 defense is charged with a personal foul."

The players, including the Steelman, took the field to finish the 4th quarter. It was their job. And the Super Bowl was ultimately at stake.

Broken Play

THE ENTIRE STADIUM WAS ON PINS AND NEEDLES. THE GAME COULD EASILY GO either way. No one seemed to notice the precipitation had stopped. Thanks to the personal foul, the Firehawks had a 1st down at the 50-yard line. Their second string running back came in and continued the momentum with an 8-yard gain to the Storm 42.

Fate smiled on the Steelman, granting temporary redemption for his two serious infractions. On 3rd and 2, the Firehawks threw a deep pass to the blocking tight end. Back-up Ezra Holmes was in for Stokes, who was out with a twisted ankle. When the ball snapped, Holmes saw a hole and charged it with his arms up, tipping the hurried pass. #52 watched the ball fall end-over-end into his extended hands. He lumbered all the way to the 'Hawks 34-yard line. Fans went wild for the Steelman's defensive turnover.

On the next play, McNulty connected with Hastings who glided untouched into the end zone. The Storm led 10-7 with eleven minutes to go.

For seven minutes neither team moved the ball into scoring position. On 4th and 4, the Firehawks finally had a chance to tie the game. Ironically, the Hawk wind blew the 43-yard field goal attempt wide right.

Only 2:47 remained. The Storm had one time-out. Firehawks had two time-outs and needed at least a field goal to stay alive. Diesel ground out yardage, running the clock down.

On 3rd and 2 at the 'Hawks 41, the Storm looked to keep the clock ticking. Harrell knew they needed the ball back and Castro would keep running. He decided to blitz, risking McNulty throwing underneath to a receiver. Hastings lined up as a wideout to add mystery to the likely short-yardage run. Harrell called a time-out to ice the Storm's momentum. Sleet was falling again. The Storm defense hoped for a 1st down to keep them off the field.

"Steelman, I'm tired and want to go in the damn heated locker room!" JB knew after this eternally cold and wet night, he was either a few minutes away from the Super Bowl or retirement. "Hopefully, McNulty can finish it."

Mike nodded. He wiped coagulated blood on his forearm and reopened the wound. He threw the bloodied towel under the bench and turned to Blackwell.

"Listen man, even if the score's 13-7, they're gonna fucking open it up. He has an eighty-yard arm and their 6′ 5″ Pro-Bowl wide-out is gonna burn your young ass. I'm just tellin' you man. You gotta listen to me calling the play and execute it!"

Blackwell listened intently. The cameras zeroed in on the Steelman, minus his front teeth, doling out animated exhortations.

"Then they try the onside kick after they score! They'll send you crying to the fuckin' locker room."

"I can do it, Steelman! For Dino and my Storm brothers."

"Cut the bullshit! Just remember what the fuck to do."

McNulty took the snap under center, dropped back five steps, and saw the blitz coming. The handoff did not develop. Diesel instinctively blocked the incoming nose tackle while McNulty scrambled right. Unsteady on the slick turf, he released the ball. The 'Hawks safety cleanly intercepted it for the game-changing pick of the season!

The Firehawks sideline and fans erupted. With the ball on their own 48, the Firehawks were in command.

"Motherfucker! Just throw the fucking game away you idiots!" Disgusted, the Steelman slammed his helmet on the ground.

It was on him to rally the defense one more time. 1:06 remaining. The 'Hawks needed a touchdown to win. A field goal tied the game, sending it into overtime. For NFL excitement, it didn't get any better.

Mike called a huddle. "Listen up! We got four fucking downs between us and the fucking Super Bowl. We're blitzing on every fucking play until we sack fucking Stafford into next week!"

The players knew full well Wallace would never let that happen. Butler figured Mike was concussed or talking trash out of frustration.

The 'Hawks fullback ran to the Storm 45 on 1st down. In a no-huddle offense, Stafford completed a screen pass to their tight end. JB read it all the way and charged, driving him back for a loss to the Storm's 49.

Harrell took his last time-out. No need to panic. Fourteen yards put them in decent field goal range. A good kick forced overtime.

The Steelman wildly waved his bare arms for maximum crowd noise. The fans responded, delighted the Steelman finally showed up. He smelled victory on 3rd and 7 with 00:38 left.

With Brookes in the ER, the Storm defense stopped the run. A 3rd down pass completion would give the Firehawks another series. They could do better than tie the game with a 1st down in the red zone. They could win. The Firehawks offensive coordinator decided to test Blackwell with a fake hand-off to the fullback. They'd throw to the wide-out on a sideline pump and go. Veteran wide-out Lavoie ran crisp routes and caught difficult passes with velvet hands. At 6' 5", Lavoie could out jump the Storm rookie in a fight for the ball. Blackwell had speed and agility. But if Lavoie found daylight, he would score.

Due to field conditions, the expectation was a short yardage pass play. Wallace signaled pass coverage. The Steelman wasn't convinced. He wanted to disrupt any play and audible "sting" safety blitz again. Only this time, Dino Rhoades was on crutches, unable to make the split-second adjustment to blitz or cover the receiver.

Just prior to the snap, Mike audibled "shadow" zone blitz. Blackwell acknowledged confirmation, but was either confused or didn't remember the play. He stunted the line of scrimmage as if blitzing the run, but panicked and dropped back into coverage, anticipating a receiver and pass were coming his way. Blackwell was laser-focused on Lavoie, fearful he would take off on a deep route. At the last second, he changed his mind again, deciding to blitz. He stunted to the line and waited in a crouched position to blitz Stafford, leaving his zone wide open.

Stafford didn't like what he saw across the line of scrimmage. The crowd noise prevented him from making audible adjustments. No time-outs. He took the ball under center. Lavoie was set in motion along with the tight end. A perfect fake handoff to the Hawks fullback, sweeping right behind the blocking tight end, was enough to get Lavoie down field and open in the flat. The defense bit on the run and blitzed accordingly, very narrowly avoiding a Joaquin Rivers' personal foul for intentional leveling of the quarterback. Blackwell hesitated and was knocked flat on his ass at the line of scrimmage by the blocking tight end. The rest of the defense couldn't get off their blocks, including the Steelman who was double-teamed.

The pass arced and dropped directly in Lavoie's outstretched hands. An easy reception, with no coverage, resulted in a 21-yard gain before he was pushed out of bounds by the cornerback at the 28-yard line. 1st down! 00:28 on the clock.

"What the fuck Blackwell? You fucking idiot! You just gave them the fucking game!"

In the Storm huddle, things got worse. The Steelman's two hard shoves to Blackwell's shoulders landed him on his ass for the second time.

Blackwell fired back. "Hey, man! I played the run like the play called for!"

"Shut up, asshole!"

"I can't believe it," O'Halleran said off-mike to his fellow Storm Predictors. "Picking a fight with a teammate in front of millions of viewers. This guy is melting down!"

Castro saw trouble brewing and was forced to use his last time-out. Butler got between Blackwell and the Steelman, yanked the cage of Mike's helmet, and pulled him away. He grabbed Mike's jersey and got in his facemask, staring into the Steelman's dilated pupils.

"Calm the fuck down, man! Gonna get your ass thrown out. Steelman, you ain't right! You either on some shit or your cage got rattled bad! Why you pickin' on Blackwell? You're the asshole who made the call."

Mike heard Butler's voice but couldn't focus on both of him, so he looked beyond to the sideline and saw his father in a wheelchair. Uncle Mike, in uniform, saluted. Lisa and Kim, both wearing wedding dresses, held hands.

Seventeen years of countless hits, drugs, alcohol, and injury, commingled with personal problems, took their toll. Unhinged, Mike looked at the huddle and back toward the sideline again. Now the grim reaper was there.

Mike screamed for a trainer. His heart was racing. He was short of breath. He pushed Butler away. JB knew Mike was unable to play. Castro and Wallace did nothing.

The whistle blew. Bent over at the waist, trying to control his breathing, he recalled his youthful voice praying. *St. Michael the archangel, defend us in the day of battle, be our safeguard against the wickedness and snares of the devil . . .*

He waved the trainer away. Reaching down for the last vestige of his old self, he trotted back to the huddle and put on his helmet. The Steelman, a bloodied and wounded warrior, was ready for battle.

On 1st down, the defense shifted into zone coverage. Lavoie and Jackson lined up "twins right." Blackwell knew he would be tested by Lavoie again. He also had to contend with Jackson.

#52 was ready to cover the middle. As he shifted his gaze from side to side, he felt sharp pain between his shoulder blades and saw double. Stafford dropped back to check down his receivers. Blackwell was stride for stride with Jackson at the 10-yard line. Lavoie was wide open at the 17. Stafford unleashed a perfect spiral that sailed just out of Mike's reach.

Lavoie snagged the pass. His long strides, with the Steelman in pursuit, carried him inside the 5-yard line. At that moment, Mike saw the grim reaper grinning in the end zone, allowing Lavoie to glide in untouched.

Game over!

The extra point was good. 14-10 Firehawks became a painful part of Storm and Steelman history.

The 'Hawks recovered the onside kick, pouring a ton of salt into the gaping Storm wound. Cold, wet, and bloodied, the Storm gathered in defeat.

Mike Stalowski sat on the bench alone.

Charlie Samples, the long-time equipment manager, was clearing the area. He had a soft spot for Mike. Most players looked past Charlie, just another cog in the Storm wheel turning to bring them NFL fame and fortune. But Mike had always gone out of his way to stop and talk to him. With no words to soften the blow, Charlie briefly stood behind Mike and patted his battered shoulder.

Sunday's Chicago Tribune sports section headline, *Firehawks leave Steel Trap Unhinged and Broken*, was accompanied by a photo of the Steelman walking off the field alone and ripping the defensive plays from his wrist. 14-10 was visible on the scoreboard. He appeared to be in deep thought, regret or pain. Probably all three. The article pretty much pinned the loss on Mike Stalowski.

The next day, the Trib's front page detailed another disaster involving the Steelman.

Last Call

"Fuckin' washed-up loser! Cost me *ten grand*," Corbin boasted.

Kim went about her business, anxiously waiting for Mike's call. *What can I possibly say?* At 11:30 p.m., Kim texted,

> Please call me baby, I love you.

Mike finally responded at 1:57 a.m. Sunday morning.

> be ther byyy 2:30

The bar emptied at 2:15 a.m. Kim, feeling a little queasy again, tallied her liquor sales. $9,657 was a good night for a small club. Unfortunately, mostly drowned game sorrows.

These tips feel like blood money! Kim's cell phone vibrated.

"Hello! Michael, where are you?"

Kim heard street noise and a slurred reply. "Done yet? I'm down by the valll . . . by the car. Let's go."

"Oh my God, Michael! I'm so glad to hear your voice! Give me fifteen minutes."

She finished quickly but had to run to the bathroom. *What am I going to do?* Kim was retching again. *How am I gonna tell him?* Her mind raced. *Should've told Momma before. Or Bethany. I have to tell him, but how's he gonna take this after losing? My poor baby Michael . . . our baby!* Once her sobs and nausea subsided, Kim grabbed her purse and coat, barely saying goodnight to the manager.

She found Mike propped against the open driver's door of his SS. Kim was shocked when he took a long swig from what looked like a whiskey bottle. Something was very wrong. Mike looked mean and ugly—he clearly hadn't left the Steelman on the field.

Cautiously, Kim approached him. "Michael, are you okay?"

"Fuck NO! I'm not okay. I blew the fucking game! And we had it fucking won." Mike took another swig.

Kim saw someone passed out in the passenger's seat. "Who's that and where the hell have you been?" she asked sharply.

"It's Blackwell! The idiot rookie. I took him out, away from all the fucking media and assholes." He smirked and took another hit off the bottle. "Out cold. Before, he was a fucking baby, crying on my shoulder in the locker room."

She'd never seen him this drunk. Kim had a sudden premonition of what life would be like for her and the baby. It scared her. "Please stop drinking! You've obviously had enough."

"Don't fucking tell me I've had enough!" He stumbled.

Standing in shitty weather, with a drunken boyfriend and his passed-out teammate, was not the life Kim envisioned when leaving Hillsboro Beach. Desperately trying to control her emotions, she asked again, "Where have you been, Michael?"

After a long pause he slurred, "I had to fuckin' square up with Blackwell . . . alone. Had a few drinks at my little dive bar. You know, the fucking Schooner. No, no. The Sewer by Chinatown. No one fucks with me there when I wanna drink myself. I mean alone."

"A few drinks, huh? What happened to the car? An accident?"

"Ya think? I fishtailed and sideswiped someone. It ain't a four-wheel drive. Shoulda drove my fuckin' truck. My $20 grand paint job is fucked. C'mon, get in! I'll wake his drunk ass up and we'll put him on the couch."

"Michael, you're in no shape to drive! Please give me the keys." Kim knew better than to demand them. She wanted to get them home safely.

"You're not driving this fucking car! *It's my baby.*"

Kim wanted to tell him she wasn't driving in his damn Chevy Super Sport WITH HER BABY. Instead, she held out her hand. "PLEASE, let me drive home, Michael! I love you, baby, but this is ridiculous. It's just a damn game."

"Only a damn game? I've got news for you, little girl. I've been beating my head against the fucking wall playing this damn game for seventeen fucking years! Don't tell me it's just a fucking game when I blew my last chance to go out on top!"

Physically and emotionally spent, Mike pulled a crumpled wad of bills out of his sweats. He peeled off a $100 and stuck it in her face. "Take a fucking cab! I'll see you there. Better yet, go to your own fucking place!" Kim wouldn't take it, so he slapped it in her palm.

Aghast, Kim burst into tears. "Have a nice life, *Steelman!*" She threw the money at him, wheeled around, and walked away. The falling sleet mixed with tears running down her cheeks.

Still clutching the bottle of whiskey, the Steelman watched her. He steadied himself against the Chevy's door and hurled the bottle against the curb. Kim didn't turn around. Mike was coherent enough to know Kim was walking away from him when he needed her most. And she might never come back.

He shouted across the increasing divide between them. "Kim! Come back here, Kim! I wanna talk. Please come back, Kim! I gotta talk to you."

Against her better judgement, Kim turned around. Inexplicably drawn to the pathetic man-child slumped against the door, she took a deep breath and walked back.

The Steelman got in the driver's seat. "I didn't mean it. I just wanna get the fuck home. I'm really sorry!"

Kim leaned in. "Michael, I'm not going to let you kill yourself or someone else. One last time. Please give me the keys." She saw the stick shift. "Does this thing have a regular transmission?"

"Yeah, it has a regular fucking transmission! 4-speed manual."

"I can't drive that. Let's park in that garage and get a cab."

Although still slurring, Mike tried to pull it together enough to sound convincing. "Listen, I'm okay."

"You're not. And neither are the streets."

"Promise, I'll take it slow. You think I want more damage to this thing?"

She looked at Blackwell. "Why is he with you?"

Mike admitted, "I owe him. Almost killed him on national TV."

"What? Never mind. Tell me about it tomorrow." She paused and took a deep breath. "We have a lot to talk about then."

"Come on, get in back. Just crawl over him."

Thinking she could help get them home safely, Kim relented. "Okay! Have it your way. If you kill yourself and Blackwell, you're taking me with you!" She walked around to the passenger side, opened the door and started to climb over Blackwell to get to the back seat, but her instincts told her this wasn't going to work. Nauseous again, Kim rationalized that she could keep Mike focused on the short drive home if she was next to him. Half-sitting on Blackwell's seat and the console, she braced her left arm on Mike's seat back. "God! Please be careful, baby. It's only about two miles. Take your time. The roads look really bad."

He shifted into 1st gear and lurched forward. Kim heard the engine's whine and felt its raw power. The tachometer needle climbed, almost redlining as the rear wheels spun. Jolted forward, she bumped her head on the rear-view mirror. She tried to focus on the road. They were heading north on Michigan Avenue, crossing over the Chicago River.

"How in the hell can you see? Turn on the wipers, baby." Kim's head bumped the mirror again when he shifted into 2nd gear. "Jeez, Mike!"

He fumbled for the wiper switch, clearing the slushy mixture. They passed Chicago Avenue, only a few blocks from the Lake Shore Drive merge, and then it was about a mile to their exit.

I can do this, Kim reassured herself.

"The windshield's fogging up." Kim leaned over, unsuccessfully groping for the defroster. "Where's the switch? Hey! Stop!"

He pulled over, scraping his tires and rims against the curb. Mike hit the brakes. Kim bumped the rear-view mirror for the third time.

"Kim! What the fuck? We're almost on Lake Shore Drive."

"You just ran that red light!" Blackwell rolled slightly. Kim bit her tongue. Pissing him off wasn't going to help.

The Steelman's eyelids were heavy. "I'm fine! JUST BACK OFF!"

This is not the guy I love. What happened to Michael?

The Steelman was in control. Or more accurately, out of it. The SS jerked forward and Mike cut off a silver Audi coupe. It veered sharply left, narrowly missing the Chevy. The driver leaned on the horn. Side by side, they were at a red light at Oak Street. The Audi's passenger window dropped and the horn blared again. The Steelman stared straight ahead, seemingly transfixed by the LSD underpass lights.

"Hey, asshole! What the fuck? You almost ran me into the fucking stoplight! You blind? ASSHOLE!"

He may as well have poked a sleeping bear with a sharp stick. The Steelman threw open his door. Kim grabbed his arm.

"What are you doing? Close the door!"

A glimpse of the imposing figure climbing out of the Chevy was enough to make the driver take off before the light turned green. He barreled north through the underpass, picking up speed despite the icy glaze.

"Michael! Let it go! Just get us home." Tears filled Kim's eyes.

He got back behind the wheel and threw the powerful SS into gear, spinning the rear wheels and fishtailing until the tires bit on the pavement. Quickly, the Steelman caught up to the Audi.

"Jesus! SLOW DOWN! Do you hear me? Leave him alone! You cut him off. What are you doing? Michael, get over, there's the La Salle exit!"

The Chevy was approaching 80 mph, under the worst possible road conditions for an old muscle car with no traction control. Engaged in a game of cat and mouse, neck and neck with the Audi, the SS passed what looked like a Chicago police squad.

Thank God! Never thought I'd be glad to get pulled over.

The Steelman rolled his window down, swerving dangerously close to the Audi. Blasted by the cold rush of wind, Kim turned away toward the ominously pitch-black lake.

"Dammit! You passed it. For heaven's sake, let him alone! Get off at Fullerton!"

Blackwell stirred. The Steelman tried to engage the Audi again.

"HEY! Pull over, motherfucker! Let's go, tough guy! PULL THE FUCK OVER!"

The Chevy swerved left again. Both Audi occupants stared straight ahead which only pissed Mike off even more. Suddenly the driver gunned it into passing gear, separating himself from the Chevy, which began to sway side to side.

Besides the Audi, the road ahead and behind the SS was empty. No flashing police lights. Picking up speed, they passed Fullerton then Diversey Harbor.

Tugging at his arm she implored, "STOP CHASING HIM! PLEASE! MICHAEL, PLEASE, we have a lot to live for!"

The Audi was several hundred yards ahead, blowing past the Belmont exit. Mike downshifted into 3rd gear, accelerating up the banked hill, intent on pursuit.

"Get off now! STOP THIS!" Near the exit, Kim grabbed the wheel, turning it hard right toward the ramp, and shrieked, *"I'M PREGNANT!"*

The Chevy fishtailed left, then sharply right. Mike pulled the wheel back to steady the SS but overcompensated. The Chevy spun around completely before sliding sideways into the curb at 60 mph. Kim's screams were followed by the sound of shattering glass and crushing metal. The SS flipped on its right side, continued down the embankment and rolled completely over again, ejecting precious cargo.

The Audi sped away. The only witnesses, besides Mike, were free. The driver, a La Salle Street lawyer on his way home to the North Shore, had received his second DUI last week.

The mangled midnight blue muscle car rolled end over end one more time, finally landing near the tree that had stopped Kim's airborne, broken body. Tail lights marked the site of death and destruction, illuminating the falling ice needles. They glowed almost blood red.

ROAD TO REDEMPTION

Spring (2007) Forward

Visiting Hours

THURSDAY WAS VISITOR DAY FOR DIVISION 5 INMATES. IN EARLY APRIL, JB SAT down in front of the glass partition and tried to keep it light. "Hey, man. I didn't know they handed out designer sweats at this club."

Jeremy Butler was the first player—and one of the few—to make the trip to Cook County Jail. He wanted his teammate to know that not everyone had walked away from him.

The only other guy who had been to County was Griff. Surprisingly, he was stone cold sober. Having known both Mike and Kim, the situation was still difficult for him to process. Neither one knew what to say during their brief awkward visit.

Butler had come to the Storm in 2004 hoping to play two or three more years and maybe get a ring. JB anchored the pass-rush. He had been chosen to be another piece of the championship puzzle, even if the piece was a little worn around the edges.

More of a loner than Mike Stalowski, Butler didn't joke or talk trash during practice and certainly not during a game. Without saying much, Mike and JB seemed to understand each other. Both were veteran warriors in a game of controlled violence, who did their jobs without much complaint. They would have respected each other on the field even if they weren't defensive brothers.

After the loss of the NFC Championship, Butler quickly realized he wouldn't make it to the "show" and quietly retired shortly after the Super Bowl. His body had been telling him "the bottle is empty—there is no more." So, JB decided to listen and was happy to hang up his cleats. He looked forward to helping provide an alternative to kids with seemingly hopeless futures—like his once was.

Retiring in Chicago brought him close to his home turf of East St. Louis, known for poverty, drugs, and crime. Life in the once-bustling industrial town was bleak. The roads in town offered nothing but dead ends for the mostly minority residents. Football was a way out for some outstanding young athletes. Some with talent made it to college. A few made it to the pros, their ticket to a world of opportunity, fame and fortune.

Jeremy Butler was one of the few who had made it to the top of the pile, just like the hardscrabble kid from Hegewisch. But unlike Mike, at the end of his playing days, JB Butler had not become a caricature of his former self.

Mike's orange shirt and gray sweatpants resembled Storm practice ones, except for the Department of Corrections branding. He was thinner. The Steelman's shoulder-length mane was in a ponytail.

Mike managed a half-smirk, and his vacant eyes became animated. "Yeah, JB. If you think my sweats are sweet, stay for lunch and I'll give you half of my gourmet cheese sandwich. Hey, man, Division 5 is like the Four Seasons. You know, concierge floor for jail VIPs. Very solitary, know what I mean?"

"I figured you'd have lots of friends in here, man. You're personable and people know who you are."

"I don't need any more friends—have enough. Besides, they keep me pretty much isolated."

"Yeah, I know how County is, Steelman."

"What do you know about County, JB? You're not even from Chicago."

"I never knew my old man other than from jail. I been to this place—and others like it—lots of times. The old man split from my mother when I was a little kid. Left me and my six brothers and sisters in that East St. Louis shit hole. Told my mother he was coming up here to make some money, but never said how. Momma suspected he was up to no good. Been locked up before for drugs. Heroin mostly.

"Anyway, Momma knew he wasn't going to work in no factory. Up here he ran with gangsters from the South Side. Took up dealing serious dope, hustling girls, and anything that made cash. Wound up killing someone after he got fucked in a kilo-deal. Heroin did it, man. I was the youngest, so I had to come up here with my mother and auntie, his sister, and listen to the same bullshit. He got twenty-five years and eventually landed in Pontiac which was a little closer. Died in there two years later from hepatitis. Only thirty-four. So yeah, Steelman, I know County."

Jeremy Butler was sharing more with Mike in these few minutes than he had the last three years.

"Hey, JB. Why did you come here? We're not tight, and the newsies will eat you up if they find out."

JB leaned toward the glass. "Look man, I know you're in hell right now. What happened to you and your lady and Blackwell can't be replayed. I'm sorry, man. Truly very sorry. I just want you to know somebody gives a shit. I know the front office and most of the guys probably don't know what to do or say. We know the news media are a bunch of assholes. You been already tried, convicted, and hung— before facing a judge and jury. I just wanted you to know this too shall pass. Have faith, brother."

JB stood up, raising his clenched fist to the glass. The Steelman nodded, silently acknowledging his gesture. "Take care, man. I'll see you again, brother. I'm prayin' for you." As JB turned, Mike saw him wipe away tears. He imagined they weren't the first JB shed at County, making his brief companionship and words of encouragement even more appreciated.

The next time Mike was brought to the visitor's room, Shel Harris was waiting for him. "Mike, I received notice from NFL counsel, that per the Commissioner, you are indefinitely banned from playing in the NFL, pending the outcome of your trial."

Two days later, Harris visited Storm team attorney Carl LeFevour. "Carl, are you saying there's nothing that will change your mind? Come on! Mike's in enough shit right now!"

"I understand, Shel, but we're taking a lot of heat from the Commissioner's office. He wants to send a message. I will tell you, Connie Everett doesn't care one fucking iota what the Commissioner wants. But he'll respect the front office's decision. And *we* decided to not renew his contract and release him immediately."

The Angels of Mercy

<hr>

"Dave, you're the criminal judge. I handle estates, refereeing family bullshit coming from inheritance and greed. Enlighten me. What's the worst that's going to happen if he's convicted? Think he'll see some real jail time?"

On a muggy August morning a few weeks before Mike's trial was scheduled to begin, David John (DJ) Cozzart, Presiding Judge of the Traffic Section, and Joseph "Stacks" Stachowiak, Presiding Judge of the Probate Division, waited for the La Grange 7:35 a.m. Metra express. They were almost neighbors and regular golf partners. Their respective North Side Cubs vs. South Side White Sox baseball allegiances often caused heated discussions over cold beers.

"It's a high-profile case, Joe. He'll be tried by the media circus on every news and sports talk show. I can speculate all flipping morning, but you know as well as I that finding an impartial jury will be tough. He's got a cult following, but he did cause the wreck killing his girlfriend and ruining another guy's career. Who knows? He may get a pass. But from some senior citizen who looks at her picture and hears she was wrapped around a tree? I don't think so. If convicted, his reputation won't help. With all the screw-ups professional athletes are getting away with, he could get significant prison time to make an example."

Boarding the train, Joe asked in a muffled voice, "Do you know who's hearing the case?"

"I might do it myself. Or maybe appoint Joan Pendleton. She's the senior female and has high-profile DUI credentials. She made it as the District's first minority female all on her own, so she doesn't owe anyone. In Cook County that's impressive!"

They both chuckled.

"She won't take any shit from the media or lawyers on either side. Why the questions, Joe?"

"I'll tell you a little secret when we get off." Both men settled into newspapers. Chicago really has two seasons: winter and construction. Rebuilding the Jackson Street Bridge was taking forever so they were forced to wade almost single-file through the commuter sea of humanity outside Union Station. Finally, across the river on Wacker Drive, Cozzart couldn't wait any longer. "What's your secret?"

Joe Stacks weighed in about 270 lbs., close to his Notre Dame playing weight. He felt the effects of being sixty-plus-years-old with bad knees. Thanks to the mercury approaching 80 degrees before 8:00 a.m., his brow dripped beads of sweat.

"Dave, I feel kind of paranoid even bringing this up. But with the feds looking over our shoulders most of the time, I have to know." Joe grinned as they rounded the corner by Sears Tower. "You wearing a wire?"

"Surely not! The County's cleaned up its act since Greylord!" Cozzart sarcastically referenced the 1970s scandal involving Cook County judges who accepted bribes.

"Never mentioned it, but I've known Mike Stalowski since he was a boy. His dad Frank and I were close. He was actually my best man. Frank's family came from Poland when he was a kid. Died young... probably only forty. That damn muscle car the Steelman wrecked was his uncle's. *I* drove Frank to the dealership to pick it up for his brother Mike! Poor kid died in 'Nam right before he was supposed to come home. The Steelman seems to be a lot like Frank, quiet but hot-headed. I lost touch with the family after Frank died, and the rest with Mike is history. Hegewisch kid living the NFL dream. Only now it's a nightmare."

"So what's the secret?"

"Recently, Father John MacKenzie calls me. Runs the Angels of Mercy Home, the orphanage on Roosevelt near UIC. Been there since the 1870s. Anyway, he calls me out of the blue and we end up talking about Stalowski's arrest and upcoming trial. So the priest—he likes to be called Father Mac—coached Stalowski at St. Michael's. They were a Catholic League powerhouse for years, until the coaching staff recently fell apart. You're a half-Jewish Northsider, so I know your world stops in the South Loop, probably at Manny's Deli near Roosevelt, the street Northsiders fear crossing."

DJ smiled when Joe busted on him. "Okay, so?"

"Father Mac wanted to know—hypothetically of course—if Stalowski got convicted and somehow sentenced to house arrest, could I maybe help get his time served at the orphanage. Crazy request, huh? And from a Catholic priest!"

"What? You actually engaged him in conversation like maybe it *can* or *is* going to happen?" Cozzart was shocked. "Where does he get off calling a judge to influence a trial? Why you?"

"Claims he remembered me from my high school and ND playing days. He played at ND in the '50s. And also from their annual fundraiser, the one Sonny goes to every year. Took a shot in the dark calling me."

"How old is this priest?"

"I don't know, probably seventies."

"I'm thinking dementia! What are you asking me, Joe? Get Stalowski convicted by instructing the jury to return a guilty verdict? Wait! I know. Talk the lawyers into a plea, count time served, and then sentence him *to rehab with his old coach at a kids' orphanage*. That's a hell of a plan. Good luck with that one! What, does Father whatever-his-name-is think he's going to save the Steelman from himself?"

"After talking to him for quite a while, Dave, I sincerely think he does. He mentored Stalowski after his old man died. Said he's followed his career—good and bad. He thinks he can get through to him—if he can get his hands on him." He paused. "He simply wanted to make it known he wants to try."

Stacks continued, "Maybe it's not so crazy, DJ. Stalowski came from a good family. I owe his dad. Thought twice about bringing it up, but figured why not? Look at all the pros who get lucky breaks, in the courtroom and from the media. Most don't deserve it. Maybe he does. I'm just putting it out there."

Judge Cozzart pondered Joe's words but remained silent. They said goodbye when they reached the County Courthouse and parted ways, heading to different floors on different missions, but both ultimately tasked with ensuring justice was served in Cook County.

Over the next few weeks, both mediocre baseball teams were under .500 again, so Chicago sports fans turned to the intrigue of Storm summer camp, minus the Steelman. The drama of Mike's impending trial remained daily news. Right through the Labor Day holiday, the Cook County State's Attorney's prosecution team strategized daily. Chicago and the greater sports world would be watching closely.

Kenneth Hairston led the prosecution. In his late thirties, he was articulate and charismatic. Unlike the Steelman, he relished media attention. Hairston was big on style and delivery, recognizing the importance of presenting a positive image, especially to the African-American community. Impeccably dressed, his Italian shoes always polished to a high gloss, he commanded attention when he strode into the courtroom.

Hairston carefully orchestrated his team. Assistant State's Attorney Dennis Kincaid, a chain-smoking, twenty-seven-year veteran of the office, put away numerous high-profile DUI defendants, despite their social status and big checkbooks. Assistant State's Attorney Nora Rodriguez, a rising star in the office, would play an integral part of jury impact. Nora was eight months pregnant.

On September 6, 2007, the bailiff declared court in session.

"Good morning, ladies and gentlemen." Judge Joan Pendleton spoke sternly. "To be clear, you should not have any cameras, phones, or other recording devices in your possession even if they are turned off. I will not tolerate any disrespectful language or behavior. Bailiff, what is today's case?"

"Your Honor, it is the People of the County of Cook of the State of Illinois versus Michael J. Stalowski."

Kenneth Hairston stood, ready to open the State's case. Across the aisle, Mike Stalowski was subdued and stared down at the table. He wore a dark gray suit. In typical Steelman style, his lavender shirt's top button was left open above the tie. Despite strong suggestions by legal counsel, the Steelman did not cut his hair or shave closely.

No matter how hard he tried, Mike could not bring himself to look at Kim's parents. Kate and Bryce Richardson sat stoically, very much out of place in the dingy Chicago courtroom, far from their oceanfront estate. They put up a united front for their only child—dead almost eight months—long enough for Kim to have given birth. No sweet grandbaby pictures to share. Instead they would be bombarded with enlarged photos of Kim's battered and broken body.

"Ladies and gentlemen of the jury," Hairston began firmly, "let me take you to the pitch-black early morning hours of January 21, 2007, on a slippery and treacherous stretch of Lake Shore Drive. We know what happened. The lives of Kimberly Richardson and her unborn child ended as the result of a reckless automobile accident caused by the defendant, Michael Stalowski. Let me also share how an athlete with a promising career in professional football was robbed of his dream, to achieve the success Mr. Stalowski enjoyed for numerous seasons with the Chicago Storm.

"The Cook County State's Attorney's Office has the responsibility to prove its case *beyond a reasonable doubt*. Some of the photographic evidence presented to you and some of the testimony you will hear are disturbing. But the evidence will overwhelmingly show, and it is my intention to prove—*beyond a reasonable doubt*—*that Mr. Stalowski is guilty* of the charges brought against him."

Hairston changed his tone to informative. "Illinois law permits a DUI or *driving under the influence* charge two ways. Very simply, having a blood alcohol level of .08 or more, or being incapable of driving in a safe manner due to the ingestion of alcohol and/or drugs. Illinois law states, 'A person commits the offense of aggravated reckless homicide when he or she unintentionally causes the death of an individual by recklessly driving a motor vehicle in a manner likely to cause death or great bodily harm while under the influence of alcohol or any other drug or drugs.' An aggravated reckless homicide charge increases the severity of the crime and must confirm impairment with a blood alcohol level over the legal limit."

The prosecutor continued conversationally. "When the State proves its case against Mr. Stalowski, you will clearly see there is more than the allegation the defendant was driving drunk. So, when you follow Judge Pendleton's instructions to the jury, requiring all parts of this statute be met, *you must find Michael Stalowski is guilty beyond a reasonable doubt.*"

Hairston had everyone's attention, especially the defense. He enumerated the legal "groundballs" Mike Stalowski hit to the State's Attorney:

"To sustain the charge of aggravated reckless homicide, the State must prove the following propositions:

"First—The defendant caused the death of Kimberly Richardson and her unborn child by driving a motor vehicle;

"Second—The defendant drove the motor vehicle recklessly;

"Third—The defendant drove the motor vehicle in a manner likely to cause death or great bodily harm;

"Fourth—The defendant was under the influence of alcohol or any other drug or drugs."

Finally, he concluded, "The evidence presented and witness testimony will prove each one of these propositions beyond a reasonable doubt. Therefore, *you must find the defendant Michael J. Stalowski guilty.*"

Clearly it was a lock-tight case. Those propositions had been covered extensively in the media.

Which is why Carl LeFevour, understanding the grave situation facing one of Conrad Everett's most popular players, had turned to the law firm of Edelstein, Conrad, and Shapiro. Harry Shapiro, who began his legal career as an Assistant U.S. Attorney in the Eastern District of New York, led the defense. A Columbia grad, he made a name for himself prosecuting political corruption embedded in the New York labor unions in the '70s and '80s. Much to the surprise of colleagues who expected he would succeed the incumbent U.S. Attorney, Shapiro left the Big Apple for the Second City to become a high-priced defense attorney. Harry found loopholes and technicalities not readily apparent to the average attorney.

Samuel Goodman was his assistant, along with Barbara Lukasik, who had a strong track record defending DUI cases with fatalities. Interestingly, Lukasik was a former Catholic nun who had left the Dominican Order after eleven years in religious life. She became a successful attorney, known for delivering impassioned closing arguments.

Mike and Harry didn't connect. First off, Harry wasn't a football fan and definitely did not approve of the Steelman's appearance or reported lifestyle and notoriety. He felt Mike didn't understand the gravity of the charges and the possible sentence he faced if convicted. Mike was disengaged from his defense.

His lawyers' questions, regarding events in the week leading up to the wreck, received short answers, if any. He did not offer insight into his relationship with Kim or the sequence of post-game events. Mike said he couldn't remember much other than getting to the Sunset Grill after an admitted drinking binge. Although he did not articulate it, Shapiro sensed the Steelman just wanted to get it over with. It seemed he was resigned to his fate and simply didn't care what happened.

Nevertheless, even with the deck stacked against him, Shapiro thought he might get Mike to plead down to lesser charges or possibly convince the jury that Mike was also a victim—of fate. If he carefully and precisely built his case as an *accidental death*, based on physical conditions and circumstance, Mike might get a lighter sentence if convicted. The burden of proof was on Hairston. Technicalities would make proving the Steelman's recklessness for conviction on aggravated charges very difficult. Shapiro knew—at the very least—he could cast doubt on witness testimony.

The order of witnesses for the prosecution was arranged methodically to build drama around the accident scene. First up was the Chicago Police Major Accidents Unit Reconstruction Specialist. His testimony was painfully technical and boring, complete with skid mark diagrams and calculations of estimated speed before the rollover crash.

Officer George Gibson, the first responder to the accident scene, was next. He looked stiff and uncomfortable in his dress uniform when called to the witness stand. Gibson did not care for traffic court, except speeders considered "grounders," which paid four hours of overtime even if the hearing took five minutes. This trial was no grounder. Out of the blue, immediately after an extremely tense Gibson swore to tell the truth, the defense requested a sidebar.

"Your Honor, we have decided to stipulate to statements regarding questions 3-14, taken during the witness's deposition May 13, 2007."

Judge Pendleton was somewhat surprised. If Hairston agreed, the enumerated questions and answers concerning Gibson's observations and actions on Lake Shore Drive—prior to the crash and immediately after arriving at the accident scene— would enter into the court record without Gibson testifying in open court and being subject to cross-examination.

Kenneth Hairston did a quick mental review.

George Gibson's deposition answers, alluding to a drag race between *what could have been* Mike's 1970 Chevrolet muscle car and an unknown vehicle, were openly speculative. His testimony could help or hurt the state's case. Proving, *beyond a reasonable doubt*, their case of aggravated reckless homicide depended on Gibson's convincing testimony. Gibson might not hold up to Shapiro's cross-examination.

The scene of the fatal accident confirmed Mike Stalowski was the driver who acted recklessly and in a manner "likely to cause death or great bodily harm" to the vehicle occupants. If Gibson testified that he witnessed a probable drag race, under the worst of weather conditions, involving a similar vehicle to the one that moments later crashed on Lake Shore Drive, the Steelman's case was over. Kenneth Hairston even had a full-size 1970 Chevrolet Super Sport advertising poster ready to refresh his memory. However—and it was a potentially monumental however—Hairston knew if the defense probed Gibson and did not elicit Hairston's desired responses, it could backfire on the prosecution implicating Stalowski *beyond a reasonable doubt.*

Of course, Harry Shapiro would try to drive a wedge of doubt into the jury. The Cook County State's Attorney's Office would describe the horrific scene in graphic detail. The defense would concentrate on limiting Mike's culpable actions. Shapiro would strive to portray that the scene was *the result of an accident—not a willful reckless act.*

Hairston decided not to risk Gibson's cross-examination.

He agreed the deposition would enter into the court record without testimony. Officer Gibson was relieved he would not have to lie under oath to protect himself and the Steelman. Keenly aware he shirked his duty and responsibility by not immediately responding when the vehicles roared past him, he had to live with the knowledge he might have prevented the accident. Harry Shapiro's strategy cut him a big break!

"Court is adjourned until 1:00 p.m." Judge Pendleton pounded her gavel. Although the defense scored a few points by avoiding the officer's testimony, Hairston was confident Drs. Scanlon and Davis would deliver a graphic description of the post mortem findings, particularly the discovery of Kim's pregnancy.

Hairston held a strategy session during lunch. Pregnancy food cravings necessitated a chili dog and fruit smoothie for Nora. Kincaid opted to grab a 32-ounce Coke and fresh pack of Marlboros. Hairston drank Evian water and read over the doctors' depositions.

"Nora, you're going to lead off. Call Jake Davis first. The free spirit from, *you know, dude, LA.* Start with questions about the victim's physical trauma, then the discovery she was pregnant."

"Got it!" Nora patted her ready-to-pop belly and smiled.

"If that doesn't impact the jury, I'll quit this God-awful job."

Kincaid nodded approval while slurping his near-empty Coke. Hairston could already imagine the jury foreman reading the guilty verdict.

After lunch, spectators filled Courtroom 104. The Richardsons took their seats. Glancing frequently at his watch, Bryce clearly wanted to be anywhere else. Janet and Tom Dennison sat two rows behind the defense team. Both mothers had experienced a grievous loss: Kate, her only child; Janet, hope for her son's future. Tragically, they shared the loss of their unborn grandchild. An elderly man with a white crew-cut, wearing a black suit, sat near the back, staring straight ahead, both hands on top of the cane between his legs. He would have gone unnoticed, if not for his religious collar.

The prosecution filed in confidently. Stalowski was led in by two Sheriff's Deputies. Mike instinctively glanced around the courtroom and fixed on the man in the black suit. For a split second, their steel gazes met. Even after thirteen years, there was no mistaking his former Dean of Discipline. Mike had heard Father Mac retired some years earlier and couldn't imagine why he was here.

Dr. Davis was sworn in. Nora determinedly waddled to the witness box.

"Do you recall your answers to the questions I posed at your deposition earlier this year?"

"Truthfully, I do not. I remember the deposition and that the questions dealt with the autopsy of an adult female who died in a car accident."

"For the benefit of your testimony today, please review your answers as I would like to ask specific questions regarding the post mortem report completed by you and Dr. Scanlon."

Davis quietly looked over the twelve-page deposition, not at all concerned that the courtroom was waiting. After five minutes, Judge Pendleton asked if he was ready to continue. He was not. A few moments later, he looked up and pushed the deposition to the side.

"Dr. Davis, can you summarize the extent of the trauma the victim sustained, which is detailed in this report?" Rodriguez held up a bound document, much thicker than the deposition.

"Objection, Your Honor! Counsel's reference to Ms. Richardson as a victim is leading the witness by providing the jury with a predisposed assumption of her fate." Barbara Lukasik spoke clearly and emphatically.

"Sustained. Ms. Rodriguez, please refer to the deceased by her name going forward." Lukasik fired the first round and was satisfied with her shot.

After a slight eye roll, Nora rephrased the question. "Dr. Davis, can you tell the court your findings from the post mortem of . . . Kim . . . Richardson . . . after her death was pronounced at the hospital?"

Dr. Davis gave a monotone, but graphic description of Kim's broken bones and multiple lacerations. His follow-up remarks should have iced the State's case for the aggravated reckless homicide of Kim Richardson and her unborn child.

"A broken neck does not always, but may cause death. The spinal cord is very sensitive to injury. If the spinal cord is injured at or above the fifth cervical vertebra, one could die from asphyxiation. Transection of the spinal cord leads to loss of nerve supply in the body including the heart, resulting in sudden death. Kim Richardson's fractured vertebrae, resulting in her death, were the direct result of her ejection through the windshield of the vehicle."

"Do you mean that because Ms. Richardson wore no seatbelt or restraint— *which were not installed in the defendant's vehicle*—her body was violently propelled through the glass with such force that her neck snapped when her head hit the windshield?"

"*Objection*, Your Honor! Counsel is leading the witness again."

"Sustained, Ms. Lukasik."

The judge's ruling didn't matter. The damage was done.

Up to this point, Mike stared at the untouched legal pad before him or rested his chin on his thumbs and closed his eyes. He seemed unaffected by Davis' graphic testimony. Nothing could be further from the truth. Repressed memories of what happened that night were coming into focus. Bits and pieces of his alcoholic haze— Kim crying and begging for the keys—Blackwell passed out in the passenger's seat— Kim half on the console, half on Blackwell's seat—the Audi—Kim screaming *"I'm pregnant!"* and yanking the steering wheel. And finally, the Grim Reaper beckoning as the Chevy SS hurtled off the embankment.

Suddenly, Mike turned to look over his right shoulder. His painful glance at the Richardsons, the only one during the trial, did not go unnoticed. Mike clearly saw Kim's face—perhaps in a vision and only for a second—between her parents, looking like an angel with sad eyes.

"Dr. Davis, do you mean that if Ms. Richardson had been seated and belted into one of the seats of the automobile from which she was ejected, her sustained injuries could have been less severe and not fatal?"

"Probably. Yes."

Harry Shapiro was taking notes when Mike leaned over to whisper in his ear. Shapiro dropped his pencil and stood up.

"Your Honor, I request an immediate side bar."

"Mr. Shapiro, you are out of order. Please take your seat until the witness is excused."

"Hey, Judge, I've got something to say—to you and everybody else in this room."

There was a collective gasp. The Steelman essentially pushed Harry Shapiro aside like a rookie offensive lineman. Mike changed the play himself—calling an audible on the field against the wishes of the defensive coordinator. The Steelman looked around the courtroom, then back at the bench.

"The whole thing is on me. My lawyer is only speaking up 'cause I told him to. If I wouldn't have wrecked out we wouldn't be here right now." Looking directly at Judge Pendleton, Mike Stalowski loudly proclaimed, "I want to change my plea to guilty."

The courtroom was in chaos. The jury was stunned. Since cell phones were not allowed, the journalists who snagged seats were taking furious handwritten notes, preparing to launch Mike's statement once they could break out of their seats. Kenneth Hairston and his team sat in disbelief.

Judge Pendleton cracked her gavel several times and shouted over the commotion. "Order! Order in this court! First off, Mr. Stalowski, you will address me as Your Honor. Secondly, I am asking you to take your seat immediately. Dr. Davis, you are excused. Mr. Hairston and Mr. Shapiro, please approach the bench."

After five minutes of muffled discussion, the lead attorneys took their seats.

"Mr. Stalowski, please rise and repeat your statement for the court record."

Mike Stalowski turned around, singled out Father Mac and looked him straight in the eyes. Father Mac didn't flinch, his hands still resting on top of his cane. Expressionless, he stared at his former student and football captain. Mike turned back to face Judge Pendleton. "I'm guilty, your Honor. That's it."

What was expected to be a two-to-three-week trial was cut short on the first day of testimony by the defendant. Mike had given his confession to Father Mac, just as he had years ago at St. Michael's, only now in a crowded courtroom. At St. Michaels, he may have been assigned prayers for penance or a Saturday jug—maybe received corporal punishment from Father Mac. But this time, Judge Pendleton would use the Illinois Criminal Sentencing Guidelines to administer punishment for Mike's admitted felony.

Yet, Father Mac was hopeful. He just might have the opportunity to save the Steelman from himself.

Judge Pendleton adjourned for the afternoon. On September 10 she formally accepted Mike Stalowski's plea, ordered a presentence investigation and set September 28 for a status hearing. In early October, Pendleton had a brief and to-the-point phone conversation. No one wanted to prolong the discussion, or dwell on favors called in, as she weighed her options regarding Mike Stalowski's sentence.

"I will consider the location, Dave. An orphanage west of the Loop, is that right?"

"Yes. Thanks, Joan."

On October 26, Mike Stalowski again stood before the Honorable Joan Pendleton.

"Mr. Stalowski, do you understand that you are pleading guilty to the aggravated reckless homicide of Kimberly Richardson and her unborn child?"

"Yes, I do, your Honor."

"Do you understand your driving privileges are hereby revoked indefinitely by the State of Illinois and any eventual restoration of your driving privileges will be determined via a petition to the Chief Judge of the Cook County Circuit Court, which may not be filed while you are incarcerated."

"Yes, your Honor."

"Very well, then. By order of the Circuit Court of Cook County, you are hereby sentenced to three years of incarceration with eighteen months suspended. If you violate any terms of your sentence, your incarceration will commence in full. Consideration is given for time already served in Cook County Jail. You will complete the remainder of your eighteen-month incarceration—confined to and performing community service at—the Angels of Mercy Home, a residential facility for orphaned children located in Chicago, Illinois.

"You will wear an electronic monitoring bracelet. You are forbidden from leaving the premises, for any reason, without petitioning this court and receiving judicial dispensation. Any visitors will require approval from Father John MacKenzie, President of the Angels of Mercy Home.

"You will be released from the custody of the Cook County Department of Corrections on November 2, 2007, and placed in the custody of Father John MacKenzie at the Angels of Mercy Home. Your confinement and community service will conclude on July 25, 2008.

"Upon successful completion of all provisions of this Order, you will be released on your own recognizance to continue your sentence of an additional three years probation, reporting to your Cook County Department of Corrections probation officer. Prior to your release date, you will appear before this court for a final status hearing. Do you understand the provisions of your sentence, Mr. Stalowski?"

"Yes, I do."

Hairston's team was surprised by the light sentence but did not challenge it. His guilty plea was still their victory.

Less than a week later, November 2, 2007—coincidentally All Souls Day— Mike was transported—body and soul—to the Angels of Mercy Home under the guardianship of Father Mac, his former Dean of Discipline.

"Somebody"

SINCE 1957, THE FRIENDS OF THE ANGELS OF MERCY CHRISTMAS GALA Luncheon had been attended by prominent and wealthy Chicagoans. Word on the street was if you were "somebody" in Chicago, you were at the luncheon. The Cardinal of the Archdiocese of Chicago gave his annual blessing, followed by inspirational remarks from other interfaith clergy. The highlight for both attendees and news media was the kids' entertainment.

A week before the 50th anniversary gala, Father Mac was tying up loose ends in his all-out effort to secure the largest audience and donations in gala history. Father Mac's Wednesday afternoon visitor was definitely "somebody."

"Mac, thanks for meeting with me. You know I had a good year, so here's a little something for the kids." He passed a white envelope across the desk to his old friend.

Father Mac opened it to find a check for $500,000. "What's this, Connie? Sure it won't bounce?" Both men had a laugh.

"Use it for maintenance," replied the perennial benefactor.

"Connie, you're good to us every year. But this is a lot of money." Father Mac closed the envelope and tucked it in his jacket. "I'm very grateful to you for all . . ."

"So, how's Mike?" Connie interrupted.

"He's definitely here! Can't miss him. Been a little over a month now, but I think it's going to take some time. He keeps to himself, and other than the rules, I really haven't talked with him much one-on-one."

"Do you think he knows we're friends?"

"Why would he, Connie? In time, I'll bring it up if you want to talk to him."

"Let him settle in. I've got many phone calls to make if he's ever going to get back in the league. Carl LeFevour called the Commissioner. We may meet with him in New York after the holidays."

The two old friends shared a cup of coffee, talking local politics and Angels of Mercy Home finances. Connie rose from his chair.

"Mac, I won't be here this year. Too much for the media. Plus, seeing Mike under the circumstances wouldn't be good for him. You let me know when you think the time is right, okay?"

Father Mac stood up and they shook hands. "Sure enough, Connie. Take care and best to the family. Good luck in the playoffs!"

"Ha, we'll need it. The defense isn't the same. I truly believe this thing with Mike rocked every one of the players and coaches, let alone the rest of the organization."

Everett turned to leave, then paused in the doorway. "Mac, one more thing. I have to tell you something in confidence only a handful of people left on earth might own up to knowing."

Father Mac sank back into his chair.

Connie spoke with heaviness in his voice. "I won't burden you with all the details, Mac. It's been a very, very long time, but I was once in Mike's shoes." Connie took a few steps forward to stand across the desk of his old friend, a priest who had not anticipated a confession almost sixty years in the making.

"High school buddies on the GI Bill home for our first Christmas break from college. We went partying one night at an Irish bar. Fitz's, I think, on Western Avenue. Remember Fitz's? My old man drank there with his crews just about daily. Chicago cops, firemen, construction guys, garbage men all drank together. Usually too much.

"Well, that night, we closed the place. I was way too drunk to drive my dad's new Cadillac even the short ride to Morgan Park. Had three guys in the car and heading down the hill on 111th Street, I ran the light at 111th and Longwood. Slammed broadside into a Ford with a kid and his girlfriend. Totaled both cars. All the guys were okay, but the girl was messed up pretty bad. She wound up in a wheelchair. My old man cut a deal with the cops and a judge he knew. I got off clean, but it cost him big money all the way around."

He looked plaintively at Father Mac. "I was blessed to get a second chance. I've tried to pay it forward and do my best to help those who need it. Off the field—Mike needs someone in his corner—and I believe it's you. No pressure, Mac," he smiled, "but there's not a lot of time left. I'm looking to you for divine intervention."

The Dean of Discipline

FATHER MAC KNEW MANY PEOPLE, REGARDLESS OF THEIR FAITH, WERE MORE hopeful and generous at this time of year. *Shining Star*, the gala's theme, referred to the one that shone brightly above the stable where Jesus was born. To spark this year's fundraising efforts, the Home presold $25,000 Gold and $10,000 Silver pledge stars which would adorn Guardian Hall during the gala. Following the children's entertainment, in honor of the golden anniversary, a live auction for *The Shining Star* would open with a $50,000 bid. The powerful combination of a sincere desire to help—and the opportunity to be photographed with the largest, most expensive and tax-deductible gold star—almost guaranteed eager outbidding by the attendees.

Although gala fundraising was top of mind, Father Mac was concerned about Mike. He hoped, during his short time here, the humble and benevolent surroundings of the Angels of Mercy Home would begin to renew Mike's faith and positively affect his judgment. The priest firmly believed what his faith promised: the forgiveness of sins, atonement, and redemption—all beginning with the birth of the baby in the manger.

Mike was tasked with Guardian Hall gala set-up. After arranging the tables, he watched older kids helping younger ones with garlands, colored lights, and posters. Mike stared at the manger, which served as his silent "Ghost of Christmas Past." He saw himself as a St. Florian's altar boy, helping with Christmas decorations, and playing a shepherd in the first grade Nativity. Mike's whole family was there, and his dad winked at him after his two lines.

His mind's eye enjoyed the Christmas lights illuminating Hegewisch homes and the little shops and restaurants on Baltimore Street. Mike remembered hanging the outside lights the first Christmas after his father died. His mother had not asked, but he had felt compelled when Anna mentioned how nice other houses looked lit up. Mike had been unable to arrange them as straight and evenly spaced as Frank. So he had hung them his own way. Some bulbs were burned out, but he had figured overall the strings brought a bit of color and light into the Stalowski house that mournful Christmas.

Mike also remembered how lost and alone he had felt searching for the lights. While rummaging through stacked boxes in the garage, he had found his father's fishing and softball equipment. The lights had been buried on the dusty tarp covering a lifeless car.

If only that fucking car had stayed there and I didn't restore it. I wouldn't be in this place. Like a fucking eternal jug!

Mike was still stinging from a lunchroom interrogation. Walter, a slight boy in a wheelchair, had rolled up to him.

"Why did you drink and kill that lady?" Walter spoke with a slight accent. The directness of his inquisition stunned Mike.

"Huh? What do you mean, kid? I don't know what you're talking about," he lied.

"I heard from bigger boys what you did and now you are here for punishment."

"It's my business!" Mike walked away, not looking for confrontation with anyone, let alone a handicapped kid.

Later, a teacher who overheard the conversation told him Walter's parents were killed and he ended up in a wheelchair because of a drunk driver. Mike began pacing, unable to face a seven-year-old kid reminding him of the terrible events he set in motion.

This kid doesn't know the whole fucking story! He's barely old enough for school. How does he know what it's like to be humiliated on national TV during a championship game? He leaned against the wall and rubbed his temples. *Everyone knows I killed Kim and cost another guy his career. What if I crawled into a cab and not the car when we left the bar that night?*

Mike's mind raced. He figured Father Mac purposely set him up to face his demons. The old Dean of Discipline was obviously using Catholic guilt as his hammer on Mike. Seeing kids like Walter would drive home that he was an alcoholic whose life spun out of control on Lake Shore Drive.

Screw him! I quit cold turkey. No shakes, no sweats. My problem is getting the hell out of here.

Mike was determined to set the record straight with Father Mac. At his office, Mike peered through the crack in the doorway. Impulsively, he pushed the door wide open and barged up to Father Mac, who was seated at his massive desk.

"Hey, Father Mac! You set me up, man! And I don't like it." He glared and pointed a finger at the elderly priest. Mike's voice reverberated throughout the room. "You can keep your Angels of Mercy Home. I don't belong here, and you set me up." The Steelman bellowed again. "Call Pendleton! I want out, now!"

Father Mac stood up, almost even-eyed with him. He took off his reading glasses. "Mike, what the hell are you talking about? Set you up how? And with whom?"

"With the kid in the wheelchair. I saw him in the dining hall. He looked up at me like I was the freakin' devil or worse. Asked me why I drank and killed that lady. What the hell am I supposed to tell a little kid sitting in a freakin' wheelchair? Why did you put this B.S. in his head? None of these kids should know who I am. Is this your idea of a joke?"

Father Mac came around his desk and locked his own icy blue stare on Mike. It brought Mike back to his first ass-chewing freshman year.

"Now you listen to me. I had nothing to do with your conversation with the 'kid in the wheelchair.' You're not thinking straight. These kids aren't stupid. They figured out pretty quickly you weren't part of the regular staff. A lot of them know who the hell you are and what happened.

"And as for that kid, Walter's family came from the Czech Republic about five years ago to build a better life. Back home his father was a concert violinist, and his mother was a journalist. To live the American Dream his dad refinished furniture and gave private violin lessons while his mother waitressed at a Polish restaurant on Milwaukee.

"Cops said the driver, who was barely scratched, spent six hours in a tavern before he got behind the wheel and broadsided the family. Walter's mother died at the scene. His father lived two more days. The boy is paralyzed from the waist down.

"Nine months and still DCFS can't locate any relatives or friends. He's mine until I can find a better situation for him. And I doubt he cares squat about football or your damn fame and reputation!"

Mike stood silently and expressionless. Father Mac got in his face. "Now, Mr. Man of Steel! Mr. NFL All-Pro linebacker! How and why did you get here? Huh? Want to know?"

The ferocious caricature of a man, who had been paid big money to cause mayhem on a football field, stood before his old Dean of Discipline, unable to look him in the eye. Mike knew what was coming.

Father Mac tore into him, each phrase more emphatic than the one before. He slammed his fist down on the desk.

"I brought you here, Mike! Do you think for a minute some lawyer cut some kind of deal?" The corners of Father Mac's mouth began to twitch. "I followed you, from college to the Storm. I watched your pro career. Seventh-round pick. NFL Defensive Rookie of the Year. I read the papers and saw the sports channels as you threw it all away, devolving into the NFL's premier bad boy—the guy with a chip on his shoulder always getting in and out of trouble. Of course, I heard about the accident.

"I called Judge Stachowiak and asked him to help me, help you. I wanted you to serve your time here, not some B.S. rehab facility for the stars. He knew you as a kid from the old neighborhood. He told me he loved your old man and he would do his best. Because you were Frank's son, not because you make asinine commercials and rock videos. Yes, I asked for a shot at helping you! That's why you're here!"

Mike shook his head. *This has nothing to do with my father.*

Father Mac loudly continued, "I first knew you as a talented kid who played high school football with all his heart, but led with his head. When you came to St. Mike's after losing your dad, you needed support and direction. And you sure as hell need it now!"

Mike balled his fists and crossed his arms. *I don't need nothing from you.*

Father Mac stepped back toward his desk but pointed emphatically. "You were given a gift, the raw physical talent to play football. How many guys from Chicago, let alone the old neighborhood, had your talent? How many even made it to college football, let alone the NFL? Not many. I can think of only one other guy from the South Side who had your talent and success. He wore #51, and he played with an attitude like you. But he knew how to handle it, off the field in his daily life. You started out as a gifted athlete but became a damn cartoon character."

Father Mac sat down and leaned back in his desk chair. Quietly, with a crack in his voice, he said, "Look at you, Mike. Look in the mirror. Who are you really? Who remembers or cares about the guy who wore Storm #52?" Sitting up straight, he returned to full volume. "You think you're some kind of badass because you have a bunch of tattoos and earrings, don't you? Well, you're not. You're a creation of the media, your fans, and some crazy, twisted image you have of yourself. Look at what you've thrown away!"

Mike stood his ground, looking down at Father Mac without so much as flinching.

"I know you had values and morals growing up. You think you're the rebel without a cause like James Dean? Well, your *fans* think you're a *lost cause,* and James Dean died in a damn car wreck fifty years ago." He shook his head. "He had an attitude and a chip on his shoulder too which ruined him at a young age. Mike, you've been successful and made a boatload of money doing what other guys only dream about. But along the way, you've made more and more piss-poor choices with each passing day."

Father Mac slammed his fist again. "Your attitude and carelessness cost a beautiful young woman her life and a talented football player a promising career. For what? Because you blew a play and couldn't handle the loss of a championship game?" He stood up and faced Mike directly. "You played in the damn NFL nine years, college and high school ball—and you never experienced failure? Of course you did! How DO you handle failure, Mike? Violence, alcohol and drugs? Your only choice that night was to drink yourself into oblivion and roll that car into a deathtrap, right? You had plenty of choices! And YOU made the WRONG one! Do you hear me?"

Father Mac was spent and sank back into his leather chair. He was done laying out the facts of Mike Stalowski's life.

"You done, Father?" Mike fired back. "I guess we've all made mistakes. How about you guys in the black uniforms with white collars?" Mike glared and pointed his finger at Father Mac. "You guys always play it straight around kids?"

"What does that have to do with you? God will judge each of us when it is our time to die. Your sins, your atonement for them, and your redemption will all be taken into account. As it always has been—your life's destiny is in your hands."

"Hasn't child abuse cost the church some rent money and news time the last few years? Did priests worry about the choices they made? I don't think so."

"Again, Mike, you weren't sentenced to jail—and now here—to discuss the failings of others."

"You've still got nerve accusing me of bad choices." His voice cracked. "What

I got," Mike emphasized his point by poking his finger into his own chest, "what I do, is because of me. Nobody gave me nothin' in life. My old man died when I was a kid. My mother barely kept the roof over our heads. Nobody came around to help except Uncle Casey sometimes. I was on my own!"

Mike noticed his hands were trembling.

"I make my decisions based on my gut," he said. "I paid my dues, on the field and off."

Father Mac sat up straight in his chair and folded his hands on his desk. "When I was a young man at Notre Dame, I thought with my fists. I was probably a better boxer than a football player. I had the same attitude as you, Mike. My way or the highway. Stand back or I'll take you out. Well, guess what? Someone took me and my knee out in a football game we were supposed to win big. Never regained my playing form. Wound up feeling sorry for myself and hating everyone. My football and boxing careers were over.

"Around Christmas, one of my professors who was a priest asked me to visit some sick kids in the local hospital while I rehabbed. He thought it might take my mind off my own misery. I said no, but I think our Lord intervened, eventually guiding me there, and changed my life. Those kids, some terminally ill, made me realize there was another calling for me. I pursued my vocation and have been helping all those in need, young and old, ever since.

"Maybe it's time for you to reflect and go in another direction. Maybe our Lord has another plan for you. Did you ever think of that? Maybe you can help someone with greater needs. You don't have to keep going through life with that chip. How long have you been carrying it? I'm guessing since your dad got sick.

"Mike, can you tell me what really happened the last few years? You're a gifted athlete who made mistakes. You're sure as hell not the only casualty of fame and fortune. But it's not too late."

With that, Father Mac reimmersed himself with the papers on his desk. It appeared the confrontation had little effect on Mike. He was still an angry man. Father Mac knew it would take time for Mike to fully—with heart and soul—accept responsibility for his actions.

Mike realized he just argued with the Dean of Discipline, who even fifteen years ago, would have invited him into the boxing ring to settle the score. Mike also knew he was confined to AOMH until the end of July and had no intention of going the distance with him. One round was enough.

"I should know when to shut my mouth. It'll never happen again." His half apology surprised Father Mac. "I'll do my time here, just like I did at County Jail."

Mike spun around and walked out. He took the stairs, but lost in thought, missed his floor, and exited by the dormitory rooms for younger children. Walking past room #11, he heard violin music from behind the heavy wooden door. He bent his ear to the door, wondering who was playing, and listened to the beautiful rendition of "Away in a Manger." Anna sang it all the time when they were kids, practicing for the St. Florian's Christmas choir. Alone in the hall, Walter's music washed over him, providing a brief respite of peace.

That night, Mike replayed Father Mac's words over and over again. Father Mac had appealed to Mike's conscience. Just maybe the Steelman lifestyle and consequences were his fault—*his choice.*

No one else had addressed his recent troubles in such cold, harsh terms. Not the clinical psychologist who worked with him at County. Not his teammates. Not even his own mother. Mike contemplated Father Mac's words again. He reluctantly admitted there was a simple truth to what he said. Father Mac still saw who Mike once was—and more importantly, who he could be.

Curled up in the youth-sized bed, Mike thought about the lives he affected. It was excruciating to focus on Kim. His first intentional thoughts about her since he woke up in the ER. Their attraction had been fast and furious. For the first time since his marriage went sour, Mike truly loved someone. He missed her terribly. How could he lose her too? He felt she was an angel now, smiling down on him. Mike so desperately wanted to be with her, that for a brief moment, he thought about making that happen. And then, the Steelman choked back a tear—the first one—that should have fallen many months ago.

The Steelman reached for his iPod and lay back to listen to one of his favorite songs, a '90s rock ballad. Previously, it helped him to deal with life in the limelight and the physical and emotional demands of the NFL.

Tonight, the soulful lyrics of "Bittersweet Symphony" held a different meaning for the broken-hearted football player. He had no intention of getting on his knees to pray, but maybe he could break his mold. He had to. There was no going back down the same road.

During an eternally long and restless night, the lyrics looped endlessly in Mike's head. Sitting alone at breakfast, he stared out the dining hall window at the nearby grotto and garden. An angel statue, arms outstretched, was in the middle of the stone path. Two thin icicles, looking like frozen tears, streamed down her face.

Maybe the angel was Kim, crying for him and letting him know it was going to be okay. Suddenly, a flood of thoughts overwhelmed him—he would never see her again—he would never be able to look into her soulful eyes and try to explain what happened that night—he would never be able to place the diamond ring on her finger—he would never experience the joy of their newborn baby's cry, or feel the peaceful warmth of the baby's breath while he cuddled their precious child to his chest.

Mike would never get to say goodbye to her in this life. Maybe not even in death. Kim was an angel—above in the vast blue heaven. Mike was here—in his own living hell on earth.

Psychosomatic Paralysis

"YOU'RE THE EXPERT, KEN." FATHER MAC CUT TO THE CHASE OVER A CUP OF coffee. He was happy to get out of his office and meet with his old friend at a Hyde Park cafe near the university. "The pediatric ortho guys at Children's Hospital can't figure it out. Neurological tests are all negative—not one solid medical reason this kid can't get out of his wheelchair. I surely can't figure it out. What's your opinion after reviewing the records?"

Dr. Ken Eisenberg was currently affiliated with the highly regarded University of Chicago Medical Center as a visiting professor and pediatric spinal research consultant. Frustrated, Father Mac turned to him for answers.

"Jack, if my assessment is right, I've only seen a few instances in forty plus years. It has to do with subliminal suppression of a devastating psychological event or fear that causes a physical manifestation of illness. In this case, maybe he linked the loss of his parents to his inability to walk. It's plausible he developed psychosomatic paralysis to rationalize his survival.

"I agree there was no identifiable trauma to his legs, neck, or spine in the accident. Luckily, he was belted in the back and did not catch the frontal impact. In the weeks following the accident, a boy his age should have bounced back from cuts and scrapes. Overcoming the loss of his parents and the psychological trauma of the accident is another whole can of worms. I'm not trained in this field. However, a competent child psychologist can help. That's what I think."

"You're telling me, it might all be in his head and not his legs." Incredulous, Father Mac asked, "Really? Why would a kid willfully sit in that damn wheelchair when he could get up and run around?" He rubbed his forehead. "But, if it's a shrink he needs, then I'll get him the best damn one I can find. Do you have anybody?"

"I do. I know a very competent child psychologist who's from the Czech Republic. Probably speaks his native language. I met her at a conference a few years back. She really impressed me in her session on adolescent post-traumatic anxiety. Dr. Helena Kovar came here from Prague as a teenager and studied at Johns Hopkins. Trust me, she knows this issue. I'll call and see if she's willing to come here for a consultation."

Father Mac nodded, somewhat encouraged. "I'd appreciate it. I've had him since he was discharged from Children's. Normally, he would have wound up with DCFS, which as you know, is a bureaucratic nightmare. Thank God, Mike O'Brien, who sits on our Board, is the hospital's Child Advocacy Director. He asked me to take Walter until relatives or the right foster home could be found. So far, no luck on either front. I've even engaged the Czech Consulate for help. They call from time to time with updates, but nothing yet. In the meantime, I know he doesn't want to be with us—no matter how hard we try."

"I know you'll do the right thing. There's no immediate fix, but I think we're on the right track." Dr. Eisenberg stood up. "I've got to get to a faculty meeting. Please call me after Dr. Kovar's visit. And let's get together sometime soon for lunch, okay?"

"Thanks. I'll call you."

Two weeks later, Dr. Kovar came to the Home, surprising Father Mac with her youthful appearance. They sat down to chat and he detailed Walter's experience.

"That is quite a story with such tragic consequences. I can only speculate about what he has gone through emotionally with the horrific loss of his parents."

Dr. Kovar volunteered that as a young teen, she accompanied her family to the U.S. from what was then Czechoslovakia. Focusing on her studies, she ultimately completed her post-graduate work in child psychology at the University of Chicago.

"I am currently in private practice and only treat referred patients with a history of family trauma. Dr. Eisenberg gave me a summary of Walter's current situation. It doesn't sound cut-and-dried. With both parents gone and no siblings, there could be several factors affecting his emotional state."

Father Mac led Dr. Kovar into a reception room adjoining his office. "The medical experts are telling me his legs are fine. The therapists are frustrated because he's resistant to their efforts. Dr. Eisenberg suggested you may understand what is going on."

"Yes, Father MacKenzie, I'm sure it's frustrating to you and your staff. I know Dr. Eisenberg and have a lot of respect for his work and research. I believe his suspicions—the boy's physical limitations are a manifestation of his mental health issues—may very well be correct. On the surface it appears puzzling, but I hope I can help. Let's talk after I examine Walter."

Father Mac concluded this would be a short meeting if she did not engage Walter on a more personal level. "You wait here, and I'll bring Walter in. Take all the time you need." Dr. Kovar insisted Father Mac remain for the interview.

He called the activity room supervisor. When Walter appeared at his office a few minutes later, Father Mac was waiting and couldn't help but notice his white gym shoes looked brand new, without even a single scuff.

"There's someone here to see you. She's a nice lady who wants to meet you and get to know you a little bit."

Walter looked puzzled. "Why does she want to meet me?"

Father Mac believed the direct approach was best and motioned for him to follow, staying a few steps ahead of Walter, who always insisted on propelling himself.

"Ms. Kovar is a friend of mine who wants to talk to you about what happened to your parents. She's a doctor. I want you to meet her and just have a little talk. It's no big deal."

Walter appeared skeptical. He slowly pushed himself through the doorway and rolled up to Dr. Kovar. Walter held out his hand. "Hello, my name is Walter Pavlik. Who are you?"

Father Mac was relieved to see Dr. Kovar's softer side. She bent down to eye level and spoke kindly with a Czech accent. "Well, hello young man. My name is Helena and I'm a doctor. I'm very pleased to meet you, Walter Pavlik."

Walter's eyes opened wide. "Oh . . . *ahoj!* Are you from my country? Do you speak Czech?"

"*Ano, trochu.* But why don't we talk in English so Father MacKenzie can understand?" Disappointed, Walter lowered his head.

"Walter, I would love to hear about you and your family."

"Well, my family was me, my mother, and my father. I have no family now because they died in our car. I lived but my legs won't stand me up. I can't walk never again." Dr. Kovar was surprised by his frank delivery.

"I am so sorry about your parents. I'm sure you miss them very much. So how did you come to live at Angels of Mercy?"

"Father brought me here from the hospital and said this is my home now. He said Jesus works in strange ways and that my parents are in heaven. Father said they love me and watch over me every minute. Everyone at the Angels of Mercy Home is my new family and they all love me too."

"I agree with Father Mac. There are many people here who are looking out for you. You can make some friends. This is a good place for you to be now."

"But I can't do a lot of the things the other kids do. I miss my parents very much and wish I was with them . . ." For several seconds, Walter seemed faraway, but he became animated and continued. "My father taught me how to play the violin. I remember some songs. We sometimes played in our church. Father Mac got me a violin and I practice in my room."

"Please tell me, don't you want your legs to get better and walk again?"

Walter said nothing, so she decided to try another angle. "Father MacKenzie tells me you're quite an interesting young man. I understand besides playing like a concert violinist, you love superhero movies like Batman and Ironman."

"Well, I pretend I'm Batman sometimes when I put on my costume and ride in the Batmobile which is really my chair."

"Walter does a pretty good job patrolling our grounds and making sure there's no bad guys out there. I got his cape and mask from the 'Batcave' where he lived."

"I'm sure your parents would be very proud of you fighting crime. Father Mac needs someone like you who is brave. What happened to your parents was an awful thing. But I believe your parents would want you to get up out of your chair and be a happy, successful man someday."

Dr. Kovar tapped his left knee with her reflex hammer. "Walter, do you feel anything in your legs when I do this?" He looked at her. She watched for, but did not notice, any reflexive movement. A similar tap on his right knee yielded the same result.

"What do you think when you see other children playing and running outside? Would you like to join them?"

"Not really. I like this chair. I go wherever I want. I like to push myself around the garden by the little lake. Sometimes I stop and look at ripples in the water. I haven't seen any fish jumping, but I think they live there. I need a fishing pole to check."

"Sure, Walter, we'll work on it," Father Mac reassured him.

"Dr. Kovar, can I go? It's almost lunchtime and then I have English class.

Maybe you can come and visit me again? We'll practice speaking Czech."

"I would love that, Walter. You're a remarkable boy and I want to be your friend. Maybe next time, we can go down by the pond to look for fish. I really enjoyed meeting you." She shook Walter's hand. "I hope to see you soon."

"Is that why you came to see to me, just to check my legs?"

"No, Walter. I came to speak with you about a very sad time in your life. It's hard to see there will be better days to come. Your future is very bright. You just have to see it."

"But I will never see my parents again until I die and go to heaven." He waved goodbye and slowly rolled through the doorway. Dr. Kovar, a seasoned professional, could not help but feel deep sorrow for him.

"What do you think? He's a heck of a kid. Smart as a whip, doesn't miss anything. He doesn't really interact much with other kids."

"I can see that, Father."

"He likes music, though, especially his violin. He's told you more than anyone else since he arrived. I think he's a little afraid of me, especially when I wear my suit and collar."

Dr. Kovar reverted to her clinical demeanor. "Father MacKenzie, I would need another interview session and perhaps some cognitive testing to render my final diagnosis. Based on the post-accident medical files and my first impression, I conclude Walter has trapped himself in a world of survivor's guilt and sorrow. As you indicated, there is no known medical basis for his condition. Some doctors call it 'survivor syndrome.'"

She continued, "Psychosomatic paralysis is a subjective illness identified within an inexact science. The paralysis can be temporary or can endure for an extended period of time. This setting should prove to be therapeutic given the structure and support of your staff. However, no one has a crystal ball with a clear picture of the future.

"I think the decision to walk again rests with Walter's ability to move beyond his parents' death and accept the fact that he survived. He's lonely, Father MacKenzie. That is very apparent. I believe he can't process the consequences he must face.

"I don't believe his legs are paralyzed," Dr. Kovar soberly concluded. "The paralysis is in his heart. If you wish, I can refer you to another child psychologist for a second opinion."

"Thanks for your time and insights, Dr. Kovar. I'll think about your comments and get back to you. We'll be in touch."

"Call me anytime. Also, have you contacted the Czech Consulate? They may be able to help search for Walter's extended family. The Consul General is a professional colleague and friend of mine. I can call him on your behalf."

"Thank you. I appreciate the offer, but I actually made that call awhile back. They are looking into it."

"Understood. Good luck. Again, call me anytime you like."

Father Mac reflected on the meeting after she left, wishing for a crystal ball with even a fuzzy picture.

Beyond the Garden Gate

"Excuse me," Mary Pat O'Laughlin, a fixture at AOMH for thirty-seven years, poked her head in Father Mac's office. "There's a call from the sister of an old friend of Mike's who passed away. Wants to talk to him."

"Really? Put her through."

It was the second surprising call this week. Tuesday, the Czech Republic Consulate notified him that a young woman from London, claiming to be Walter's distant cousin, wanted to meet with him as soon as possible. Although encouraged, Father Mac was somewhat skeptical. And now a call for Mike Stalowski.

"Hallo, Father. This is Stella Janowik. From Hegewisch on the Sout'side. Can I talk wit Mike? The football player der at your place for kids. The orphanage, right?"

Father Mac immediately recognized her South Side Polish accent. She sounded elderly. He checked his mental Rolodex but couldn't recall her name.

"I gotta tell him my brother Chester died. He knew him from the old neighborhood. Chester told me a couple times what happened to Mike in the car accident. Said he knew him from his fishing stand since Mike was a kid."

Chester . . . Chester? Oh! Probably the guy in the lobby a few weeks ago. The one who tipped his WWII veteran's cap.

Later, he learned the old man had dropped off a long narrow package for Mike. It was accepted without question by a new teenage volunteer who didn't know about Mike's mail restrictions. She had passed it to another uninformed volunteer, who put it in the Steelman's room.

". . . So Chester said if anything ever happened to him I should tell Mike. I dunno why, but please, I can talk to him now? I told Chester I would do it. So I'm calling your place and she said I had to talk to you. Since it's Holy Week I gotta plan his funeral so I can bury him before Friday, right?" No answer. "Hallo Father. You still there? Father, this is Stella Janowik!"

213

"Yes, Stella! Sorry, I was trying to remember something. I'm very sorry for your loss, but Mike can't come to the phone now. Please tell me what happened and I'll let him know."

"When he didn't answer the phone after five times, I called the police. Chester always answers the phone when I call. It's right by his chair in the living room where he watches the TV. They found him in his chair. Told me he musta had a heart attack or something. I dunno. The TV was on when the police got in the house. He liked to watch the news a lot. You know Father, he's my only brother. Just me an' him. Now everybody's gone.

"It would be nice if you could come to the wake. It's gonna be at Oprondek's Funeral Parlor on 135th by Brainard. Close by where Chester's house is. I'll let you know for sure. Maybe you can come with Mike and you guys can say a prayer."

"Stella, I'll see what I can arrange. I'll get back to you. I promise."

"Okay. Good-bye, Father. Thank you!"

Later that morning, Mary Pat notified Father Mac of the call he was waiting for.

"Thanks, Joe. Yes, everything's okay. No, I don't think many people will be there. Only a few hours for the funeral home and cemetery for graveside prayers. Please tell Judge Cozzart I appreciate his help. I'm very sorry you had to disturb him on a weekend. God Bless!"

Father Mac needed a break from the pile of correspondence on his desk. He turned around to look out the window and was astonished to see Mike Stalowski and Walter Pavlik fishing by the old campus pond. Lines from Chester's poles were in the water.

What the hell? Holy Christ and St. Michael! I can't believe he's out of his wheelchair, sitting on the grass. Father Mac recalled Walter tell Dr. Kovar, *"I like to push myself around the garden by the little lake . . . I think they live there. I need to find a fishing pole to check."*

On warm sunny days in early spring, hope was palpable. The end of Chicago's long, cold, gray winter was near. New growth and longer light-filled days were transformational.

Only a week away, Easter would mark the Resurrection of Jesus Christ and bring the promise of eternal life for mankind. Father Mac recalled a favorite Lenten sermon line. *Faith also brings the light of hope and intercession in our daily lives.*

Maybe things were looking up for Walter. In Father Mac's experience, miracles happened when needed most. He believed guardian angels worked 24/7 interceding in shattered lives. In this case, they guided two lost souls to common ground. *But how the heck did Mike get Chester to bring those poles?*

———————•———————

Mike befriended the Home's cooks, who spoke only Polish to each other and very broken English to everyone else. Recently after doing some heavy lifting for them, Marysia, who resembled his *Babcia*, handed him a plate loaded with pierogis. She was a widow from Back of the Yards, where the stockyards once thrived, and a WWII labor camp survivor. Sometimes when she was cooking, Mike could see the faded *11317* on her left forearm.

Pierogis in one hand, ominously waving her knife with the other, she yelled, "I cut you hair! You look like hippie! Where's you net?"

Mike quickly put it on before thoroughly enjoying the ethnic dish he ate at Christmas Eve *Wigilia* with his grandparents. When done, much to the cooks' surprise, he said, "*Dziekuje*,"—one of the few Polish words he remembered besides *ryba,* which means fish—and it provided a potential solution to a problem he faced.

Glancing around the kitchen, Mike's eyes landed on a hanging clipboard with an attached pen. He scribbled Chester's address on the back of an inventory sheet, then held it up for the cooks to see.

"*Kolega*," he said and pointed to his chest. "My *kolega*, Chester Janowik."

They looked at each other quizzically and nodded at Mike.

"*Woda*." Mike moved by the window that overlooked the pond in the distance and pointed. "Water."

Marysia and Helen nodded again, half-smiles breaking on both their faces.

Mike began motioning like he was casting and reeling in a fishing line. "*Ryba*. I need *ryba* pole. From *kolega*." He went back to the clipboard and held it up. "Please, I need pole for *ryba* from my *kolega*. Chester."

Mike looked earnestly at the cooks, who could no longer contain their amusement.

Chuckling, Helen elbowed Marysia. "*Zapytaj go po angielsku*."

"You want Chester bring fishing pole?" Still brandishing her knife, Marysia grabbed his ear. "Why you no just tell us that?"

———————•———————

Father Mac decided to investigate. Approaching around the bend of a hedgerow, he stopped when he heard their voices.

Walter held his pole with both hands and concentrated on his red and white bobber. He saw a small ripple. He had one! As quickly as the bobber submerged, it popped back up.

"Uhhohh! The fish is gone."

"Hey, don't worry, little man. Probably didn't set the hook like I showed you. So he took your worm. No sweat, he'll be back and bring his big brother. We've got some big fat worms for these guys. Reel it in and we'll check the hook."

Walter slowly cranked the reel. The bobber jumped again and took off in the opposite direction.

"Hey, Walter! Look, man. He didn't take the worm before and he's back for it! Keep reeling it in. You gotta set the hook!"

Mike had taken great care to position Walter so he wouldn't fall over. His legs stretched out before him, he was intent on catching the condemned bluegill. Mike showed Walter how to whip the tip of the pole up. For an instant, Mike swore Walter's left foot moved, ever so slightly, when he set the hook. Walter struggled but kept cranking the reel. The pole bent. The bobber went under.

"Wow! That's some bluegill, little man. Gotta be at least eight inches long. Keep reeling buddy. Don't let go!" Mike stood up and trained his eyes on Walter's left foot. He definitely saw a twitch.

"Help me! He's going away again!"

Grabbing the line, Mike remembered a similar scene. He had been a bit younger than Walter and afraid to reel in what was no doubt a sea monster lurking near the breakwater rocks.

Frank had encouraged him. "Don't be scared and let go, Mikey! Keep control. Keep fighting. You gonna win!" A minute later, the speckled perch wiggled on the hook. Smiling, Frank had held the line to display his son's catch. Frank had given him the push, the courage to reel it in. Another fisherman had taken a picture with Frank's Kodak. Once proudly displayed on the Steelman's locker shelf.

Mike held the line and showed Walter the big flopping sunfish. "See! You did it! Here, you wanna hold him?"

"Sure. I'm not afraid!" Mike showed Walter how to lay the gills down so he wouldn't nick his fingers. "Where's the worm? Did he eat it?" The fish jumped out of Walter's hand and landed near the edge of the pond. "Oh no! I let him go! Grab him, Mr. Mike!" Walter's left ankle twitched again as he leaned forward.

"Yep, he ate the worm." Mike nudged the fish back in the pond. "Good fishermen catch and release so the fish stays alive. There you go fat sunfish buddy! See you again. Don't worry, Walter. There's plenty more like him in that pond. We may even catch the same one again. Sometimes I let running backs and receivers get by me, but I'd get 'em on the next play."

"What is a play?"

"A football play. They're called *downs*," he explained. "There's four on every offensive series." Walter looked quizzically at Mike. "Me and the rest of the defense *would try to stop them* so the ball wouldn't go in the end zone, past the goal line. Kind of like playing soccer. You know, keep the ball out of your net."

"Oh, I know a little bit about soccer! I watched my father play in the park. Sometimes he would kick the ball to me and we would practice. I like soccer!"

"Maybe we can practice sometime." Walter did not take the bait.

Mike pulled another worm from the bait bucket and put it on Walter's hook. "Here, little man, toss it out." Walter cast over his head, watching it go *kerplunk*.

Father Mac waited for an opportune time to join them.

"When I was a kid, I fished with my dad on Lake Michigan. On the big breakwater rocks by where I grew up. He took me there to catch perch in the summertime. Taught me about live baits, how to handle the hook, and when to set it to snag the fish. We'd either use minnows or worms, sitting on the rocks and casting into the lake. Sometimes we'd fish right off the dock.

"At first, I was a little scared when I felt the pull on the line. I thought maybe it was a big ugly and scary fish, like carp. They're scavengers! But my dad told me every cast is different. Don't be afraid of what's on the end of the hook. I learned he was right. Kinda like when I played football. I was sometimes nervous at the beginning of the play. But if we did bad on the first down, there were three more to do good."

"I'm not sure what you mean exactly, but I think you got another chance."

"Right, little man, *another chance*. On the next play, football players get another chance to make good." Mike's words unintentionally struck a chord with himself.

"Are you still afraid sometimes what is on the other end of the hook?" Walter asked.

"Huh, whatta you mean?" He paused. "Not afraid. I guess just a little anxious to see what's on the other end. Why, little man? You afraid of what you're pulling out of the water?"

"Not really. But sometimes I wonder what's going to happen to me. Where will I go? I have no one." He paused then asked, "Are you afraid of other things?"

Mike was baffled. "I dunno. I guess I'm a little afraid of what I'll do if I don't play football again. Don't really know what else I *can* do. I like to make things with my hands. Maybe I'll build things, like houses. I'm leaving here this summer. But I don't think I can play anymore. It's over for me, little man. So I guess I have some decisions to make, right?"

"What do you mean, Mr. Mike? I know you got hurt too. Like me. I heard you had to stay here, then you would be a football player again. Don't you still want to play?"

"Who told you that?"

"Well, I listen pretty good to other people. I heard you were punished to be here with Father Mac because it was your fault a lady died when you smashed up your car. That's why I was mad when I first met you. My mother and father died in a car because a man wasn't careful. Now I can't walk and have to stay here." Walter looked ahead at the bobber. "So you are leaving."

A concrete block of reality and regret fell onto the Steelman, weighing down his already heavy load to bear. Walter was too young to understand DUI's, vehicular aggravated reckless homicide, incarceration, and autopsy findings. But he understood right and wrong.

"Listen, buddy, you're almost right. Only you can't understand what caused it really. I dunno, maybe you could. I made some really dumb decisions that night. The lady who was killed was my girlfriend. She was my best friend and I wanted to marry her." Saying it aloud cut Mike to his core.

"Are you sorry what happened?"

"REALLY sorry! I wish I could make it different, but I can't. I don't want to talk about it anymore now, okay?" Remembering the twitch in Walter's foot, he decided to probe himself. "How about you, Walter? Don't you want to walk again?"

"Yes, Mr. Mike. I want to be out of my wheelchair. But I'm afraid. Maybe

Father Mac will make me leave if I can walk. Where can I go?" He paused. "Are you afraid to leave and play football?"

The Steelman was clotheslined. "Maybe, little man, maybe." Walter's simple question forced Mike to face reality. Up to now, ignoring football, along with the physical pain and mental anguish he had inflicted upon himself and others, was easier.

"We can try to help each other. If you try to play football again, maybe I can try to get up by myself. Then we can leave here together and go fishing somewhere."

Father Mac was stunned to hear both fishermen were anxious about the future. Time for him to step out of the shadows.

"Hey, guys! If you two are fishing for dinner you better pick up the pace. I don't see a lot of fish. As a matter of fact," he chuckled, "the bucket's empty."

"Ha ha, Father Mac! You know it's pizza and movie night, like every Saturday. We're practice fishing. You know, catch and release."

"Oh, I see," he nodded. "Walter, it's great to see you outside, sitting on the grass. Feels good, right?" The boy nodded silently. Father Mac did not push it.

"Mike, just kidding about the fish. Of course it's pizza night! The movie is *King of Kings*."

"I think we watched that when I was a freshman at St. Michael's."

"Yes, but it still tells a great story. My friends, Palm Sunday tomorrow begins Holy Week. What better time to watch the story of Jesus' life. Come on, Walter. I'll get you in your chair and back to your room, okay?"

"Thank you, Father, but Mr. Mike will help me. And I can get back myself." Walter reeled in his bobber and laid the pole at his side. Mike shrugged and picked Walter up, carefully positioning him in his chair.

Walter took off, his arms quickly propelling the wheelchair. Father Mac pointed down the path. "Okay then, Mike, let's go."

After about fifty yards, Mike stopped. "Hey, Father, I forgot something."

"What?"

"Something back by the pond. Go ahead."

Curious, but wanting to give him space, he agreed. "Okay, see you at dinner." Father Mac remembered one of the first freshman practices when the raw St. Michael's recruits were herded back to the locker room. A young Mike Stalowski brought up the rear. *Remember Stalowski, the defense leaves the field as a unit. You forget your helmet? Hurry up! It's dinner time!* He smiled at the memory.

Once Father Mac was out of sight, Mike looked at the downtown skyline. The sun reflected a majestic mosaic of color off the glass of high-rise buildings. The Home bordered Holy Family Church, whose neighbor was St. Andrew College Prep. While fishing, Mike noticed what looked like the tips of goal post uprights. After his discussion with Walter, he was curious to check it out.

Past the garden and pond, he confirmed two metal pole tips far off in the distance. Approaching the fence line, they disappeared from sight. Due to Holy Family renovations, canvas-covered construction fencing blocked his view. About twenty yards away, he found a rusty, padlocked gate. Peering through the one-inch gap, he saw a portion of a scoreboard and green turf with white markers. Beyond the garden gate, St. Andrew College Prep had a football field.

Taps for Chester

After dinner Monday, Father Mac passed by Mike's room. The door was open, so he poked his head in. "What are you reading? That wizard book, Harry what's-his-name? That's all these kids talk about."

"Nope! Going back to *The Catcher in the Rye*. I barely read the *Cliffs Notes* senior year! Next is *The Grapes of Wrath*."

Father Mac smiled wryly. "Nice to see you're catching up on classics. Listen, I've got some calls to make now, but can you come to my office in about half an hour? There's something I want to discuss."

"Sure." Mike wondered what he had done. The last time he went to Father Mac's office was not pleasant. Mike couldn't focus on his book, so he anxiously watched the alarm clock on his nightstand. Right on time, he knocked hesitantly on the Dean of Discipline's office door.

"Come in. Mike, please sit down. I need to share something with you."

"What?"

"Chester Janowik's sister called to let you know he died. He wanted you to be notified if something happened to him."

"Wow! He was just here a couple of weeks ago."

"She asked if you and I could go to the wake. She'd also like me to say graveside prayers. The funeral home is in Hegewisch and she said Holy Cross Cemetery isn't far."

"I can't leave, though." He pointed to his ankle monitor. "Remember? This thing explodes if I go too far off campus. That really sucks. Chester was a good guy. My last real connection to the old neighborhood. Was it like a heart attack?"

"I don't think they know for sure. Look, I've cleared it. We're leaving at 8:00 a.m. tomorrow in my car. Just you and me. Although we're going to have a shadow hanging back. Those are the rules."

"I don't know what to say, Father. I don't have funeral clothes. I have my suit from court, but I think it's a little tight from all this good food the Polish ladies cook. Maybe I have some khakis and a sweater."

"Don't worry, Mike, you'll be fine. Wear what fits. "

"Okay. I know that cemetery. A lot of my family is there."

Hegewisch families like the Stalowskis were well-acquainted with Oprondek Funeral Home bereavement services. Opened in 1920 when the mills belched smoke 24/7, "the parlor," as locals called it, hadn't changed much. It remained a family business, priding itself on tradition. Mr. Oprondek, an usher at St. Florian's Sunday Mass for over forty years, knew every family by name.

They arrived at 8:30 a.m. and easily parked. There were only a few cars in the lot. Mike wore a windbreaker over his sweater to ward off the steady drizzle. His hair was trimmed but still a little shaggy. He looked like a typical neighborhood guy coming to pay his last respects.

They walked under the faded maroon canopy that protected caskets being loaded into hearses in inclement weather. Father Mac opened one of the massive double wooden doors with arched stained glass windows. In the lobby, an old black letterboard with yellowed changeable letters announced Chester Francis Janowik was in Chapel A.

Almost immediately, a stout woman with gray hair and glasses hobbled over. Father Mac was easy to identify with his priest's collar. "Hallo, Father. I'm Stella. . . Chester's sister. Thanks for coming today. I'm so happy." She glanced at Mike, who tipped his head and half-smiled. "So you are Michael, the football player. I'm happy you could come too."

Stella led them into the parlor. Mike noticed the subdued, mournful lighting still cast traditional pink and purple hues, especially over the casket bier, intended to reflect sorrow, pain and the great loss of a loved one. In the not-too-distant past, wakes had been three days long. Agonizing for families, especially young children. Mourners had likely been dressed in all black and spoke in hushed tones as they honored and remembered the deceased. While mourners still gather, usually for much shorter periods of time, to share stories, their love, and their loss, wakes had become less formal, some even semi-festive—affirming life goes on—but ultimately leaving people to contemplate their past with the deceased and their future without them.

There weren't many suits at Chester's wake, but a lot of baseball caps. About a dozen WWII vets sat together. All wore their coveted caps declaring the ship or military unit they were assigned to decades ago. Chester had frequented the local VFW Post, sharing memories and grabbing an occasional shot and cold beer with them. Some may have been recipients of Mike's ticket and transportation generosity.

Chester lay peacefully in the casket. His Purple Heart was pinned to the chest of his navy suit. Next to him were his treasured USS Indiana cap and a red and white fishing bobber. Mike and Father Mac made their way to the foot of the bier and bowed their heads. Father Mac said a silent prayer and assumed Mike was doing the same.

Staring at Chester in repose, Mike remembered his first wake. He could still smell the sickeningly sweet aroma from the dozens of flower arrangements encircling the parlor. Despite the rose-colored light, his third-grade classmate had looked like a heavily made-up mannequin wearing his recent First Holy Communion suit. Mike's grandparents' wakes were a blur, although he remembered parts of the Mass had been recited in Polish.

His father's wake was the most vivid. He could still see a few photographs of Frank that had been on a small table. In a family favorite, Frank held Anna's tiny hand while Janet held Mike's. They were enjoying Rainbow Cones from the popular South Side Beverly ice cream shop. Next to it was the photograph of Frank and Mike fishing that found its way to the Storm locker room.

In stark contrast to Frank, full of life in the photographs, was Frank Stalowski in the gray metal casket. The finish resembled the steel he had toiled over. Makeup couldn't disguise his gaunt face or sunken eyes. He had been buried in an ill-fitting dark gray suit and black tie. His weathered hands had held a rosary from Mike's *Babcia*.

Only Mike and Janet had remained after the mourners filed past Frank's casket for final goodbyes. Anna had been spared and was waiting in the lounge with Janet's mother. Janet had openly wept, tightly clutching her son's hand. The lid was closed. Mike had not shed a tear. Internalized anger had taken its toll. Finally, thirteen-year-old Mike had been liberated from his onerous obligation—and simultaneously imprisoned by deep shame and guilt for feeling free.

Father Mac gently nudged Mike. They both made the sign of the cross and stepped away from Chester's casket.

Chester would be buried in the military section of Holy Cross Cemetery in nearby Calumet City. His plot was next to an aerated pond, near where the pump sprayed a cascade of water plumes. Often in the bright sun, a rainbow would appear. The rain, a steady drizzle all morning, inexplicably stopped the moment Father Mac began to speak, surprising the small graveside gathering.

"Let all of us gathered here begin by reciting the Prayer of St. Francis of Assisi, Chester's favorite.

"Lord, make me an instrument of your peace;
where there is hatred, let me sow love;
where there is injury, pardon;
where there is doubt, faith;
where there is despair, hope;
where there is darkness, light;
and where there is sadness, joy . . .

"Chester Janowik proved he was a hero in many ways. I didn't know him personally, but learned he selflessly fought for his country in a foreign land. He came home to Hegewisch, a true hero, and lived a quiet life of service to his family and the community he loved. He did not seek praise for the price he ultimately paid. Chester was a husband, brother, friend, and mentor. Always giving of himself. Asking nothing in return.

"Let us pray. May our Lord accept our brother into His heavenly paradise as we say goodbye to Chester and commend him to the light of His presence . . ."

The brief committal ceremony concluded with military taps played by a VFW brother. The flag draped over the casket was folded and presented to Stella. Father Mac sprinkled holy water on the casket.

It started raining again. Stella grasped Father Mac's and Mike's hands. "Thank you for coming. I know Chester is smiling on us." She grabbed Mike's forearm and pulled him down to whisper in his ear, "You gonna be okay, Michael." Patting his arm, she repeated, "It's gonna be okay. You'll see." Stella hobbled away.

Back in the car Mike asked, "Hey, Father, can we go to another part of the cemetery on the way out?"

"Which part? This is a big place."

"I don't remember exactly. It's been awhile. Our family plot on the other side."

"Truthfully, I promised we would return immediately after the service. How about we make a quick detour to the cemetery office and look it up. Everything's computerized these days, even the deceased! If it doesn't take a lot of time, we'll stop."

The computer database made it quick and easy to find the Stalowski family plots. In the older Resurrection Hill section, Mike jumped out and disappeared over a small ridge. Father Mac grabbed his cane, opened his umbrella and followed. Several purple lilies were in place for Holy Week. Easter Sunday there would be an abundance of white lilies and gold crosses to celebrate Christ's Resurrection—a triumph over death and darkness—the promise of new life.

Father Mac caught up with Mike. Down on one knee, by a marker bearing the family name and inscriptions for his grandparents, father, and Uncle Mike, Mike pushed aside the overgrown and matted grass, then gently ran his fingers over the names and dates. "I haven't been here as much as I should have. Looks a little neglected."

Mike stepped to his right and stood over a marble stone engraved with a cherubic angel. Father Mac moved closer to read the inscription.

MICHAEL ROCCO STALOWSKI
OUR LITTLEST ANGEL
OCTOBER 19, 2004

Shocked, he glanced at Mike, who was soaked with raindrops streaming down his face. Father Mac thought perhaps they were co-mingled with tears.

Father Mac understood Mike was a troubled man with a complicated past and an uncertain future, but he had no idea Mike and Lisa lost a son. Two years later, another baby had been conceived and destined to die with their mother. An overwhelmingly heavy burden to bear.

Northbound I-94, heading downtown, was backed up by 11:00 a.m. Father Mac exited at Stony Island Avenue. "Thank God I know another way home," Father Mac chuckled.

"I remember driving down Stony after we beat Resurrection in the playoffs senior year. I was concussed, but I know we rocked the hell out of that bus on the way back to school. Screaming out the windows like a bunch of idiots. We had a caravan, like a whole motorcade behind the bus, remember? We were rock stars! What a riot!"

"I remember it well! Even though you guys won, I was ready to double-jug the whole team for Saturday and Sunday! It almost *was* a riot. I'm surprised the police didn't pull everyone over, especially parents who might have had a tailgate beer, or ten, that night. Funny, the things you recall. If we had more time, I'd drive past the school. They're hurting for money you know. Rumor has it they're merging with St. Theresa the Little Flower. Saints preserve us! Girls at St. Mike's!" he lamented. "Can you imagine?"

"You know, I was supposed to speak at an alumni fundraiser right after the accident. Guess I could've done more to help out along the way. I hear Lattrell Simpkins has been back pretty regularly since he joined the NBA. Remember him? He was my locker mate freshman year." It was the first time Father Mac heard Mike utter the word *accident* since he arrived at the Home.

"So I hear. Well, that's up to you, my friend, but it would be a nice gesture if you reconnected in the future." He added, "Don't worry, Mike. You still have time to figure things out before I cut you loose."

Father Mac turned east on 57th Drive through Jackson Park, to South Lake Shore Drive near the Museum of Science and Industry. The normally breathtaking view of downtown was cut off by low-hanging clouds. Mike surveyed the ominous horizon and three-to-five-foot white-capped waves crashing on the Lake Michigan shoreline.

About ten minutes from the Home, as they merged onto I-55 from the Drive, Father Mac broke the silence. "Mike, I expect this has been a tough day. I think I saw some pretty raw emotions earlier. May I ask what's going through your head?"

Mike fidgeted in his seat. "What's this? Confession or something? Yeah, it was tough to go back to the old neighborhood and the cemetery. What do you want me to say?" Mike looked squarely at Father Mac. "But hey, Chester's in a better place, right? Isn't that what you're going to tell me? Don't worry, I said my goodbyes to him. And going back to the family plot wasn't exactly a day at the beach, Father! Lisa buried the baby there because of me. She insisted we cremate him, and I refused! Truthfully, I haven't been back since."

They exited at Roosevelt Road. Waiting for a red light, Father Mac pushed a little further. "I'm very sorry, Mike. But here's something to consider. Have you *really* said your goodbyes to *all* the people that were important in your life?" He paused. "I don't think you have! You've lost loved ones, early on and recently." Mike was stone-faced. "That may be the real ball and chain you're dragging.

"Today, I saw pieces of your past that shed light on the present. Look, I know you've been through hell these last couple of years. We never really discussed it. You're leaving in a few months with some big decisions ahead. Some will be made for you, some won't.

"Have you thought about where you're going and what you're going to do? What about football, Mike? Are you ready to walk away from your career the way it ended? *If* you get another chance—will you take it? *Can* you still play? At thirty-two, do you *want* to play? Not easy decisions. But I want you to know I'm here to help. That's why you're at Angels of Mercy." The light changed to green.

"Really?" asked the Steelman sarcastically. "So, what? I'm like Rocky now? A down-on-his-luck, washed-up linebacker? I don't think so! It's more complicated. My story's different. My Adrian is gone, and I don't know if I can play anymore."

"No one's saying you're a movie character, Mike. You've traveled a rough and winding road, no doubt. You'll be at a crossroads soon. The past is past. The next turn you choose on life's highway is going to make a difference.

"You probably don't realize people still believe in you, despite the accident. And seeing you with Walter the other day? Surely you remember our last discussion about him. I believe he's had an influence on you—and you on him." Father Mac pulled into the parking lot. "Come on, I've probably got twenty messages waiting for me."

After changing, Mike resumed scraping and painting the metal frames of the stained glass windows inside the chapel. Father Mac informed the authorities Mike was back, then picked up several messages. He expected the first and was puzzled by the second.

"Yes, Dr. Dvorak. I look forward to seeing you both at 10:00 a.m. No, I haven't said anything to Walter. Quite frankly, he's made a lot of strides recently. He's more engaged and he's made some friends. See you both Thursday."

"Hello, Mr. Kendall, returning your call. I understand attorney-client privileged information, but if it involves the situation with his wife, I should have some idea what's going on." Father Mac listened. "Okay, I understand. I'll have him call you before 5:00 p.m." He left to notify Mike.

The gloomy weather had given way to patches of blue sky. When Father Mac entered the chapel, sunlight brought the stained glass windows to life. He was amazed by the surreal image of Mike in a pew—head bowed and hands clasped together—illuminated by the stained glass image of St. Francis of Assisi, whose prayer still rang in Mike's ears. Father Mac waited until Mike crossed himself and stood up.

"Wanted to make sure this wasn't becoming the Sistine Chapel. Run out of paint?"

"No, I was taking a little break. I'll finish up this window tomorrow."

"Okay. Your attorney wants to talk to you today. You can call from my office. I think it has something to do with your separation."

"Great! More good news. Nice way to end the day of a funeral."

As it turned out, Lisa had another man in her life. She was ready to take what she could get now—instead of banking on Mike's future. Without a moment's hesitation, Mike told Kendall to draft settlement details.

"Yeah Steve, I know. The condo has to get emptied. I can't do anything until I get out of here, so it's on you. There's not much there I give a shit about except a ring."

Mike shared the conversation with Father Mac, omitting the ring. "So you know what I know. Father, her decisions caused a lot of collateral damage. Especially serving me right before the game. She gets what she wants and I'll pay for the rest of my life. If this happened in the fall of last year, I might not be here today. The dominoes may have fallen differently. Timing is everything, right? But I'm gonna move on. Hey, if you're good with it, I'm going out by the pond for a minute."

"Sure Mike, but no fishing! And you know what? If I hadn't blown my knee out at Notre Dame, *I* might not be here today. *Neither would you.*"

Mike walked toward the pond and diverted to the gate separating AOMH from Holy Family. He pulled a key out of his pocket. Mike tried to turn the lock, but it wouldn't budge. He applied more pressure. Finally, the tumblers released.

He slowly opened the gate, trying to silence the rusty hinges, and walked across church property toward St. Andrew's. He wasn't sure at what point his electronic bracelet would trigger an alert, but he pressed on. Through some foliage, he saw their football field.

"I hate this tarp, Mike. Kills our view of the skyline. Never tire of looking at it, especially at night." Mike thought he was *really* busted, but Father Mac continued as if nothing was wrong. "It's the best athletic field in this part of town, maybe the whole city. St. Andrew's isn't that good, though. The program came back a few years ago after shutting down in 1964. The field is brand new, courtesy of an alumni benefactor. Those poor kids went 1-8. You know, if I had time, I'd resurrect my whistle and playbook to help out."

It seemed he wasn't going to get jugged for another six months or read the riot act for theft and trespass. Perhaps Father Mac wanted him to see the field.

"Why the record? Bad coaches or no talent?"

"Probably both. St. Andrew's is a highly-regarded academic school. One of the best in the state. But not too many kids want to play football. They only suit about thirty guys for varsity games, and they definitely aren't the size you were. Not a Catholic League powerhouse like your alma mater!"

The Dean of Discipline threw a right hook. "On another note, why *did* you do this, Mike? It's a construction site. The fence is up for a reason. I'm curious to hear why you popped the lock. Planning to attend church through the back entrance?" He smirked and crossed his arms. "Let's hear you get out of this one."

Mike sighed. "I dunno. I saw the tips of the uprights before and thought it was a football field. Then you got me thinking today. I had to look and see for myself."

"Here's my take. I think you were *really* wondering what's beyond the Home's garden gate. You know why? Because I think you're *really* thinking about football. Pro football. Specifically, what's left of your career.

"Problem is, you need answers. There are league questions, team questions, legal questions, medical questions. Many issues to resolve before you can play again. That's a long 100 yards ahead of you. But first, what's left in your gut? In your heart?"

Mike was staring at the field. Father Mac wondered if he'd heard a word he said. He correctly suspected Mike was reliving his football days in a flurry of emotion. After-school practice at St. Michael's—running out of the Veterans Stadium tunnel wearing Storm silver and blue, the prominent "C" on his jersey—winning the high school state championship—and losing the NFC championship. From a shy high school freshman to the larger-than-life Steelman—wins—losses—concussions—injuries sustained and injuries inflicted—cheering fans—battle scars.

"Honestly Mike, it all starts with the private meeting Connie Everett wants to have." Mike was shocked. "He always wants to know what you're saying about your future. Obviously you haven't said a word, and I didn't ask. I told him I'd talk to you when the time was right."

"You know him? And talk to him?"

"For many years. I probably knew you were getting drafted before the team scouts. You should know he's supported you from the shadows throughout this whole ordeal."

"So that's why I ended up here."

Father Mac nodded. "Mike, we both thought it best if you could be here during your confinement. I wanted to help you myself. People care. It may not seem that way, but it's the truth."

"Wow! Guess I shoulda gone to your big fundraiser when the front office asked me. The GM made sure we knew it was Connie's pet project."

Father Mac pointed toward St. Andrew's. "I know those guys. They might let you workout after hours. On the QT of course." He laughed. "I kept my stopwatch and can still run linebacker drills in my sleep. They haunt me every now and then. I'll bet you still remember some of the Crusader defense I drilled into your head, right?"

"Yeah! I know all about being haunted by drills. You know, I actually came to like the Machine Gun Drill," he chuckled.

"You put everyone down on their ass!" Father Mac elbowed Mike in the rib and smiled. "Come on, let's lock this gate—for now."

As they walked past the pond, Father Mac advised, "I'd start with Connie Everett first. He usually brings Easter baskets for our kids. I'll call him."

The Steelman looked skyward. He was thinking of Kim and looking for a nod of approval.

The London Eye

WALTER'S SITUATION WAS DISCONCERTING. GIVEN THE UNIQUE CIRCUMSTANCES, Father Mac planned to proceed with caution. At the Czech Consulate, he met Dr. Radomir Dvorak, the Consul General, and Gabriela Tesar, a striking woman who appeared to be about thirty-five years old.

Dr. Dvorak invited them to sit around a coffee table, ornately carved by a Czech artisan. An assistant placed a coffee service on the embroidered table linen and offered ethnic pastries. Father Mac welcomed a cup of black coffee, but politely passed on the sugar and carb-laden goodies.

"I am pleased we finally have a chance to meet, Father MacKenzie." Dr. Dvorak spoke with a heavy accent. "I see you *are* in fact a priest."

As usual for religious functions and meetings, Father Mac wore a black suit and priest's collar. When circumstances permitted at the Home, he wore casual attire, occasionally donning his old St. Michael's hat. Since Mike's arrival, it had been on an office shelf next to his Notre Dame hat.

Dr. Dvorak smiled. "I wasn't sure from our telephone conversations when you identified yourself as Jack MacKenzie. I researched the Angels of Mercy Home and learned your official title is President."

"That's correct, Doctor."

"I read reviews of the wonderful work you do and assume the Angels of Mercy Home is a Roman Catholic institution. It's certainly not a governmental facility with that name. I want to thank you for coming today to discuss Walter Pavlik's situation."

Dr. Dvorak looked to set the diplomatic stage. He did not share that the Czech authorities conducted a thorough background investigation to avoid embarrassment.

"I would like Ms. Tesar to gather as much information as possible. I anticipate, after speaking with her earlier, we will collaborate on Walter's behalf. Please tell us a little more about yourself and your institution."

Quickly assessing the situation, Father Mac cleared his throat and responded with a friendly but assertive tone. "I see. Yes, I am a Roman Catholic priest for more years than I care to admit! My last parish priest assignment was Associate Pastor at nearby Holy Name Cathedral. When I retired, Cardinal Gleeson asked me to assume oversight of the Home for a short period of time. It's been extended to almost a decade!

"Our residents have varying needs. Some have both physical and mental health challenges; some none at all. Walter, I'm sorry to say, has experienced both. Unfortunately, he was seriously affected by the untimely loss of both parents in the accident.

"Dr. Dvorak, I'm guessing Dr. Kovar shared Walter's diagnosis with you." The Consul General nodded his head and removed his glasses to rub his eyes. "Although multiple medical opinions are consistent, finding no physical damage to his limbs or spine, he remains confined to a wheelchair.

"Walter is very intelligent, polite, and talented, both academically and musically. Initially, he was isolated. Lately, he has become more engaged with residents and staff. Last Saturday I was surprised to see him really enjoying himself fishing in the pond on our grounds. As a result of these changes, I plan to call Dr. Kovar for a follow-up visit.

"But I'm saying too much. It's a pleasure to meet you, Ms. Tesar. I can't thank you enough for making the trip all the way from London! I'm encouraged that Walter does in fact have extended family and would love to hear about you."

Gabriela formally folded her hands. "Thank you, Father MacKenzie. It's a pleasure to meet you as well." Father Mac was surprised to hear a British accent. He'd expected an Eastern European one. "I have only seen a portion of your great city, but it reminds me of London somewhat, with its eclectic mix of buildings and people. It appears to be a beautiful city, very cosmopolitan. I know a little bit of Chicago's history from the internet. But I guess you can't believe everything you read about gangsters and Al Capone."

Appreciative of a good sense of humor, Father Mac laughed. "It is a unique city, Ms. Tesar. I assure you the Capone era is long over. As a life-long Chicagoan, I've seen a lot of change since I grew up, mostly for the better. I'm curious, by the sound of your voice, I would think you're originally from England." Father Mac sipped his coffee.

"My background is not that intriguing. About 1980, I was a young girl, much the same age as Walter, when I left Prague with my parents who sought opportunities in the UK because times were difficult in our country. My father was a medical technician, and my mother a primary school teacher. Like my parents and most immigrants, I imagine the Pavliks wanted a better life for themselves and Walter. Until their dreams were snuffed, in such a tragic way." Gabriela became momentarily melancholy. "My father passed away in 1999 from sudden illness. My mother in 2004. I have no siblings."

"Can you tell me how you learned about Walter?"

"I can answer that," said Dr. Dvorak.

"No, please let me. Very simply, I received an inquiry, shortly after the holidays, from the London Czech Embassy regarding my extended family in Prague. My married name is Hill. My husband David, whom I met in university, is British. We live in London, in Chelsea. I don't know if you're familiar. You can see it from the London Eye, our enormous Ferris wheel overlooking the city. It's like one here I saw from my hotel window."

"I'm not familiar with London. I've been to Rome, but never to England."

Gabriela glanced at the Consul General. "I believe, correct me if I'm wrong, Doctor, a passport search produced my maiden name." Dr. Dvorak nodded his head. "I was curious because I haven't had contact with any relatives for many years. When I last visited with my parents, I was thirteen.

"Walter's mother was a Tesar. So I can best assume Walter and I are distant cousins. This is how I see it and wish to explain my kinship to him. I am very curious though and am further investigating our family tree. When I learned of Walter's situation, my heart immediately went out to him, all alone in the U.S."

After a brief pause, she continued with a smile. "So David and I live in a flat with our two dogs Chip and Pitch! David owns a football production firm. That's how we named the dogs. A chip is a shot that gets the ball in the air, and a pitch is the lovely green turf where football is played. My husband is crazy about football, and he thought up the names. He played goalie in university. Still helps as a coach with a local youth team."

"They are unique names!" Father Mac smiled. "I know our American football. Not too familiar with yours, although I've seen a few games."

"Actually Father, American football is growing in popularity in the UK. I believe some games are staged in London."

"Yes, you're right."

"And as for me? I work as an editor for the BBC."

"That sounds like a very interesting position, Ms. Tesar. I'd love to hear more about your work sometime, but I have a question about your family. Do you have any children?"

"No, we do not. Truthfully, we put forth quite an effort to adopt after learning I am unable to bear children. We decided not to pursue it anymore."

"I was hoping we could briefly discuss next steps." Dr. Dvorak glanced at his watch apologetically. "Unfortunately, I have another commitment in thirty minutes."

"Of course. My husband and I have discussed this at length. I would like to meet Walter before departing Saturday evening. We know there are many hurdles to secure approval, but perhaps Walter can come in mid-August for a short visit when we're on summer holiday."

"Father MacKenzie, I believe further developments regarding Walter will come from you and Ms. Tesar. The Consulate will help in any manner we can. I think Ms. Tesar's proposal is reasonable and could lead to a favorable outcome. What is your opinion?"

"I will be honest with both of you. Walter's situation is complicated by the likelihood of 'international red tape,' as Ms. Tesar indicated. Truthfully, I have to confer with our attorney and the child advocacy authorities who make official decisions.

"Before we get too far, my instincts tell me the next step is for Ms. Tesar to have an informal visit with Walter. We'll see how that goes. This is Holy Week and Easter weekend is a very busy time. I have commitments tomorrow, Good Friday, beginning at noon, but I'll check with my staff to determine if there's a window of opportunity. Saturday is busy, but perhaps we can meet briefly after breakfast. I need to be mindful of your departure time, which is equally important, Ms. Tesar.

"Dr. Dvorak, you are more than welcome to join us. It is my preference not to surprise Walter. He is perceptive." Father Mac concluded, "Honestly, I don't know how he'll respond."

On his way out, Father Mac agreed to take some Czech pastries back to AOMH. Mary Pat had a sweet tooth and loved homemade cookies. So did he when no one was watching.

Rites of Passage

U<small>PON</small> <small>RETURNING</small>, F<small>ATHER</small> M<small>AC</small> <small>FOUND</small> M<small>IKE</small> <small>OUTSIDE THE</small> <small>CAFETERIA</small>. "Mike, I spoke with Conrad Everett today. Confirmed he's coming with *all* of his grandkids to the Easter basket blessing on Holy Saturday."

"Okay."

"You can sit down and talk about football. It's the first step toward leaving here with some direction. July 25 is coming quickly."

"I'm not..."

"Think about it and let me know tomorrow morning." He patted Mike's shoulder. "Stop at Mary Pat's office. There's a box for you."

Mary Pat handed him a nondescript 18″ x 10″ box. "Here you go, Mike. A courier dropped this off. He said the lady at the address instructed him to deliver it here. From your team headquarters."

Mike headed to his room. Shaking the light package revealed nothing. He tore into the box and found the packing list.

Locker Room Cubicle Inventory

#52 Michael Stalowski

(4) framed personal photographs

Mike took a deep breath. Tentatively, he unwrapped the *gone fishin' with my dad* crayon drawing, followed by the others from his *office*.

These past few days bittersweet memories of his youth had flooded his brain. Now, looking at these pictures placed Kim, who wasn't even in any of them, front and center. He smiled remembering their first date when Kim told Harry she was his fiancée. Only she wasn't. Because he killed her before he proposed. His mind raced through the last eighteen months: their chance meeting—whirlwind relationship—the championship game—the accident—the isolation of jail—and now facing an unknown future.

He went to find Father Mac. His office door was ajar, and he looked up from a stack of papers. "Come in, Mike. Please, sit down."

"No thanks. You're right, Father Mac. I want to speak to Connie Everett Saturday. We good?"

"Sounds like you made a decision. If you're sure, then we're good. I'll call him tomorrow. One question though. What was in that package?"

"Personal stuff from my locker. Just some old family pictures they sent to my house." Sarcastically, he added, "Only it's not mine anymore! At least Lisa was decent enough to send them here."

Early Friday morning, Father Mac was at his desk skimming the Tribune and sipping coffee. After last week's spring tease, the weather forecast was foreboding. Highs in the 40s with afternoon thunderstorms and high winds. Looked to be a perfect storm for Good Friday.

Father Mac was ready to face the solemnity and sorrow of marking the day Christ died as he did each Easter Triduum. People often asked what is "good" about Good Friday given the circumstances. Father Mac believed it was because it led to the Resurrection of Jesus and the promise of new and eternal life. Not a guarantee of life without challenges, but the promise you won't face them alone. First however, Stations of the Cross would remind his flock of the suffering Jesus endured on our behalf.

Later that morning, Dr. Dvorak and Gabriela Tesar arrived with an unexpected companion. Worried about Walter's psychological issues, Gabriela asked Dr. Kovar to accompany them.

"Good morning everyone, please come in." They gathered in his conference room.

Mary Pat followed. "Would anyone like a cup of coffee?" Smiling, she added, "Unfortunately, I don't have any delicious pastries like the ones Father brought back yesterday. He did leave me a couple though!" Father Mac grinned sheepishly.

"Father MacKenzie, it's good to see you again. I hope you don't mind I was asked to join."

"Thanks, Dr. Kovar. I intended to keep this first meeting with Walter and Ms. Tesar a little more intimate. If it went well, I planned to have you meet with Walter and render an updated opinion. As I mentioned yesterday, Walter is more engaged recently. But you're here, so let's see how this goes."

"I can excuse myself," offered Dr. Dvorak.

"Thank you, but at this point it doesn't matter. We can always give Ms. Tesar a chance to speak with him alone." Father Mac added frankly, "This will either go well or it won't. We'll know pretty quickly."

"Walter has a twenty-minute recess before his next class, so we should head over now." Curiosity was killing him. "Ms. Tesar, may I ask what's in the box?"

"A small gift for Walter. Something I thought a boy his age would like."

"That's nice of you. Hopefully it's something to do with fishing. He loves to sit by that pond with one of our staff members."

She smiled and shook her head "no." Gabriela took in the old institution's ambiance as they walked to the annex. "The building is in very good repair despite its age. It's a bit gothic looking. With all this dark wood, it reminds me of London's old public buildings."

"It's pretty old. But not as old as the church and school next door. They survived the Chicago Fire of 1871, when the city almost burned to the ground. The flames went around them. Divine intervention!" he declared. "Our Board of Directors is very focused on preserving the original look. But wait till you see the annex."

The two-story multi-purpose room was modern, with lots of light, color, and open space. Walter was parked upstairs at a table, engaged in animated conversation with classmates. Father Mac directed his guests to the ground-level hub, an open atrium with a large skylight in the center that flooded it with natural light, even on gray days. He approached Walter's table.

"Hi guys, how are you doing this morning? You know classes end early for Good Friday services this afternoon. Then cheese pizza tonight."

"Yeah, we know. Tomorrow we can eat meat and chocolate again, like three times!" exclaimed Gabriel.

Gabriel, an eight-year-old African-American boy from a poverty-stricken West Side neighborhood, was here for the second time. His father was a gang member, who regularly beat him, his siblings, and his crack-addicted twenty-three-year-old mother. He had run away from every foster home he'd been placed in, but at AOMH again since January, Gabriel was thriving socially and academically, defying the odds and proving to be a math whiz. Some might say, under Father Mac's stewardship, the Angels of Mercy Home worked miracles.

"Walter, please come with me. There are visitors I want you to meet."

"Where are we going, Father? I have science class next. We're learning about wind power so I can't be late."

"Don't worry, you won't be. We're going to the hub. And there's always plenty of wind in this city! We may have some big gusts today. Get rolling!"

An ADA circular ramp allowed Walter to scoot his wheelchair in a corkscrew down to the first floor. Father Mac took the stairs.

"Come on. They're over there."

Walter glanced ahead. "I remember that lady. She's the doctor I talked to before."

He tipped his head down and rolled slowly behind. Father Mac wasn't surprised.

"Hello, everybody!" Father Mac waved.

Dr. Kovar and Gabriela smiled brightly. Dr. Dvorak hung back.

Gabriela's heart raced when she felt an immediate connection to Walter.

"Dr. Kovar, Walter recognized you right away."

"Hello, it's good to see you again." She smiled and extended her hand. He cautiously shook it.

"Walter, this is the Consul General from the Czech Republic, where you were born. He helps all the people from your country who live here. His name is Dr. Dvorak."

"*Dobry den Valtr.*"

"*Dobry den,*" Walter whispered.

"This is Gabriela Tesar. She came from London, England. All the way across the Atlantic Ocean to meet you! Isn't that something? Gabriela's a distant relative of yours!"

Walter looked suspiciously at Father Mac.

Gabriela bent over, reached out her hand, and softly greeted him. "Hello, Walter! It's so very good to meet you."

"Well, you don't sound like a relative of mine." Walter's eyes met hers. "You talk kind of funny."

The adults laughed and relaxed a bit. Walter kept his hands on the wheels of his chair, rolling it back and forth a few inches.

"I suppose that must be my British accent."

Dr. Kovar interjected. "I understand you've been fishing in the pond. I remember you wanted to do that last time we visited."

"I was right. Fish do live there, and I caught one! But we released it back."

"You have good instincts, Walter. Father MacKenzie tells me you're doing very well in your classes and music. You seem happier today than before."

"Yes, I like it here now. There are more interesting things to do, and I have friends."

"That's wonderful!"

"I know." He continued rolling back and forth in the wheelchair. Turning to Father Mac, he asked, "Isn't it time for my class?"

Father Mac glanced at his watch. "You still have fifteen minutes. Plenty of time. I have to show our guests something in the theatre. Ms. Tesar has something she wants to give you. Why don't you two visit for a few minutes and then meet us up top?"

Father Mac waved to Drs. Kovar and Dvorak. "Follow me, please." Once out of earshot, he turned to them. "Let's hope my instincts are good!"

Meanwhile, Gabriela reached over and placed the package on Walter's lap. She sat down on a stool next to him. "Go ahead and open it. I brought this all the way from home for you."

"Why did you bring me a gift? You don't know me."

"Oh, but I do. I learned a lot about you and your family. I didn't know any of this until Dr. Dvorak told me you lived here in Chicago. Your mother and I are related. I never met her, but I have the same last name she did."

"Our name is Pavlik. Yours is different."

"Well, it was her name before she married your father and became a Pavlik. I think that makes you and me cousins." She continued, "I also have a married name. It's Hill. My husband's last name. His first name is David. My full name is Gabriela Tesar Hill," she said proudly.

"Wow, that's a long name. So you did not know my mother, only you think you're my cousin?" Walter opened up a little. "If you live in London, how come you came all the way here? I know London is far away, in Europe, on the British Isle. Did you come just to see me? Because maybe we are cousins?"

"Yes, I did! I wanted to meet my *far-away* cousin in the United States! And I brought you something. Please open it."

Walter carefully opened the box and pulled away tissue paper, revealing a soccer ball with the official England National Football Team crest. He punched it a few times. Then he tossed it up over his head, deftly catching it. "This is very nice. Thank you!"

Gabriela detected a gleam in his eye. "Do you like football, Walter? Oops! I'm sorry. It's called soccer here. The U.S. version of football is very different I believe."

"I do like soccer. Sometimes my father and I kicked the ball in the park. I can't play now, but I have a friend here who plays football. I mean he used to. His name is Mr. Mike."

The Steelman reference meant nothing to Gabriela. "So Walter, my husband's company sends balls all over the world to football teams we watch on the BBC. I believe you have those broadcasts on ESPN."

"What's the BBC? I don't watch ESPN, but I like Discovery Channel!" Walter said enthusiastically.

"I like it too! BBC is like one of the big television stations here in the USA. I work for them. It stands for British Broadcasting Company. We have a lot of really cool programs."

"What do you do?"

"I edit programs so they make sense when people watch them."

"Oh, I like when things make sense."

"I'm sure you do. So do I—like me coming here to meet and visit with you!"

"Do you have a son who plays soccer football?"

"No, we don't have any children. But we have two really cute dogs, Chip and Pitch. Those are football words. David always plays with them and the football in the park. Chip and Pitch love to chase the ball!"

Walter giggled.

Trying to keep the momentum going, Gabriela got down to business. "Walter, I have a really, really, exciting idea!" She leaned in and looked directly into his eyes. "Why don't you visit us in London? The plane ride over the ocean is fun and you'll see *sooo* many new things! You could meet Chip and Pitch. They're Yorkshire Terriers and would love to play with you.

"You don't have to stay long. Consider it a vacation. Perhaps you can come in August when British children are on summer holiday. We can show you around London like a tourist—or a family vacation. You could take lots of pictures to show Father MacKenzie and your friends.

"We have this really neat Ferris wheel near my house that looks over all of

London, as far as the eye can see! That's why we call it the London Eye. I can point out our house from the top. Like we say in England, it's the bee's knees!"

"The bee's knees!" Walter roared with laughter. "What does that mean?"

"It's a British saying meaning something is awesome." She glanced at her watch. "We have to be mindful of our time. Your class is starting soon."

Walter tossed the ball up. This time, instead of catching it, he head bumped it. He extended his arms to grab it, but it bounced just out of his reach. For a split second, Gabriela thought she saw Walter's left foot twitch. She handed the ball back to him.

"Well, should we go meet the others?"

"I'll race you to the top," he challenged.

Gabriela paced herself.

"I win!" he yelled.

"You're quite a competitor. I lost my breath." She pretended to pant.

"If I visit, you're going to have to keep up with me."

"Should I take that as a maybe or a yes?" She bent down to speak to him at eye level. "Walter, I must return to England. This was only a short visit." Walter's demeanor changed. "But I'll call and we can send emails. We can also use Skype! We actually see each other on the computer screen while we talk!

"I'll check with Father MacKenzie. Maybe we can try it next week." She grabbed his hand and held it. "Tell you what," she continued, "why don't you think about it and let Father know."

Walter nodded okay.

Gabriela kissed his forehead and turned away teary-eyed. They headed to the group.

"Well, I see you got one heck of a present. Did you thank her?"

"Yes, Father Mac. I have to go to class now. Goodbye everybody." Smiling, Walter waved to Gabriela. "See you!"

He rode away and noticed Mike with a pushcart full of food. Walter called back to Gabriela. "That's my friend over there! Mr. Mike, the football player I told you about." She recognized he was clearly important to Walter.

In Father Mac's office, Gabriela reiterated her intentions. "David and I would love to bring him to London in August. I believe he is interested and hope we can make it work." Her enthusiasm was apparent.

Father Mac welcomed the return of sunny skies Saturday morning.

He called Mike into his office and noticed he wore an AOMH embroidered polo. His khaki pants were pressed. He was clean-shaven and apparently got a hair trim yesterday from the Home barber.

"Connie Everett will be here with his entourage at 11:30 a.m. for the Easter egg roll and basket blessing. He wants to talk to you first. You can meet in the hub or outside somewhere. Your choice. Right now, you have to help spread 400 plastic eggs."

"Absolutely!" The Steelman smirked. "Can't wait. I already stuffed about a hundred of those eggs!

"I think we'll just find a spot outside. Never figured I'd be talking to Connie Everett about football in the Garden of Intercession. You'd think my last contract negotiation would be me, my agent, and him seated behind his big old wooden desk. You know, he's got about a hundred pictures of his family on a cabinet behind him."

Father Mac took silent note of Mike's use of "last."

"He's a family man, Mike. Say what's on your mind and don't pull any punches. Funny the effect that Garden had on you this week."

Connie Everett arrived in a packed Storm passenger bus. Mike avoided the PR staffers brought along to help. Father Mac directed them to the grassy north grounds, next to the Garden of Intercession. Between AOMH residents and the Everett clan, it looked and sounded like grammar school recess.

Father Mac led Connie to the pond, motioning for Mike to join them. Before the accident, Mike had been ready to go head-to-head on a new contract, even if it meant getting released. Not today.

Everett shook Mike's hand with a firm grip. "Mike, it's good to see you," he said sincerely. "I have to say," he chuckled with a gleam in his Irish eyes, "it doesn't look like you've been hitting the gym regularly."

"Yeah, you're right. How are you doing, Mr. Everett? I see you brought some of your family with you." His response was as stiff and awkward as he felt.

"I'm good, Mike! I brought the younger grandkids, at least the ones who still believe in the Easter bunny!" Connie smiled. "I think there's about a dozen of them here, give or take. Look around. Father Mac does a great job for all these kids on Holy Saturday, doesn't he? I've been coming for a few years and wouldn't miss it. The blessing of Easter baskets is something I've done all my life. I want my family to know tradition. It's important to me. Nice of you to help out."

Like I'd be doing this if I didn't have to! Mike said nothing.

"Let's sit down on that bench, Mike."

Connie led him away from the raucous swarm hunting for hidden treasure. The Easter bunny was tossing eggs to the Home's physically challenged kids or their assistants. Mike watched Walter stuff them in his basket, grinning each time he caught one.

As in business, Connie took control. "This is a special place. Nothing else like it in the city. Things are changing in Chicago, and not all good. Neighborhoods my father built, once thriving with hard-working people who cared about family and faith, have deteriorated. Many are poverty-stricken and crime-ridden. But in the midst of that, Father Mac is doing wonderful things.

"My kids and grandkids are blessed in many ways. But they need to understand not everyone is lucky. See people who need help and someone to love them. I want them to experience what the Angels of Mercy Home stands for. It's important they learn to support people who need a helping hand. That's why I love this place. I think the world of Father MacKenzie and what he does for everyone. Although he should be taking it easy in retirement."

Mike thought, *This guy never said more than ten words to me at once. Now he sounds like Father Mac.*

Connie looked over at Mike. "I'm curious to know what you think of Angels of Mercy? I'm guessing you have a better idea now than last November."

"Yeah, Mr. Everett, it's a special place." Mike was guarded. *I can't say anything stupid.*

With a serious look on his face, Connie Everett shifted his whole body to face Mike. "Look Mike, I'm not here to rehash what's been said in court, the media, or on the street. Father Mac told me you've adjusted here. I trust him when he tells me you're doing well.

"There's a lot of things in life that don't make sense but happen anyway. Bad things happen to good people. I may not like or understand a lot of what happened the last few years." He paused and pointed a finger at Mike emphatically. "But you have paid a dear price—personally and professionally.

"Me?" Connie shrugged. "That morning, when I heard what happened? At first, I couldn't believe it. Then I was pissed when I thought about the end of the game. The coaches should have followed medical advice." At the other end of the bench, Mike tensed up.

"And when I thought about it more, I realized you must have felt like hell battling other demons." Mike tipped his head down and lowered his eyes. "My heart went out to you and your family. And your girlfriend's parents. You experienced a horrendous trauma and loss." Trying to maintain his composure, Mike looked up at Connie and gave a small nod. Connie waited briefly before continuing.

"You know Mike, that championship game was a blip on my radar screen of life. And yours, if you can believe it. But others felt it was the end of the world."

Connie stood up, squarely in front of Mike. "This is life. Forget about the past. You can't change it." Emphatically he advised, "You need to *focus only on what you can control!* Going forward—think about your decisions—personal and professional." Connie sat back down, closer to Mike.

"Playing football is a critical decision because it is *both personal and professional.* Plain and simple. I want you back on this team. The one you led, in a Storm jersey with #52 on it. Understand?"

Definitely didn't see that coming! Mike's eyes opened wide, but he didn't know what to say.

"But there's a process with hurdles ahead. Some are pretty big. Are you up to the challenge? Do you want to go out like you did or do you want to fight back and go out your way? The only way you and I both know—as a winner. Right now, you're in limbo with the Commissioner and the League. What about your fans?"

Connie didn't expect Mike would have immediate answers and saw that Mike was getting overwhelmed.

"Mike, I don't give a rat's ass about public opinion, but some in our organization do. I'll deal with the Commissioner myself. Blackwell was a popular rookie. We really liked him. His career is over, but I hear he's gone back to school to be a doctor."

"Wow!"

"Summer camp will be a fresh start. There will be room for rookies, free agents—and walk-ons." Nearing the end of what he came to share, Connie stood up. "It's been years since I drafted you as a rookie, and technically, you're not part of the team or the league anymore. But *you're a veteran who earned his scars and stripes.* You should be there—and you can be there. If you accept the challenge, *you can walk back on the field and the team.* You have my invitation to prove you want to be a member of the Storm."

Mike swallowed hard and nodded.

"We have a new Head Coach and several assistants. I want your answer

Monday morning. If you're willing to try, we'll talk about next steps. If not, know that my door is always open. You'll always be part of this organization. You paid your dues—served your penance. If you want your old job back, put your head down, and go for it. *Be a walk-on, Mike!* And may God Bless and keep you!"

Connie grabbed Mike's hand, shook it firmly and walked away to join Father Mac, his young flock and the Easter bunny. After a few steps, he turned to add, "Just for the record, Mike. I was going to give you a new three-year contract, despite what Castro and the front office advised."

Crossroads

WALTER ZIPPED BY MIKE AFTER DINNER TUESDAY. "HEY! COME BACK HERE, little buddy!" He stopped and spun his chair around.

"Yes?"

"What's with the soccer ball, little man? You join a team?"

"No, my football is a gift from my cousin in London."

"Really? Football huh? London cousin? What's up with all that? Was that lady with Father Mac on Good Friday your cousin? You and her were talking, right?" The Steelman sounded like a cop bracing a pint-sized perpetrator.

"Yes, that was her. She came here with a man named the Consul General of the Czech Republic! And a doctor lady who was here before. Gabriela is my cousin who lives in London. Her husband delivers soccer balls. She came *just* to meet me, *and* she invited me to come for a summer visit." From Walter's enthusiasm, Mike surmised it was true. He'd get full details from Father Mac. "She said we can see each other on Skype when we talk on a computer."

"Wow, man! So you gonna ride around with that ball on your lap now? You know we can toss it around."

"Okay! Maybe *one day* I can kick the ball to you like I used to with my father."

Mike recalled the first time he grabbed his fishing pole after Frank's death and sat on the breakwater rocks at 95th Street Beach alone. *Maybe Walter's ready to move again.*

That weekend, Gabriela and Walter had their first Skype call. Father Mac agreed to thirty-minute visits on Saturday mornings.

The St. Andrews head football coach was a nephew of Coach Grogan, Father Mac's St. Michael's colleague. He helped Father Mac stage surplus free weight equipment in the Home's maintenance shed. Mike started slowly but regained some bench strength. After a month, he was able to bench press nineteen reps of 225 pounds. The 2008 NFL Combine record by a defensive player was thirty-seven reps. One late April afternoon, Father Mac led the Steelman to the wide-open north grounds. More daylight allowed for agility drills. Father Mac set five orange cones at 20-yard intervals. His old stopwatch and whistle hung around his neck.

"Mike, I have to ask. Why the hell did you call a blitz with a minute to go when you had the Firehawks on the ropes? You already took out their whole running game when you injured the rookie. I thought you'd play the pass and not gamble. Should have won that damn championship and gone to the Super Bowl."

Mike sat on the damp grass, stretching his quads. "Yeah, maybe. At first, I put it all on Blackwell for not covering the pass when I changed it up. I thought we'd recover on the next play, but it didn't happen. Don't worry, I realize it was my fault and have felt bad ever since, but that play clock can't be reset."

"I remember the Resurrection game senior year. I called the safety blitz and you took out Lorenzo White on your own. You covered me on that one. Coach Grogan chewed me out even though we won. I called the wrong play. He thought they were going to pass." He smiled, "We're even."

"You know Father, that ended up being the least of my worries that night."

Father Mac put a hand on Mike's shoulder and nodded sympathetically. "Although I don't understand why—it was part of the Lord's bigger plan. The time has come to move forward, Mike. " He reached out a hand to help him up off the turf.

Mike headed to the first cone.

"All right, let's go," directed Father Mac. "What was your best time in the 40 during the 2006 season?"

"6.2, I think. Not sure."

"What did you run it in the Combine?"

"5.1," Mike laughed.

"I heard an outside linebacker from LSU got drafted in the 1st round today. He ran a 4.42 in the Combine."

"Yeah, but he's a black kid and they run faster than white guys," Mike kidded.

"I'd JUG that attitude if you weren't already in detention!"

The Steelman ended his third 40-yard trial huffing and puffing, beads of sweat forming on his face. "Well, what do you got?" He felt the old physical demons awakening. But the newest one, the right tibia fractured in the accident, hurt the most. The Steelman silently ate the pain.

Father Mac ran down the numbers on his old St. Michael's clipboard. "7.4—6.8—7.6! You have a way to go, my friend."

Mike bent over at the waist trying to catch his breath. The garish pink and purple scars from the accident stared at him.

"How's the leg?"

"Doesn't feel too bad. I can plant and make cuts." *Racking up mortal sins lying to a priest.*

"I'm sure the team staff will get you right when you report to camp. We're a little limited here."

For the second year in a row, the Storm had made the playoffs, only to lose their shot at the Vince Lombardi trophy to another wildcard team. Connie Everett had struggled with letting Don Castro go after he had allowed Mike to play against medical advice, but his failure to get to the Super Bowl demanded change. New head coach Ty Miller and his hand-picked staff would focus on an explosive offense to win.

With aging veterans to replace, the front office was busy. Miller and his staff planned to emphasize youth and speed. Diesel Cummings indicated the 2008-2009 season would be his last. So did Brandon Stokes. Dino Rhoades and Jeremy Butler were gone. The defense needed to be rebuilt.

Dr. Cowan was busier in April than during the season, buried by the added load of reviewing prospects' medical profiles which affected their NFL stock. At Connie Everett's request, he agreed to evaluate Mike on Sunday, April 27. Coincidentally, it was the last day of the NFL Draft and Mike's birthday.

Father Mac brought Dr. Cowan to the medical suite. The space met current standards for institutional medical care but lacked sophisticated imaging equipment needed for a comprehensive diagnostic assessment.

"It's good to meet you, Doctor. Thanks for coming. With your schedule, I suppose it's your only day off."

"I'm far from being off today, Father MacKenzie!" he chuckled. "I just got cut loose when we made our last pick, a kid out of USC. Mr. Everett must have listened to our new scout from California."

Kendrick Clements, the seventh-round pick from poverty-stricken South Central Los Angeles, was an over-achiever raised by a single mother. Connie preferred Big Ten programs. He figured local guys would bust their ass to make the hometown team. Of course, Notre Dame was the exception to that rule, due to his South Side Irish roots. Coming at a time when the Storm needed another unlikely hero, Clements planned to simply run his ass off and score touchdowns.

"A Trojan!" exclaimed Father Mac. "We used to eat them up when I played at Notre Dame. One of the oldest college football rivalries."

"It should be interesting. That's great you played football at Notre Dame! Connie told me you coached Mike in high school."

"I did. Not too many like Mike come along. I think I did a pretty good job with him on the field. It's the off-field stuff I wish I could have been around for the last several years."

"It's been a very tough road for him. I'm curious to see how it goes this afternoon. Haven't spoken to him since the 4th quarter of the championship game. I told him—and the coaches—he shouldn't play. If he didn't have a concussion from the hits on Brookes, he wasn't human.

"I will tell you this in confidence, Father Mac. If he plans to put the pads on again, there are many obstacles to overcome. But I've been around him since he was drafted. He's the guy that pushes aside a pallet of bricks to get to the ball. It's in his heart. His DNA. I'm glad to help."

"Thanks." There was a knock on the door. "Come in."

Mike tentatively opened the door.

"How are you, Mike? Good to see you." Dr. Cowan felt there was no need to get into an extended dialogue about anything other than the business at hand.

Father Mac excused himself.

Mike felt like a draft prospect getting the team doctor's once over. Dr. Cowan did a quick visual check down of the former Pro Bowler, whose medical history he knew well. It was apparent Mike had added girth to his previously chiseled abs. As expected, the Steelman's arms, shoulders, and chest had lost muscle mass and tone. When they shook hands, Dr. Cowan saw the garish zig-zag gash on his right arm. The right leg looked worse.

After a cursory exam, Dr. Cowan determined Mike lacked arm strength, flexibility, and range of motion. His labored breathing while jogging in place and kicking up his knees was an obvious sign of the absence of aerobic activity. Elevated blood pressure, not previously part of his medical history, could have numerous causes.

"Tell me Mike, is this something you really want to do? I assume you've thought hard about it, maybe with some divine intervention."

"Doc, look I hear you loud and clear. Yeah, it's my decision to do this."

"As your doctor and friend, I have to be candid. It's an uphill climb to walk on this team."

"You know, my neck pretty much feels the same. With sitting out last year, maybe I've got a couple of years left. Then I go out my way."

"Training camp is going to be a bitch this year. Starting with being in the middle of an Indiana cornfield. The new philosophy is youth, speed—and offense over defense. No bullshit! They want to rebuild."

"New injuries I'll work through. No Vicodin or Toradol here, Doc. No alcohol for the last what, fifteen months? This place forced me to think about things. That was the intention, right? I gotta see what's left and what I can still do."

Dr. Cowan nodded. "You've done it your way since I met you. But your neck? The damage is still there," he reminded him. "And it's two years later. Don't kid yourself. Adding the new injuries to the old stuff, it's going to be the biggest challenge of your career.

"Father MacKenzie told me about potential access to the field next door. You just have to hope there are no #52 jerseys to autograph. I'm guessing it would be hard to stay under the radar. Push-ups, pull-ups, stretches, core work, jump rope . . . you could do right here. Your rehab favorites, remember?"

"Oh, yeah. Couldn't forget if I tried."

"You take care now. We'll talk soon."

As the countdown clock ticked closer to the Steelman's release from the Angels of Mercy Home—and the beginning of summer camp—he made steady incremental improvements toward regaining a semblance of his NFL form. It was more difficult than any previous off-season.

It seemed Walter's suggestion was prophetic. *If you try to play football again, maybe I can try to get up by myself.* Since Easter, Walter pushed himself to get stronger. Between regular physical rehab sessions and weekly visits with Dr. Kovar, he made consistent strides physically and emotionally. Walter could stand for short periods of time with crutches and move himself forward on parallel bars.

Walter and Mike fished when time permitted. Mike promised to take him fishing on Lake Michigan during the perch run. They enjoyed tossing around

Walter's soccer ball or a football. With Mike's insistent urging, Walter could drop-kick the ball a short distance by the Fourth of July. Clearly, without realizing it, Mike had become his mentor. In return, Walter softened the jagged edges of the Steelman's hardened heart.

Working at his desk early Monday morning after a full weekend of patriotic celebrations and fireworks, Father Mac glanced at his calendar, confirming what he already knew. Mike's days at AOMH were numbered. He needed to double down on his efforts to prepare Mike for freedom.

"As you know, your sentence here ends Friday, July 25. Don't worry, no F's in my report for your final court appearance! Literally time to move on, Mike. You'll need to hang your hat somewhere else."

Mike nodded. "Yeah, I know. It seemed like forever, but it's coming up pretty quick. Even if I could, I don't want to step one foot in the last place I lived. That condo was really for Lisa all along, and I only moved in because it was a place to go when we separated. But I do need to make sure some stuff is out of there before she officially gets her key back. "

Mike didn't share the sole item he wanted. Hopefully, Steve Kendall had Kim's diamond ring secured.

"You know, I get to keep my Harley and old Corvette. Have a spot here? God only knows if I ever get to legally drive again."

Father Mac figured it was Mike's attempt at gallows humor. "Sure, Mike, we'll figure something out. I've thought about your driving privileges. It's my understanding you can petition the court to reinstate them, with limits. That's for your probation officer and lawyer to sort out.

"More importantly, Connie Everett called yesterday. Training camp officially begins Monday the 28. You have to leave early Sunday morning."

"Don't worry, Father. My attorney is already looking for a condo. Where the heck is camp this year? Independence, Indiana? Sounds like a *fun* place to get back into it."

"I'm sure it's not as nice as your suburban facility, but the campus is nice. I've been there a few times on retreat."

"Doc said it's the middle of a cornfield."

Father Mac laughed. "Yes, you'll absolutely see the corn growing around the athletic field. The football team is D-3, but they're pretty good. Connie Everett paid for a new fully-equipped athletic facility. He has a connection to St. Joe's. Spent another $3 million to spruce up the field and stadium."

Mike heard the words but drifted off to training camp 2006. Kim had just appeared in his life. Back then she was the light at the end of the training camp tunnel.

Father Mac cleared his throat to refocus Mike. "Look, there's one thing you should *always* remember. You can return to Angels of Mercy if you need someone to confide in, or just to check in and say hello. We started this leg of your journey together, and I'm going to walk with you the rest of the way."

Their steel-blue eyes met. Mike nodded to acknowledge his understanding and acceptance of his Dean of Discipline's help. He stood up and shook Father Mac's hand.

"Thanks for everything, Father Mac. Really. I never told you before but should have. I appreciate everything you did for me ever since back in high school. You never shut the door. I won't forget it." There was a pause. "Hey, when is that charity benefit this year? That Shining Star thing?"

Father Mac was surprised. "I think it's on the books Sunday, November 30."

"Well, count me in!"

The final days peeled off the calendar, each one passing a bit more quickly. Mike knew he had to say goodbye to Walter but didn't want to make a big scene. He stopped by his room after the Saturday night movie. Walter was seated in a chair near his desk reading a geography book. A child-sized walker stood next to his wheelchair.

Mike had hated the limitation of his walker after the last knee surgery. Walter's embodied his courage to embrace a new life. One step at a time.

"Wow! Walter, look at that! New wheels, man. You're getting ready to trade in that old wheelchair for good."

"Yes, Mike!" Walter had recently dropped Mr. "My therapist said I won't even need it in a few weeks." Proudly, he exclaimed, "Look! The left one moves pretty good already." He slowly lifted his left leg a few inches off the ground and straightened his knee. Dormant muscles were coming to life.

"That's great, little man! Good work! Keep it up." Mike bent down to eye level. "Hey, Walter, remember I said I might see if I can play football again? Guess what? I'm gonna try."

Walter nodded. "I knew you would go."

"I'm heading to Indiana to join my old team for summer camp. When it's over, we'll go fishing. I promise! And get pizza at my favorite restaurant afterwards, okay?"

"It's okay. Are you leaving here now?"

"Tomorrow morning, little man. My ride comes early."

"Well, I will miss you, Mike. But when I see you again, you can't call me *little man* anymore because I'll be taller when I stand up."

The Steelman double fist-bumped Walter and gave him a hug, the first outward sign of affection exhibited by the Steelman in many months. He fought to suppress his emotions. Uncharacteristically misty-eyed, he stood up. "Listen, we'll still be buddies. You'll see. Okay?"

"Okay." Walter smiled and high-fived Mike.

"Keep working with those therapists. Do your best, right?" Walter nodded yes.

As July drew to a close, months of plans, preparation and logistics were coming to fruition. Walter's and Mike's lives had intersected due to tragic losses. Now at crossroads, their paths diverged, but the marks on each other's hearts were indelible.

Sunday, at dawn, Mike took one last mental picture of his home for nine months. He was conservatively dressed in a long-sleeve blue dress shirt, khaki pants, and brown loafers. Almost unrecognizable with his short sandy-blond hair.

At the curb, Father Mac patted his shoulder. "Here, Mike, almost forgot to give you this." He pulled a clear plastic bag with a cell phone and charger out of his pocket.

"Thanks! For everything."

"Don't worry, Mary Pat charged it. Remember my number!" Father Mac smiled. "Good luck in camp. Hustle it up, Stalowski!"

The Steelman threw his gear bag in the trunk and climbed in the back seat, headed to independence at last.

Independence

THE ONLY REASON TO DRIVE THROUGH INDEPENDENCE, INDIANA, WHOSE population doubled every August when 3,200 students arrived, was to get to the College of St. Joseph.

Connie ensured the St. Joseph's Eagles athletic facility improvements, partially funded with his $3 million contribution, would be ready for his grandson's upcoming senior season. He also recognized the opportunity for the new regime to establish themselves in a secluded environment. Media and public were not invited. Traditional Storm football—strong defense and bruising running game—was subject to change.

Don Castro had been old school. He had believed in squeezing the last ounce out of aging veterans. Ty Miller, on the other hand, a thirty-six-year-old wunderkind successful in D-1 college ranks, built teams around young, well-disciplined, and focused players.

Connie Everett had explicitly instructed the new coaching staff to evaluate Mike Stalowski objectively and provide Connie with a comprehensive report. "Stalowski has been a proven veteran and leader for the Storm, and *I* will make the final decision on whether he makes the roster! Understood?"

Miller didn't care for distractions caused by Steelman-type characters. Despite Connie's mandate, he intended to make Stalowski expose his limitations.

Bored with the farm landscape, Mike turned his phone on. The picture from Warren Dunes almost stopped his heart. Quickly closing his phone, he tried to get Kim's image out of his head. He sensed the car slowing down and looked up to see the lush green lawns of the Division 3 campus.

"Can you drop me off by the big tower? I don't know where I'm going, but it looks like a good place to start."

He slung the weighted gear bag over his shoulder and found a campus directory near the quad. Nearby was a small chapel, surrounded by headstones. *Can't get away from cemeteries and chapels.*

Although he was far removed from 1994 Champaign, Illinois, Mike had felt the same butterflies in his stomach when he left Hegewisch for his first collegiate football camp. Thankfully Connie Everett made sure there were no distractions—no red tape—no media trucks and microphones in his face—no general public. He wanted Mike Stalowski to concentrate on winning back his old spot.

In the distance, the Steelman singled out the athletic center. The parking lot was almost empty. No exotic sports cars or expensive SUV's indicating the arrival of his teammates. Clearly, the Steelman had been brought in early.

"Hello, sir!"

Two young men, wearing Eagles jerseys, didn't seem to recognize him. They were probably team managers helping direct Storm personnel.

Looking around, Mike saw the Eagle logo and an inscription. "Soar like an eagle—champions rise above the storm." On the adjacent wall it read, "Fate whispers to the warrior, 'You cannot withstand the storm.' The warrior whispers back, 'I am the storm.'"

Holy shit! Going to be a long two weeks! "Can you tell me where I can find the coaches' office?"

"Sure, that way, sir. Room 13."

"Thanks, man."

He readjusted his gear bag on his shoulder and headed in the direction they indicated. Although the college boys waited until he was out of sight, Mike heard their whispered argument. Yes, it was definitely "him."

Mike paused before the half-open door. He raised his fist to knock, then hesitated. He replayed the promises he had made to himself and those who helped get him here. *Time to face my football future.* The Steelman stood up straight and knocked.

"Come in."

The spartan surroundings reminded Mike of the jail visitor's room. At least there was no glass partition. Only a yellow note pad was on the table. Seated before him were two young clean-cut guys, dressed in gray khakis and Storm-blue polo shirts. He figured they were barely older than him.

Mike knew very little about Miller: from college ranks; never played in the

NFL; former PAC 10 receiver who believed the West Coast offense was the greatest thing since sliced bread, which explained drafting the USC running back. Storm smash-mouth football, which the Steelman and fans were accustomed to, was going to change.

"Good morning." The youngest-looking guy stood up and extended his hand. "I'm Ty Miller. Mike Stalowski, correct?"

"Yeah . . . I mean yes. I was told to report here. How are you guys doing?" Mike reminded himself to smile and establish a positive image.

"Mike, I'm the new Head Coach. We appreciate you getting here early. We've retooled coaching and administrative staff this season. Some faces will be familiar, but many will not." Miller was business-like. "This is our Defensive Coordinator Mark Slaughter." Miller chuckled. "The defense will play under Slaughter's Rules."

"Pleased to meet you, Mike. I've followed your career for several years." Slaughter extended a firm handshake, but his "deer in the headlights" expression made him seem uncomfortable.

This guy is gonna run the defense? "Thanks, I'm glad to be here."

Both coaches sat down simultaneously. Mike wondered if Connie had scripted their speeches. Miller cleared his throat, folded his hands on the table and glanced at Slaughter, who no doubt would influence Mike walking on the team. Or would he?

Miller stared at Mike authoritatively. This wasn't Connie's script. The Steelman was getting called on the carpet.

"Look, Mike, here's what you should expect. We have two full weeks of team meetings and coaching staff one-on-ones where we're all going to get down in the weeds of learning about each other, on and off the field. Everyone's going to learn what playing football for the Chicago Storm means *going forward*.

"You must understand it's our job to change the Storm's direction. Our goal is to maximize talent to win a championship. You probably realize many people in this organization want you at St. Joe's today. But I'll tell it to you straight—there are ALSO those who *don't want you here*.

"You will have every opportunity to play for this team." Miller paused briefly. "But it's on you to win that spot. No free rides. We're putting the best fifty-three guys on the field. Period."

Then Miller honed in on the real issues. "I've been briefed about your personal life the last couple of years. I was told it is not reflective of your career and achievements as a leader and captain of the defensive unit. We all know what the media said. I expect the truth is in the middle." Mike sensed his words lacked sincerity. "So my position is simply your personal life is personal to you. It has no bearing on your ability to play football for the Storm this season. Period.

"As you know, Mike, camp begins with ninety players. Only fifty-three make the roster. You're a free agent walk-on. That is your official status, and you're not the only one. I am deliberately not assigning numbers during camp. Names will be on practice jerseys. Numbers will be on seventy-five jerseys for Family Night, the day after camp folds.

"Mike, a lot of hungry players want to be on this team, including your replacement. So let's be clear. I wish you well, as does Mark. But you will have to earn a spot. Period."

Slaughter, an obvious company man, simply nodded. The one-way conversation was done. Mike had counted three emphatic "periods." He had to conform and perform. Although unstated, the alternative was clear. Period!

"Is there anything you want to say?"

"Look, Coach, straight up, my life was turned upside down. I went through stuff I don't wish on anybody. Truth is, I decided to come here to see what I have left to contribute. I know it won't be easy, but I will work my ass off to get back in shape and see where I'm at as a player.

"I have some physical limitations, but I can still play." He paused. "I owe Connie Everett a lot, including this second chance. I want to help win a Super Bowl championship. We were close. I want to help *this* team get there—this year."

"Fair enough, Mike. See you at noon in the auditorium. Wait outside. A team assistant will take you to your dorm room. Mr. Everett is bringing everyone by bus around 10:00 a.m."

Luckily his worst fear, rehashing the NFC Championship fiasco, was groundless. As expected, the Steelman would have to prove himself on the field. The question remained, could he?

Slaughter spoke up after Mike stepped out.

"I know what you said before, Ty, but I see a guy who's cleaned up his act. Almost didn't recognize him. We gotta give him a shot. You know what Everett said."

"Yeah, but *I'm* the Head Coach. As far as *I'm* concerned, it's *my* call. We'll give the Steelman his shot. But I'll tell you now, none of his previous bullshit! And I promise there *will not* be any shadows of former Pro-Bowlers darkening *my* sideline. *Period.*"

The closed-door discussion was muffled, but Mike heard the emphatic fourth utterance of *period.* He knew his football fate hung on whatever preceded it. After ten minutes of impatiently waiting in the hall, he heard a familiar voice.

"Well, look who the Storm blew in! All cleaned up like a La Salle Street banker. Thought I was coming to grab some lost rookie." Charlie Samples, the equipment manager, grinned widely, exposing his gold front tooth. He reached out both hands to Mike. "Good to see you, man. Knew you'd come back to us!"

Mike was happy to see a familiar face and bent over to give Charlie a bro-hug. He had met Charlie his rookie season. Mike was amazed that Charlie, in his seventies with a bad limp from a construction accident, was still quick on his feet with a spring in his step.

"Hey, Charlie, good to see you. How are you, man? Hear you're taking me to my hotel room."

"Yes, sir, Steelman! I do gotta say I miss Don Castro. Family's good, kids, grandkids all good. Wife still naggin' after fifty-four years," laughed Charlie. "How 'bout you?"

"I'm good, Charlie. It's been a little rough. But I'm back and gonna see what I can do."

"I gotta get this out." Charlie paused to wipe his beaded brow. "You listen to me. These next two weeks—you hold your head up high. You been a leader and everybody knows it! I know you had troubles, brother. Trust me. It ain't easy. I played the hand I got dealt. Mr. Everett didn't count me out. Told me to pick myself up and come back to work. He give me another chance like he's givin' you one, Mike.

"What you been through would test any man. But you know what? I am a South Side church-going man. The Lord, he only gives you so much to handle. And I know there's folks watchin' out for you." He chuckled. "Your angel been workin' overtime.

"You give these young guys hell-fire on that field. Show 'em what you got in the tank. *There's a storm comin'!* Ain't the end of your story, Mike, it's a new chapter! And I am truly sorry for your loss. I been prayin', man."

Mike nodded. "Charlie, I appreciate it. You've always been good to me."

Inside the dormitory, Charlie pressed the elevator button several times to no avail. "Come on, Steelman, let's take the stairs. These guys have you with a Notre Dame rookie O-lineman named Settles. Miller wants big bros helping little bros, defense and offense, one big happy family. You gotta know, Mike, I didn't make the assignments. I was gonna take care of you 'cause I like you. I switched names on the bed so you was roomin' with Stokes! Thought they wouldn't notice, but I got caught."

"All good, Charlie. I've been hangin' around a lot of kids lately. Don't worry, roomin' with a rookie is cool, even a Golden Domer. I found religion, man. Anyway, I roomed with Stokes last camp. He snored like a bear all night."

"Here we go, Steelman, Room #22. It ain't the Four Seasons Presidential Suite."

"Ha! I've seen worse!"

Mike checked out the twin-size beds on either side of a large window. The right-side placard read *Mike Stalowski—Defense,* and the left *Orlando Settles—Offense.* Two large Storm gear bags were on each bed. Mike had an extra box.

"You got some extra essentials. Mr. Everett himself told me to make sure you got what you probably didn't bring. Tell me what else you need, and I'll make it happen."

"Appreciate it! Thanks, man." Mike peered out at the quad.

"Who's all those people? I thought campus was closed."

"Oh, I heard they had tours for freshmen and their families. Kids don't come back until you guys are out." Charlie looked at his watch. "Steelman, I gotta move along. That bus full o' your teammates is gonna be here in an hour. Still got a ton of stuff to do. I ordered local barbecue. This farmer is smokin' up some meat. You guys'll eat about five cows I figure."

"Charlie, thanks for everything, man. Although I could use some food now!"

"I know you lookin' for some double cheeseburgers and fries, but a couple of those protein bars gonna have to tie you over. No restaurants open around here."

The Steelman sat on his bed. His thoughts bounced between football, freedom, and his last summer camp. Hearing laughter from the crowd, he looked out again, fixating on a blonde with her back toward him. The hair on his neck stood up. *Holy shit!* She looked just like Kim.

Breaking into a sweat and feeling more anxious than ever, Mike rested against the headboard and closed his eyes. A knock woke him up, disoriented because he wasn't in his AOMH room.

"Who's there?"

"Orlando Settles, man. Your roommate."

"Come in."

The door slowly swung open. Filling the entire doorway was a young black man in brand new Storm gym shorts and T-shirt. He had cornrows and both of his arms were completely tattooed.

"What's up? I'm Orlando Settles."

"Mike Stalowski."

The 6' 6", 310-pound offensive tackle shook his hand. "I know! I'm a fan. Even though I'm from Texas, I always followed the Storm. Hope you don't mind being roommates." Settles chuckled. "We sure gonna fill up this room!"

He dropped his bags and rustled through one.

"I know this ain't your first rodeo. Is there lunch before the meeting? I'm starving, man."

"No, I think it's gonna be a lunch meeting. Don't worry! We'll get fed. And I didn't see a cafeteria. Here, you want one of these protein bars?"

"Hey, thanks! Can I call you Steelman? That's how everybody knows you." Settles pushed down on the college-sized X-Long twin mattress. "You know the beds in our ND athlete dorm were a hundred times better. And we had a loaded snack pantry. It's going to be a long two weeks."

"Get used to it. You'll do okay. Just don't roll too far!"

"Ain't that the truth," laughed Settles. He fished out a small picture.

"Who's that?"

"My baby girl, Jasmine! And my fiancée, not a baby Mama!" He laughed. "Although I have to say my dad, who's a pastor, would have been much happier if we married first."

Mike peered at a little girl in a pink dress with pink bows in her hair, nestled in her mother's arms.

"She's two-years-old, Steelman. She's my world and always gonna be. Whatever happens the next two weeks don't matter. If it don't work out, I'm going home to build a life."

"Wow, man! Nice family."

Here was a 22-year-old rookie from small town Texas, who seemed like he would be able to avoid the temptations and pitfalls of the NFL. Orlando Settles had plans A and B, with or without an NFL contract. Mike had no real plan, whether he made the team or not.

"I do hope, though, Steelman, you know for that first home game, that I run out of that tunnel through the Storm cloud right behind you!"

Thoughts of Kim and her baby were in Mike's head. He quickly stood up. "Hey, I gotta go explore a little. I'll come back and get you in about half an hour for the meeting."

"Where you going? Explore what?" Settles was unsettled by Mike's reaction.

"For a walk."

The group from outside his window was headed his way. Taking a long look at the blonde, he realized she did not resemble his dead girlfriend at all. Actually, she looked like Lisa. As if Lisa and Kim had morphed to remind him that despite being in Independence, he wasn't really free.

Mike came upon the campus chapel and climbed the cobblestone steps. He plopped down in the second pew and looked around. Mike was drawn to the St. Joseph statue, with a kind, nurturing face and an arm around adolescent Jesus' shoulder.

Dad's middle name was Joseph. But it wasn't that way the last two years. Was the other way around.

He tried to focus. Summer camp was the opportunity to rebuild his career. Not time to deal with his personal life. Nevertheless, Mike felt his personal past was entangled with his football future. *It isn't 2006. Period. Kim is not here. Period. I won't find her at St. Joe's or anywhere on earth. Period. I have to accept, as she once willed, her spirit is now on the wind, over the water, and in the bright stars of the night. Period.*

The door creaked. Mike glanced backward and saw 11:30 on the choir loft clock. *Jesus Christ!* He charged out, hoping to make it to the meeting with five minutes to spare. Jogging briskly, he got to the dorm at 11:46, tucked his binder in the right steel trap and took off at a full sprint. A dull pain surfaced in his right leg.

The Steelman's shirt was soaked for his 12:01 p.m. grand entrance. Sweat dripped down his face. On the dais, Ty Miller glared, barely masking his disdain for Mike as he grabbed the nearest aisle seat.

Someone poked him in the rib. With a Cheshire cat grin, Stokes whispered, "Brother, some things don't change! You get lost man?"

The Steelman covertly fist-bumped him. "Took a wrong turn out of the dorm."

Mike listened to Miller's vision. He looked over the ninety players assembled—eager rookies, wary veterans, and recycled free agent walk-ons—knowing full well only fifty-three would wear a Storm uniform for the season opener. The old #52 didn't know if he would be one of the fifty-three.

Under Miller's direction, summer camp would break Don Castro's mold. Offense over defense. Speed over force. Touchdowns over turnovers. He would be leading the Storm in a new direction. Roster cuts would separate the wheat from the chaff, the weak from the strong, and the committed from the entitled.

The daily schedule was onerous. Breakfast call was 6:30 a.m. sharp, followed by team meetings from 7:00 a.m.–9:00 a.m. The next three and a half hours were intense contact drills and scrimmages. At 12:30 p.m., they had a 90-minute respite from the heat for lunch and additional instruction. Back on the field until 4:30 p.m., followed by one hour of mandatory weight-training and aerobic conditioning. The last meeting included breakout sessions until 6:30 p.m. Finally, dinner until 8:00 p.m. afforded teammates a small window of opportunity to refuel and socialize.

At the first dinner, Miller had players stand up and share something about themselves. Rookies went first. Thankfully, free agents were last. When it was the Steelman's turn, Mike felt all eyes on him. Some younger players seemed awestruck. The coaches appeared eager to watch the disgraced player introduce himself.

Mike had rehearsed for a moment like this. In a reserved tone with no bravado, he simply stated, "My name is Mike Stalowski and I'm a middle linebacker. I've been in the league since 1998. I'm from Chicago and played for the University of Illinois. I've played this position since high school and hope to continue this year." Mike paused and added, "I'm looking forward to camp."

The infamous captain of the Steel Trap defense kept true to his old self, not sharing much. He sat down. Brandon Stokes, Joaquin Rivers, and Ezra Holmes stood in unison and began clapping. Some of the younger players followed suit. Ty Miller scowled.

The first week of practice, temps hovered in the mid-90s with extremely uncomfortable humidity. The second week was worse. Though never a big fan of aerobic conditioning, Mike knew full well that he either met Ty Miller's mandate or went home, wherever that might be.

Stokes was sweating profusely on the stairclimber next to the Steelman. "Damn, son! You better up the level and get your big ass moving! You look like you're draggin' a damn piano."

Earbuds in, Mike was blasting an old Guns N' Roses favorite, "Paradise City." Peering through beads of sweat clouding his eyes, Mike was preoccupied with the pink and purple accident scars on his arms and legs.

"Hey! Mike? You listening?"

The Steelman finally noticed Stokes. "What's up?"

"I said pick up the pace, Steelman. Season starts in a few weeks. You ain't got time to play the piano. Quit draggin' it around! You and me are gonna study the playbook later, right? Like Coach said. Even us veterans, the guys who wrote it!"

Mike wiped his brow. "I may not have to. After today's practice, I could be washing cars! That rookie running back can juke, cut, catch, run, and stop on a dime, man. I thought I was tackling a ghost. He kept slipping through my fingers. Made *me* look like a rookie who didn't tie his cleats. You looked good, though."

"It's that damn new offense. Give it a couple of days, Steelman. We'll make the adjustments, right?"

"Absolutely. Hey, Brandon, I'm hitting the whirlpool."

"Okay, I gotta stretch, but I'll join you." Stokes thought about how tough it must be for Mike to be a walk-on. He honestly wondered why the Steelman wanted to be back on the field with the organization he failed to lead to the Super Bowl. And that was only the professional side. Mike's personal nightmares Stokes couldn't even begin to comprehend.

Miller and Slaughter monitored the defense competition closely, especially aging linebackers. During practices and drills, Mike relied on instinct and years of experience to "play smart" instead of simply doling out the brute force that had built his headhunter reputation. He was alcohol- and drug-free. Nothing to mask physical pain, which had been difficult while running drills with Father Mac at AOMH. On the field, Mike had some success proving he could still make plays. However, in certain new defensive schemes, he got beat: blowing opportunities to showcase his old form, missing key tackles.

Most NFL teams shy away from giving highly-paid athletes a chance to intentionally inflict pain and injury on a teammate. But Mark Slaughter, who had never participated in one of the drills himself, thought it would be a good idea to conduct the Oklahoma drill. He felt it would either reveal what was left of the Steelman's Pro-Bowl form—or make his roster cut a no-brainer.

Under the blazing 2:00 p.m. sun, Slaughter painstakingly explained the drill fundamentals. "Okay, men, the Oklahoma drill showcases the foundations of football: getting off blocks, shedding them and getting to the ball carrier."

Stokes poked the Steelman's ribs and whispered through his facemask. "Is this dude for real? Don't he know this is the NFL, not Pee Wee football?"

"You have to be tough and physical! *Wrap up* your opponent and *tackle* them! Remember football fundamentals, men! Stay within the cones. Start when the whistle blows. The drill is over when one of the players is on the ground. Linebackers, you're up."

"C'mon man!" Mike whispered sarcastically. "You might learn something."

Kenny Lynch, #52's replacement, was in an unenviable situation with the potential return of the Steelman. He had been released from Cleveland after tearing an ACL and not returning to form. Actively looking in a thin market, the Storm front office took a gamble, offering Lynch #56 and a cheap one-year contract. The coaches were pleasantly surprised.

"Let's go, Lynch!" The whistle blew. Diesel Cummings got low and rumbled forward. Lynch shed the O-lineman's block and cleanly tackled Diesel for no gain.

"Stalowski, you're up." Mike was across from the second-year guard. Behind him stood the Trojan rookie. Clements showed no fear. He wasn't fazed one bit by the infamous veteran Pro-Bowler.

The whistle blew. Clements shot out of the hole, straight at the Steelman, furiously churning his legs. In a flash, Clements shifted left. To make the play, Mike planted to twist right—stunned by sudden sharp pain in his right tibia. Instead of grasping Clements with his steel traps, he barely delivered a glancing blow to the swift rookie running back. Clements quickly blew past him for a 5-yard gain.

What should have been a routine tackle by the Steelman was an eye-opening performance by the rookie. The Steelman tried to hide his leg pain. Stone-faced, Miller made notes on his yellow pad. Mike clearly fell short in the coaches' eyes—but more importantly, his own. It was crystal clear he had to deal with what his body was telling him.

The end of two weeks of isolation, blood, sweat, and tears finally arrived. Fifteen players were trimmed from the roster Friday, August 8. The big surprise to Mike was back-up outside linebacker Ezra Holmes. Mike had always respected him as a player and felt Ezra performed better in camp than he did. Mike was glad Orlando Settles made the cut. The following night, the remaining seventy-five players would have the opportunity to make big plays in front of fans, under the bright lights of Veterans Stadium at *Chicago Storm Family Night*. Twenty-two more players would be cut shortly after. The Steelman survived the first hurdle. Making it to the season opener was TBD.

Mike stared out the bus window at acres of flat cornfields along Interstate 57. The Steelman was apprehensive about looking in the locker room mirror—and not seeing the reflection of the player he once was. There were no guarantees he would assume his position or wear #52. Mike thought about what it would take to bring the Steelman back. Alcohol and painkillers were not options.

Mike self-assessed an at-best mediocre camp performance. He had received accolades from some assistant coaches and veteran players. Miller and Slaughter were a hard read. Neither said much about his performance, let alone had an intimate conversation with him. So much for getting to know everyone. Mike figured Miller didn't want him on the roster. It was clear he was at St. Joe's only because Connie Everett said he would be.

And now, he was heading to an empty condo. Truly on his own for the first time. Steve Kendall had hastily arranged a six-month lease in a South Loop high-rise close to the stadium. Preoccupied, Mike barely noticed the cameras waiting at Storm headquarters. Word had spread like wildfire the Steelman was making a comeback. He slipped to the back of the building, avoiding the media, and called Steve.

"I have a driver there, Mike. In a black Suburban. He'll take you to *Harbor View Luxury Condos*, 1901 South Calumet. You're on the twenty-second floor."

"I don't need luxury. Just a place to lay my head."

"It's just a name. You can afford it. Don't trip over the boxes when you walk in. Your condo stuff is there. Plus what was sent to the Home. The priest okayed it. There's only a few boxes, maybe eight.

"Look Mike, we'll talk about the personal items and legal docs when I see you."

"What about the Harley?"

"In storage." Mike had one more question. "Yes, I have it in the original box."

Family Night

Kendall paced in the lobby. "Hey, man, great to see you! Looking good. Here's your condo and Harley keys. Sorry, I gotta run."

What's with the bum's rush?

"I know there's a lot to talk about, but I have dinner with a big new client. I'll call Monday."

Another big client? How about sitting your ass down with your current biggest client? Mike was hungry and wanted to put down temporary roots, so he let it go.

Kendall pulled a small manila envelope out of his suit jacket. "The ring as promised."

Mike grabbed the envelope. "Thanks for everything, Steve. I'll call after practice Monday. You know I gotta figure out how I'm getting to Lisle without wheels."

"Oh, yeah! I spoke to your probation officer. We can petition for limited driving privileges, to and from work. I have pretty good hooks at the DMV. In the meantime, there's a car to drive you wherever you need. Don't worry, I'm covering it! Also, you'll be glad to know the final settlement numbers aren't that bad. Lisa actually left you something to live on. Although I'm sorry about the old 'Vette, Mike. I think it was her way of getting the last word."

Mike opened Unit #2233 and was immediately struck by the impersonal décor. Not at all like Lisa's luxurious tastes. He sat down on a wobbly wooden stool at the breakfast bar and pored over a list of eateries that delivered, finally deciding on Chinese which Lisa hated. He couldn't remember the last time he ate alone out of white cardboard cartons.

The condo had a picturesque Lake Michigan view which he enjoyed while sitting on the couch and eating dinner. His mind drifted, in and out of lake memories. The most vivid were of Kim and their water's edge encounters. No longer used to receiving calls, he jumped when his cell phone rang.

"Hey, Mom! Good to hear from you."

"Michael, how are you doing?"

"Condo's okay for now."

"How was camp?"

"I made it through, right? We'll see how it goes."

"What about your neck?"

"Feels pretty good. Let me know if you want to come in and see a game."

"I called to talk about watching you play, Michael. I'm actually at the airport for a flight to Chicago . . ."

"You're coming here?" he interrupted. "Where's Tom? Is everything okay?"

"He's home. Everything's fine. Mr. Everett called last week. So I booked my ticket to support you at Family Night. But now I'm at the airport, waiting to board and I started feeling a pit in my stomach. And I realize I just can't go and watch you dish out and take what made you infamous. I'm sorry, but I just can't do it."

"Don't be sorry! You always worried even way back in high school. It's okay, Mom. I never expected you would come."

"Listen, I know the hell you've been through. No matter what happens next, Michael, do what's best for you."

"I get it. I really do."

"You have a lot of life ahead, and football doesn't have to be a part of it. Your Steelman has been gone awhile. You don't have to bring him back."

"You're my only son and I love you! I really wanted to be cheering for you. I'll support you any other way. *But I just can't watch anymore.* Not after the toll football's taken on you physically. How it's affected your personal life and your personality. I'm *really* sorry."

"Mom, it means a lot that you planned to come. Please don't worry about the Steelman. I got a lot of religion this past Easter, and I don't see him being resurrected too. I gotta see what *Mike Stalowski* can do when *he* shows up to play."

After the call, Mike decided to see if his X-Box was packed. Previously, when the season started, Mike liked to play video games when he was alone to think about anything besides football. Hopefully some of his favorite "black ops" hero games had been packed. He ripped into tape and bubble wrap, smiling at his good fortune when it was in the first box. Tucked among the video games was an 8.5″ x 11″ envelope labeled PICTURES. Hesitantly, he opened it.

Mike froze when he saw Kim's headshot proof. It seemed she was alive, looking directly at him. He clearly remembered taping it back together and putting it in the dresser drawer with the ring. The second photo, a black and white, was initially unfamiliar. Then he realized it was the picture from the dunes bike trip. A sticky note on the back, in Kim's flowing script, read *need black frame.* He quickly stuck the photos back in the envelope and tossed it in the box.

I gotta take a shower and chill out. Been a long fucking two weeks. No, it's been a long life.

Twenty minutes later, Mike plopped on the couch and fell asleep. Later, he dragged himself to bed and didn't wake up until 9:30 a.m., groggy and unsure of his whereabouts.

Mike made coffee and sat on the couch, looking out over the lake. Glancing north, he saw the stadium's parking lot. He figured it was only a few blocks to the pedestrian bridge crossing Lake Shore Drive, a convenient way for South Loop residents to get to the lakefront and Storm fans to the stadium.

Screw it! I don't need a fucking driver. I'm a walk-on, right? Today, I'll be a walk-in, too!

Mike got down to business sorting through boxes. The envelope with Kim's pictures and ring went into yet another dresser drawer. Out of sight, but within reach.

At 1:00 p.m., he grabbed his gear bag. Mike wasn't taking any chances on being late for the 4:00 meeting. The doorman barely acknowledged him. *Probably not a football fan.*

It felt weird walking to work. Previously, he cruised Lake Shore Drive onto McFetridge, descending to the player's garage. Barbi Santiago's interview at the top of Ramp 41 popped into his head. Given any opportunity, media vultures would swoop down on him. Thankfully he wasn't in a chauffeured vehicle, reminding everyone he could not legally drive.

Family Night was a popular preseason showcase, especially for families. Tickets were only ten dollars, with kids under thirteen free. Fans young and old delighted in watching rookies and idolized veterans scrimmage. For years, the Steelman had been a fan favorite, evidenced by the swarm of #52 jerseys throughout the stadium and around Chicago.

The offense was expected to score points passing and running the ball. The defense was expected to make tackles, but not full-force injury-inducing sacks or violent hits. The front office honored recently retired players. Tonight, Dino Rhoades and Jeremy Butler would receive accolades.

In his hometown stadium for the first time since the national TV meltdown, Family Night was the Steelman's comeback litmus test. Normally, there would be hordes of fans, parking in the South Loop and clogging the bridge hours before kickoff. Most fans arrived just before 7:00 p.m. for Family Night since tailgating wasn't allowed.

Seeing the stadium's tall Romanesque columns in the distance tightened the knot in his stomach. Built in the 1920s and dedicated to WWI veterans, it was in dire need of a facelift when the Storm won their only Super Bowl. Many disappointed Chicagoans, not just architectural purists, thought the renovated exterior looked like a gray spaceship landed in the old stadium. Some declared it looked like a toilet bowl surrounded by the original walls. Only Connie Everett's closest confidants knew he planned to build a state-of-the-art domed stadium, along the lakefront near the old steel mills, if Chicago won the 2016 Summer Olympics bid.

Mike approached Gate 0, the original main entrance. The four 20-foot-high locked metal doors opened into an expansive atrium with an enormous overhead banner. *Welcome fans! Warning—There's a storm coming!* Luckily, a service door was propped open. Peering through the crack in the doorway, he saw an unattended Stadium Operations cart. The driver must have left the door ajar.

After the short walk to the stadium, the Steelman had soreness in his right leg. *I can drop it off at the locker room. They leave these things all over the place.* But he opted not to push his luck. The last thing he needed was Miller reminding him the carts were not for players' use. Period!

He had never been in the atrium as a player. It was one of the stadium's largest concession areas with a mega-store full of team merchandise and memorabilia. Mike didn't see any #52 jerseys on display. Two seasons ago, they had been a bestseller. He shrugged. *Doubt they sold out last season.*

Team and sponsor advertising banners were everywhere. "Legends of the Game" caught his attention. It included record-setting players' pictures and statistics from the team's early days through the 1990s. Game clips brought them to life.

Mike skimmed the legends backwards. As the photographs and game-clips became grainy, Mike didn't recognize them. *Chester could have rattled off these guys from the '30s, '40s, and '50s like it was yesterday.* He pictured Chester and his old war buddies hanging out at the Hegewisch VFW or Old Tyme Tap, watching a game over shots and beers.

What would Stalowski #52 look like on that banner? Which game clips would loop endlessly? Will I be remembered as Mike Stalowski who showed up to play—or the infamous Steelman? In twenty years, will fans remember me as a dominant player—or someone who spun out of control at the end of a productive career? Will I only be remembered for the car accident that killed Kim and ended Blackwell's career?

Mike passed the Section 138 tunnel, near the 50-yard line and directly above the Storm Family and Friends Lounge where Lisa Stalowski had once reigned supreme. Before entering the locker room, Mike had to take the most difficult step on his NFL journey.

Emerging from the tunnel, he walked on the field alone. No inflated Storm cloud—no fireworks—no flyovers—no cheering and screaming fans. The Steelman would not be taped-up, padded-up, and drugged-up to play.

From the corner of the endzone, Mike soaked it all in. He surveyed the 100-yard gridiron from goalpost to goalpost—Storm bench—50-yard line—blank scoreboard and jumbotrons—and empty stands. Nine years of memories, pain and euphoria swirled in his head, accompanied by echoing cheers of fans and Storm sideline chatter.

"Hey, Steelman!"

"Charlie, Holy Christ! You scared the crap out of me."

"Some shit never changes. Always the first guy here!"

"I had to come out here. Before everyone else."

"Yeah, I know. It's a big step, man. Take 'em one at a time."

Mike nodded. "Let's go, Charlie. I'll need some tape to suit up!"

"Absolutely, Steelman! Whatever you need, brother."

Precisely at 4:00 p.m., Connie Everett welcomed his team in the locker room. "Gentlemen, you are members of the Chicago Storm. Your jersey bears your name and a number. Show our fans and this organization what you are made of." Ty Miller noticed Connie went out of his way to shake Mike's hand.

"Hey," Stokes asked, "did you know Dino and JB are coming tonight? To get recognized. We should set something up to celebrate their retirement. Just a few of the defense."

"Sure, man. I gotta hear what they're gonna do now to occupy their time."

Later, when the team assembled at the tunnel, which reflected hues of silver and blue from spotlights inside the cloud, Ty Miller led the charge, followed by the offense. Behind defensive free agent no-names, the Steelman strapped on his helmet. His infamous hair—cut and blue-streak free—no longer cascaded out the bottom.

Showtime for the Storm. Exploding fireworks signaled the moment of truth. Just like Connie wanted. #52 STALOWSKI was part of the team. A shock to some and prayer answered for others.

Since high school, Mike's heart had raced before each game. Family Night was no different. His heart pounded like never before when thunderclaps and simulated crackles of lightning strikes reverberated through the stadium speakers. The anxiety of being on trial again—in the court of public opinion—weighed heavily. Determined to face judgment, he ran onto the field through a gauntlet of teammates, receiving unexpected high-fives and fist-bumps. The Steelman took his place on the Storm sideline.

Mike stood at attention facing the flag. Initially, he was shocked to hear the familiar chant—*Steelman—Steelman—Steelman*. Then loudly and clearly—*Your steel traps look a little bent and tarnished—Welcome back ladykiller.* Good and bad shouts from the sidelines seemed about evenly split. *Welcome Back #52—Nice haircut, get it in County Jail?—Steelman we love you!* Mike Stalowski stood stoically, helmet in hand, as the opposition pumped up the volume, drowning out the Steelman chant with—*DUI—52—DUI—52—BOOOO—52.* Brandon Stokes glared at the stands. At last, the national anthem drowned out both cheers and jeers. The Steelman stared straight ahead, the taped fingers of his right hand over his heart.

Standing at the 50-yard line with their families, Dino Rhoades and Jeremy Butler waved as the crowd cheered in their honor. Mike watched his former teammates, almost enviously, knowing in his heart the Steelman would never receive the same sendoff.

JB Butler, a man of few words, simply thanked the team, fans, and his family. Dino Rhoades, never at a loss for words, stepped up to the microphone.

"First off, I want to thank God for guiding me here. I lived the ultimate dream in this stadium. Fortunately, I've had positive role models throughout my life, who encouraged me to do the right thing and be the best I could be. Secondly, I want to thank Mr. Everett and the entire Chicago Storm organization for the opportunities they gave me. Most importantly, I want to thank all you fans—the best in the world—for being an extended Chicago family to me, my wife and our children. You are all now and forever in my heart."

A five-minute cacophony of applause and cheers filled his eyes with tears. When the applause subsided, Dino's voice cracked. "And finally, thanks to all my teammates and coaches, present and past, for being with me on this field, both in good times and bad. It's time to move on."

Mike hung on every word.

"Many of you know about The Rhoades Scholars' work supporting under-privileged students in their educational endeavors. That will not change. I will now devote more time to mentoring and inspiring young adults, leading and guiding them on their path to becoming the very best they can be, in the classroom *and on the field*. You can still find me on the gridiron—working with student-athletes to help make their dreams come true. But I can't do it alone. I need you on my team. Please continue to support The Rhoades Scholars. I sincerely appreciate it."

It was time to watch Family Night with Jerome Butler, behind the bench in Section 138. Leaving the field to another round of thunderous applause, Dino scanned the players bench looking for his former teammate. Their eyes met. He flashed Mike a big thumbs-up. The Steelman nodded and returned the gesture.

Anticipated starters usually played the first few series. Free agents and rookies were next, and then a mix of all three groups executed plays. Diesel Cummings waited at the 20-yard line to return the first unofficial yards of the 2008-09 season. The high kick fell right into his numbers. He ran it straight up the middle to the Storm 36-yard line. A decent return for the aging veteran.

Automatically, #52 strapped on his helmet, ready to head out on the field. "Lynch, get in there," announced Slaughter, stopping the stunned Steelman in his tracks. Kenny Lynch knew he was getting looked at hard, but he had fully expected the Steelman to get the first call.

On the opening play, Lynch fought off a double team, cleanly tackling Diesel in the backfield for a five-yard loss at the 31-yard line. Lynch earned a dirty look from the new offensive line coach, but Diesel fist-bumped his teammate. Ty Miller remained deadpan.

Shit! I could've walked through that gap pushing a wheelbarrow full of bricks. But Mike knew Lynch's tackle for lost yards was impressive.

On the next play, Miller wanted to evaluate the young talent. Orlando Settles went in at left guard. Kendrick Clements lined up ready to take the handoff and run up the middle. An undrafted rookie receiver lined up wide right.

The Steelman watched from the sidelines. Linebackers Stokes, Rivers and Lynch readied for Slaughter's unfamiliar 3-3-5 defense. In anticipation of a pass, Lynch gambled and dropped back 10 yards to cover the flat. The ball snapped. Clements took the handoff from McNulty and charged the gap opened by Settles. Clements side-stepped, just out of Rivers' and Stokes' reach. Lynch finally dragged him down from behind for a 1st down at the 49-yard line. The crowd went wild for Clements' power run and Lynch's come-from-behind tackle.

Ty Miller whispered to Slaughter, who motioned Lynch to the sideline, giving him a congratulatory pat on the shoulder pads. "Stalowski, you're in. Let's go!"

Mike checked his helmet straps and took a deep breath. His first steps on the familiar turf seemed surreal, but the former captain of the Steel Trap defense and veteran Pro-Bowler was in command, instinctively sizing up the next play. Diesel and Clements lined up in the Power I-formation. Mike recognized the triple option. If they ran the ball, the fullback would block for Clements. One of the receivers could get thrown to. McNulty, a mobile quarterback, could also take off running if he saw daylight.

Mike knew the Family Night game was a place to play conservatively, but the Steelman wanted to pay Clements back for the Oklahoma drill embarrassment.

The Steelman came to life, bellowing a familiar 4-3 formation in anticipation of the run. Slaughter was not surprised. "Old dogs don't learn new tricks."

McNulty was under center. The Steelman yelled "Zone black" meaning cover the pass or blitz on a running play. He looked side to side. Both outside linebackers were in position. His heart was racing waiting for the snap.

McNulty faked a hand-off to Clements, then dropped back for a screen pass to the H back. Rivers and Stokes bit on the run, blocked at the line of scrimmage before they could scream, "Pass!" Orlando Settles manhandled two defensive linemen, preventing them from disrupting the play.

The "Steelman sixth-sense" felt the screen pass coming. He zeroed in on the receiver's hands going up to grasp McNulty's bullet pass. Like hundreds of times before, the Steelman needed to change directions in pursuit. He pushed off his planted right foot. His right leg almost collapsed from pain in his tibia, causing him to stumble. The 6' 3", 235-pound H back T-boned Stalowski, crashing him to the turf. His degenerated vertebrae snapped, crackled, and popped, reminding Mike the damage was still there. The free safety tackled the receiver. Another 15-yard gain and 1st down.

Mike was on his hands and knees, listening to the crowd noise clearly dominated by jeers. His right leg was on fire. *I gotta get up! Son-of a bitch! What the fuck happened?*

Sensing trouble, Brandon trotted over. "Get up, man! You gotta get up!" He reached to pull his captain up before the sideline and stadium realized the obvious.

Dr. Cowan knew something was wrong but didn't move, giving Mike a chance to save face. Now clean and sober, in all his years of eating pain, the Steelman drew from reserves of determination and grit. Never before had he needed to dig so deep to find the strength to simply stand up, let alone trot 15 yards to the 34-yard line.

Miller and Slaughter conferred. McNulty nodded after the Offensive Coordinator signaled. The next play was a "trips right" three wide receiver stack at the line of scrimmage. Cummings and Clements were on either side of the quarterback. McNulty was under center. "Green 88—Green 88—Hut-hut." He pulled the ball in, dropping back to check down his receivers.

The Steelman called "sting blitz" and saw daylight in the B-gap. Just like he called a blitz January 20, 2007, when another Storm rookie caught his wrath—and a blitz thirteen years before that saw him barrel down on Lorenzo White. Now Kendrick Clements saw the Steelman's fierce blue eyes with the thousand-mile stare. The hobbled, one-legged middle linebacker barreled down on Clements. McNulty read the blitz. With all three receivers covered, he released the ball into the stands.

Although he should have—the Steelman did not let up. Head down, he plowed into Clements' numbers, knocking him airborne. The rookie's helmet snapped forward and then back when he slammed onto the turf. The referee blew the whistle. In a game, Mike probably would have drawn a personal foul. The Steelman ran another ten yards before stopping. Clements was flat on his back. No movement. The stadium was silent. The medical team assessed the damage.

"Holy shit, Mike! You leveled the kid!" exclaimed Stokes.

Mike panted, bent over with hands on his hips. "He had it coming, bro. We shut them down." It seemed the Steelman was back.

Clements sat up and then stood up on his own. The crowd cheered and clapped.

Slaughter signaled Mike off the field, replacing him with an unsigned rookie. "Stalowski, what the hell was that? We're playing a scrimmage, not the damn conference championship!" Mike glared at him contemptuously.

The remainder of the scrimmage was uneventful. Players rotated in and out while Mike mostly sat on the bench. With a few minutes left, Slaughter put the anticipated starters back in. The Steelman's right leg still throbbed, superseded only by neck pain. A fog had rolled into his helmet after the hit on Clements.

Unexpectedly, Orlando Settles sat down next to his summer camp roommate. "Hey, Steelman, it's almost over. I just want to say thanks for everything while we roomed together. You been a big inspiration, man."

Mike turned to look around the stadium that once cheered his every move. He saw only a handful of #52 jerseys.

The assistant linebackers coach came over. "Only a couple more plays. You good to go back in?"

"Yeah, I'm good," he lied. The coach sensed his insincerity, and the Steelman did not step onto the gridiron again that night.

Requiem for a Linebacker

S ELF-CONSCIOUS ABOUT HIS ACCIDENT SCARS, MIKE SHOWERED LAST. THE super-pulsating jets of hot water loosened his stiff neck. They kneaded his sore muscles at all angles, top to bottom and sideways, like a car wash. He moved his right leg across the side jets to soothe his tibia. Hopefully, the throbbing headache and fogginess would soon fade. If the coaches realized the impact of his head hitting the turf, he'd be in a concussion protocol. Behind the eight-ball before the season was even underway.

Although he really didn't want to socialize, Mike decided to stop briefly to wish Dino and JB well. Connie Everett would surely make an appearance. Mike didn't want to face him after tonight's performance. At least it was unlikely that Miller and Slaughter would still be there.

Feeling somewhat human, he wrapped a large towel around himself and moved to the long row of sinks to look at his reflection. Mike always assessed the collateral damage sustained by the Steelman, worst pain first. Bending over, he ran his fingers over the surgical scars on his right leg. Throbbing but tolerable. He planted his bare foot on the hard tile and winced.

What the fuck happened? All I did was make a cut and push off my fucking foot. Something's really messed up! Shit! How the hell am I gonna play sixteen games? He tossed a few disposable ice packs in his bag.

"Just seeing who's still here." The Director of Security poked his head into the locker room. "No rush."

"No worries. I'm out of here in a few."

Mike stood in front of the mirror fixated on his arm tattoos, intermingled and overlaid with purple and pink scars, a constant reminder of the accident. St. Michael and the infamous steel traps were most prominent. *Like it or not, looks like the Steelman will always be a part of me. These scars will probably fade pretty good, but tattoos sure as hell don't wear off.*

Mike leaned over to rest his arms on the counter. He slowly lowered his chin and stretched his neck side to side. He closed his eyes and replayed the horror movie reel seared into his brain—the last minutes of the fateful NFC championship game. To escape the hard reality, he fantasized about what could have happened *if they won that night*—winning the Super Bowl—marrying Kim—having a baby.

Reluctantly, Mike opened his eyes. His vision was blurry. The mirror reflected another stark reminder he no longer held the keys to the Storm kingdom. His old locker stall was empty. Mike visualized Kim's last headshot and the dunes photo added to his practice locker. Not tucked away in a dark drawer, along with the dazzling diamond-encrusted ring. Its brilliance snuffed out like a flame, entombed in the tiny black velvet box.

When he looked back in the mirror, he was stunned to see Kim standing next to him—looking exactly like she did in her headshot, except her dress was white.

She whispered, "It's gonna be okay, baby. You'll see."

She raised her left hand and blew him a tender kiss. Her ring finger was glaringly bare, not sparkling with the halo diamond ring. In a flash, as quickly as she appeared, his heavenly angel disappeared. He felt she was real. *I heard her sweet voice. But that's impossible.* He had to find his own way.

On his way out, Mike tried to sling his duffel over his left shoulder. Due to sharp shooting pain, he couldn't hoist the strap high enough. *Shit, must'a tore something. I'm gonna have to let Cowan know. This ain't no sprain.* Two quotes in bold black letters were taped on the door.

> # A CHAMPION
> ## IS SOMEONE
> ## WHO GETS UP,
> ## EVEN WHEN
> ## HE CAN'T

```
PLAY UNTIL

THE CLOCK

SAYS 00:00
```

Post-It notes as we hit the field! Is this Miller's way of inspiration? Where's the "PERIOD?"

The bruised and battered Steelman took a long look around the silent locker room. *Fate whispers to the warrior, "You cannot withstand the storm." The warrior whispers back, "I am the storm."* The words from St. Joe's were stuck in his head. *Been one fucking hell of a storm for me. Could use some clearer skies.*

The locker room door slammed shut behind him. He walked toward the Family & Friends Lounge. Mike was startled to see Father Mac, sans priest collar but with his cane, chatting with Connie Everett outside the reception. Mike had noticed Father Mac used his cane more frequently around AOMH.

Holy shit! What the hell am I supposed to say?

He heard Connie's gravelly voice. "Hey, Mike, come over here." *Busted.* The team owner and his AOMH guardian were looking straight at him.

Be cordial. Act like you feel like a million bucks, not a sack of shit! He attempted to walk straight and tall to hide any visible signs of injury.

"Hello, Mr. Everett. Hey, Father, good to see you. How's it going?"

"We were going to ask you the same thing," Connie answered. "Saw you down on the field. It must have felt good to be back out there."

"Yeah, Mr. Everett, it was good. I still have to get used to the new playbook. I'll study it more," he fibbed.

Father Mac smiled. "Mike, I remember in high school I made you reread the X's and O's several times in the library. Don't worry, you'll get it right."

"Looks like you took some shots, and dished 'em out too," noted Connie. "I was a little worried about the rookie."

"I just wanted to make the Clements play. Old habits I guess."

"It was only a scrimmage. Seems like a tough kid; he took the hit."

Shit, now I really fucked up!

"It's okay, Mike. I've seen you play a few games. I know your capabilities. By the way, please stop by my office Monday after practice. I want to follow up on some things we discussed before camp. I'll be there all day. Going in bright and early." Connie's tone was matter-of-fact.

"Sure, Mr. Everett." *Is this about my contract? Something else?*

"Good to see you both. I have an early morning at Mass, so I'll say goodnight. Father Mac, we'll talk soon. Mike, see you Monday after practice!"

Under normal circumstances, Mike's agent would attend a meeting with the owner, but this seemed personal.

Father Mac had a surprise. "Mike, someone inside wants to say hello."

"Yeah, who?"

"Go on in. You'll see. I'll be in shortly."

Mike opened the door. About sixty people were milling about, trying to mingle with JB and Dino. How on earth was he supposed to find "someone" who wanted to "say hello?" A young boy on the other side of the room looked familiar. Just like Walter, minus a wheelchair or walker. A soccer ball and cane were on the chair next to him. *My little fishing buddy and friend.*

Completely forgetting he was there for JB and Dino, Mike hurried over. Walter looked up and smiled with a mouth full of hot dog. Mike dropped his duffel bag and put his hands on his hips.

"Hey, Walter! What the heck are you doin' here?"

"Hello, Mike! I came to see you play."

"It's good to see you, buddy!"

"I watched from the big skybox where Mr. Everett brought me and Father Mac. Wow, this stadium is big! I saw you out there in your uniform. I don't understand all the rules very well, but I saw you running around chasing the other team." Walter exclaimed, "It's not like soccer, Mike!"

Seeing Walter warmed the Steelman's heart. He momentarily forgot his own physical pain and emotional angst.

"It is *not* like soccer! Yeah, Walter, I was running around out there all right. Trouble is, I'm a little rusty and didn't do as well as I thought I could. I see you brought your ball, huh?"

"Well, Mike, at least you tried your best. Isn't that what you told me? Remember? Try your best. I brought my ball because I want to show you something. Can we go by the field?"

"If you can, show me in here."

Walter planted the cane in front of himself, grabbed it with both hands and slowly pulled himself upright. With the cane in his left hand, he leaned over the chair and picked up the ball with his right hand. Stepping away from the chair, Walter carefully guided the ball down his right leg, resting it near his foot.

"Watch this, Mike!" Walter cocked his right leg back and swung it forward, launching the ball about forty feet. Timing his entry perfectly, Father Mac intercepted the kick.

"Nice job, Walter! Right, Mike?" Father Mac winked at Mike.

"Walter! Wow! Look at you, man! Up and running, ready to hit the turf. I'm so proud of you, man. You said you were gonna give it your best and look at the results." He gave Walter, who was grinning from ear to ear, a fist-bump and high-five.

"Can we go out to the field, Mike? I'd like to kick it again on the grass."

Father Mac saw in Mike's eyes that was the last place he wanted to go. "Walter, I don't think we have time. Mike has to say hello to his old teammates. Remember? The ones this party is for. And we have to be ready for our trip tomorrow night."

"What trip?" Mike looked quizzically at Father Mac.

"Please, Father, let me tell him!"

"Okay."

"Guess what? I'm going to London tomorrow night! I'm going to visit my cousin for a week! We came to tell you and see you play."

Father Mac added, "Yes, I'm taking Walter."

"Well, isn't that something! All the way to London. I hear there's a lot of stuff to see there. Old stuff, like museums and castles. That's great, buddy. You take care of Father Mac!"

"We need to say goodbye to Mr. Rhoades and Mr. Butler." Father Mac handed Walter the ball. "Why don't you stop by the dessert table and pick out a couple of brownies or cookies to take back?"

"Yes, Father." Walter turned to Mike. "So, Mike, I'll tell you all about it when I get back. I can't wait to play with Chip and Pitch!"

"Who are they? More cousins?"

Walter roared with laughter. "No! Dogs who love to play soccer. I'm going to kick to them! Goodnight, Mike!"

When he was thirty feet away, Father Mac called out, "Hey, Walter! Send that ball back here!"

Mike kept his eyes on Walter while he positioned it, almost like a placekicker. Walter's once limp and lifeless leg launched the soccer ball about a foot off the floor. The Steelman tried to block it with his right leg. The ball bounced off his reassembled tibia, sending excruciating pain throughout his entire leg. Proud of his kick and oblivious to Mike's pain, Walter went to grab a treat.

Father Mac knew something wasn't right. "Are you okay? You look a little foggy, my friend. I see it in your eyes. You took some punishment tonight. And doled some out. Contact the trainer Monday or talk to Dr. Cowan. Your leg needs to be checked out." Father Mac's eyes showed genuine and serious concern.

Mike was unable to look the priest in the eye. "I'm all right, Father Mac. Just a bit nauseous from the heat," he lied.

"Okay, Mike, I get it. But I know when someone's cage is rattled. Look, at least call me in the morning. We're leaving about 12:30, but I'm up early."

His point made, Father Mac changed topics. "You know I haven't been to Europe in ten years. Last time, I went to the Vatican. Beautiful place, even if you aren't a Roman Catholic priest!" He laughed and pointed to Walter over by the desserts. "Once he's settled in, I'm looking up an old cousin in Ireland for three or four days. Might even have a Guinness or two. Ha!" Father Mac winced, thinking that probably wasn't funny to a recovering alcoholic, and quickly looked at his watch. "Wow! It's getting late. We have to go."

"It's great you guys are going. Looks like Walter is moving on."

Mike wondered how Father Mac did this mentoring thing, day after day, year after year. Half a lifetime ago, he had taken a troubled teenage boy under his wing, helped develop his raw talents and positively channeled his anger and frustration. Seventeen years later, Father Mac was still working to put his runaway train back on track. Mike watched his young mentee and old mentor, both propped up by canes, walk over to Dino and JB.

"Thanks, Father. And you too, Walter." Dino Rhoades grinned widely. "Hey, Walter, that Storm hat looks good on you, man. Make sure you don't give it away in England." Walter fist-bumped the former All-Pro.

JB high-fived Walter and shook Father Mac's hand. "See you guys. Thanks for coming."

Mike was surprised it was already 10:20 p.m. Time to talk to JB and Dino.

"Well, well, look who's here. Hey, Steelman! You hangin' around just for us?" Dino extended a brother's grip to his old friend and gave him a hug.

"Good to see you, man," was all JB said.

"Congrats man. Good to see *you* guys!" Mike managed a worn smile. The trio, who fought hard together, felt a little awkward. The Steelman recalled Dino, writhing on the ground with his torn ACL. His decision cost Dino the right to *choose* when he would retire, on *his own terms*.

"Hey, Steelman, it was only a scrimmage! You really gotta show off on Family Night in front of the fans? Everybody knows how you hit, man! You almost killed the rookie," Dino joked. When he remembered Blackwell, he felt horrible. "Hey, Mike! Just kidding, man. I didn't mean to say something stupid. Bro, I'm in your corner. You know that!"

JB clenched a fist in solidarity.

"Hey, Mike," Dino continued. "I got something to ask you. Was gonna wait, but I'll do it now since I won't be seeing you much."

"One thing first, Dino." Mike fidgeted but looked him directly in the eye. "Dino, you gotta know something. Look, I'm sorry for the play man. When you ripped your ACL. You paid the price *because of me*. I wouldn't listen to you, man. I'm sorry." Mike's eyes welled up and he held out his hand.

Three trench warriors understood what the game of controlled violence did to men playing to win—making split-second decisions—before thousands of screaming spectators and watched by millions more on screens that replayed the good, the bad and the ugly—over and over again.

"Listen, brother, things happen for a reason. Everything does! We played it the way it was supposed to happen. No looking back! Understand?"

His words did not comfort Mike.

"So, listen, Steelman." No more reflection on their collective football past. It was time to look ahead. "There's this team of young boys in a program that hasn't won a game in like three years. West Side kids who need guidance and good coaching—*time invested*—not just cash for uniforms. You get where I'm coming from, Steelman? I'm the head coach." He pointed at JB. "He's the defensive coordinator.

We know he don't know shit about coaching linebackers. I figure maybe you'd help out when you could. Bottom line, *I need you, brother. They* need you."

"Tell you what, Dino, a lot of things have to fall in place. Let me think about it." Mike had no way to predict his immediate future, let alone the weeks and months ahead. "Listen, guys, I wish you both well. You know that. It's getting late, so I'm gonna head back. We'll make the time to hang out, man. I promise!"

Mike retraced his earlier steps, up the ramp to the Gate 0 atrium. *It's late. I should be able to get out of here without being noticed.* Security officers were herding the last few fans out of the restaurants and bars.

Mike had a sudden urge to look at the south end zone. A man and a boy about Walter's age were staring at him. He kept walking and overheard the father. "Yeah, I think that's him. Go ahead, Richie. Ask him."

The wide-eyed boy, dressed in a kid-sized #52 jersey, cautiously approached. The Steelman stopped. Shyly, the boy asked, *"Sir, are you the Steelman?"*

With his tattoos covered and short hair, he could deny his Steelman persona. The boy was getting nervous. He turned to look back at his father. Mike saw *Stalowski* stretched across the jersey.

"Well, uh . . . yeah . . . I am. And uh . . . c'mon closer. What's your name, little man?"

"Richie. You're my favorite player, Steelman."

"You a football player?"

"I play defense, too. Umm . . . can I have your autograph? Please?"

Mike relaxed a bit when he learned the boy's intentions. "Richie, that's great. What've you got for me to sign? How about your jersey?"

Richie's eyes lit up. "Sure!" He quickly fished a black Sharpie out of his pocket.

"Okay, turn around." Mike pulled at the jersey above his name and scribbled his name and number.

"Thanks, Steelman!" Richie shook Mike's hand and scooted back toward his dad.

His father stepped forward. "Mr. Stalowski, can I say something?" He appeared to be in his early forties with graying temples, like a thousand other faceless fan-dads over the years. But this man's face told another story.

Mike nodded.

"I just want to say thanks. This means a lot to him. More than you know. His mom has breast cancer, and he's been down for a long time. We were all here a few years ago. He asked me to bring him tonight. We heard you were in camp and hoped he'd get a chance to see you play. You're his idol, Steelman. *Thank you for taking the time.*"

Mike grasped his outstretched hand. Rarely speaking to fans, grunting monosyllabic words when he did, the Steelman was at a loss. "I wish your family all the best. I hope your wife gets better. See you, Richie."

Mike continued to Section 233, near the south end zone. Only a few perimeter lights illuminated the field where he had toiled for nine seasons. The Jumbotrons were off. The play clock was dark, but its ghostly gray numbers clearly signaled 00:00. Maybe it wasn't Ty Miller, but the football grim reaper who had posted *Play until the clock says 00:00.* Time had run out.

Gazing into the night sky, filled with bright and shining stars, he thought about Kim. The Steelman took a deep breath, exhaled and walked away. The atrium was empty except for impatient security officers at Gate 0.

"Time to go, sir."

Mike Stalowski stopped on the 18th Street bridge. He lifted his rebuilt right leg to rest it on the railing's lowest rung. It still hurt. His throbbing head was the cherry on top of his sore-neck sundae. Watching the red tail lights race by on Lake Shore Drive, Mike was envious of the cars' occupants who knew their destinations—unlike himself.

Mike passed a young couple walking two small dogs, reminding him of Walter's excitement about Chip and Pitch. Mike was on a parallel path with the boy who had become his friend at the place they once called home: taking incremental steps, one at a time. Walter was no longer paralyzed by his excruciating loss. Over time, he would find a home in London with Gabriela and her husband and fully open his heart to them. Most importantly, he would learn to accept the loss of his parents. Thinking about Walter's future should have been encouraging to Mike regarding his own.

But as he opened the door of his spartan condo, the Steelman was tired and banged-up, weary of the day's emotional roller coaster. In the past, he'd hit the refrigerator for beer to help him get right with the world. Not an option. Almost midnight, Mike's body told him it was time to shut down for the night. His rattled mind agreed. He dragged himself into the bedroom and fell into a restless sleep.

Hillsboro Beach— Where Fallen Angels Fly

<hr>

Eyes wide open, Mike lay in bed. His thoughts wandered between the scrimmage, physical pain, mostly his right leg, and the nearby dresser drawer. Entombed in its little black box, Kim's diamond-encrusted ring was a constant reminder of his loss.

As the hours dragged on, he tossed and turned, unable to shake the vivid locker room vision. *She appears and then she's gone? Teasing me . . . which she loved to do. What the fuck was she trying to tell me? What's gonna be okay?* The clock advanced to 3:22. Mike tucked the pillow under his chin. His eyelids grew heavier and finally closed.

Dressed in his Crusaders uniform and carrying his battered helmet, he walked alone down the pristine hall to St. Michael's chapel. It was strangely silent. His cleats didn't click on the floor. He opened the heavy wooden door. Faceless Storm players, their jerseys bearing random numbers, filled the pews. His eyes were immediately drawn to the illuminated portrait of St. Michael.

The Archangel gazed lovingly at Kim, who was wearing the red tasseled dress from Griff's. In slow motion, Mike approached her. She smiled and softly whispered, "Michael, please put your helmet down."

Mike obeyed, then slowly extended his taped and game-bloodied fingers, reaching for her left hand. Her ring, positioned between his thumb and forefinger, sparkled brilliantly. Their eyes met. Their fingers almost touched.

With a soft smile, she pulled back her hand. "No, Michael, it's time. I have to go now, baby. Good-bye." Her delicate fingers gently brushed his cheek. She disappeared.

Expressionless, Christian Blackwell, wearing his Storm uniform, emerged from the darkness of the side aisle. The Steelman turned to approach Blackwell. The chapel was now empty. Christian back-peddled, disappearing into the shadows. Looking back for Kim, Mike was startled by the illuminated Archangel's piercing eyes now glaring at him.

Mike shot up in a cold sweat. The jarring movement caused agonizing neck pain. *Jesus Christ! Why is this happening?* Mike was afraid to close his eyes and felt he was spinning out of control. It was 5:11 a.m.

"Hey, Father Mac, I know it's early. I was thinking I'm gonna stop by to see you for a little bit."

"Never too early to call me Sunday morning. I've been up since 4:30. I was having some crazy dreams. Probably worrying too much about this trip with Walter. Are you okay, Mike?"

"Yeah, pretty much. I think I took a few good shots, but that's the price I pay, right? I'll be all right. I'm just not thinking real clear right now. Anyway, I want to visit before you leave. I won't take much of your time."

Despite his imminent flight to London, Father Mac was glad Mike reached out to him. Hearing that Mike wanted to "visit" this early on his first real Sunday of freedom, Father Mac knew something was very important—or very wrong.

"Grab a cab and get over here."

"Okay. Be there in fifteen minutes."

"Sit down, Mike." Father Mac glanced at his watch. "Listen, we're having a special breakfast at 9:00. Father Orozco, a young associate priest from Precious Blood, is going to be here in my absence. The school kids there love him. He's a lot of fun and evidently speaks their language." Father Mac laughed, "He knows what YouTube is and what an iPhone does. Maybe he can be my replacement! Anyway, I have to introduce him."

"So look, Father, I don't know where to start. I've had crazy dreams. Feel like I'm losin' it. You know my condo's pretty close to the stadium so I walked there and back. Something I never did because people would hound me for autographs and stuff. Well, guess what? Nobody knew who the heck I was. I wasn't the Steelman."

"But surely you realize you don't look as menacing anymore. Were your arms exposed? That's a dead giveaway!"

"I was wearing a long-sleeved T-shirt. Anyway, then I pass the team store inside the atrium. No #52 jerseys or cutouts of myself anywhere. No Mike Stalowski."

"Where are you going with this?"

"You saw the scrimmage. I played like shit!" Mike realized he swore. "Sorry, Father!"

"I've heard it before. Go on."

"Look, I told you I'd give it a shot. Well, I did, but I don't know *if it was my best shot*. I honestly don't know what that is anymore. I think there's more going on inside my head I gotta sort out. I don't think I can play the way I used to."

"I've been around this game many years. I know what style of play made you famous. You're a warrior in a brutal game. You proved that season after season."

"You know what I did learn, Father Mac? *Pain keeps you honest.* That's why I'm here. Pain keeps you honest and makes you realize things—in your head—your heart—or your body!

"I put the Steelman on during that play against the rookie running back. Almost took him out before the kid even wins a roster spot. At that moment I just wanted to hurt him. Put him in his place." Mike looked his former Dean of Discipline and assistant coach in the eye. "You know what? The Steelman died that night with Kim."

Father Mac knew Michael Stalowski accepted the inevitable.

"I gotta be honest about the last few years. I listened to this old Pink Floyd song, "Comfortably Numb," like all the time. You know why? Because that's the only way I could play! Jacked up on stuff I should never be taking. Hiding stuff from the League. Drinking like a fish without even realizing it.

"Look, I know these coaches don't want me to be part of their X's and O's." Mike's eyes welled up and a river of tears flowed. His voice cracked. "Father Mac, I . . . I just can't play hurt anymore. I can't."

"You don't have to," Father Mac said gently.

"And I won't do what I did before to play like I was expected to. I really did try reaching deep down inside these last few weeks, but there's not much left. It's next man up."

Father Mac remained silent, waiting for Mike to find the words he still seemed to be searching for.

"One more thing. I don't think I ever dealt with what I did to her that night. I loved her, Father Mac. I loved Kim and I killed her! She keeps coming back telling me things."

"Last night I saw you were hiding something. Only I didn't know why or to what extent." Mike hung his head in shame. "I heard you talking to me. Not sure if it was the Father Mac to my right or left . . .

"Connie Everett came to me because he thought you got a raw deal," continued Father Mac. "Not so much the arrest, but the circumstances leading to the accident. He thought you deserved a second chance at your career—at life. That's why he came to me. I told him playing football was secondary. Look at me, Mike."

The Steelman raised his head and wiped his eyes. He was ready to receive his penance, fully expecting more than the usual penance of his youth—three Our Father's, ten Hail Mary's and three Glory Be's.

"As for Kim, this is the first time you said her name. I believe you loved her, and it's clear you have a lot of emotions to deal with. People can help you with that, including me. You may not want to hear this, but our Lord and a legion of angels are watching over you. You have to believe they never left your side, especially our Father."

Father Mac waited a moment. "There's nothing more to prove on the football field, Mike. In time, you'll be remembered for the way you played and what was in your heart. Reclaim your life by freeing yourself from what haunts you. If it's the specter of playing professional football, then make peace with your choice.

"Tell Connie Everett yourself. *That you want to retire.* There's no shame in that. You don't need to explain. He will understand, trust me. He said he wants to see you after practice tomorrow. Go see him first thing. Know what you want to say. He'll hang on every word." Mike nodded. "One more thing. Promise me you'll see a doctor."

"Yeah, I will. You said the word I never thought I would—*retire*. You know, Kim wanted me to retire. She saw what I couldn't accept. If I only listened."

"Remember what Kim meant to you. Hold on to the good memories forever. I'm sure that's what she would tell you. You have to accept God's plan. Something is out there for you. Let Him show you the way.

"Mike, look at how Walter's life changed direction. Clinically, his paralysis was *in his head*. Yet it was real. Confined to his wheelchair from the devastation of losing his parents. Unwilling and unable to face his fears and live his life. You had an enormous impact—*positive influence*—on Walter. He committed to work through his emotional and physical pain—to move forward with his life. Walter will never forget what he lost, but he is letting go. *You* helped him do that, Mike. *Can you do that for yourself? Will you?*"

Father Mac stood up. "I'm five minutes late. Remember what I said. We'll reconnect when I get back. Make good choices in the meantime."

Mike Stalowski had all day to choose the right words for Connie. Mercifully, he did not relive or invent terrors in his dreams that night.

After a shower and a protein smoothie, he met his driver promptly at 6:30. Mike saw Connie's Escalade when they pulled into Storm headquarters. "Thanks, man," he told the driver. "Can you wait here? Probably less than an hour."

Once inside, Mike needed to get past an unknown security guard to reach mahogany row. "Can I help you, sir?"

"Yeah, I'm Mike Stalowski and want to see if Mr. Everett's around."

"May I see your identification, please? Do you have an appointment?"

Mike fumbled unsuccessfully for his state ID card. "Uh, sorry. I left without it. I was in kind of a hurry this morning."

"You don't have an access card or an ID? And you expect to walk in and see Mr. Everett?"

"Please, can you let someone back there know Mike Stalowski is here to see Connie . . . I mean Conrad Everett?"

"We're not supposed to. But I'll ring his assistant."

It was 7:45. Thirty minutes until practice. Mike was shocked to see Connie come out. "Surprised to see you here, Mike. Thought I told you to come after practice."

"Mr. Everett, I was hoping we could talk this morning instead. Do you have a few minutes?"

"Okay, follow me."

Connie was dressed conservatively in one of his custom-tailored suits. After folding his hands on his desk, he leaned forward. "What's on your mind? I was waiting on some phone calls before we spoke after practice." Connie glanced at his Presidential Rolex. "Which you should be at in about fifteen minutes, right?"

Suddenly it didn't feel like the right time to bare his soul. But there was no turning back. Unlike yesterday, Mike intended to keep his composure.

"So, Mr. Everett, I know your time is tight. You've been straight with me, and I owe the same to you. When we met at the Angels of Mercy, around Easter, you said you were going to give me a shot at making the team as a walk-on."

The Steelman cleared his throat. "Mr. Everett, I tried. I tried to play the only way I know. Truth is, I can't do it anymore. I proved it to myself and probably everyone else during the scrimmage. I thought hard about it and decided yesterday morning. I talked to Father Mac. He told me I should tell you in person."

"Tell me what, Mike? What do you have to tell me that's so important at 8:00 a.m. on the first day of practice?"

"It's time for me to retire, Mr. Everett. The biggest reason? I can't do it anymore. I can't play like I used to. It hurts too much. I can't keep playin' in constant pain. *I decided I'm not going to continue as of today.*" The finality in Mike's voice left no doubt in Connie's mind. "Please, tell me what I gotta do next, Mr. Everett."

Connie walked around to Mike. "It's not what I hoped would happen, but I respect your decision. Evidently you listened in the garden when I told you to *only worry about what you can control.*"

Conrad Everett's eyes teared-up a bit. He pointed at Mike. "*You* gave this team your all, Mike Stalowski. For a lot of years, *you* brought us success. There were games where you carried this team on your back. I remember them. The *hard* wins. I recognize your efforts, and I respect your accomplishments. That's why I wanted to give you a chance to go out *your* way and on top.

"To prove to people *who you really are.* Not some crazy Steelman character in a football uniform incessantly talked about by the media. If you're telling me there's nothing left for you on the football field, then I sincerely wish you well. Know that you will always be a part of the Chicago Storm family."

"Thanks, Mr. Everett. I'll never forget what you did for me. I want to let you know straight-up—I played my ass off for this team."

Connie smiled, "I know, Mike, I know. Listen, I'll take care of the rest. Our PR guys will put out a statement. If you want a press conference to publicly announce your decision, we'll do it right."

"You know what, I appreciate it, but I've never been a big media guy. The fans should know, but I don't want to stand in front of a bunch of cameras and answer questions. I'd rather go out under the radar."

"Understood. Let the dust settle for a few days. Our legal staff will help you with League administrative issues, and the operations folks will set you up in the transition support systems for NFL retirees. You can join Dino and Butler with a clear conscience. I'll be in touch again, I promise. God Bless!" The two men shook hands.

Without fanfare or a good-bye reception, Mike Stalowski was chauffeured away from life in a fishbowl, the NFL in his rearview mirror. He left the building of his own volition, his future unknown.

Mike had a message from Steve. "Good news. Just heard from the Secretary of State. I know you're at practice, but I'll courier a temporary certificate authorizing you to drive to and from work."

Won't he be surprised? The only thing with wheels he had access to right now was the Harley. *Hopefully, I can park it at the condo. God only knows where she took the '63 'Vette. Probably sold it.*

Mike had no idea what to do with himself. Replaying the sequence of events since Independence overwhelmed him. There had been so much to think of—and now nothing. He was totally on his own. He should call his mom with the news.

But first his probation officer. "Hello, Mr. Carpenter. This is Mike Stalowski. I'm supposed to call you to set up a meeting."

His probation officer was a huge Storm fan. "Hey, Mike, I just got your file Thursday. Was going to go over it and then call. Listen, your attorney's given me basic information. I want to set you up with a good group of guys in an AA chapter near where you're living and a counselor who works with professional athletes. She's good. How about we set up a meeting for end of next week. We'll work around your schedule. I heard this morning about the provisional driver's license. Driving is restricted to work-related purposes. You can't leave the state without notifying me. Got it?"

"I understand." The very recently retired Steelman knew his decision wasn't public knowledge.

"We'll meet next Thursday or Friday. Call me with any questions."

"Same here. Thanks a lot."

After hanging up, he scrolled his contacts, stopping at KIM. With trembling fingers, Mike accessed his texts.

11:30 p.m. 1/20/2007

> please call me baby, I love you

1:57 a.m. 1/21/2007

> be ther byyy 2:30

Mike tossed the phone on the floor. Seeing the messages while clean and sober reopened unhealed wounds. He went to his dresser and pulled out Kim's headshot. The taped tear, a manifestation of her anger and frustration, caught his eye. *Couldn't throw this away. Must have kept it for a reason.*

Two sticky notes fell out of the envelope. The first he'd seen before. The second was also in her neat and flowing script.

To my rebel with a cause.

You're my Leader of the Pack . . . Be my baby

I'll always love you . . .

He had been right. She was singing to him at Griff's. Mike pulled back the ring box's black velvet lid, releasing the diamonds' brilliance. *Man, she would've died when I put this on her finger . . . if only I didn't kill her first.*

Mike held the ring in his hand, closing his fingers around it tightly. He thought about his recent visions of Kim, his nightmares, and the unresolved feelings bottled up inside. He wondered if Kim had been telling him that *he'd be okay.* But first, he had to say *goodbye.*

He took the headshot and ring with him to the living room and plopped down on the couch. While looking out at Lake Michigan and turning the black box over and over in his hand, he was suddenly inspired.

"It's probably under Steve Kendall's name. Yeah, a black Harley stored a few months ago. Yep, I own it. I'm coming before three o'clock. You're on frontage road by I-55 and Route 83, right?"

Patches of sun broke through hazy clouds. Cautiously he steered the rumbling Harley onto the frontage road, the remnants of Route 66—America's Mother Road. Mike passed familiar County Line Road. Lisa briefly crossed his mind. His life with her was finished, legally and emotionally. What he had to face did not involve her.

Back home, MapQuest routes materialized before his eyes. *Wow, Nashville is like eight hours down I-65 through Indiana and Kentucky. Florida another twelve frickin' hours? Holy shit, that's a long, lonely road.* Mike followed the route on the screen with his fingers, ending at Hillsboro Mile, a road Kim knew well.

That's it! Hillsboro Beach! Almost frickin' Miami! The last time Mike had been there, he'd traveled on a chartered aircraft. Ironically, he thought of Kim the whole way down and back.

That night Mike slept soundly and jumped out of bed when the alarm buzzed at 5:30. With his four-day growth, he looked a little like the Steelman again, sans long hair. Dressed in his favorite worn jeans, riding boots, and black Harley T-shirt, he looked in the mirror and was satisfied with his appearance.

He checked the time and gulped down a protein shake before laughing. *Ha! No worries about getting to practice!*

Mike grabbed his provisional license and state ID. He stuffed a credit card and stash of $20 bills in his right front pocket. *All's I need is a change of clothes, a rain jacket and my shades.* Mike retrieved the envelope with Kim's pictures and secured everything in the Harley's fringe-trimmed saddlebags.

I'll take the Indiana Toll Road to 65. Thanks to an overnight storm, he roared off under clear skies, enjoying the lake breeze. Mike caught the light at 95th and Ewing. Instinctively he turned into Cal Park. Near the public boat launch, he looked out over the lake at the breakwater rocks where he had fished.

He clung to the memory of his first date with Kim, the Hegewisch show-and-tell tour, when he had parked the Harley in the same spot. He thought about their picture at the dunes, tucked with his angel's headshot. He felt for the bulge in his left front pocket, reassured the Asher & Klein box was safe. There was one important stop on the way. Mike kicked the bike into gear. He hit shuffle on his iPod and pulled out of Cal Park blaring "Paradise City."

At 3:30 Mike pulled onto Vanderbilt's campus. It was larger than expected and he didn't know where to begin. He saw a University Police Department cruiser. Mike approached the officer.

"Sorry to bother." Mike kept his distance. The last thing he needed was to startle the officer. "I'm from out of town, looking for an old buddy I used to work with. All I know is he's going to school here to be a doctor. Can you help?"

"What's his name? I can look him up in the Student Directory."

"Christian Blackwell. He's a black guy."

The officer smiled. As if a racial reference would identify him in the student directory. "Here he is. Children's Emergency Medicine. That building has a big common area connected to all these buildings. Like a big lounge where the students meet and eat 24/7! Try walking through there. If you don't see him, the reception desk might be able to help."

"Thanks, man. Really appreciate it." In the lounge, Mike was amazed at the number of student doctors, representative of the League of Nations. But not one of them resembled his former teammate.

He sat down to wait and soon saw an approaching trio, chatting and laughing. Two young women walked on either side of a man with closely cropped hair. He had a leather valise in one hand and a cane in the other. It was Christian Blackwell.

Mike froze. Blackwell passed by, glanced at Mike and kept walking. Ten paces later he turned around.

"Man, you look like someone I know. Mike? Steelman? Is this for real?" Blackwell turned to his friends. "You guys go ahead."

Mike faced the man whose life he changed. "Yeah man, it's me. Don't be too shocked. Is there someplace a little quieter we can go?"

"How did you know I was here? I thought you were back with the team, man. Heard you were in camp."

"Well, I'm here. I officially retired yesterday, but no announcement yet. I found out you were going to school."

"I see. You came here just to see me? Come on, let's go in there." Blackwell led him to a study room. "Hey, Steelman, you want a water or something?"

"No, I'm good. Thanks. I'm passing through Nashville today, heading to Florida. There's some stuff I've got to say to you."

Blackwell put his materials down. "Okay, I'm listening."

"I don't know how to say this, but all I want you to know is *I'm truly sorry* for what happened, man. At the game and afterwards. It haunts me every day. Probably always will. I know I can't change anything, but I learned I have to make things right. For me and everyone I touched. Look at what I did." Mike hung his head. Shedding the weight of his guilt, pound by pound, was difficult.

Blackwell contemplated Mike's words. "I was angry at first . . . confused. Then I resigned myself to what happened and asked the Lord to show me the way. My faith brought me here." He stood up without the aid of his cane. "This is my journey. I'm going to help people, kids that were traumatized. That's what I'm supposed to do.

294

"You know, football for me was a game. It didn't do for me what it did for you. It wasn't supposed to. I prayed for you a lot. Still do. And look. The Lord brought us together. That's all that matters. I kept up on your life after the accident as best I could. Heard you were on the road back. I sincerely believe you are."

Mike extended his hand. Blackwell pulled him in close for a hug.

"Mike, it's all good. Look, I have to go. That lady I was with . . . we're together, planning a future. I have to catch up with her." Blackwell held Mike's hand. "I know how hard it must be for you to think about the lady with us that night. I pray for her too. You take care, brother. You know where to find me." Mike nodded and double-fist-bumped Christian, before resuming his own journey.

He reviewed the route to Hillsboro Beach, twelve hours at best. It was 5:20 with about three hours of daylight left. He planned to ride until exhaustion set in. Heading south on I-24 out of Nashville, he picked up I-75 by Chattanooga, heading for the Georgia line. Five hours later, he had covered a lot of asphalt paved over Georgia red clay, stopping only for fast food and gas. A passing thunderstorm brought him to a halt under an overpass in a desolate stretch of Crisp County, Georgia, a few miles from the "Watermelon Capital of the World." The sheets of rain subsided, but the roads were slick with oil. Time to call it a night in Cordele. Mike pulled his Harley into the Southern Hospitality hotel lot.

A skinny young girl, with chipped nail polish and wearing an ill-fitting business suit, barely greeted him. "All that's left is a double bed near the elevator. That okay?"

"Yeah." Mike put his credit card and ID on the counter.

"Do you know your Rewards number?"

Mike smiled. "Sorry, I don't have it." The Steelman would never step foot in this place. His keys were presented to him in a five-star hotel, along with a briefing sheet including nearby high-end restaurants. "Can I get a 5:30 wake-up, please?" The girl nodded without looking up.

Fully clothed, Mike plopped onto the thin, sagging mattress and fell asleep. In the morning, he grabbed a soggy breakfast burrito from under the breakfast bar hot light and wolfed it down. After topping off his tank, he continued south on I-75 in the heavy humidity. Almost four hours later, Mike reached the Florida Turnpike split, an hour north of Orlando. The Florida sun bore down. His shades created raccoon eyes. Determined to reach his destination before sunset, Mike roared on, often exceeding speed limits. Some things would never change.

Close to the Atlantic, Mike merged onto I-95 near Jupiter. Hillsboro Beach was within reach. It was only 2:30. He slowed down, passing West Palm and Delray Beaches. Near the Boca Raton Airport, he checked his fuel gauge. A quarter tank. 4th and goal—inches to go. Mike pressed on.

Heading east on Route 810, he stopped at the 3rd Avenue Shell station. He passed a tattoo parlor that seemed out of place in the neighborhood. The *Rebel Ink* sign said it all. He was about a mile from A1A. South of Route 810 it became the even more upscale Hillsboro Mile.

Mike cruised the Mile, taking it all in. Just as Kim did when he rolled her through Hegewisch, past Patriot's Park to Mancuso's.

Why she shunned the gated villas, high-end restaurants, and ocean clubs of the ultra-rich for Chicago was a mystery. Her life had begun near Hillsboro Mile— next to the blue-green water of the Atlantic Ocean. It ended not far from Chicago's Magnificent Mile—beside icy-cold Lake Michigan.

So this is where the little rich girl cut her teeth. He imagined Kim behind him, her arms tight around his waist and her hair blowing in the wind.

Fate caused their paths to cross at Griff's, where neither of them wanted to be that night. But Kim needed money and Mike was helping a friend. They chose to stay together. The memories would have to last his lifetime. Mike would always wonder how life might have been—blessed with a baby neither of them expected, but both would have loved.

Kim lived most of her life near the white sands of Hillsboro Beach—the Hillsboro Club where Kate left her to play as a little girl—and the Hillsboro Inlet Lighthouse, her special place. He felt close to her right now, as if she were on the back of his bike, telling him to pull over. She would lead him there.

Mike parked along a concrete breakwall north of the Hillsboro Club. He stretched his sore legs, limping a little as he went to feed the meter. He pulled the pictures out. Her haunting hazel eyes looked at him. The black velvet box wasn't in his front pocket. He breathed a sigh of relief when he felt the fuzzy cover on the bottom of the saddlebag. Mike removed the diamond ring and put it in his pocket, before tossing the velvet box back into the saddlebag.

Stepping through a break in the wall to get to the water's edge, he noticed a large flock of seagulls take off. Momentarily following their flight, he saw a lighthouse in the distance looking exactly as Kim described it. This was *her special place* where she spent countless hours playing and dreaming, beneath the sun and stars with the ocean stretching as far as she could see.

"*You should see the lighthouse at Hillsboro Beach. It stands out like a beacon. I dreamed it was my house and the ocean was my backyard. In high school, I'd go to clear my head. Lay in the sun or look at the stars. It still makes me happy when I think about being there.*"

Now Mike understood. He walked along the sand, feeling her next to him. "*Told'ya it was nice here, Steelman.*"

There weren't many people on the beach. Near the lighthouse, a little blonde-haired girl in a yellow bikini was throwing shovels of dry sand in the air. Her mother, talking on her cell phone, swatted at the toddler to stop.

As he drew close, the little girl put down her shovel. She smiled and waved. Her big green eyes sparkled. Mike imagined she was Kim, playing next to an impatient Kate, preoccupied in conversation with one of her club friends. Twenty years earlier, he would have been right. Mike smiled and waved back.

Passing by, he heard a bit of the mother's conversation. "No, *I don't know* how we're gonna make it. He worked *so hard* and put everything into this business. *We're really broke!*" He kept walking toward the water, stopping where the rushing tide lapped at his dusty boots. He turned around. The little girl was watching him.

Alone at the ocean's edge, staring at the undulating waves, he felt the rush of Kim's presence in the soft wind on his face and the rhythmic breaking of waves on the shore. Mike felt a deeper connection to the blue-green water than ever before. More intense, yet peaceful, than his time on Lake Michigan. Here at Hillsboro Beach, he was mesmerized by the rushing tide which came to him and then pulled back—over and over—like his memories of Kim.

This is what she wanted me to see and feel.

They were linked by the ebb and flow of the tide, washing over his boots. Mike recalled the push and pull of their lives. The calm and stormy times of their few months together. Perhaps their mutual love of the open water had drawn them together—sitting in Cal Park along the shores of Lake Michigan—becoming one at Warren Dunes—and simply holding hands on the bow of his boat. Kim had told him what Hillsboro Beach meant to her throughout her life. Ultimately, it was here she found peace. Kim had said she wanted her "*ashes spread by the ocean, carried by the wind across the waves, in front of a setting sun.*"

For Mike, Kim's spirit would live forever at Hillsboro Beach—alive in the ocean water and on the warm sand—shining brilliantly like a star in the night sky—beaming a beacon of love from her lighthouse. Although Kim and the Steelman were gone, they would always be part of him. But now, as she told him in the chapel, under the watchful eye of St. Michael the Archangel—*he had to say goodbye*. It was and would *"be okay."*

From his pocket, he pulled what he had wanted to give her so long ago and admired its brilliance. Looking out over the waves, he whispered, *"For you, baby."* He palmed the ring and cocked his arm. Mike heard the little girl crying over the crashing waves. His hand dropped to his side and he turned around. She was still standing next to her mother. Watching him.

He shook off the interruption and cocked his arm again. Suddenly, but intentionally this time, he stopped. Rubbing it gently between his fingers, Mike thought of a better purpose for the ring. Intuitively, he believed Kim would have approved. *"I think you're sweet . . . nothing like the guy your fans want to believe you are."*

Mike walked toward the little girl. Her mother was still on the phone. Mike tossed the ring on the sand right in front of "little Kim." The diamonds glittered brilliantly. She stopped crying and scooped it up in her shovel. Mike picked up his pace. One hundred yards away, he turned to look. She was holding her treasure and tugging on her mother's arm.

Seagulls on the sand marked the break in the wall. Mike glanced at the lighthouse. Back at the Harley, he examined their picture closely. Her white T-shirt was hiked up just enough to expose the top half of her wingless angel. He had intended to leave the pictures behind with the ring. But now Mike understood that eliminating reminders of Kim wasn't the same as letting go.

He slid the pictures back in the envelope and safely tucked them in the saddlebag. Mike donned his shades and climbed aboard. He revved the engine and looked toward the beach one last time. The flock of seagulls flew away in a heart-like formation. There were storm clouds to the north and west. Mike decided to make a stop.

By the time he came back outside two hours later, the quick-moving storm had given way to patches of setting sun in the orange and purple sky. The ride to Chicago was going to be very long and lonely. In his heart, Mike knew he had accomplished what he set out to do.

He dialed Dino's number. After eleven rings it went to voicemail. "Hey, Dino, decided I'm gonna take you up on that coaching gig. I found some time to help out. Call me!"

In a sleeveless Harley Davidson shirt, exposing a bandage on his left arm, Mike was ready to face his uncertain future. Pointing his wheels north on A1A, he plugged in headphones and scanned for "Fly to the Angels." The first stars of night were sparkling. He twisted the throttle. The Harley roared to life. The wind blew the loose gauze off his arm, revealing his fresh Rebel Ink tattoo. Carefully positioned beneath his battle-scarred St. Michael was a replica of Kim's angel—*blessed with wings*—nestled under her protector's care, to be watched over until the end of time—by the Archangel himself, the guardian of departed souls on their journey to Heaven.

Acknowledgments

WITHOUT THE TIRELESS EFFORTS OF MY AWESOME WIFE PATTY, THIS BOOK would not exist. She transformed my voluminous first draft into a manuscript that reflected the story that had been in my head and my heart since 2007. I assure you it was not an easy process. Suffice it to say that I had not been quick to listen to or accept constructive criticism. However, throughout the roller-coaster ride of our forty-plus years together, she has stuck with me and the task at hand. I'm very lucky and grateful, blessed actually, for her dedication to bringing this story to life while juggling the responsibilities of raising a family, running a small business, and keeping the household humming.

Thank you to both of my children and all the friends who listened to my incessant talk about Mike the "Steelman" Stalowski and encouraged me. I greatly appreciate all my early readers, especially Pam O'Hara and Karen Soenen, for plowing through multiple versions. And Jeanne Manning, for telling me, "It has legs."

I want to express my sincere gratitude to Holly Kammier, Jessica Therrien, and the entire Acorn Publishing team for their vision and support. Specifically, many thanks to Molly Lewis, for elevating my story to the next level, Damonza.com for the outstanding cover design, and Leslie Ferguson, for her invaluable insights and management of the myriad details needed to pull it all together.

Last but not least, I extend my heartfelt thanks to you, the reader. I truly hope you connected to the characters I've created.

I know from experience you can find your way back after a wrong turn on life's highway.

About the Author

Richard Podkowski, a native of Chicago's South Side, began writing fiction while studying criminal justice at Loyola University Chicago.

As a United States Secret Service special agent, Richard protected U.S. Presidents and foreign dignitaries and investigated major domestic and international financial crimes. After retiring from the Secret Service in 2003 as a supervisory special agent, he became a management member of a Fortune 100 company's global security group. For the last several years, Richard has been a private sector strategic security consultant.

Inspired by professional athletes who lived in a fishbowl under constant media scrutiny and made life-altering mistakes, Richard wrote *The Walk-On*. Other projects include a Christmas romantic comedy screenplay and a crime story. In his free time, Richard enjoys riding his road bike, working out, and making Christmas ornaments. He currently resides with his wife in Los Angeles.

Made in the USA
Monee, IL
04 March 2023